THE WATER THIEF

THE
WATER THIEF

Claire Hajaj

ONEWORLD

A Oneworld Book

First published in North America, Great Britain and
Australia by Oneworld Publications 2018

ISBN 978-1-78607-394-5
eBook ISBN 978-1-78607-395-2

This is a work of fiction. Names, characters, places, and incidents are either
the product of the author's imagination or are used fictitiously, and
any resemblance to actual persons, living or dead, businesses, companies,
events or locales is entirely coincidental.

Typeset by Hewer Text UK Ltd, Edinburgh
Printed and bound in Great Britain by Clays Ltd, Elcograf S.p.A.

Oneworld Publications
10 Bloomsbury Street
London WC1B 3SR
England

'*There are three great rivers with which sinners purify them-selves in this world: a river of sincere repentance; a river of good deeds that drowns the sins that surround it; and a river of great calamities that expiate sins . . . So swim . . . and have patience.*'

Ibn Qayyim al-Jawziyya,
Madārij al-Sālikin (Stages of the Wayfarer)

Two men are taking Nicholas away. I see them through the police-car window. One takes his shoulder, one his arm. They swallow his skin, like mouths.

Nagodeallah, she fears them. She wriggles and cries on my knees. She grows heavy as a goat. Goggo says I hold Nagode too tight. She says: 'Eh, boy, let her loose. Let her cry like she should.' But Goggo knows nothing. Her mouth has no teeth. All she does is cry for us and lick the water from her gums. But Nagodeallah is mine now. So I squeeze her. I say shush, *like Mama would.*

Nicholas has not seen us yet. He looks back, towards the runway. At the end is the aeroplane, waiting. Big, like a beast. Like the horse from Mama's stories, the white horse with wings. A knight's horse for Nicholas, to fly away from us.

Those men have angry faces. I know it. Because I am angry too. They tell me that in the special lessons. They ask me to draw everything that happened. But I could only draw the well. Your well, Nicholas. The one you stole like Robin Hood, that you said would save us all. I drew how it was when I looked down inside it – big, and black. These men are big and white.

I hear one man speak. He says Nicholas is lucky. He says it like this: 'You don't know how lucky you are, mate.' Mate. Nicholas uses this word too. It means 'my friend'.

But these men are not his friends. They have locked his hands together. And his face is white, white as the spirits. When he came to us, he was pink. Mama, she used to laugh at him. But the fires burned him away. They burned us all away and left only bones.

1

When the policewoman came to tell us about Nicholas, Goggo said: 'Praise Allah. Good riddance.' She has not forgiven him. She wants blood in her mouth not tears. Sometimes, I see the blood in my dreams. I see them, Mama, Nagode and Adeya and the others, and their cheeks are running red.

It was Adeya who made me come. The police lady said: 'He asks for you, JoJo, every day. Will you not see him?'

Goggo spat. But Adeya, she came to stand by me. She grew so tall, as tall as Mama. After the fires I told her: 'You can come to live with us, like you are our sister. And I will care for you the same as Nagode.' And Adeya, she said: 'Yes, JoJo. But when we are grown, remember that I am not your sister.'

So I said yes to the policewoman, for Adeya. The word in my mouth was no but yes came rolling past my teeth. So the police car fetched us at first light. It had electric windows. I wound them down, so the wind could feel Nagode's hair.

Now the policewoman stands by my window, waiting. The car door is closed. And I am afraid to open it. Doors are tests, Baba said. We choose to pass or stay. I do not know if the right way is through or back. But I am a man now. So I must choose.

I lift my hand and open the door. Nagode holds me as we climb into the light. The policewoman steps back. And then Nicholas, he sees me.

He says: 'JoJo.'

I want to say: No way, Nicholas. No, mate. We have nothing for you, Nagode and me. We came only to see you go.

But my throat hurts and the words are stuck in it. My arms shake, and I cannot hold Nagode. I give her to the police lady. One day, my arms will be stronger. One day, Nagode will speak. On that day, I will tell her our stories. I will tell her about Mama and Baba. I will tell her about you, Nicholas, and The Boys, about the fires and the well. When we are grown, we will still remember. That is what I have to say to you, Nicholas. We will remember.

Will you remember, too? When they take you from here, will you think of us, and the things we did together? Like when we built our castle. It was great, that castle. Strong, with a moat, and towers, and the flag Mama made for it. You taught me how to make it strong. Each wall pushes and pulls against the others, you said. If even the smallest falls, then all become weaker. But together they are balanced. This is how the building finds its strength.

I want to tell you, Nicholas, that I understand this now. I do not need your lessons any more. I go to a good school. I am the best student. Each night I sit with Adeya and we study your language of numbers. Adeya, she says the numbers speak to us. Like the spirits, Nicholas. Sometimes the spirits speak to me still. They push and pull me inside. It hurts and I cry when Adeya cannot see. But I, too, will become strong one day.

'Please,' you say. 'Please.' And now I am crying. Because I am not ready for you to go. I do not forgive you yet, Nicholas. I have important things to tell you.

But now there is no time, they are pulling you away from us. So it must be my turn, Nicholas, it must be me who saves us. I will stop these men with their strong hands. Because we promised, Nicholas. We promised we would stay together.

I open my mouth to call you. But the words are stones and my heart is deep water. The police lady pulls my shoulder back as I put my hand out to you, and I pull forward with all my strength.

And then I feel it, the balance inside. I can speak your name. And you look around one more time; you are turning from the big men and the jet plane back to us.

Do we see each other, you and me? Do you see my hand, and what I have there? Because I know, Nicholas. I know what I must do. I know how to finish it.

DRY SEASON

The airport terminal doors swung open; Nick stepped through tempered glass into blinding daylight. Two porters reached for his suitcase as he passed through, palms sand-dry, their eyes dark with need.

He rested his back against cool brick, breathing in the afternoon's ragged clamour. The porters had moved on, drawn away by richer opportunities, their skinny forms swallowed in a heated blur of bodies. A woman brushed past him on the narrow pavement, shoulders swelling from a tight jungle-green dress, matching fabric crowning her temples, arms opened wide like a carnivorous flower. She squealed as she reached into the melée of expectant faces and trundling baggage, pulling someone into a strong embrace – a mother perhaps, or a sister. Nick watched, transfixed by their joy, the fierce press of skin against skin, the careless flow of tears.

Ahead, the airport road curved away from him. Cars flowed along it bumper-to-bumper, a slow-moving river under a bottomless sky. Exhaust fumes circled lazily over nameless trees, their dark flowers collapsing onto the roadside.

Purple cloudbanks curled and deepened on the horizon, over jammed clusters of houses, red-roofed and low. The city centre was just visible beyond them, a blurred shimmer of glass and steel reflecting the coming storm. The sky seemed to grow as Nick looked up, becoming vaster and heavier. Waves of wet heat pulsed downwards, soaking through his shirt. He felt his skin rejoicing, drinking them in, as if quenching a lifetime of thirst.

Nine hours earlier, he'd been cushioned by the soft ascent

from Heathrow, the sky racing soundlessly from grey to blue. It was the longest trip he'd ever taken, and when they'd first burst through the clouds into the bright void above it had taken Nick's breath away, filling him with awe. Here at last was the feeling he'd been hoping for: an old chain finally snapping, clear air opening between his past and future.

The jolt of touchdown had woken him from sleep, catapulting him into an altogether different world. They had lowered steps onto the runway and he'd walked out, dazed under the curdling sky, through the confident jostle of bodies at the baggage carousel and out through customs into this new daylight, with its miasma of car fumes, cigarettes, perfume and sweat. Loud smiles and bright voices overshadowed him on every side. *What are you doing here?* they seemed to demand. He had no easy answer to give, even to himself; it made him feel young, insignificant, and above all *not ready*.

He closed his eyes, shaky, suddenly grateful for the wall at his back, sensing people rushing by on their way to the taxi ranks. He felt the sky's heat spreading inside him, the dense closeness of rain overhead, probably sweeping in from warm ocean waters just beyond the city. Their rhythm pounded in his temples, green waves beating onto a wide, white shore. But then a tiny, cooling thought blew into him: he knew that ocean. He'd watched it countless times as a small boy, four thousand miles away on its northerly edge, under a sky grey as marbles, digging clams out of the sand between stinging rocks, the cold a blue knife raking bare feet. Somehow even then, before he was old enough to imagine what lay beyond the horizon, or that there could be a *beyond*, the hidden arc between that moment and this one had started to form.

The memory steadied his breathing. *A sign*, he thought – a turning point in the story, a straight road glimpsed through the haze. His excitement woke again, a warm rush. *Look out of the window at exactly noon*, he'd told Kate, at their goodbye. *I'll be waving right above you, au revoir at thirty-five thousand feet.* Her face had been pale in the flicker of the departure board, one fist outlined against the blue wool of her pocket. *Like Superman*, she'd replied with a strained smile, as his lips touched the almond-scented skin of her cheek.

That kiss lingered in his mouth; the taste of guilt. When he'd first confessed his plan to her, her laughter had been sympathetic, the compassion of the sane for the deluded. But under the departure board, her hand had clutched his arm in a last, anxious appeal. *It's not too late, you know.*

Too late for what? he'd asked gently, torn between admiration for her determined composure, self-reproach for the hurt it concealed and desperation to be gone. He'd felt her fingers pressing through his shirt, as if she could penetrate his skin to reach the many doubts still lurking beneath. The curtain of dark hair he'd parted on their first night together a year ago, falling shining and straight across her face, was swept up tight into a ponytail, betraying a tremble of mouth and chin. Her engagement ring winked up at him like a third eye. *To change your mind*, she'd replied. *To stay here with me, where you belong.*

'Nicholas? Hey! *Pardon* – you're Nicholas?'

Nick opened his eyes into a present full of warm light. A hand was reaching out to him; he followed it up to a stranger's face, vaguely familiar from a grainy snapshot in his deployment folder. Steel-rimmed glasses beneath an anxiously receding hairline, the forehead a worn pink over watery eyes. Pale lashes blinked rapidly against the glare, like a burrowing creature's. Nick had a sudden memory of moles ripping through his mother's lawn, their pointed noses testing the air as she sat motionless by her easel.

'Jean-Philippe?'

'J.P., please. Welcome! At last. No problems with the visa? They can be devils, you know.' He glanced sideways at Nick. 'But look at you! You're not like I imagined. No offence.'

Nick laughed. 'None taken. It's Nick, by the way.'

J.P. dragged the suitcase through the melée of waiting taxis. Bodies buffeted Nick, warm and bright with sweat. His senses were jumbled: corn roasting on a roadside stall filled his mouth with the taste of mellow gold; the air was smoky green at the back of his throat – with something else, darkly sweet, like sewage.

They reached a brown sedan among the chaos of double-parked cars, exhausts belching fumes. Behind the dust-smeared windscreen a crucifix dangled off coloured beads – strings of chocolate, grass, gold and blood.

'I mean, you're younger than I thought,' J.P. said as he opened the boot, hoisting Nick's suitcase inside. 'Twenty-seven? Twenty-eight?'

'Thirty.'

'They usually send them older. The mid-career crisis, you know. Ha!'

The car's seats were stripped bare, metal bones shining through. Nick cranked down the window to let in the sluggish air. Small children wandered through the traffic, clutching packs of gum and rotting baskets piled with fruit and flies. Most scattered at the blare of car horns. But some pressed in, thin fists hammering on the glass.

J.P. started the engine. 'But anyway, here you are.' Buildings loomed ahead, black-streaked and crumbling. 'Young blood.' Music crackled to life from the radio cassette player – a full-throated wail over sax and drums that pulsed through Nick like wingbeats. J.P.'s hands tapped its rhythm on the wheel. 'Femi – you like him? He's a god round here, so say yes if they ask. It's his latest. *Mind Your Own Business*. Good advice for our nice new nineties, no? Personally I prefer Ali Farka Touré. The greatest blues man on earth – but from a few borders north of here. Oh, they'll tell you: this is all West Africa, borders are just colonial importations, like French and English – and they have a point, mind you. But when it comes to music, football – the important things in life – the patriotism here is crazier than Europe. So I keep my opinions to myself.'

The lyrics were English, Nick could tell – and yet he couldn't quite catch their meaning as they slipped past, sucked through the window into the whirlwind of street noise: the cry of hawkers over a boom-box's tinny pulse, long-tailed birds piping from a passing tree, the dark rumbling sky overhead. He took a deep breath, conscious of J.P.'s briskly tapping thumbs, of the importance of first impressions. *Don't look so overwhelmed, idiot. This has to work out.*

'I don't know much about music, I'm afraid,' he replied, taking refuge in honesty. 'Catholic mother – I was brought up on hymns.'

'No Geldof? No Live Aid? I thought that was a basic requirement for you British.'

'I missed the Live Aid thing. Too busy studying for the second stage of my architecture qualification. My girlfriend loves U2, if that qualifies?'

'U2, my god. They grow up on hymns here, too. In the south, anyway. Not in the north, where you'll be. There, it's mostly *allahu akbar*. Well, by the time you go home, you'll know what to sing where. And what do you think of this warm welcome you're getting? Femi . . . all this sunshine. Nice for the swimming pool. But not so nice for the farmers.' Sweat pooled on the Frenchman's temples. 'The rains failed.'

Nick's hotel, booked for one night before his journey north, was fronted in mottled colonial brick. Black birds squatted on its casements around a central swimming pool. J.P. went across to the bar, to negotiate with the waitress for a drink.

Nick waited for him by the water. Red flowers fell from overhanging trees onto the listless surface. He watched, hypnotised, as the water swallowed them, petal by petal. His pale reflection swam between them. *Such a sad little fellow*, his mother used to say. That was in the early days, when her arms would still wrap around him, baptising him in warmth. He caught the ghost scent of paint on her hand as she stroked his hair. *Don't give the boy these ridiculous ideas, Mary*, his father would tell her, back turned to them as he worked on patient records, his disdain cold as a knife. For a moment Nick imagined a grey figure materialising beneath the water's cloudy surface, before he wiped his hands over his eyes.

11

J.P. came back with two cold beers and Nick's recruitment papers. He flicked through them with a whistle. 'You did a lot already, eh? Engineer, architect?'

'Structural engineer.' His voice sounded thin in the heavy air. The beer was malty, with a metallic aftertaste. 'My firm built public spaces and infrastructure in London.'

'That's great. Working for the Iron Lady. *Vive le capitalisme!* Lots of money for that, I bet. Happy mama, happy papa, happy wife.'

'Fiancée. And my father wasn't so happy.' Talking of him felt bold, like an exorcism. 'He wanted me to be a doctor, like him.'

'Even more money.'

'Not in his practice. He was a local GP, a country doctor.' Now Nick regretted the conversation. The subject was still too sharp – a splinter buried deep.

'So you give it all up to come here?' J.P. raised his eyebrows. 'Is the fiancée a pain in the ass?'

Nick laughed despite himself. 'It's just a sabbatical. A year, that's it. Then I head back home.'

He remembered saying the same thing to the recruitment panel, after all the exams and application essays. *We need to know you can last the year*, they'd said. *That you're not going to drop out because you're too lonely, or it's too hot, or the sky is too strange and you can't sleep.*

And he'd given them his too-plausible assurances – the same ones he'd served to Kate, as she stood frozen in their kitchen, a cork pulled halfway out of the bottle of Saint-Émilion. *I want to do something meaningful*, he'd said. *Before I settle down – before we start our whole life together.* It was meant to reassure, but he felt the unsayable truth hovering just beneath – that he could feel that life solidifying around him, trapping him into one of a billion diligent, purposeless existences that faded in the living.

He'd taken Kate's hand, her engagement ring cold and solid between them as she tried to pull him back to her. *But everything's already organized – I ordered stationery for the invites*

– we've started writing our vows. The argument had run on into the small hours, exhausting them both. She knew he was afraid, she'd said; a lifetime is a lifetime after all, and she was scared too – but running away to another continent was no solution. He'd countered that he wasn't running away but preparing himself; he'd be back in just a few months, ready to make good on every promise, more able to be the man she wanted him to be. Finally, she'd asked, bewildered: *Is this all because of your father?* She'd thought that his father's death had filled him with the helium of wild ideas, that he risked floating off unless she could pull him back to their safe, defined spaces; evening meals and weekend escapes, the wedding plans taking shape with colour schemes and honeymoon brochures.

A treacherous voice in his head had whispered: maybe she's right. Maybe this is just fear – the coward all over again, afraid to step up when it counts. It had all happened so fast – a race from first kiss to engagement in a year, a proposal coming straight after his father's funeral. She'd been an object of desire in his office for months before he'd dared to ask her out – an icon of self-assurance and faultless lines, deftly presenting communication strategies to senior management, her hair a dark banner sweeping down her back. *You're a natural persuader, he'd told her. You make people want to do what you tell them.* It was the clumsiest pick-up line.

She'd absorbed his compliment with a wry shrug. *That's what everyone thinks about women in PR. Other people have talent, we just talk. I should put it on my business card. Communi-Kate.*

He'd felt for her then. *Compli-Kate.* They'd laughed – and again later on, during a dim evening in the flush of alcohol, Nick feeling a voyeur's thrill as she unbuttoned her professional confidence, exposing the hidden fears beneath. She could never smile at a man without wondering if he'd one day resent her for not sleeping with him. She despised herself for playing on her looks, but her face looked so awful without make-up – like a mannequin without its paint. Her mother had been a QC; Kate worried her own life was trivial by comparison. She wanted too much from people, so maybe she was doomed to be alone. They'd been so tantalising, those half glimpses of weakness, like sensing deeper currents under a lake's still surface. And then at a spring party, in the middle of some forgotten conversation, his awareness had drifted slowly from light office jokes to the pale ridge of goose bumps pricking the flawless white of her arms, her silk camisole too thin, clinging to the stubborn swell of stomach that gym sessions couldn't flatten. As she'd turned her face up to him, the wine was still sharp on her breath, lips pale and cool as a swan's wing. Later she would claim he'd kissed her first – but he remembered nothing except that taste of wine and almonds, the mix of thrill and alarm.

If his father hadn't had a heart attack, the old man would probably have sat grudgingly at the back of Kate's family's Anglican church watching his only child take his wedding vows, disdain spreading in a poisonous wave over the muted Christ pinned up behind the vicar, the neat peony bouquets, their two corporate incomes and aspirational house hunting. This flight across continents would have taken the two of them on their honeymoon.

But the telephone call had come six months ago. And when Kate found Nick frozen in their hallway, the receiver humming a flat dial tone in his hand, they'd both felt the tremble of a hidden rudder, a subtle shift of course. *I know you weren't exactly close*, she'd said as he walked dry-eyed from the synagogue. *Even so, you're handling it well.*

But in the night watches he'd quietly filled in applications for volunteer work abroad, listening to Kate's even breathing. She claimed never to remember her dreams, but he could imagine them. They'd flickered through his mind as he wrote: happy dreams – dappled sunlight on an ivory dress, kites soaring over parkland, small wellington boots outside a townhouse, family holidays in the Alps. His own dreams could not be shared with anyone: a playground filled with screams and shattered glass, his father's half-moon spectacles staring him down, the pale wash of his mother's landscapes on silent, sunny walls.

'Well,' J.P. said, 'you did the training so I won't bore you with everything again. This project will be easy for you, perfect. The north is tough and the governor is a piece of work. But Dr Ahmed is a great host. Ten years working together and never a problem. His place is just outside the Town – but you'll see it's better that way. Our consultant, Eric, will be your liaison. He has a team of locals, but not one who can reach the same total twice.'

J.P.'s beer was already gone. He shouted to the bar for another. 'I went to university too. I could have been a lawyer. But then I followed a girl, the usual story.' The second round of beers came, one for Nick, as well. 'The main thing I learned here is not to try too hard. Many things can't be helped. Many people, too.'

Nick smiled. He'd heard the same thing countless times, at farewell dinners over glasses of chilled wine.

'That's a great recruiting line,' he teased. 'Sign up, it's hard and hopeless!' A worthy life should be hard work, his father used to say. He'd been fond of quoting what he liked to call the only sensible part of the Talmud: *no man should rely on shortcuts and miracles.*

J.P. shrugged. 'Perhaps for your British charities. So Victorian. And the Americans are worse, by the way. Quakers and Evangelicals. Too many rules, too many virtues. Just be a human being, Nick, that's my advice. Someone who can keep a spread-sheet and knows how to build a hospital.'

Nick offered to buy their third round, peeling dollar bills out of his wallet as he headed to the bar. The waitress serving drinks had woven her hair into a maze of braids, her orange T-shirt pulled tight across a dark slash of cleavage. Her eyes were young and wary as she took his money, pulling two beers from the refrigerator and handing him change from a wad in her jeans.

After a quick mental tally, Nick said quietly to her: 'Twenty dollars.'

Her face was blank in incomprehension. 'Twenty dollars,' he repeated. 'I gave you twenty dollars.'

'You gave me ten.'

'No,' he said. 'I gave you twenty, you gave me change for ten.'

She waved her finger at him, mouth set in a stubborn pout, her head turned deliberately away.

'Hey.' Alarm turned to annoyance. 'Please give me my money.'

J.P. wandered over.

'What's the problem?'

'Nothing. She didn't give me enough change.' He dumped his notes on the bar.

J.P. poked them. 'Give the man his money,' he said to the girl. She looked at the floor and shook her head, wordless.

A man in a hectic floral shirt came over. 'Can I help you?' His voice was a pleasant baritone. Nick saw the girl's head come up like a fallow deer's, fear surfacing.

'I'm so sorry, sir,' the manager said, once J.P. had explained. He turned to the girl and spoke softly. Tears came to her eyes. 'He gave me ten.' Her voice was very quiet. She looked sideways at Nick, in shame or appeal. Patches of sweat were visible under her arms.

Frustration wilted in a sudden rush of doubt. He pulled out his wallet; the notes stared blankly back at him. The humidity was oppressive. Nick's chest hitched as he breathed, panic twining around it like prickly shoots.

'It doesn't matter.' He reached out to touch the manager's sleeve. 'It may have been my mistake.'

'These beers are on the house,' the big man said.

Nick took them. 'I'm sorry,' he told the girl. She didn't respond, her eyes falling to the notes as J.P. scooped them off the bar top. Reluctant to leave, Nick followed J.P. towards the table.

'Will she be OK?' He was fighting the urge to run back, to halt the unknown dance of consequences.

J.P. shrugged. 'They'll sort it out themselves. These things happen all the time. You did right, don't worry.'

They agreed to meet again the next morning, to see Nick off. When they left the table, he looked around for the waitress. The bar was deserted except for the hum of the refrigerator, his empty beer bottle still standing on the warm counter.

That night, under the hiss of the air-conditioning, he dreamed once again of Madi. They were sitting together as they'd always done, after school on his mother's kissing gate at the end of the garden. *How did you find me here?* he asked, panic rising inside him, his mouth still fizzing from swigs of Dr Pepper as the older boy looked up at him, a sad smile on his face. *I'm always here. Blood brother.* Then Madi jumped down, running ahead towards the hotel swimming pool, thin arms flung out like jackdaw wings. *Please!* Nick wanted to scream. *I'm sorry!* But the words flew out of his mouth in silence. And Madi was laughing as he tumbled in to the dark water, as the red flowers pulled him under and he vanished into black.

The long drive north began at dawn. Somewhere beyond the capital's outskirts Nick realised they'd crossed an invisible boundary between living world and desert. Lush greens faded to gold, the rolling fields flattened into plains of yellow earth. The land became vast and encircling, cast out to a remote horizon, pathless and bright with a parched sweetness that moved him. It was like sailing alone into unchartered seas.

Nine bone-shaking hours later, a single jacaranda tree broke the landscape's pale palette. Red-tipped buds were pushing through dark branches, ready to burst into brilliant bloom.

The tree marked the end of the northward ride; their car swung off the highway onto a smaller road. The village appeared over a rise, swift as a mirage. The road narrowed towards a central square where a mosque lofted its white minaret. Beyond that, the road disintegrated into a sand track leading around low houses of coloured stone. Market stalls and mud-brick houses were scattered unevenly beyond these, closer to the lowering sun.

The car swung west, trundling over dirt. Families strolled home in the late afternoon. The men wore pants and shirts, or light robes of peach and blue. Some bore the black-checked keffiyeh he'd only seen in news reports from the Middle East. The women's heads were wrapped in vivid scarves, dark orange and sherbet-pink. Dust rose as the car passed by, blurring them into a weary haze. One old woman sat on her porch, rolls of skin clinging to a shrinking, orange-wreathed frame. She leaned forward, baleful eyes following Nick around the final bend.

Dr Ahmed's clinic stood at the edge of the village, behind a low wall enclosing a garden. Yellow fronds of flowering sennas climbed over whitewashed brick. A trellised gate marked the house's boundary. Inside, a path framed by sprouting vegetables led up to a wooden porch. Its neatness was dwarfed by the wild sweep of the desert beyond. Something about the scene struck Nick as poignant, an out-of-place sense of familiarity.

The driver sounded his horn. Nick climbed out of the car, limbs aching. Earthy smells filled the air – soil, smoke and somewhere the deep rot of decomposition.

A man came striding down the garden path. 'My dear fellow!' he called, his faded jacket swinging from an angular frame, a slight limp in his gait. His hair curled grey at the temples like an aging scarecrow's. All his vitality had been sucked into the smile beaming from under half-moon spectacles.

He took Nick's hand and pumped it. Nick was taken aback; this was not the conservative village healer he'd been expecting. *For him it's not just the money*, J.P. had said. *He's a good guy; he likes to have us around.*

'You must be Dr Ahmed,' said Nick.

The old man's face creased in delight. 'And you must be Nicholas! Come in, come in! What a long journey you've had, my goodness. How can we refresh you? Some tea? My wife has already put on the kettle.'

The living room was small and dingy, dominated by a vast grandfather clock. It shone from its corner, rich walnut and gilding topped by a white-faced procession of roman numerals. Its elegance was slightly marred by a gaping side panel – exposing melancholy cogs and a still pendulum. A large wooden box lay open at its feet, filled with odd tools.

Dr Ahmed laughed at Nick's expression. 'Yes, I'm afraid I'm a terrible tinkerer.' He ducked under the low doorway as they entered the kitchen.

A young woman stood at the sink peeling vegetables, head bent and hair knotted behind her. Light from the window framed a long neck and slender shoulders.

'Margaret, my dear. Here is our guest.'

She did not turn immediately. When she did look up, the movement was quick, almost reluctant. Her skin was lighter than Dr Ahmed's with sharp planes and pale hollows under her eyes. Something in her expression disconcerted him, an echo of his mother's unreachable distance.

'Thank you very much for having me,' he said, his awkwardness returning.

'It is our pleasure,' she replied, her quiet English precise but deep with the fullness of African vowels. Her hands worked continuously, pausing only to wipe themselves on an apron over the blue cotton of her dress. A circle of stillness seemed to spread from her, causing even Dr Ahmed to moderate his jovial tone.

'Where are the children, my dear?' he asked.

'Nagodeallah sleeps,' she said. 'JoJo is out, I don't know where.'

'Boys,' he said to Nick. 'What can you do with them? But tonight at least we will give you a proper welcome. To us Muslims, a stranger is sacred. The Prophet, peace be upon him, advised even his brother-in-law to be like a stranger. I know how it is to be far from home. Margaret too, isn't that so?' He put his arm around his wife, dwarfing her.

'That's so,' she said, looking into his face with an odd smile. Her throat gleamed in the dim light as she turned; her skin seemed luminous, as if lit from a source within.

A tour of the house followed: Nick's office and bedroom were next to Dr Ahmed's clinic, both doors opening onto the main porch. Dr Ahmed was proud to display his surgery: a desk, examining table and small cupboard of medical supplies. On discovering that Nick was a doctor's son, his enthusiasm knew no bounds. 'Indeed!' he cried. 'A London doctor?'

'Country doctor. A small village on the southwest coast. We didn't see many outsiders. A bit like here, I suppose.'

'Outsiders are the lifeblood of humanity,' Dr Ahmed said. 'Every man should experience another culture. I myself was lucky enough to train for two years in London, at University College Hospital. Every Saturday I would go to Portobello Road. Do you know it?'

'Of course.'

Dr Ahmed sighed. 'Now, *there* was a place to teach us things. A mix of old and new, East and West. The latest music and fashions, too. I was quite the dashing fellow back then!' He chuckled, and Nick grinned back.

'But also they restored such wonderful antique pieces.' Dr Ahmed was lost in reminiscence. 'Those grandfather clocks – they were perfection. All the little parts working together, in such a delicate balance. Too much tension here, too little there, and the whole will collapse. Even as a young man I saw the similarity with the human body and also the human spirit.'

Nick looked around at the bare little room and found his heart strangely warmed. 'So your clock is a souvenir?'

Dr Ahmed smiled sadly. 'A tribute. I bought it when they sent word my father had died. He never wanted me to leave home, you see. But he would have loved those old clocks. He was an accountant, very fond of balances. I brought it back – but it has never worked properly since. The folly of youth!'

Nick heard himself saying, 'My father died recently too. He would have been glad to see me here. This was the kind of service he believed in. We used to argue about my choices.' He felt the familiar swelling in his throat, painfully harsh, and swallowed. *I didn't cry when they buried you; you won't get tears from me now.*

Dr Ahmed put his hand on Nick's shoulder. 'I am sorry for your loss. But time is the best judge of our choices, more than men – more even than fathers. Like I tell my son: never decide things are broken while there is still time to fix them.'

Margaret's voice sounded from inside, calling them in for dinner. Guests were arriving soon; Dr Ahmed, distraught at his lapse in politeness, hurried to show Nick to his room.

As Nick followed him through the falling dusk, something jarred, diverting his attention to the garden's edge. It was a makeshift cross – two small pieces of wood tied together and pushed into the earth by the wall. A fading bunch of yellow blossoms lay at its base. It was unassuming, like memorials to the nameless fallen. But something about it filled Nick with disquiet; it reminded him of an English grave.

Today I join The Boys. Everything is fixed at last, and no one can stop it – not even Baba. A man is coming to see him from the capital – some English man. So Baba will be busy all day and Mama will be with Nagode.

We waited for one year already, Akim and me. Since Juma joined The Boys. He is sixteen and big. You could not know they are brothers, Akim and Juma. Akim had a sickness when he was small. Baba says this is why his arms are like dry sticks. They break so easily. He tries push-ups after school. We tried it together one day. Juma saw us, and he laughed. 'You two look like you're fucking the sand,' he told us. But when we are in The Boys, no one will laugh any more.

When we sit in the classroom for the first lesson Akim whispers: 'After the last bell Juma will come for us. Then he will take us to Mister, and he will give us the test.'

I ask Akim: 'What is the test? Is it hard?' Akim says: 'Wait, JoJo. You will see.' Then the teacher shouts, 'Stop this noise.' And I bend to my books.

I see the nervousness in Akim's eyes then. He pretends he is not afraid. But Akim just turned twelve last month. I will reach thirteen before the next rains. I am more nearly a man than he is.

I told him and Juma: 'It must be after school.' Baba takes me there every day and watches when I go in. He says: Be a good student, Yahya. Listen well, Yahya. *No one calls me Yahya except Baba.*

When the bell goes at last, I feel my heart start to beat fast. We run outside. Juma is waiting for us by the school gate. I still have my uniform shirt on.

'Take it off,' Juma tells me. The buttons catch and my arms get stuck. Akim laughs until I tear it free. I want to push him. But not with Juma here. He fixes cars and motorcycles in the shop with Mister. No one will trouble Akim because Juma is his big brother. I was a big brother once. Until Bako died. Now there is only Nagode. But she is still a baby. She only needs Mama. She doesn't need me.

Juma takes us to the square. They've finished prayers already. I see Juma's father Mr Kamil, speaking with Imam Abdi. He looks so fat and clean. Juma pinches Akim's arm. 'Quick,' he says. He does not want Mr Kamil to see him. We bend low behind the cars. I see black birds sleeping on the mosque roof.

The cars have too much dust on them. Juma drags his finger across one. 'Bad rains are good for business,' he says. 'All the engines in the village will stop working soon.'

Two years before, we had good rains. The ground was heavy and the lake was green. There was mud as far as the village. Akim and me, we painted ourselves red. How Baba howled! One day it rained so much the lake came to the square and made Baba's car into a boat. We pretended that I was the captain and on the top was a big sail. Even Mama laughed at us.

Today, Akim is complaining: 'Man, it's too hot. I want some Fanta. Let's stop at Tuesday's place.' But Tuesday is not in his shop. Instead there is one of Tuesday's ladies. The refrigerator is not fixed, she says. There is no Fanta. I smell the hot glass when I put my hands on it. Juma asks her: 'Where are the magazines, darling? You know the ones?' He leans close to her and she hits him on the side of his head. I take some stickers from the shelf and put them under my shirt, into my trousers. They are shaped like flowers. Later I will give them to Adeya for her schoolbag. Her bag is very ugly.

'Get out,' Tuesday's lady says. 'You are only trouble, you boys.'

When we leave the shop, Juma's face is red where she hit him. But he is still laughing. He says: 'How many times has Tuesday fucked that one? Maybe she's tired of him now. Maybe she wants a change, eh?'

Akim is giggling like a donkey: eeheeheehee. Juma punches him, and he gets tears in his eyes. I do not want Juma to hit him again. So I say, 'How do you know about Tuesday's ladies?' Juma, he laughs. 'I know all of Tuesday's ladies,' he says. 'I fucked some of them, too.'

Akim has his stupid smile again. Juma pinches my arm. He says: 'That is how you get a big dick, JoJo. You give it lots of exercise.' Then he pulls down his pants so we can see it. His dick is not so big.

We walk through the garden of the mosque. Akim wants to go another way. He whines, 'Maybe Father will see us,' he holds onto Juma's arm, but Juma, he pushes his brother away. 'Leave me be,' he says. 'Father went home with the imam. Men will come to the Town to speak with them about the election.'

Akim's eyes go wide. He says: 'The governor's men?'

'Fuck the governor,' Juma says.

I say nothing. But I think. My baba does not like Mr Kamil or Imam Abdi. When Jalloh brings the meat to our house after Friday prayers, he tells Baba: 'Good sermon, eh, Dr Ahmed?' And Baba just smiles and says: 'Thank you, sir, for the best cuts as usual.' But sometimes he says to Jalloh: 'We must all be very careful.'

Baba is an old man. He is not strong like Juma, like Mr Kamil, like Mister. He does nothing. Instead he stands, like a tree. The winds here are too strong, they take down the trees. This is what Juma says. He says: 'Mister teaches boys how to be strong.'

We reach the shop where Juma works. I can smell burning inside. Suddenly I do not want to go in. But Juma pushes me. He says: 'Hurry, yallah. Mister is at the back. He waits for you.'

A radio is playing Michael Jackson. 'Beat It'. Now Akim's eyes are down. He is afraid.

But I will not be afraid. I want to look at Mister. I never saw him close. So I turn my eyes up – and there he is, looking straight at me. And he smiles.

At first I think – but he is smaller than Juma. Just a boy, like us. He sits so still, on a box under the shelf where the radio is. He has bare feet. His toes are long, like white fingers. One tooth is gone. There is a scar from his shoulder down to his hand. His eyes are not brown. I never saw such eyes. They are white. His hair is white, too. Like Baba's. Baba's is old-man-white. Mister, he is spirit-white.

Juma says: 'So here is my brother Akim. And Lady JoJo, too.'

'I'm no lady,' I say back fast. But my heart is beating.

Juma says: 'Your mama and baba treat you like a girl. Drive you to school, JoJo. Don't be in trouble, JoJo. Dress nice, JoJo.'

Akim is laughing too. If we were at school, I would hit him. But here I swallow the words. They feel hot in my stomach.

'So, boss.' Mister is talking. Juma and Akim, they go quiet. 'How old are you?'

I say: 'Thirteen. Soon.'

Mister smiles: 'Almost grown, eh? I know your father. And your mama, she's a pretty one.'

Mister stands up and comes close. I can smell him. He smells of burning. He asks me: 'Do you know who we are?'

I answer: 'Yes, I know.'

'We are the knights of the village,' he says. 'You know what a knight is?'

'Yes,' I say. His eyes make me cold inside. So I try again. I tell him: 'The knights fight to protect the weak ones.'

He puts out his hand to squeeze my arm. It hurts. I hear the music behind and the dogs barking in the field. He is so close. In his belt is a knife. Its shape is long and slim. He opens his shirt for me. I could touch it.

Then he lets me go. I rub my arm where he has marked it. He turns to take an oil can from the shelf beside the radio with Michael Jackson singing. Akim moves back, away from me.

'You want to be a knight, boss?' Mister asks me. 'You want

to join us?' His eyes are white, white as his knife. I feel like they cut me.

'Yes,' I whisper.

He smiles. Then he tips the oil can. I see it pour out onto my school shoes. They go yellow where it touches them.

He says: 'Your brother died. Your mama can't have strong sons. You are one of the weak. How do I know you will even live to be a man?'

He is close to me, so close. I know what he is telling me. I know what he wants. He wants me to take the knife from him, right now. I must show no fear.

Inside I shout: 'Now, JoJo, now!' Behind me the dogs have caught a bird. I can hear it screaming. When they cut Mister's arm, did he scream? Is his blood red, like mine? Or white as his skin?

Mister, he waits. With every breath I think: Now! Now! But I do nothing.

Then Mister, he smiles.

'Go home, boss,' he tells me. 'Be good. There's no place for you with us.'

I run.

Margaret had laid the table, fire-roasted meat filling the room with its warm thyme smell. Beside it lay a bowl of maize porridge, dumplings made of groundnut, rice and lime soaked with strong yogurt. There was a salad of tomatoes and a green, viscous soup. The meat was paler than lamb and darker than chicken. A plump man with scarred hands and a vast belly nodded gratefully when Nick complimented its flavor.

'I bring the best cuts for Dr Ahmed,' he said. 'They are always tender because the animal is never afraid when I slaughter it. I hypnotise it with my voice.'

'He really does.' Another man spoke from the table's end. 'I've seen him at it. One minute they struggle and then Jalloh here whispers in their ears. I don't think they even see the knife.' His beard looked thin and small against the splendour of his peacock robe. He had been introduced to Nick as Mr Kamil. His wife, Aisha, wore a full emerald abaya with dark embroidery and a towering hairpiece. Her nails glinted like beetles as she waved her husband's remark away. 'Oh, Kamil, please. At dinner it's disgusting.'

Across the table sat the hunched old woman Nick had seen on the porch of the house opposite – Miss Amina. No English, according to Dr Ahmed. But she nodded vigorously, saying, 'Eh, eh.'

'It's my personality,' Jalloh continued unperturbed. 'The animal knows its master. Once it knows, it forgets its fear. Fear sours the meat. The best butchers have strong personalities.'

Dr Ahmed leaned over to Nick and whispered, 'Jalloh is a great hypnotist. He thinks he has hypnotised me into imagining his goats get thinner every month. I don't mind making my little contribution to his Friday supper, though.'

Margaret served the food, her hair covered in a pale scarf. It slipped as she bent to spoon rice onto Nick's plate, her wrists fragrant with thyme. The carelessness of her dress seemed almost disdainful; he saw Miss Amina's frown and Aisha's pursed lips as their hostess placed the bony meat on the table. She met Nick's eyes, her own coolly deliberate.

'This is the wrong lesson, Jalloh,' another man said – the village imam, wrapped almost to vanishing in a heavy white shawl. His narrow mouth worked even when empty, as if in permanent argument. A thin hand burrowed into the folds over his lap, the other plucked at the meat like a hungry stork. He had more to say, but in a language Nick did not understand, waving his finger at the butcher. A slick of grease shone on his knuckle.

Dr Ahmed listened with intent politeness. Margaret came through from the kitchen and took a seat behind Nick, a plate of food on her lap. He looked back at her. 'They're upset about something.'

'It's an old argument,' she replied. 'The imam says no death is ordained except by Allah, and any man who challenges Allah's authority is the pawn of Shaitan. Now they are talking about politics, not goats.'

'Forgive us, Nicholas,' Mr Kamil broke in. 'Our village is like a house of many rooms, a different family in each one. Allah is the rightful master of the whole house. But some men place themselves above Allah. And wherever men challenge Allah's authority, the poor and weak suffer first.'

Jalloh's broad face was creased into a dark frown. He moved to answer, but Dr Ahmed spoke over him. 'Another time, Kamil. Let's enjoy our dinner.' Mr Kamil leaned closer to Nick.

'Let me ask you something. In England, if a man takes the food and fuel from a house and makes the family inside beg to take back what is rightfully theirs – what would you call such a man? Master or thief?'

'Politician,' answered Nick, and Mr Kamil laughed, slapping the table with puffy fingers. Yellow grains of rice flew from his beard like flies.

'That's right! Politicians are the biggest thieves. We will have elections here soon. There must be a return to the rule of law. Allah's law is a fair law. Man's law is easily corrupted.'

'You are a Christian?' the imam interrupted in halting English.

Nick sensed Margaret stirring behind him. She picked up her plate and walked into the kitchen.

'My mother was a Catholic,' he said carefully. 'She had her faith. My father wasn't a religious man.'

It had been one of Kate's wilder efforts to talk him out of coming here, an uncharacteristic resort to terror tactics. *They hate Jews, you know*, she'd said. *They could find out and kidnap you. I'm not Jewish*, he'd reminded her, gently. *Only my father is – and he hates Jews more than anyone.* She'd snorted at that. *Like they'll know the difference.*

But he'd thought about it later, about the strange compulsions that drove his father to marry a fervent believer despite his contempt for faith. He remembered the tense day of his grand- mother's burial – feeling cowed by the sight of his father in a long black coat, singing in an unknown tongue that transformed him into a stranger. The women were eerily alike: the same hard black shoes, the same shiny hair emerging from caps, curling around their chins. *Wigs*, his mother had whispered. The men wore fringed tallits, stringy curls jerking as they bobbed over their prayer books. There had been dark knots of silence under the falling rain and shouting behind closed doors while his mother cringed, then a silent drive home. Later Nick made a hesitant pilgrimage to his father's study to find him hunched over a thick book, strange letters slanting across its pages like fine strokes of a paintbrush. *Is that Grandma's book?* he'd asked in a whisper. His father looked up at him, gaunt, deep lines scored down his cheeks by the grey light. For a split second Nick had a wild urge to run to him, to bury his face in his chest and feel the constant, steady thud of his heart. But his father turned away, closing the book with a snap. *God is for people who can't find the right road without a map*, he'd replied.

'Many good men do not practise a faith,' Dr Ahmed said. Nick had seen passages of Arabic script framed on his wall, presumably from the Qur'an.

'He would say the same thing.' Margaret's eyes were lowered, but he sensed the light touch of her attention. 'He believed the only important values were human ones. Honesty. Honour. Valour.'

'And here you are following his teachings,' Mr Ahmed said. 'Like a good son.'

Before Nick could reply, the group turned at the sound of the door opening. A reedy boy slipped into the room, heading for the kitchen.

Dr Ahmed stood up. 'Yahya? Yahya, come here. Where have you been? Your mother is angry with you.'

His father's voice pulled the boy back – shoulders set in tense unwillingness. He said something quietly to his father.

'Speak in English,' said Dr Ahmed. 'We speak in English to the children, you know. It's better for their education.'

The boy cleared his throat and turned his eyes to the kitchen doorway. Margaret stood there, her face the troubled mirror of her son's.

'I was out with Akim,' he said, spacing each word carefully, speaking to the floor. 'I forgot the time.'

'It is impolite to be late, Yahya.' Dr Ahmed sounded pained. Mr Kamil was nodding sagely. 'You know we have a guest here.' The old man seemed to notice his son's disarray for the first time – the white shirt dirty and torn, his shoes leaving oily prints on the tiled floor. 'And what happened to your clothes? What kind of state is this?'

The boy looked over at Nick, disturbance plainly written on his face. Their eyes met. And Nick remembered a kindred moment, standing in front of his own father after one of many nameless failures, his chest filling up with the old man's disappointment. It was the first feeling of real comradeship since his arrival.

'I don't feel well, Baba,' the boy was saying. 'I need to sleep.' His father walked over and felt his forehead – love plainly wrestling with irritation in him. 'Nonsense, Yahya. Please wash and come sit with us.'

The boy looked into his father's eyes, and Nick felt the strain between them. Then the boy turned and ran back through the door into the night.

Margaret reached out an arm, calling, 'JoJo!' But the door slammed behind him. The boy had left a dark trail on the floor that stank of oil.

I am not afraid of the dark. I am fast. If I run, nothing can catch me. Not even the dogs. Dogs will try, if they are hungry. Hyenas will take even big children. A boy was taken two years before.

But I will not go home. Baba, he shames me. Mr Kamil will tell Akim and Juma. Tomorrow they will laugh at me.

Akim is stupid. Mister, too. What does he know? My brother was the weak one, not me. He could not fight the fever. And Baba was weak – he could not save him.

Baba lies, too. He says we must study to lead a good life. But look at him. His books, they are useless. He could not even save his own boy. Only the poor people go to him, like Miss Amina. Or Tuesday, for the sickness in his dick. Everybody knows. If you are sick and you have money, you go to the Town. If Baba had taken Bako to the Town, he would be well now. I would be his big brother still.

The houses look different in the dark. The road is awake, and the houses sleep. There are lights on the road. Oil and water, Baba says, cost more than blood here. But I like to hear the generators. They sing after dark. They beat, like hearts.

The lights make everything white. The houses are white. The road is white. Only the desert is black and the lake. We don't go there at night. There are witches there. But I will not be afraid of them. I am not afraid of Mister. I am a man, too.

I am still running, away from the mosque and the generators. There are no lights here. Here the sky is bright. The wall of the school is low. I can cross it, easy. We used to play catch here, Adeya and me. She is fast. For a girl. But that game is for children.

My shoes hurt. So I take them off. Baba bought them for me. Good leather and a buckle. Shoes show respect, Baba says. Respect for learning. But the oil is inside the soles. Now they stink.

I want shoes like that white man's. I saw pictures of men wearing shoes like that in Tuesday's magazines.

There is my classroom. I see the window near my desk. The teacher says I am smart. She says: Smart boys don't stare out of the window, JoJo. They look at their books. *But what is in those books? Stories and numbers. They are not real. Mama used to read me stories, sometimes. Dragons and castles and knights from long ago.*

But not any more. Now I know what is real. The fevers are real. The dogs are real. Mister, his knife is real. His scar is real.

I drop one shoe. The other one is heavy in my hand. Like a stone. It pulls me down into the ground.

I can see the window of my classroom. I think: knights do not take classes from the school. Knights fight the wicked. They fear nothing.

So I reach back my arm and I throw. I throw the shoe with all my strength, far away from me. Then the glass breaks, and I feel my heart still running. But beneath my feet the ground is sharp as knives.

OCTOBER

Light floated down through high, yellow curtains, stirring behind Nick's eyelids. He lay still in the early heat, each new breath tugging him gently up towards consciousness. Senses returned one by one – the sweat filming his skin, the cool whir of a fan, the mattress wire-thin against his back, the taste of last night's meal still warm and bitter in his mouth. For once, he couldn't remember his dreams.

He sat up, feet tentative on the floor's bare tiles. They were cool to the touch, soothing his heated skin as he looked around him. *My new home.* His suitcase was wedged against the door separating the small bedroom from his office beyond. A plastic curtain divided the bed from a sink, a squat toilet and a shower hose attached to the wall. Outside, he thought he could hear birdsong.

After a cool rinse and a rudimentary shave, Nick stepped into his office. The filing-cabinet drawers were rusted. A bulky Codan HF radio was connected to a portable generator. His desk was chipped, sporting a telephone and a walkie-talkie, with a worn plastic chair to sit on. Nick thought of his London office – all plush carpets and artwork, wide windows sweeping down onto a world of bustle and steel.

Soft human sounds were audible from Dr Ahmed's clinic on the other side of the wall. Already at his morning rounds. Nick's watch read 9:30. J.P.'s fixer, Eric, would pick him up in half an hour to take him into the Town – to view the hospital project site and meet the region's governor. *Our partner in crime.*

Kate's stationery set and fountain pen lay on the filing cabinet where Nick had placed them before he slept. Light deepened the watermark into swirls, glossing the twinned embossed initials. *N&K.* Those letters sent a rush of unexpected fondness through him. The stationery had been intended for use in their wedding announcement; it had arrived the week before his departure. *Take it with you,* she'd said. *It'll remind you of what's here to come back to.* She'd given him the pen at their last meal together, over braised chicken and chablis. He'd kissed his thanks, their lips numbed by the chill of alcohol. *I'll miss you,* he'd whispered, willing it to be true.

Now he sat at the desk, resting his fingers on the crisp white of the top sheet. Picking up the pen, he wrote:

Hello from deepest darkest etcetera. I've survived so far. It's not so bad. Actually, it's quite beautiful. I've spent so much time filling spaces with shapes that I forgot how stunning empty space can be. Driving up here through miles and miles of nothing, I had this bizarre feeling that it wasn't really empty at all – but part of something bigger, too big to see from the ground. Very disorientating. Or maybe it was just the jetlag . . .! My hosts are interesting. The doctor's an Victorian gentleman – Dickens in the desert. I thought he was putting me on at first. But he seems genuine enough. He even hauled a grandfather clock here all the way from Portobello Road. He worships it, like an idol. His wife is much younger than him. She seems out of place here – a closed book.

He paused at a sudden, disconcerting flash of recall – her laying down dinner plates in silence, a long arm brushing against his sleeve; that shared flicker of contempt, separating them briefly from the table's chatter.

Anyway, today I'll find out what I'm supposed to be doing and hopefully not make a complete mess of things. Wish you were here.

A bubble of ink burst from the nib, staining the white sheet. Nick cursed, watching the words smudge under the spreading purple. He scrunched the paper into a tight ball. Now he'd have to start again.

Outside, the world was wrapped in easy stillness. He stood in the doorway, his rucksack on his shoulder, shielding his eyes from the daylight's brilliant surge. Dr Ahmed's vegetable garden rolled away to the gate, dotted with dark green shoots. Miss Amina sat on her porch in her tangerine-coloured wrap. Nick raised his hand; chicken fat wobbled under her chin as she replied with a wary jerk of the head. A car's engine pulsed far away; closer, Nick heard the bleating of unseen goats.

He walked to the corner of the porch, looking around it and into the garden. A flash of colour made him draw back – Margaret, tall and oblivious, came out of the kitchen with a basket full of wet clothes. Nick watched from his hidden corner, the long line of her back twisting as she reached up to her neck, wiping beads of sweat from under her hair's dark knot. He pulled his eyes away, feeling the furtive guilt of a thief.

Dr Ahmed's surgery door was open a crack, an antiseptic reek slicing into the soft outdoor smells. Nick could see the outline of shapes: the frail curve of a limb stretched out, a white rectangle obscuring part of it – and then suddenly a sharp line of steel.

As he stepped backwards, the voices inside hushed. Steps crossed the floor. A moment later, Dr Ahmed's beaming face was framed in the doorway. One gloved hand was visible in the morning sunlight, the pale latex streaked with blood.

'Nicholas! You slept well?'

'Very well.' He averted his eyes from the bloody glove, looking over the doctor's shoulder to where two other pairs of eyes glowed white in the dimness. A girl stood by the examination table, her face bird-thin, barely emerging from a clinging circle of black fabric. One pale hand clutched the folds of her abaya, drowning her small frame in its dark waves.

Beside her, a little boy lay on the table – legs poking from his dirty shorts. A pink-stained cotton pad covered his right shin. His eyes flicked towards the sudden light, and Nick saw the clouded whiteness at their centre.

'Just in time,' Dr Ahmed was saying, gesturing for Nick to enter. 'I need a surgical assistant.'

He stepped reluctantly inside, feeling the clench in his stomach. The girl drew her robes around her, fingers dark yellow against the cloth.

'Hello.' Nick bent his head to her. She looked to Dr Ahmed, bewildered. He spoke to her quietly, his large hand dwarfing her shoulder.

'Here.' He pointed to the little boy's leg. A surgical needle was pinched between thumb and forefinger, thread dangling towards the ground. 'We are fixing a very small accident. But I need you to hold the leg. Yes, just like that. This fellow is an old patient, eh, Hassan?'

The milky eyes swivelled in the small face, searching. Nick fought an urge to reach over and close them against the hopeless strain. The skin of the leg felt rough and hot under his hand, jerking slightly with each tug of thread as Dr Ahmed worked away. The girl reached across the child's face, passing an anxious hand over his forehead. Nick realised with shock she must be his mother.

'Nearly done,' the doctor said. Nick sensed a note of reassurance, perhaps meant for him. He wanted to apologise for his queasiness – to explain why he could not look at the wound, why he was fighting the urge to run while the boy lay with stoic stillness. But honesty was a habit he'd buried long ago. Instead, he hid the rising bile with conversation. 'So these are your patients?'

'I spread my net wide.' Dr Ahmed bent over the leg, lips curled in a smile. 'These two are from the Town. They come on market day with the vegetables. I started treating this boy's injuries two years ago. He does not know he is nearly blind, you see.'

Dr Ahmed stretched, rubbing the small of his back. He took off his glasses with his clean hand and wiped his eyes.

'How can he not know?'

'Wishing can create many illusions. This boy wants to run and play like his friends, so his mind tells him he can see. During my clinical training we learned about it as a rare brain disorder, nothing more. But his mother might say its roots are in the heart's desire. And sometimes,' he pressed the wound gently under the dressing, 'there are consequences.'

Nick forced himself to meet the white pupils, the ghost of a reflection staring back at him. 'Could his sight not be cured?'

'It is a service I cannot provide.'

'But when this hospital is built in the Town . . .' Nick felt a renewed surge of purpose. He reached up to the boy's face, heard the small catch of breath as he touched the round cheek.

'Ah, yes. Your hospital.' Dr Ahmed cut the final thread and put the needle down on a tray behind him. Intrusive shards of daylight speared off the metal; the old man's gaze followed them to the door's crack and the invisible world beyond. His jaw worked silently for a moment, eyes unfocused, and Nick wondered what he was seeing. Then he turned back to Nick, with a renewed smile

'Did you know, you are already an important figure in young Hassan's life, Nicholas? And in this little enterprise of mine? The rent I get from your organisation goes to fix many of these little accidents – and more besides. So these strangers,' he gestured to the girl and her child, 'are not really strangers in a way.'

Nick smiled back at him, feeling a tug in his chest. His father had taken him on house calls every summer when he was a little boy of six or seven, too young to resent wasting his school holidays. In dark country lanes and narrow fishermen's cottages, he'd watched red beads swell from drawn splinters or around the knotted lips of wounds pierced by the suture needle. He'd loved it back then: the silence, the sharp scents of iodine and Dettol, the sound of his father's laughter as he soothed and reassured – a kinder man at these moments, less godlike – the almost sacred presence of healing.

'And long may that last,' he replied, sincerely.

A sharp sound outside caused the little boy to jump. From the doorway, Nick saw a Jeep pulling up by Dr Ahmed's gate, yellowed by dust. Its driver was bull-shaped, a flaming red beard punching out of his chin. One thick, freckled arm waved from the window.

Nick picked up his bag, smiling apologetically. 'I think that's my ride.'

'Of course.' Dr Ahmed raised a hand in farewell. 'Have a wonderful first day.'

'Morning!' the driver roared as Nick hurried down to the low gate. His booming voice chewed up the quiet. 'Welcome to our little castle in the desert!'

Nick met the bruising grip of the outstretched hand. 'You must be Eric,' he said.

'Guilty.' The blue eyes were friendly, slitted above slab-like, bristled cheeks. As Nick climbed into the passenger seat, Eric's muscled forearm slammed on the horn. 'Good health, Dr Ahmed!' he yelled towards the open surgery door. And then Nick was pinned to the seat by the Jeep's acceleration, shooting towards the village square.

'So they finally fucking sent you, eh?' Eric stank of sweat and stale leather. 'Did they have to wait for school holidays? Teacher let you out?' He roared at his own joke. 'Sorry, can't help it. Anyway, it's about fucking time. Six months I've been waiting here, construction stalled and everything. Fucking bureaucrats.' His guttural accent made Nick think of drunken Norse gods.

'I'm sorry I'm late.'

'Why should you be sorry? We're a team now. All hunky-dory.'

The Jeep tore along past the mosque, swinging northwards past market stalls heaped with tyres, rubber shoes and decomposing vegetables.

'I still don't really understand why they need me here,' Nick said. 'You know the ground and the people. Why bring in an outsider?'

'Well, I'm no bloody architect, am I? J.P. says you have degrees from here to Copenhagen. Half these bloody buildings don't last five minutes. And then there's the cash. The boss doesn't want a naughty little boy like me fiddling with it, does he? Outsiders are always honest.'

The northern highway was fast; a red wind whipped through the car. Eric shouted over it – a list of complaints: J.P.'s meddling, never being paid enough or on time, the arrogance of foreigners and the thievery of local hires. He even had some words of friendly enough scorn for Dr Ahmed. 'Nice guy, but completely bonkers if you ask me. Wants to be an English gentleman in the middle of nowhere. His wife, though . . . She's fucking beautiful. You can't say that about these Islamics, mind. But she is.'

Nick was silent, but Eric needed no encouragement. 'They should hire Dr Ahmed in the Town, not leave him stuck out here. He's another one with degrees coming out of his arse. But it's all politics, eh? There was some trouble once, between his family and the governor. Anyway, Dr Ahmed isn't welcome in the Town, I know that much.'

Nick replayed Dr Ahmed's almost obsessive civility compared to his firebrand guests at last night's dinner. To picture him as any kind of revolutionary seemed nonsensical.

'And what about us?' Nick asked. 'How welcome are we?'

'Very fucking welcome. We're the ones with money. The governor really wants his hospital. He's had planning permission for a year now – that's what the last of you boys managed before he buggered off. It took bloody forever, all this participatory bullshit – local consultations and everything. But the rains were so bad, the governor had to give extra money to his farmers to buy water. He's been waiting a while for someone to come with more cash, and he's not a patient fellow *at all*. There's a construction firm on standby. You've the plans – some clever bastards from the capital made them. They're supposed to be architects, too.'

'They're bad plans. And overpriced.' Nick had sat up late into the night memorising them, desperate to make a good first impression.

'So make them better. Make yourself bloody useful. Keep the books, pay the bills, kiss the governor's arse and moan to J.P. all about us lazy, thieving fuckers. Ha ha ha!' Eric's laughter was propelled out of the open window, speeding towards the dark and busy horizon.

As they neared the Town Nick noticed more trucks, massive dust clouds spinning in their wake. They swept past like hallucinations, lurid ribbons of paint around silver mirrors and warped iron trellises, trailers piled high with strange cargoes: wooden chairs, old mattresses, salvaged metal. Men clung to the top, turbans wrapped close against the stinging wind. As one truck passed, Nick breathed the stench of defecation. A cow's eye caught his as the metal slats whipped by, a dark brown circle of uncomprehending fear.

Some of the trucks were marked with bright blue logos, ragged lines leaking onto the road behind them. 'Water,' Eric said. 'The governor controls the only reliable source, an hour or so north. It's his company that sends out the tankers and sets the prices. Good management, he says – making sure there's enough to go round. And we'll need it. It's going to be a bitch of a dry season.'

Dry season. The land around them looked like it had never seen water, lying flat under a haze of dust, as pale and hard as bone. This was nothing like the deserts of Nick's imagination, the smooth, sculpted gold of sand and light he'd first marvelled at on the television screen, curled up next to Madi watching

Lawrence of Arabia. It's not real, Madi had assured him. *Those places don't look like that.*

They might, Nick had said, still dazzled. *How do you know?*

Coz I saw them, English. So I know.

The highway narrowed; suddenly Nick saw billboards advertising washing powder and shampoo. Smoke rose from busy street stalls over charred maize. Aerials bristled from apartment blocks, their balconies bright with draped clothes.

They circled a central roundabout, around men hard at work planting flowers. One stood up as they swung past, dust tracing hungry lines down his face. His blue T-shirt screamed *Go Dodgers! World Series Champions 1988.*

The signposts were now all in English – one to a university, another to an Islamic school. At the third turn they reached a checkpoint. A skinny youth in dark green came to the window, clasping Eric's hand with a quiet, 'Hi, man.' A long-barrelled gun bobbed over his shoulder as nervous eyes scrutinised Nick.

'For the governor,' Eric said. The soldier stood back and waved them through, Adam's apple pale in the hollow of this throat.

'I thought we were meeting at the hospital construction site,' Nick asked, puzzled.

'That we are.'

The road opened into a wide forecourt. To their right, a fountain threw out arcs of foamy water; behind it stood a large mansion of white stone.

Opposite was a hospital – with ambulances parked in the courtyard and electric doors opening onto a raised porch. A doctor in an immaculate white coat smoked by the entrance wall.

Nick was bewildered. He turned to Eric. 'There's already a hospital here?'

'One hospital.' Eric pulled up the handbrake and hopped out of the Jeep, dusting the sweat off his khakis. 'And you're building another. You saw the site plans, didn't you?'

'Yes, but . . .' His recruitment files had described a children's hospital planned next to an old administrative centre. In bed at night, with Kate's back turned to him, he'd given it shape – standing out from its background in clean, white stone, an island in a sea of sickness. He'd even captured it in a painting, setting aside his slide rule and compass and bringing out his mother's watercolours for the first time since childhood. He'd laid it at her unresponsive fingertips on the plastic table during his final visit. *See, Mum? I'm going to build this.* One of the nurses had peered over his shoulder, patting his mother with brisk condescension. *Isn't that nice, Mary? And what a rare treat to get a visit from Nicholas, eh? I'm sure he's very busy.* His mother just stared ahead, her eyes a blue fog. And he'd thought of the quotation she'd inscribed under her portrait of Madi, still hanging in their old kitchen. *And God shall wipe all tears from their eyes. And there shall be no more death, neither sorrow, nor crying.*

Cigarette smoke drifted over their heads from the hospital lobby. He breathed it in with the sharp taste of disappointment. 'They said it would be the only hospital in the region. A life-saving project.'

'And so it will, the only children's hospital. What's the big fucking worry? Come, the governor is over there.' Eric pointed to the white building. 'All will be revealed.'

The governor's office was on the second floor of his residence. As the heavy doors swung open, Nick became conscious of his damp armpits and palms, the treacherous scent of uncertainty.

The governor sat behind a desk, signing papers. He looked up as they entered, removing large-framed reading glasses.

'Ah, Eric.' A gold watchstrap circled his wrist. Smooth flesh swelled around it, vanishing into a white tunic.

'Good morning, sir. How are things?' Eric shook his hand and eased himself into a chair on the other side of the desk.

'And you must be our new brother-in-arms.' The governor took Nick's hand with courteous attention, his palm as large as

Dr Ahmed's. But while the doctor's was bone-hollow, the governor's was full, power pulsing under the skin.

He motioned Nick to sit down. The chair rocked awkwardly on the carpet; he had to clutch the desk to keep his balance. 'I'm very happy to be here.'

'And we are happy to have you. The delays have been frustrating.' The governor's English was flawless. Behind his head, Nick saw framed degree certificates. One showed a white shield quartered with a red cross, around a rising sun. The governor turned to follow his gaze.

'Brown University, in Rhode Island,' he said, 'Economics major. An Ivy League school. Did you study economics?'

'I'm afraid not,' Nick replied. 'I stick to buildings, they're more predictable.'

The governor laughed. 'You're lucky. People and systems are rarely that. How to make them work is a constant puzzle. Coffee? It's a local variety, from our tropical south. This country sends all its best home-grown coffee abroad. In the States, they sold it back to me as American coffee. Human economics, you see.'

The coffee had a rough, burned flavor. Eric topped his up with sugar. The governor sipped slowly, the thin china vanishing behind his full bottom lip.

'Did Eric show you our site yet?'

'He did.' Nick steeled himself. 'Just to be clear, sir – my plans are for a hospital. But the one you have downstairs looks very . . . complete. Why build another?'

The governor shook his head and pointed at Eric. 'You need to do a better job of these briefings. We haven't time to waste.'

Eric was unfazed. 'I'm just the contractor, not the project manager.'

The governor sat back, the red leather of his chair creased by his weight. 'Look, young man. Our hospital was not functioning for many years. The building was going to be condemned. Your organisation offered to co-finance its reconstruction. But you took too long. So this year I made a personal donation to bring it back to working order.'

'I see,' Nick said, 'but . . .'

'What I need now is a children's wing. A fully modern wing, to lower our child mortality rate, which is very high.' The governor put down his coffee cup. 'Do you understand supply-side economics?'

Nick's face flushed. 'A little.'

'Your Mrs Thatcher does – though your countrymen seem not to appreciate her. There are two different types of society. In one, the people drive. Leaders are always chasing them but they can never do enough. This is a recipe for exhaustion and anger. In other societies, leaders drive. They create the desires of their people by showing them what can be theirs.'

He leaned forward. 'We talk of modern societies now in this last decade of the millennium. But you cannot modernise by consensus. Someone always has to lead. This specialised clinic will draw people from the whole region, the whole country. People who now think they can cure their children with witch doctors and potions. We will see an effect that trickles down through our whole society. Is it clear to you now what we are trying to do?'

His absolute assurance was like a pressure wave, pushing Nick back. 'It's clear,' he said. 'You have a mission.'

The governor smiled at that. 'A mission,' he repeated. 'Yes. A voice in the wilderness.'

The audience was over; he dismissed Nick with a friendly clap on the arm. 'I hope you have a fruitful time with us. And give my regards to Dr Ahmed.'

The head of the local construction firm had appeared at the door, a ferrety man holding rolled-up architectural plans. Their site tour began in the existing hospital, white rooms layered with smells of chlorine, faeces and sweat. The hospital administrator hovered anxiously, pointing out the newly installed X-ray machine, electric beds and nursing staff trained in Europe.

But Nick's disquiet grew. He noticed that half the ward beds were empty. As they left the building, he looked over to the checkpoint – its long metal bar keeping the world at bay.

After a brief review of the construction schedule, Nick agreed to start after Friday's holiday. They said their farewells, returning to Eric's Jeep. The barrier lifted silently to release them.

They drove back into the Town's fringes. Nick wound down the window, closing his eyes against the sun's glare. Eric was silent. Eventually he cleared his throat.

'So how do you like the professor? Brown University!' He spat out of the driver-side window into the parched air. The desert was a cloud of dust, white and thick as the little boy's eyes this morning. Restless eddies rolled back and forth in it. Nick turned to look at Eric. 'Who exactly uses that hospital? The building's so far from the centre. There's no public transport. How could people even get there? And why all those guards and barricades?'

Eric shrugged. 'I saw sick people plugged into machines, beep-beeping away. It smelled like shit, but all hospitals smell like shit.'

'Something's not right.'

Eric shook his head. 'Look, Nick. This is why I tell them not to send these fucking volunteers. Like that French bastard J.P. would say, a little *je ne sais pas* never hurts when you come to a new place. Wouldn't you say?'

The horizon loomed, far and featureless, an optical illusion caused by a faint swell in the landscape. It was disorienting; the road pointed straight ahead, but Nick already felt lost.

But then the village's familiar outskirts appeared over a rise, the tall mosque beckoning them in. Dr Ahmed's house materialised around the bend in the road; the sight of it eased Nick's heart. The yellow flowers spilling over the gate could have been climbing roses; the pale sky was the same colour as a midsummer evening. Even the sense of sorrow inside the house was familiar – the silence of people living together in separate worlds.

Eric said he'd be back on Saturday. Before leaving, he reached into the glove compartment and brought out a large envelope.

'Twenty thousand dollars,' he said. 'For the site manager, the workers and the rest. I'll bring you all the names and job descriptions later. So over the weekend you can make a nice spreadsheet for J.P.. Here, count it if you like.'

'I don't need to.' Nick got out of the car and offered his hand. 'Thanks for everything today. I'm glad you're here.'

Eric laughed. 'A fucking Viking is always useful, even in the desert.'

The next morning Nick tried to make the telephone and radio work. A faint hiss over the generator hum suggested the radio was transmitting – but J.P. did not answer. The phone line was an echo chamber filled with shrill cicadas, clicking and whistling.

Dr Ahmed had been out the previous evening, seeing patients. Nick had eaten alone – a plate of jollof rice left by Margaret on the kitchen table.

But soon Dr Ahmed came striding into Nick's office, brimming with good cheer. He apologised for their poor telephone connection. 'A lack of insulation on the wires,' he explained, voice mournful. 'They corrode during the wet season and then crack with the heat. Another casualty of our bad weather, I'm afraid.'

Nick remembered the water trucks rolling down from the Town. 'Where do you get your water?' he asked. 'Do you ever have shortages?'

Dr Ahmed adjusted his glasses. 'Ah, well. You see, we buy our water from the Town. A standing arrangement with the governor. We pay a collective fee every month and the tankers come. But, of course, sometimes the fee is higher than others. The governor sets the price and quantities.'

'I met the governor yesterday,' Nick said. 'He told me to give you his best regards.'

'Did he, now?' Dr Ahmed was no longer smiling. 'And what did you think of this hospital, if I may ask?'

'I thought it was empty. Do you know why that would be?'

Dr Ahmed turned towards the radio and started fiddling with the dials. His shoulders sloped thinly in his dark jacket.

'I did want to work at that hospital once,' he said. 'But the jobs went elsewhere. My father was active in the opposition party. I stay out of politics, but . . .' He looked over at Nick and smiled sadly. 'Memories are long.'

'I'm sorry.' Nick thought back to the largely empty wards, the smell of the pristine new floors. 'It's really their loss.'

'Well,' Dr Ahmed straightened up, 'here I get to help my own community, the people I grew up with. I feel useful, which is no bad thing when you get old. You have a while to go yet, Nicholas. Come!' He opened the office door. 'Let's have some tea.'

He followed his host into the kitchen, passing the deep walnut of the grandfather clock. Today it was decently closed, ticking sleepily. He stepped over the box of tools spread out on the floor.

Dr Ahmed busied himself lighting the kitchen stove. Tea came, ferociously dark and sweet. 'English tea was a revelation to me,' he explained. 'When I was a boy, tea was powder in bottles. I brought some English teabags back for my older sisters, but they could not get used to it. Now it's imported routinely – but I can claim to be one of the first to drink it here.'

One of Dr Ahmed's sisters was still living, it seemed, a widow with a small apartment in the Town. 'She is much older than me. Yahya calls her "grandmother". Goggo is how we say it. His real grandmother died when I was Yahya's age, birthing a girl.' Nick saw tears behind the thick-framed glasses. Feeling the old man's embarrassment, he asked, 'You call your son Yahya, and your wife calls him JoJo?'

'Oh, yes. You see, Yahya means John in Arabic, in the language of the Qur'an. We chose the name because John the Baptist is a prophet for our two great religions – Christian and Muslim. John is the one who leads the way. My wife is a Muslim now, but she was born a Christian. She speaks to our son in the language of her childhood. The language of the heart.'

'Where is JoJo now? I mean, Yahya?'

Dr Ahmed frowned. 'In his room. I hope he is thinking. He was disobedient – reckless.' He put down his cup and folded his hands around it, an oddly protective gesture. 'Do you want children, Nicholas?'

The question took Nick aback. He thought of Kate, of the laughing days after their engagement. They'd joked about naming their children after architectural marvels – Sofia, Petra, Ben. 'I don't really know. I feel as if my own life has barely started.'

Dr Ahmed smiled. 'This is a question no African person of my generation could ask another. For us the entire purpose of life is children. When a man has sons, he stops thinking about adventures and starts thinking about traditions. If I am honest, this is what disturbed me most about life in England. There were many West African communities there I knew – Yoruba, Fulani, Igbo – and others, too, Indians, Arabs, all living well and making good money. I could have been one of them. But many grew up without truly knowing themselves. This is a terrible thing for a child. If you do not know your starting point, how can you chart your course?'

Nick heard it as a plea, watching Dr Ahmed's knuckles tense and flex around the cup. He remembered the awkward misery in JoJo's eyes, the painful barbs of frustration hooking father and son over the dinner table.

'I was an only son, too.' He tried to make his voice gentle. 'It's a lot of pressure.'

'Yahya was not always an only son.' Dr Ahmed looked upwards. 'He had a younger brother. Bako. But a fever took him.'

'I'm so sorry.'

'Yes, we grieved. Margaret especially.' Dr Ahmed sat up and shook his shoulders. 'We loved that boy. Bako was always happy. But Yahya . . .' Another sad smile touched his face. 'He takes after my wife. And something beautiful in a woman can be dangerous in a man.'

A voice screeching from the garden gate made Dr Ahmed

48

look up. 'Ah, my day begins!' Nick looked out of the window to see Miss Amina leaning over the gate, her chest heaving with angry exertion.

'An emergency.' Dr Ahmed's smile had returned. 'Margaret once made me some very good sketches as a birthday present – my patients represented as clocks of different kinds. Miss Amina was the alarm clock.'

Nick laughed. 'Your wife's an intelligent woman.'

'Oh, yes, very. She sees us doctors as artists of the body. Science is not the strongest force in our lives. You have to know the spirit before you can cure the flesh.'

He stood up, and Nick rose with him. 'So – once more unto the breach,' the old man said, heading to the door. 'And may God grant you a good day.'

Nick found Margaret in the back garden, hanging washing. Her hands were framed with bright beads of water, staccato drops falling to stain the orange ground.

He watched her, relaxed in the peace of the morning – lifting, shaking, laying over the clothesline and bending back to the basket. Every time she shook the clothes, droplets took to the air in wild clusters of refracted light.

After a while he walked over, bending to pick up a pair of child's dark trousers. She stood back as he handed them to her, wary. 'Thank you.' Her voice had a quality of reluctance, as if not much used.

'You're welcome.' He noticed that her features had the precise grace of technical drawings. He picked up another bunch of wet fabric from the basket. But this time it slipped from his grasp as he struggled to rise, falling into the dust.

'I'm so sorry.' He blushed at his clumsiness, scrambling to retrieve it. *Idiot.* I'm not helping, I guess.'

Her eyes met his as he straightened, a cool and intelligent scrutiny. At last she indicated the basket again with a small tilt of her head. 'But if at first you don't succeed . . .'

He smiled, abashed; he realised he'd misjudged her. The next shirt passed carefully from him to her, her fingers deft as they slipped it over the line. Nick searched for some key to conversation. 'Does Dr Ahmed usually work on a Saturday?'

'He is always working.'

'My father was the same. No rest for the wicked, my mother used to tell him.'

A small stool had been placed beside one of the flowering cassias. She sat on it, wrapping her long blue dress around her legs. Two tin pots lay at her feet, one filled with bulging root vegetables, another with rough, beige grains. A kitchen knife was balanced between them.

Behind them under the flickering shade a baby lay on its back, arms splayed in sleep. Sweat dappled its forehead, plastering thick black curls to its skin. The strange little English-style cross cast a spindly shadow over it, sending a shiver of superstitious anxiety through Nick. He thought of asking about the cross, and the child – but then remembered talk of a little sister.

'She's beautiful,' he said to Margaret. 'How old is she?'

'Ten months.' Margaret took up a stone plate from under one of the pots and laid it on her lap. Pouring the grains onto its surface, she picked up a second, smaller stone shaped like a pestle. Her arms moved back and forth in slow, circular waves, fine powder escaping to the edges with every motion. Her wrists were bare except for one knotted bracelet spaced with blood-red beads.

'What's her name?'

'Nagodeallah.' A smile came to her lips; it transformed her face, illuminating tides of emotion beneath. 'It means: *thanks be to God*. My husband chose it.'

'It's beautiful,' he said. 'It suits her.' The baby was round as a fruit, her mouth puckered as she breathed. 'It's better than Nicholas, anyway.'

Margaret shrugged. 'Nicholas is not so bad.'

'My mother wanted to call me Theodore. Much more romantic.' Nicholas had been his father's choice. He'd looked it up with Madi in the *Encyclopædia Britannica* once; it meant *victory of the people*. 'She was an artist – like you.'

She looked at him in surprise. 'What do you mean?'

'Your husband said you made sketches. He was very proud of them.'

Margaret fixed her eyes on the grinding stone. But after a moment she said, 'I liked to draw as a girl. It was a hobby. I made storybooks for my sister.'

'Like cartoons?'

'No.' She looked over at him with that amused smile. 'Like *once upon a time*.'

'Oh.' He felt heavy beside the light flash of her mind. 'So . . . do you still have them? I'd love to see them.'

'Somewhere,' she replied. 'I used to read them to JoJo. Now he thinks he's too big for stories.'

Something dark brushed her face. She bent her head over the grinding stone, her arms picking up an angry pace.

What did I say? He cleared his throat, casting around for a fresh start. 'People here must be grateful to have a qualified doctor so close by.'

Her forehead creased. 'Few men would do so much for them.'

Nick remembered Mr Kamil, with his small hands and smooth words of persuasion. 'Were those your husband's friends at dinner the other night?'

'They are from the village council. My husband grew up with them.'

'But you didn't?'

'No.' She lifted the grinding stone and swept the flour back into the centre of the plate. 'I grew up in the capital.'

Nick was surprised – but then remembered Dr Ahmed's words: *she was born a Christian*. He wanted to ask more, but didn't know how. So he picked up one of the ugly root vegetables. Margaret looked at him with a quizzical expression.

'I'm pretty good at this at home,' he said. 'May I?' She nodded. He started to attack the skin with the flensing knife. It was harder than it looked, the brown hide clinging to white flesh underneath. The knife scraped across one knuckle, leaving a pink smear.

He put the bloody finger in his mouth so he wouldn't have to see it, swallowing his revulsion at the bitter iron tang. Margaret put down the stone plate and walked into the house, returning with a wet piece of cotton and a bright strip of cloth. He took them sheepishly. *You drop her washing, you bleed on her food. What must she think of you?* He dabbed the stinging liquid onto the cut and tied the cloth around it, a bow at the top, trying not to interpret her slight smile as scorn.

'Very stylish, right?' He waggled his decorated thumb at her. 'Hmm,' she replied, a teasing note that stirred Nagodeallah into urgent, sleepy squeaks. Her mother turned to lift her; she tucked the child under her long throat, dark skin against gold.

Nick reached over and stroked the baby's cheek. *Liquid eyes.* He'd read it somewhere – perhaps under the bedcovers in one of the magazines they'd stolen from the newsagent's top rack. But it was perfect for the little girl, blinking back tears of awakening.

Margaret watched him in silence. Then she said, 'Here.' Handing him the baby, she ran quickly into the kitchen. The child was a warm weight, smelling of sourdough. Margaret emerged a minute later with an apricot headscarf, carrying a loaf of bread and a Pepsi bottle filled with white liquid – yoghurt from yesterday's meal, thick and viscous beneath the plastic.

'I'm afraid I must go out,' she said. 'You can give me Nagode.'

'May I join you?' Nick was reluctant to lose her company. 'I haven't seen the village properly. I could help carry something.' He indicated the bread and the bottle with his spare hand.

Margaret hesitated, then nodded. She traded the food for Nagode, and together they turned towards the front gate.

They walked out towards the desert, along a rough dirt track. Clusters of grain stores lined the path, mud-baked circles with their yellow thatched roofs. Crop fields stretched beyond – man's last barrier against the wilderness. The houses were small and squalid, built of stained concrete, corrugated iron, mud and plastic sheets. Nagodeallah's small head swivelled towards endless sources of fascination.

Margaret stopped at one of the houses. Its concrete walls were softened by yellow curtains at the windows. Nick stood below the porch as she knocked on the door.

A girl of JoJo's age answered, her face lean with childhood's remote beauty. She smiled at Margaret, reaching up to squeeze the baby's fleshy thigh. Nick thought her body looked strange and lumpy behind its concealing abaya.

An older woman came to the door behind her. A tight abaya covered her from hair to toes; she was tucking in the last strands with distracted fingers.

Margaret turned to Nick. 'This is Hanan,' she said. 'And her daughter Adeya. Hanan speaks little English, but Adeya speaks well. Don't you?' She touched the girl's cheek. Hanan took Nagode from Margaret's arms.

Nick nodded to them both. 'Nice to meet you, Hanan, Adeya.' The girl broke into a smile of shy delight, one foot squirming at the door's threshold. 'Nice to meet you,' escaped her lips, her English soft but precise.

'Adeya is a friend of JoJo's. She takes good care of Nagode, too, if I have an errand.'

Adeya blushed at the praise and raised her face to Nick. 'JoJo is in my class. We are the top students.'

Then her eyes darkened. She turned away, and Hanan pulled her daughter to her wide chest; the gesture spoke of apprehension.

Margaret made their farewells and they left, the door closing fast behind them.

'She seems smart.' The girl had reminded him of Margaret somehow – that same impression of fragile intelligence unfolding, like a butterfly's wing.

Margaret reached across to take the bread and yoghurt from him, tucking them under one arm. 'My husband saved her life. She had a sickness in her bowels. Hanan brought her to us, screaming. Ahmed drove her to the Town and paid his savings for her operation. Now she needs a bag to make her business. They tease her at school.' She looked up, eyes blinking at the horizon. The sun was at its zenith, a dry yet penetrating heat. 'It is hard to be different in this place.'

A nearby enclosure jostled with goats, spilling warm, pungent air. Margaret reached one hand in through the wooden fence. Soft noses nibbled at her fingers.

'Nothing for you, greedy,' she said, dipping her head with a half smile, her shape occluded by the light.

It's hard to be different in this place. It was something Madi could have said to him once – maybe not in those exact words, but making a sort of joke of it in his casually fluid English, one of the hundred times they'd sat on the kissing gate at the garden's end, their uniform hoodies pulled up against the afternoon drizzle, savouring the fizz of Dr Pepper as the green fields rolled away before them. Or maybe it had never happened. It hurt that Nick wasn't sure. Once he'd believed he could never lose a single memory of their friendship, that every day would be indelibly preserved in its exact place, sacred, like a missing child's bedroom. But the door had been locked for too long, and he could glimpse only broken fragments as if through a keyhole: the thrilling bitterness of their first beer after Madi's triumphant return from the off-license (*they never check a blackie's age round here*); the wet sting of sand as they chased the returning Atlantic along the wet sand flats, Madi's longer legs kicking spray high into the air; the celluloid smoothness of *National Geographic*, the bumper edition Madi gave Nick for his thirteenth birthday, with Mount Etna roaring red on its cover, costing him a month's wages earned gutting stinking sardines at Saturday's fishmarket. *It's nothing, mate, don't worry about it. Happy birthday, blood brother.*

Now Nick looked at the woman walking beside him, bread and yoghurt nestled in the pale crook of her arms. A Christian woman in a Muslim village. An outsider like Madi – only this time the difference lay beneath the skin. He wondered who she confided in.

'Is it difficult for you?' he asked – half afraid of being too intrusive, but driven to offer now what once he'd failed to give.

Her head turned slightly towards him, eyes not quite meeting his. Then she stepped back from the fence, turning to face the desert as the goats brayed their protest. 'You are not the only stranger here.' For a moment she looked him full in the face, her expression frank, unexpectedly young – before she was striding off again, forcing him to hurry after her, the red beads on her wrist blazing a path through the sunlight.

The village was behind them; now the land was dissolving under his feet, water spreading through the dust in a dark stain. As they paced through reeds, a light wind stirred them into peaceful ripples. The sky arched overhead, a glorious umbrella of light. Beneath it, a moving shadow streamed north, dark wings shattering and reforming. Birds, he thought, migrating. He wondered where they'd come from; maybe they were the same swallows that used to pierce the autumn skies over his mother's garden with whizzing arrows of flight.

Silence ticked by, bounded by the tread of Margaret's feet and light intake of her breath. The quiet pulled at the space inside, a gap that opened when his father died. Margaret's eyes were fixed beyond the lake, oblivious: but why had she asked him to come with her, if not to speak to him?

'Dr Ahmed said your family is originally from the capital.' His voice sounded thin in the vast space. 'So how did you come to be here?'

She raised her eyebrows, scanning the expanse before them. 'It's a long story,' she replied.

'I'd like to hear it.'

She walked on without replying, hoisting the bread into her

other arm without breaking her stride. Nick had a sudden image of her in jeans, moving through a London street with the long beat of those legs, or folding them under a café table, a book in her hand.

Just when he'd given up, she answered. 'I came here on my marriage. Thirteen years ago.'

'That must have been a real change for you.' The dark water was muddying his toes as they skirted the lake. In the distance, Hanan's goats were braying.

She smiled, a curl of the lips that bordered on scorn. 'You saw the capital. What do you think?'

He paused. 'I don't know. I just thought . . . I wondered if you ever missed home?'

She stopped walking and turned towards him, her face a challenge. 'Why do you want to know these things?'

He blushed, realising he had no clear answer. 'I'm sorry,' he said to her. 'I didn't mean to pry.'

He felt her eyes scour him, the harsh scrutiny of judgement. Small lines traced the sweep of her long cheekbones – laughter lines, his mother would have said, though the sunlight turned them silver as tears.

Finally, she sighed. 'No. I am sorry. Most people here do not ask questions. Perhaps I forgot how to answer them.' She gestured with her head towards the far side of the lake. 'Come. It's not far now.'

They resumed walking in silence. Nick felt curiosity burning stronger than ever. But couldn't find words to frame his questions, the sun in his face blank and dazzling. He was surprised when she eventually spoke again. 'I have no home left to miss. My mother died long ago.'

'I'm so sorry.'

'Save your tears.' She raised her free hand to her eyes, shading them from the light. 'That's what the priest said when she passed. My sister and I. They said: "It was God's will to take her."'

'That's what they said to my mother when she became ill.' He struggled to keep bitterness out of his voice. 'She was a believer, too.'

Margaret smiled. 'They told us England has no real Christians any more.'

'Well, she felt real enough. She prayed and went to Communion every Sunday, until she couldn't.' But the Church hadn't dried her tears as her mind dissolved, hadn't soothed away that certainty of damnation, of the unforgivable sin and unpardonable wrong. It was the burden of faith without its comfort.

'Is your mother still with you?'

'No.' It was the first time he'd acknowledged the truth since her committal. The memory of their goodbyes still flayed him – her paper-thin face staring at him as he promised to come back soon, the soul-bleaching smell of antiseptic, the itch of her gaze on his departing back.

'Her body's alive,' he explained to Margaret's questioning glance. 'But she has an illness – a psychiatric illness like depression. She knows she's alive, but I'm not sure she wants to be.'

Margaret nodded, wrapping both arms around her chest, hugging the yogurt and bread to her. 'Who cares for her now?' she asked. 'Your wife?'

'I'm not married.' He realised he didn't want to talk about Kate. 'My mother went into a facility after my father died. They're experts there.'

He read surprise on Margaret's face, an arch to her eyebrows that verged on scorn. 'This is how love ends in your country? Alone in a hospital?'

The words stung. 'It's not a hospital and she's not alone. They look after her.'

'*Look after* is not the same as love.'

'I told you,' he said, feeling the old chameleon shift from guilt to defensiveness, 'it's the best way. She doesn't love me any more – or anyone. Love doesn't come into it.'

Margaret shook her head, unflinching. 'Mothers love,' she insisted. Her hand went again to the beads on her wrist. 'Love ties us to the world. Only God should break the thread.' Her face was flushed, peach scarf blowing into the sky in a brilliant flare. He felt the force of her condemnation, her form sharp and vivid against the blurred white of the landscape, everything else just a background sketch.

Unsettled, he tried to turn the conversation. 'You have a sister, you said?'

She seemed taken aback. 'Sarah.' He saw her draw a breath, resuming her steady walk. 'And a brother, too. But my marriage has separated us.'

'Why?' Nick was surprised. 'How could anyone object to Dr Ahmed?'

She smiled, biting her lip. 'I was a university student when I met Ahmed – studying English literature, if you can believe it. I hurt my ankle falling off a bicycle. My friend told me of a doctor who treated students for free.' She wiped her forehead with the back of her wrist. 'He mended my ankle. Then he asked me for coffee. I read him Tennyson, and he told me stories of England, of his travels there.'

'Had you never travelled?'

Margaret's headscarf whipped in the rising wind; her bracelet glinted as she reached up to adjust it. 'It was my dream to travel. My father had a big travel agency. He brought brochures to the house. See the world – cities and museums and all these things.'

'Where did you most want to go?'

'Many places,' she said. 'Italy. France. England. The cities I read about in the poems. The place with the daffodils – that was my favourite. You know: *I wandered lonely as a cloud that floats on high o'er vales and hills.*'

Lonely as a cloud. He looked up to the white shapes racing across the sky, vast and solitary, endlessly chasing each other through the void.

'So what happened?' he asked. 'Why didn't you travel?'

She sighed. 'My father died from a heart attack. I thought he died rich. But David – our brother – he knew the truth. My father had debts we could not pay.' Her laughter cut. *'Pride goes before a fall.* I was clever, rich and beautiful, and I had always laughed at those who were not. But then David took me from the university and put me to keeping his house. And that was my life – until he came for me.'

'Who came?'

'Dr Ahmed. He offered to send me back to university and pay my fees. But David would not permit charity from a Muslim.' She threw the word out like a challenge. 'So Ahmed offered me the protection of a husband. I would have to convert to Islam. He said it was only for show. Faith is a matter of conscience, he said. We all love the same God.'

Nick's mind turned to his own marriage proposal, made while he and Kate packed boxes after his father's funeral. As he'd watched her hands busily folding and arranging on his mother's kitchen table, a terrible vacancy had spread through him; he'd felt like a clock with its mainspring unwound – and he'd clutched Kate like a lifeline, asking her to marry him. Her face had turned red, eyes filling with tears. *Do you really want to marry me?* she'd asked, the words escaping from the depths of her insecurities. *It's not just . . . this?* She'd indicated the table filled with old books and yellowing letters, the debris of a once purposeful life. *Yes,* he'd replied instantly, terrified of confessing the truth, that he was afraid of an empty life. Later she'd regained her composure, laughing on the sofa. *That was so you, Nick,* she'd teased. *Spur of the moment, nothing organised.* She'd insisted on a more traditional repetition, a mechanical process of jewellers and kneeling declarations on a bridge over the Thames.

Now Nick's heart filled with respect for the old man – and a kind of envy, for the sure inner compass that guided the Dr Ahmeds and Kates of this world, while his own spun so wildly at every crossroads. 'That's real goodness,' he said. 'How could your family reject him?'

Now he heard the scorn in her voice. 'When I told David, he

said to me: "There is no marriage outside the Church. Only whoring." It made me glad to defy him. But in the end . . .' She laughed again. 'I did not finish my degree, and I never saw my daffodils. The year after our marriage there was sickness in the village, and they begged Ahmed to return. In his goodness he could not deny them. So we came here at last. I was twenty years old.'

She turned towards Nick – a swift, fierce focus. 'Do you know why I am telling you this?'

Nick shook his head; her stare was hypnotic, lights on an oncoming car. 'No.'

'It is to warn you,' she said. 'You people always try to mend things that are broken. But perhaps they were broken for good reason. God does not want us to escape His judgement.'

'Doesn't Christianity teach redemption?' *If God can forgive us,* his mother once wept to him, *then why can't we forgive ourselves?*

'Jesus opened the door to heaven,' she said. 'But before we pass through, there is penance. That's all.'

They'd reached the top of the lake. Beside it, Nick saw what could only be called a hut, reeking of ash and defecation. A piece of red cloth blocked the doorway.

He stopped, instinctive revulsion warning him away from it. But Margaret walked onwards with her bread and yoghurt. Barely breaking her step, she laid them down before the door. Over Margaret's shoulder, he saw a hand emerge and snatch the food inside.

'Who is that?' he asked, as Margaret returned.

'Her name is Binza.' Margaret's face had lost its animation. She walked past him without meeting his eyes, heading back towards the village.

For a moment Nick stood, rooted to the earth. The dark water, the slit in the red cloth, Margaret's story – they twisted together in his mind. *Who is Binza? And what is she to you?* But Margaret was already far ahead, dry stalks at the lake's edge snapping under her brisk footsteps.

As they neared the house, Nagode restored to Margaret's arms, Nick saw the boy sitting on the porch. He stood up as his mother approached, his frame tense with expectation.

As she entered he ran to her, burying his face in her side. Her spare arm wrapped around him. 'My wild son,' she whispered to his bent head. Her eyes slipped up to meet Nick's, her lips pressed to JoJo's tight black curls twisting up in a wry smile.

It occurred to Nick that he'd not spoken to JoJo since his arrival. Now he knelt down in the dirt and tried to catch the boy's eye. One curious brown orb peered at him over his mother's arm.

'Hi, JoJo,' he said. 'I'm Nick. I met a friend of yours today. She said you were top of the class.'

JoJo turned towards him. 'I'm not the top.' His voice was soft, tiny catches running through the pre-adolescent sweetness.

'JoJo broke a window at his school.' Margaret said. 'His father is angry.'

'My best friend got into trouble at school, too,' Nick told JoJo. 'Because he was too clever, and he got bored. He needed something to keep him interested.'

JoJo's eyes were fixed on him, a penetrating stare. The accelerating forces of manhood were just beginning to push through his features, lengthening his jawbone and filling out his lips. It gave him an aura of uncertainty – like someone on the edge of a precipice. The loneliness of Nick's own childhood returned as they regarded each other, bringing an unexpected sense of kinship.

He stood up, coming to a decision.

'Is JoJo interested in how things are made – like . . . buildings and machines, that kind of thing? Are you?' He addressed the boy, saw his eyes widen in surprise.

'I like cars,' he replied. 'I have all the Top Trumps.'

'It's the same idea,' Nick said. 'Learning how things work in the real world. Maybe you would like to come and see how we build this hospital? Would he be allowed – after school one day?' He directed this question to Margaret, who looked at her son.

'Would you like to?' she asked him.

JoJo looked up at her and then at Nick. Nick could see the boy's mind working, new ideas pushing and pulling inside him.

'Yes.' The word sprang from him, his body straightening as he spoke. 'Yes, I would like to.'

So today I am going to the Town – with Nicholas! He said I must be ready at eight o'clock SHARP. I say: 'Like a knife.' But Nicholas, he laughs. 'Sharp means exactly,' he says. 'Engineers must be very precise or our buildings will fall down.'

There are so many cars on the road to the Town. Expensive ones. Big engines. Some of them are from my Top Trump cards. I showed the cards to Nicholas, in my room. My favourite is the Jaguar XJ6. It goes from nothing to 100 kilometres per hour in 11 seconds. The size of its engine is exactly 3,442 cubic centimetres. Nicholas says cubic centimetre means capacity. He says capacity is the power that sleeps inside.

Nicholas wants a Ferrari. Bad choice, I told him. Someone will steal it. So he said, 'OK then, a Lamborghini.' Still bad, I told him. They are fast but not strong. He laughed again. 'You choose a car for me,' he said. 'You're the expert.'

The fat man who drives Nicholas, he smells. His teeth are bad, like Imam Abdi's. He laughs too loud and spits. He says: 'So you're coming with the men today, boy? Child labour, eh, Nick?'

Nicholas, though, he is quiet. He asks me questions, but not too many. What is your favourite subject? Do you have a best friend? My favourite subject before was mathematics. But I am not so clever any more. I get the red pen on my workbook. And my best friend was Adeya.

He asks me about Adeya. 'She seems very smart,' he says.

Nicholas tells me he did not have many friends at school.

'Some people are not good at friends,' he says. Then he is quiet for a while. Afterwards he says: 'I made one friend. His name was Madi. He was my best friend for a while. You remind me of him, JoJo.'

I ask: 'But was he English like you?'

Nicholas says: 'Many English people do look like you. But in our village all the English people looked like me, so Madi was very unusual. He was a refugee, you see. They put him in my school when he was a few years older than you.'

I do not know this word: refugee. But I do not want Nicholas to think I am foolish. So I ask him: 'Are you still best friends?'

'Not any more,' he says.

I ask: 'Were you sad?'

'Yes,' he says. 'I miss him very much.' Then he smiles at me again. 'It's why I'm so happy to be here with you. It reminds me of the time we spent together.'

I like to talk to Nicholas. I was afraid Baba would not let me go with him. But Nicholas asked Baba, and Baba came to talk to me in my room. My heart was beating. He sat on the bed and he looked so sad. Then I felt ashamed. I said, 'Baba, I know I'm trouble for you.'

He said, 'I do not want your sorrow, Yahya. I want to know if you understand the difference between right and wrong.'

In my mind I thought: how can you tell me what is right and what is wrong, Baba? All men think you are weak. They laugh at you. I hear them, after Friday prayers. I heard Mr Kamil speaking to Imam Abdi and Tuesday and the rest behind the mosque wall. He was saying: 'We must deal with Ahmed – he is too afraid to fight, and he will make others afraid, too.'

But I can say none of these things to Baba. Instead I told him I was wrong to break the window in the school. This is true. Adeya – her desk is by the window. The morning air is cold and she is not strong.

Baba had many more words but then he took my hand. He

asked if I wanted to take some time to go with Nicholas and see the new hospital.

I said: 'Yes, Baba.' Then he took my head and pulled me close. He smelled of oils and medicines, of the polish he uses for his clock. His heart beat like the clock – tock tock tock.

'It is a long time since we measured you,' he said. 'Shall we see if your body is growing as well as your throwing arm?'

'Yes,' I said, so I followed him into the hall. 'Come, Margaret,' he called, and Mama was there with Nagode and Nicholas.

I stood with my back to the clock. Its bones felt thin. But its skin shone. Baba has a trick to make the shine come. He rubs groundnut oil on there with a soft cloth. But the real trick, he says, is love.

'Stand straight,' Baba said. With his knife he cut a small line above my head. There are many lines beneath it for me – and three for Bako too.

'There,' he said. 'At least an inch.' He went to Mama, and took Nagode to kiss her. 'Our boy is growing up,' he said to us.

There are soldiers outside the governor's hospital. The fat man talks to them and gives the tall one a cigarette. They are not older than Mister, but taller, with nice uniforms. Maybe they eat meat every day, not just on Friday. Goggo once told us that if Baba worked for the governor we could buy a long table. She meant, to pile high with all the food we would buy with his big salary. But Baba, he said: 'I already have a long clock.'

We drive inside, to the place where the machines are working. The fat man stops the car. But I don't want to get out. The whole world is roaring, like a storm. Nicholas comes to me with a plastic hat. He opens the door and shouts: 'Very peaceful, isn't it?'

I shout back: 'It's too loud!' He smiles and puts his hand to his ear like he can't hear me. So I punch him in the arm.

Nicholas shows me the machines working here. There are men who want to speak to him. But Nicholas tells them to wait. He takes me to see the deep hole. He says: 'The foundations will keep *the building stable. This soil here is sand and clay. Rock is much harder to dig through – but also much stronger. Sand and clay cannot carry as much weight. So you have to compensate for this in the design of your building.*

I ask, 'What is compensate?'

Nicholas takes my hand and asks me to hold it loosely. He pushes it down fast, and my hand drops. He says: 'This is weak ground. Now,' he says, 'push against me when I push you.'

This time I keep my hand strong. He tells me: 'You see, my hand is one force. You are compensating with a force that is equal to mine. And now we are balanced, you see? When you build a strong building you have to find this kind of balance. Do you understand?'

'I do.'

The fat man is laughing at us. 'Listen to the fucking professor,' he says.

But Nicholas, he says: 'JoJo is smart. He might be your boss one day, so mind your manners.' Then he winks at me.

We go inside the other hospital, where Nicholas must pay his men. The walls are white, like the coats on the men. One of them stops to greet Nicholas. He has a gold pen in his pocket. His shoes are shining, like Baba's clock. Even his hair shines. He smiles at me and says something. I want to smile back. But I cannot. I hate this shiny doctor. Baba went to a university. He was in England. And now he has old shoes and old hands with nothing in them.

Nicholas' office has drawings on the wall. They are made of straight lines and circles. It is a kind of language, Nicholas says. He can teach me to understand it.

Men come and go from the office. Nicholas gives them money. He says to the fat man: 'October's wages, materials and hire, bloody money to resubmit the amended plans – but we may as well do the right thing.'

'Matter of fucking opinion,' says the fat man.

Suddenly they both stand up. Nicholas says: 'Sir, good to see you.'

I turn. And he is right there. The governor.

My stomach twists. On the poster he looks smaller. In life he is bigger than Baba. A friend of Shaitan, Imam Abdi says. The one who challenges Allah.

He says: 'Good to see you too, Nicholas. And who is this young man?'

His eyes are on me. He puts out his hand. I have to take it. If you touch the devil, does he drain your strength from you? Or can you take strength from him?

Nicholas steps behind me. He says: 'This is JoJo, Dr Ahmed's son. I'm bringing him on some field trips. He has a gift for science.'

'Ah,' says the governor. He lets my hand go, but his heat – it stays inside me.

'Your father is a good man.' The governor is speaking to me now. 'It's a shame we could not persuade him to lend us his talents here. But maybe his son will do us the favour one day.'

'Yes, sir,' I say. And I think: I can be an engineer in this place or a doctor with a gold pen. Only children like Akim believe in the devil.

The governor takes off his hat. It is a baseball cap. On it I see the word BROWN. Next to that is the head of a creature that snarls. I know this animal. It is a bear.

The governor holds out the cap. I take it. It feels hot when I put it on my head.

The governor, he laughs. 'It suits you,' he says. 'A leader in the making.'

I watch Nicholas. I see he is not happy. His eyes are thin, like knives.

The governor says to him: 'I'm glad to meet your apprentice. Blessed are the teachers, isn't that what Jesus said?'

'"Blessed are the peacemakers",' says Nicholas.

'Ah,' says the governor. 'Close enough.'

Nicholas, he says: 'Did you want to talk to me about something, sir?'

'Later,' says the governor. 'You have a lot on your plate, I see.'

Then he turns to the door. He puts his hand on my head. I feel his weight, like a stone. It pushes me down.

He says: 'The most important lessons are learned outside the classroom, young man. Study well. I'm sure I will see you again.'

Nick took JoJo home at sunset. The boy was breathless with exhaustion, his forehead pressed to the window under the brim of the governor's cap, staring into the sun's brilliance. Light lent the boy's features adult definition. Nick could almost feel his concentration, filtering new ideas into purposeful order.

'So was it interesting?' he asked, 'at the site?'

JoJo tilted his head towards the sound of Nick's voice. 'It was much better than school.'

'School's important, though. The men pouring the concrete didn't finish school, but the men who designed the building did.'

JoJo raised a hand to the governor's cap. Lifting it off his head, he brought it slowly down to his lap. His fingers wandered over the roaring bear emblazoned on its front. 'What about the governor? Did he finish school?'

Nick fought the urge to warn JoJo against the man. He didn't like to see that hat on JoJo's head – and nor would Dr Ahmed, he sensed. But he'd received too many childhood lectures to feel like dishing them out. 'I suppose he must have.'

'Is he your friend?'

The question took Nick by surprise. 'No. Not like you are.'

JoJo fell silent, the cap clutched in his fingers. Nick glanced at him in the rear-view mirror as the Jeep reeled southwards. *What can he possibly make of his life, all the way out here?*

Then the light shifted in the rear-view mirror, and JoJo's face blurred into another's – Madi, his forehead creased in concentration as he peered at quadratic equations, Nick beside him correcting his answers. He could still feel his hands sticky from half-eaten jam sandwiches with their mechanical strawberry scent, hear the clatter of plates in his mother's usually silent kitchen.

They are so alike. When Nick's headmaster had announced the arrival of a new boy at the start of Year Eight, there'd been no inkling of what it would eventually mean for Nick, no warning of how many lives were about to switch course. The name itself was strange, like the other word they'd used. *Refugee.* The headmaster's pronunciation emphasised its strangeness, rolling the *r* and drawing out each syllable. *Rrrreff-uu-geeeee.* 'I expect you all to be on your best behaviour – that means you, Phillip, and you Jonno – and show him how we do things in England. He's missed some school so he's got to make up a year.'

'Why are they putting him here, sir?'

'Because they are, Amanda. Ours is not to reason why.'

'But he's so old, sir.' That had been Jonno, grinning as Phil whispered *besssst behaviaaaaa*r behind his hand. 'Fourteen already – he must be thick.'

'Any more from you, Jonathan, and it will be detention all week.'

Word had gone round the village, too. 'There'll be more curry shops than pubs round here soon, mate,' the sweet kiosk owner had told Nick and his mother. 'Don't know what the government's thinking sticking them down here, poor buggers. Send them up north with their mates, I bloody would.'

He must be thick. Even Nick had secretly believed it. But the boy escorted into class the next day had been rapier-thin, cropped brown head held high in defiance, eyes flaring blacker than any Nick had ever seen. The uniform shirt had hung from his frame, flapping loose like a white flag. Nick saw the boy's Adam's apple jerk upwards as he folded his body into the empty seat in front of him.

For two days Nick watched the back of the new boy's head, sand-brown skin on his neck deepening into a dark curly cap of hair. Often Nick would see the boy's face twist towards the classroom's high window, eyes wide and unfocused. Once a careless jerk of his arm sent a ruler clattering from the desk to the floor. Instinctively Nick bent to pick it up, meeting the black eyes and seeing *thanks* mouthed quietly before the teacher called out: 'Eyes forward, everyone, please.'

During lunch break later that same day, Nick had taken his usual station alone by the far school wall. The playground's other side belonged to Jonno and Phil, their thick fists fattened on the local housing estate – reigning over the school climbing frame and the puny bodies that dared to play between its arches.

He was deep in his *Beano* when someone slumped down beside him, a dark hand reaching over to take the comic from his hands. The new boy flicked through panels of *Dennis the Menace*; his eyes slid across to meet Nick's.

'Where are the girls in this one?'

Nick shrugged. 'There aren't any.'

The boy handed the bright pages back to him. 'So why read them?'

Nick started to answer, flustered – but the hand came out again, this time offered open. Nick took it, embarrassed. It was such a grown-up thing to do, shaking hands. But then this boy was already a grown-up, who'd seen things Nick could not imagine.

Cries drifted down from the climbing frame. Phil had chosen his victim of the day, an old favourite with thick lenses and runty arms, hair as red as his face as he strained towards his twentieth push-up at Phil's feet.

'You're friends with them?' Madi asked, watching intently.

'No way.' Phil's gang had gathered round, counting down push-ups in vicious delight. 'They'd never be friends with me.' He wondered where the playground supervisor was: but it wouldn't help anyway. Miss Tinner was as loathed as Phil, from the same heavy-skinned, angry-faced stock. She ignored Phil's macho infractions and forgave his undone maths homework. But otherwise she was hard-eyed and vicious – particularly to 'fancy boys' like Nick with their careful manners and BBC accents. And Madi had come in for even worse treatment. She found everything about him offensive: she scoffed at his kindergarten-level mistakes and the slouch of his gangling form in the classroom's narrow seats. She found a reason to call him up in front of the class every lesson, drawing her scorn slowly across him like a blade as he stood at the board, tense and silent, scratching chalk desperately across the black slate.

Madi's eyes were still on the red-haired boy puffing at Phil's feet. 'Phillip – the big one. He's a dick, right?'

Nick squirmed. 'What?' It was unthinkable to bad-mouth Phil. In your head maybe, but never in the treacherous open air.

'Dick. It's English for this?' The boy pointed at his crotch.

Nick laughed in embarrassment. 'Your English is good.'

'I watched movies back home. American ones. And my father was an English teacher.' His fingers were long, drawing circles in the loose gravel. 'Here he drives a taxi. He taught me all the bad words first. So I could ask the English girls to – you know.'

'You're lying.'

Madi grinned. 'Maybe. They wouldn't, anyway. Girls don't like me here. They like ones like you.'

Nick looked over to the chapel steps, where the oblivious classroom queens held court. He sensed that Madi was being kind; he'd seen girls staring at the stranger, with his nut-brown, unblemished skin and deep-lashed eyes.

'They don't like me either. That's why I'm here reading this.' He brandished the *Beano*. And Madi had laughed. This wasn't the cruel jibe of the Phils and the Jonnos; it was the rare sound of empathy.

Now Phil was coming towards them, tailed by Jonno and his friends, seeking fresh game. Nick stiffened by instinct, Phil's meaty finger stabbing towards him as he approached. 'Yeah, that's right, nancy boy. I'm watching you.' His eyes flipped to Madi – but the moment had passed. They kept moving, heading off to smoke behind the school shed. Nick breathed out, and Madi rubbed the playground dirt with his trainer, casting Nick a curious glance.

'Is it always like this here for you?'

'Sometimes.' The question shamed him; his unpopularity must show on his skin, as disfiguring as eczema.

But Madi didn't seem to notice. Instead he shifted his body closer to Nick's.

'See this.' He drew a piece of paper from his pocket, dropping it on Nick's lap. He unfolded it – a page ripped from an exercise book – to see a cartoon sketch of razor-sharp accuracy: a large pig with Phil's face gazed out at him in porcine ecstasy; its puckered mouth rested on the backside of a girlish cow – Miss Tinner to the life – with ringlets and buxom udders, holding a giggling hoof up to her lips.

Nick gasped. 'You're mental. He'll kill you.'

Madi grinned. 'I'm no good at anything else here. And I haven't any friends. So I make these.' His English was almost perfect, warmly accented with only the occasional stumble. 'It's what they're really like, isn't it?'

It was; even Nick could see the cartoons had their own savage justice. 'My mother draws too. You're nearly as good as her.' He felt strangely grateful, as if the picture was a coded message confessing *I'm lonely too* – a suicidally brave admission in the playground's dog-eat-dog world. And he was suddenly embarrassed that he, Nick, hadn't been the one to reach out – that all he'd offered this new boy so far was surface admiration at a distance, for the casual way he walked through the halls in his long, loose gait, ignoring the whispers and turning heads. But now he noticed tell-tale signs of other stories – a fine scar arcing down from one eyebrow and into the pale hollow under the boy's eye, deep scuffs marking his trainers, their laces almost frayed through, bands of bright string tied around too-thin wrists that Madi worried constantly with his fingers, like rosary beads.

'Just ignore them.' He hoped he sounded authoritative, convincing. 'They're stupid anyway. They're not worth it.'

Madi shrugged, his shoulders like rails under his shirt. 'OK. If you ignore your little piggy, I ignore my big cow. Deal?'

'Deal.' Nick hugged his legs, smiling into his knees. Out of the corner of his eye, he saw Madi smiling too, gaze fixed on the gravelled concrete. 'Here, mate.' He offered Nick his drawing. 'Keep it in your no-girls magazine.' *Mate.* How strange, how cautious that English colloquialism had sounded on Madi's tongue, screaming its need to belong.

'You keep it,' he'd replied, wanting to say more but not knowing how. 'That thing's a death sentence.'

The bell rang as Nick handed it back, sending a hundred pairs of feet scurrying for their classrooms. Madi tucked the picture into his back pocket as he followed Nick into Miss Tinner's, sliding into his chair. As he sat, the folded paper tumbled from his pocket on to the floor beside him.

Nick quickly reached under the desk to pick it up – but it was too late. Tinner had already started striding down towards them, bending to snatch Madi's sketch out of his hand.

'No notes in class.' She unfolded the page, scanning it. At once her sallow cheeks shaded to deep puce; she slammed the drawing down on Madi's desk. The girl next to him gasped when she saw it, leaning over to whisper to her friend. Titters began to spread across the classroom, reaching Phil in the back row.

'Yours, I take it?' Tinner's tone had dropped to a hoarse bass, dyed ringlets trembling around her eyes. Madi looked up at her in silence. Nick wondered where his thoughts were racing, along the long road here, the spoiling of a second chance. The boy's fingers twisted the coloured bands tied at his wrists, rubbing them back and forth across his skin.

'Well?' Tinner demanded again. 'Is this how they do things in your country, Madi? You're in England now, you know. A civilised place.' Another outbreak of laughter. Madi's hands came together on the table, fingers clenched. He seemed about to speak.

'It's mine, miss.' It was a moment before Nick realised he'd spoken.

The class had fallen silent in expectation. Miss Tinner bent over Nick's desk, her cleavage a dark slash as her stare drilled into him. Nick could still remember the thud of his heart as he returned it, unflinching.

'I don't believe that for a minute, Nicholas,' she said at last. 'Detention, both of you. And I'll be sending a letter home to your parents.' But Nick had seen Madi's head swivel as she marched past him, catching his eye for the briefest second, full of wonder.

Now the desert road arced ahead of him, through a wasteland blank and empty. Nick gripped the wheel, pushing away the ache of longing. *If wishes were horses*, his mother used to tell him, *then beggars would ride*. What would Madi say if he could see what Nick was doing now? *Laugh at me, probably. What's the matter, mate? Tired of the good life?* He heard his friend's voice so clearly, it made him laugh despite himself.

JoJo stirred by the window. 'What is it?'

'Nothing, mate. Just thinking.'

JoJo's eyes were visible in the rear-view mirror, glazed over with sunlight and exhaustion. For a moment they filled the sliver of glass with a half-focused intensity that seemed to pierce through Nick. Then they shifted back to the landscape.

Dusk was falling when they reached home. Nick opened the garden gate as JoJo pushed past him, hurtling up the steps towards Margaret waiting at the front door.

'Mama!' he shouted, pulling off the governor's cap and holding it out to her as she caught his hands, the day pouring out of him in a tangle of words.

'Thank you,' she said, when the boy finally skipped off to his bedroom to change his clothes.

'For what?' Nick teased.

'He has so little excitement here.' Her face looked lighter than he'd ever seen it, without its usual wariness – JoJo's delight in a more resonant key. 'His father tries. But the old do not remember what excites the young.'

'It's a father thing,' he said. 'My mother could make me feel more with one painting than my father could with a hundred lectures.'

JoJo's high tones drifted down the hallway, summoning her. Margaret hesitated, her eyes still on Nick; she seemed to have more to say. But then she shook her head, her hand on her chest as if to quieten something there. He watched as she slipped away, feeling both pleased and disturbed. The day lay heavy on him as he collapsed on the sofa, emotions churning inside him. Dr Ahmed opened the front door a minute later, peering into the room to make his apologies – he'd planned some house calls for that evening and would miss the family meal.

'Was it a productive day?' he asked Nick. 'Did Yahya behave well?'

Nick gave his assurances and Dr Ahmed left, calling his farewell to Margaret. Soon the familiar song of dinner preparations surrounded them, the kitchen stove hissing over the concussive ring of pots. A warm rice smell unfolded through the house.

Now JoJo wanted Nick's attention – bouncing in and out of the sitting room to bring him sketches of imagined buildings, each one more fevered than the last. 'When I grow up I will build them all.'

'It's a big responsibility to be an architect,' Nick told him. 'Architects take ideas and make them real.'

JoJo was silent, absorbing this truth. Then he said, 'You can teach me.'

Nick laughed. 'You'll have to study hard.'

JoJo shrugged. 'I can.'

Then let's start with something small,' Nick said. 'Something we could build in the garden.'

JoJo's forehead creased. 'Like what?'

'I don't know. We don't need to decide right now.' A sudden absence of sound distracted him; the kitchen had fallen silent. Through the doorway he could see a fresh bowl of rice on the table, Margaret's hand gripping the table's edge beside it. Steam traced its way up a slender arm, in soft pulses like breath.

JoJo took his drawings back to his room. Nick closed his eyes and relaxed back into the narrow sofa. The sour scent of rice blended with the vibration of the evening generators – a deep hum that soothed his mind, like a lullaby, floating him gently down towards sleep. Some drowsy part of him wondered when he'd started to feel like this – this comfortable ease. He could barely remember his first day driving here – how dazzled he'd been, how new and alive the world had seemed, its strangeness surging through him like electric shocks. Somewhere an unseen alchemy had been at work, blurring the line between them, reshaping each to the other.

A sound startled him out of his thoughts. Margaret was framed in the hallway, something rectangular held to her chest, colour in her cheeks. It was a sheaf of papers, mottled with dark stains and bound with a ribbon. A title was visible on the front page, above the shadow of her folded arms.

'The storybooks I made,' she said. 'When you helped me hang washing in the garden – you said you would like to see one.'

'I remember.' Nick read the title silently. *The Thorn Princess.* The upright letters were printed in a child's hand – careful yet uncertain.

'I made many as a girl.' Margaret's arms loosened as she bent to hand it to him. 'Sarah loved to read them. But this is the only one I kept.'

He took it gently. The pages were yellow and stiff. Uneven smudges of colour dotted the cover, as if the book had been left out in the rain.

But when he opened it, the first image stunned him: a vivid silhouette in black charcoal, far too sophisticated for a child's imagination. The girl at its centre was tall and faceless, her body a storm of dark lines and circles more conjured than drawn, the spikes of her crown shaded to razor-sharpness. She was set against a dream-like landscape of fantastical turrets and blood-red flowers. He flicked through page after page, each one holding an ominous power. 'Margaret, these are magnificent.' He looked up, simultaneously disturbed and moved. 'It's a work of art.'

Her eyes met his. 'Read it. If you like.'

He cleared his throat, turning to the front page. '"Once upon a time,"' he read, '"a princess was born in a castle. But this princess was not like the nice ones from the stories we know. She was beautiful but proud and selfish, and her words pricked people like thorns. And so everyone called her the Thorn Princess, and soon no one was brave enough to be her friend.

'"Then one day, another girl came to live in the castle. Her heart was kind, so she played with the lonely Thorn Princess. She made braids for her hair and sang songs to make her smile. She brought two beautiful roses from her garden and gave one to the Princess. 'We can be sisters,' she said.

'"But the Princess wanted both roses for herself. So when her friend fell asleep in the grass, she stole the rose straight from her hand. At the same moment, the sleeping girl turned white as death. And every petal in the Princess' garden fell to the earth.

'"Seeing the garden empty and dead and her friend lying so still, the Princess felt great sorrow and shame for her cruelty. She clutched the bare rose to her heart and cried, 'Forgive me!' The thorns pricked her skin to the bone and drew out great drops of blood. And to her great wonder, each drop grew into a new rose as it fell. She plucked them as they grew and laid them on her friend's heart . . ."'

Nick broke off as Margaret stood, hearing a faint cry from the inner bedroom. 'Nagode,' she murmured. 'She's hungry.'

JoJo appeared in the doorway, freshly washed. 'Mama, Nagode is awake.' The wailing grew louder; Margaret smoothed down her clothes and wiped her forehead, before vanishing into the dark corridor.

The book remained on Nick's lap. Turning to the last page, he read: '"So the girl forgave the Thorn Princess, and from that day they were truly sisters. They played forever in their garden, and this was the start of many wonderful adventures."'

The picture under the words showed two small figures, hand-in-hand against the light of a dark sun. Underneath, more lines ran down to the bottom of the page – an adult's script, hasty and flowing. He squinted to make it out in the weak light.

Sarah – this message is the only way to reach you now, since David will watch for any letters. Please don't blame me for leaving as I did. You know what our house became. A prison. I could not stand it. And do not listen to David's lies. I swear to you Ahmed never dishonoured me. He's a good man, Sarah, an educated man. Does David think I am blind, that God is blind? If an honest Muslim like Ahmed is damned, then what about a false Christian who brings his whores into his parents' bed? After we marry, Ahmed will buy a house near the diplomatic quarter – or maybe return to London. He has friends in all the best hospitals. They respect him. We will plant roses for Mama, and there will be a room there for you, Sarah. So be patient for just a little while longer. On Mama's soul, I swear I will send for you the first minute I can. Until then have faith, keep on with your studies and say nothing. Don't let David frighten you into a small life. God's promise is bigger than they tell us, if we are brave enough to seek it. I will wait every day for your reply. May it bring me your forgiveness and your arms around me soon again.

Nick closed the book, his pulse quickening. Evening shadows were pressing in from the desert's emptiness. They moved through the small room like grey fingers, tracing the Quranic hangings, the stained walls and the rigid pillar of the grandfather clock.

The note must have been written just after Margaret's marriage, while they were still in the capital and the promise of their life together was still new. The ink was smudged with haste. *He has friends in all the best hospitals.* Understanding trickled into him, and compassion. Margaret had run from one prison to another, from the notoriety of a rebel to the invisibility of a silent helpmate. *Thirteen lonely years cleaning an old man's house, feeding his neighbours and bearing his children.* The same desert road that had thrilled him coming here had probably filled her with despair, each mile bleaching the bright canvas of an imagined future.

He felt a sudden, brutal urge to tell Margaret the truth: that England might have been even worse – that the eyes following her would have burned no less for being in suspicious white faces instead of Miss Amina's or Aisha Kamil's. They too might have offered contempt instead of welcome, made her feel stupid for violating one of their thousand provincial sanctities: standing too close in the bus queue, clasping someone's hand too warmly. He still remembered the looks people gave Madi, the day after Miss Tinner's detention, when he'd slung his long arm over Nick's shoulder as they wound homewards through the village High Street. *Queer.* Nick could almost hear the word in people's minds. He'd been so torn, loving the unfamiliar weight and warmth of the touch, but embarrassed, too. 'Guys don't do that here,' he'd explained later to Madi, when they were sitting on the kissing gate. 'People think it's gay.'

'But it's normal,' Madi had said, puzzled. 'It's a mark of respect. It's not like I want to fuck you. Those people don't know anything.'

He'd tried to restrain himself afterwards, to keep a proper English distance even once they'd become inseparable, their arms swinging side by side on their way to school, to the beach with Madi's football or to town to spend Nick's pocket money on Dr Peppers and Quavers. But Madi, Nick knew, resented this unnatural restraint of soul and body. And sometimes he'd forget. Until once, when they were waiting their turn at the sweet kiosk checkout, Madi had unconsciously reached for Nick's wrist. The assistant's eyes had narrowed. 'Leave off, poofter,' someone had whispered behind them. And Madi's fingers had dropped away, curling into a fist. 'Fifty pence,' the assistant told him. 'And get out.' It had been December, a bitter wind hunching them down into their puffa jackets as they'd walked out under a darkening sky. Nick had been painfully aware of Madi's hands thrust deep into his pockets, his eyes fixed on the garish festoon of Christmas lights winding from lamppost to lamppost.

'You just have to remember, that's all,' he'd pleaded, feeling shame burn against the ice in his lungs. 'I *told* you.'

'Why should I?'

'It's embarrassing, that's why.'

'I don't care shit about them. You shouldn't either.'

'I don't,' he'd lied. 'But – I mean, you're here now. You've got to do what people here do. What's the point of making trouble?'

Madi laughed, a bitter sound. 'That's what they used to say to my dad, before. So why did we bother coming to this country then?' Nick couldn't answer. Madi's fingers suddenly closed on his wrist, hard as wire. 'What you did for me with Tinner – that was so cool, man. Seriously. No one else here's brave like that. We hang out every day – but why, if you think I'm what they say?'

'I don't think you're anything.' They were the wrong words; Nick meant to say: *you're braver and better than anyone in this place; I don't know why you chose me for your friend; I can't imagine life here without you.* But the fairy lights were dazzling, the winter air a steel trap in his mouth, and he could only feel the cold bite on his wrist as Madi dropped it, watch as he pushed ahead into the swirl of passers-by: the sharp, hunched ridge of his shoulders, an island in a lonely sea. And Nick had been left alone under the sparkling Christmas lampposts: strings of seraphim blowing their jaunty trumpets over the heads of oblivious shoppers.

Now Margaret's shadow was moving through the hall, Nagode whimpering over the light tread of feet. *It's history repeating*, he thought, in a rush of sorrow. *Your new life broke its promises.*

He closed the book, but she passed through the sitting room without looking back. As she crossed the threshold, the baby stretched her arms over her mother's back. For a moment Nick imagined she was reaching out for him, standing up in a blind impulse to answer. But then she was gone, vanishing through the doorway, her outflung arms making the dark silhouette of an angel's wing.

When I get home from school, Nicholas asks if our building can be a castle. He says: 'We can have a lot of fun making a castle. You can be the knight and your mother the queen.'

Together we make the first drawing. This is called the schematic. I draw the lines with a ruler and we measure angles. We must calculate the load, Nicholas says. Load is how much something can carry before it breaks. He writes on the page – letters and numbers and lines. I tell him it looks beautiful. Then Nicholas smiles. 'Yes, it does,' he says.

We collect rocks to burn for the mortar. Nicholas says these rocks are the right kind for cement. They are heavy in our barrow – but I push them home myself. Nicholas asks to help me many times. 'But I am strong enough,' I tell him. 'I can see that,' he answers. 'Probably stronger than me.'

Adeya and her mother are in their millet fields when we pass. Their patch is so small. But their crop is good. Each plant is fat and white. Adeya goes after school every day to pick the beetles and bring water. It is hard work. But Adeya, she does not tire. One time she told me she gave each plant a name, so she could call to it to grow. 'They listen,' she told me. 'No plant listens, stupid,' I said. But she smiled. She said: 'They listen to me.'

Nicholas sees Adeya and her mother working. He stops to call: 'Good morning, Adeya! Can we help you?'

Adeya, she looks up and sees me. She starts to smile at me. Hanan puts her shawl over her mouth and looks away. She does not like Adeya to smile at boys. She might beat her later. So I tell Nicholas: 'Let's go.' But he says: 'Friends should help each other, right?'

So we go into Adeya's field. Adeya, she is quiet at first. But Nicholas makes jokes with her, until she laughs. She shows him how to pick blister beetles from the leaves. She is patient even when he breaks the leaves by mistake. She tells him: 'When it is time, we will cut this millet and hang it over smoke, so we can eat until the next harvest.'

I wish Adeya would smile at me again. So I tell Nicholas that each plant has a name. She names them to help them grow. Nicholas asks her to tell him the name of each one he touches. When he picks off the beetles, he calls the plant by its name. He says: 'Very nice to meet you!' Adeya, she laughs. I come close to her by accident, to watch her fingers move. Sometimes I feel she is watching me. But when I look, she does not see me at all.

We burn the stones in Tuesday's oven, to get the powder to make the cement. Nicholas pours water on some of it, and it hisses like a snake. We bring the lime bags back to the garden, singing a song that Nicholas is teaching me, about going to England on a jet plane. It has funny words. Kiss me! Smile for me! I sing it to Miss Amina as we pass her. Miss Amina, she yells at us. She is like a bat, an orange bat with big ears. 'Boy, what is all this noise you make? Stupid boy. I will tell your father.'

Baba comes out from his office. He is wiping his hands. Jalloh is hiding behind him. He does not want Miss Amina to see him there. Ha! Maybe he has a disease in his dick, too.

'Ah, Miss Amina,' Baba calls to her. 'I have your medicine here when you want to come. Free of charge!' He winks at me. I am happy, so I wink back.

Every day we make a little more of my castle. First we dig the foundation. Then we make the outside walls and inside walls — the support walls they are called. Then three towers — two on the side and in the middle a big round one. The schematic is on Nagode's sleeping tree behind us. I stuck it there with a pin.

Mama comes often into the garden now. She helps to mix the quicklime with sand and small stones. Once Nagode tried to put some in her mouth. I had to say: 'Hey, Mama, watch her!' But Mama is too busy watching us.

On the last day of our project, Mama comes into the garden with something rolled up in her hand. I try to take it from her, but she gives it to Nicholas.

He opens it and says: 'You made a flag.'

'A castle should have a banner,' Mama says. She holds the corner still, so Nicholas can see. It is a white flag and in the middle Mama has drawn a yellow flower. She says: 'A daffodil.'

I do not understand why this makes Nicholas smile at her. He winds the flag onto a stick and ties it on. We make some extra cement to put the flag on the tower.

Baba comes back from his rounds then, as we are setting the flag. 'Very good, very good,' he says. He shakes the hand of Nicholas. And next he shakes mine. 'My son the master builder.' His hand is dry and I feel his bones. He goes inside to bring his camera that he brought from England. We line up, me, Nicholas and Mama, with the castle in front. Nagode is putting brown grass into the moat. 'Smile,' says Baba.

After it clicks, I think Baba looks sad. He tells Mama: 'I will make some tea.' But I see him go to the office instead.

Mama looks happy, though. She is picking flowers from Nagode's sleeping tree. The tree was bright before, but now it is brown. She puts them on the castle tower.

'Now a real queen would agree to live here,' she says to Nicholas.

Nicholas, he goes down on one knee and opens his arms. In a deep voice, he sings: '"My good blade carves the casques of men, my tough lance thrusteth sure, my strength is as the strength of ten: because my heart is pure."'

Mama, she smiles. She says: 'So, Sir Galahad. And is this Arthur's castle?'

'No,' says Nicholas. 'In that castle, Guinevere was sad.'

'It's a strong castle,' I say. 'I can make soldiers from the rest of the cement. We can put them around the moat to protect the queen inside.'

Nicholas gets up. He says: 'Lady Margaret, will you dance with me?'

Mama laughs. 'No, sir.'

But Nicholas, he holds out his hand. He says: 'Please, my lady.'

*She covers her smile with her hand. I think she looks small,
like Adeya.*

I say: 'Go on, Mama.'

*So she takes his hand. And he pretends they are dancing around
the castle. Their feet make the dust rise, with the small biting flies.
Nagode, she is laughing to catch them, reaching in the air.*

*In the window of the kitchen I see a shadow, watching us. I
want to call to him: Baba! But then he is gone.*

*When the day ends, Akim comes to see my castle with Juma. Juma
has something to tell me. He comes close. I can smell him — broken
cars and cigarettes.*

He says: 'Mister, he knows what you did at the school.'

I say nothing.

*Juma wants to pinch my arm, like he used to. His hand, it
comes near me. But then he stops. He says: 'Come with us tomorrow, JoJo. He will see you again.'*

*I remember the knife in Mister's belt. It was white, like his skin.
White like the sky is now, when the sun falls low. I turn the governor's cap so the bill shades my eyes.*

*Juma thinks this means yes. He is smiling. He lights a ciga-
rette and walks to the schematic that Nicholas and I made.*

*He takes the paper off Nagode's sleeping tree. He says: 'What is
this?' He turns it this way and that. The ash is dropping on the
ground. But Juma cannot read this language, the numbers and
the lines. He will never read it. All Juma can do is clean a car, like
Baba cleans his clock.*

I take it from him. I say: 'It is nothing. Juma. Don't worry.'

*He can see my meaning, I know. His smile fades. He looks
smaller than before. Like Akim. It means I do not need them. I do
not have to follow them.*

*And then Nicholas calls from the door: 'JoJo! Dinner time!'
Juma and Akim, they are still looking at me, waiting.*

*I go inside to Nicholas. I run with our paper, and I leave them
behind.*

NOVEMBER

The *harmattan* arrived early – a relentless, hair-dryer wind sweeping a red curtain across land and sky. Workmen turned up to Nick's site muttering about bad omens. Day after day dust choked machinery and shrivelled Adeya's millet plants into spears of yellow bone.

The wind was a harbinger, Nick's foreman told him, a bad omen, the earth surrendering to the sky. Men feared for their crops; they were harvesting early, to save what they could.

'How do people stand this every bloody year?' Nick asked, beside the rattling corpse of one dust-clogged digger. Eric frowned at the horizon, already dark at noon. 'It's not usually this bad.'

By mid-November Nick finally surrendered, too, shutting the site until the worst passed. The crew covered their machinery with tarpaulins, as he and Eric headed back down the highway, under the ominous haze.

The haze intensified as they neared the village, thickening into eerie darkness. As they rounded the square, Nick grabbed Eric's arm. People were racing towards the lake, carrying bundles of cloth. Others gripped brooms and buckets, yelling through smoke.

'Fuck,' Eric said. Smoke was billowing directly ahead of them now, from the village edge where Dr Ahmed's house stood, and Adeya's fields. Nick's heart thudded to a hollow stop. Eric slammed down a gear and accelerated forward, towards the village millet fields. A strange sound filtered in through the window – chaotic, agonised keening. Behind a wall of flame, Adeya's goats were screaming.

Nick jumped from the Jeep, stumbling as a huge body slammed into him, leaving a grimy trail on his shirt. A burning stench coated the air – the stink of charred hair and meat. Adeya's field was a furnace, black and boiling. Wet fabrics had been laid over the shrubs all the way back to the outlying grain storehouses – bedsheets and towels stained dark with earth and soot. But not enough; the tail of the fire was curling around to encircle the thatched roofs of Hanan's millet store.

Nick ran towards these new cries of alarm, gathering armfuls of soot-stained sheets to join the circle of desperate, beating arms. Pieces of thatch were already aflame; he could picture those soft white ears, so lovingly tended and carefully harvested, blackening and withering inside, consumed to nothing.

The sheets were heavy in his hand as he beat the flames, frenzied now, his shoulders aching with effort, delaying the inevitable surrender. The heat was incredible, a red wall pushing him back. Smoke choked his nostrils, violent and sickening. Eric grabbed his shoulder. 'Forget it!' he yelled. 'It's already gone.' Eric was right; the whole thatch was now a roiling orange. As Nick stepped back, half of the grain store collapsed, flames arcing into its heart.

He turned away, his chest tight, fighting against nausea – and saw Dr Ahmed on the ground, cradling Adeya as she sobbed. Hanan sat beside them, grey with cindered flakes, one scorched stem lying on her lap. Adeya's hands were held out palm up, as if in prayer – and then in horror he realised why: they were a raw, swollen mass of red and white blisters. A foul-smelling brown fluid trickled from her dress over Dr Ahmed's legs.

Margaret knelt beside Hanan, taking the dead plant from the older woman's hands. Hanan sat motionless, as if dead herself. *Mazed*, his father used to say of his mother. *Away with the fairies.*

Margaret drew back her hand and slapped her – hard enough to draw some faint recognition. JoJo beside her, red eyes in a smoke-streaked face.

Dr Ahmed looked up. 'Her bag has broken,' he said to Nick. 'Help me. We need to get her to my surgery.'

Wordless, Nick bent to lift Adeya out of Dr Ahmed's arms. Her stench enveloped them both, raw aromas of fire and faeces. Her body weighed pitifully little. Tuesday, gold-toothed owner of the village corner store, pushed onlookers aside to let them through.

Murmurs followed as they passed, faces turning from Adeya's stinking robes. Nick gripped her closer as she flinched into his chest through the rolling smoke, held earthwards by a heavy sky.

Dr Ahmed and Margaret stayed in the surgery with Adeya till nightfall. Eric smoked outside and Nick made JoJo bread and jam. The boy was silent as he chewed, pink crumbs gathering at the corners of his mouth.

'How did this happen?' Nick asked him. JoJo twisted in his chair.

'It was a bushfire,' he said, eyes downcast.

'How do they start?'

'Allah starts them.' JoJo took another mouthful of sandwich.

'That's not a scientist's answer,' Nick said. 'It's just a way of saying, "I don't know".'

JoJo looked up, defensive. 'Maybe He sent lightning.'

Eric had come back into the kitchen and picked a slab of bread from the table.

'No storms today, boy.' He took a huge bite. 'And bushfires are for April, not November. This ground is too fucking dry. When are they going to start calling this a drought? That's what I fucking wonder.'

Nick remembered Adeya's sure hands, plucking beetles from her stems. All those months of sowing, seeding, nurturing and growing, of back-breaking trips to fetch water. For what?

He looked out to Miss Amina's house, her orange abaya now grey and dripping over her porch railing. A water tank sat on her roof. He wondered how much was left inside.

He turned to Eric. 'What if it were a drought? Dr Ahmed says water prices are higher every day.'

Eric rubbed his chin. 'You know they used to have their own water here? A well, some sort of underground system.'

Nick looked out over the darkening land, swirling dust a yellow mockery of England's misty sunsets. 'How was that possible?'

'Oh, there's an aquifer hereabouts. There was a survey. I've still got the papers somewhere.'

Dr Ahmed came into the kitchen from the hall, wiping his hands with a towel.

'Ah, hello my friends.'

'Adeya is OK?' JoJo was on his feet.

'It could be worse.' Dr Ahmed was falsely jovial; he seemed to be looking through them all. 'Their house at least was saved. Margaret will take them home now. I am sorry, you must be hungry.'

'Don't mind me, sir.' Eric clapped Dr Ahmed on the shoulder. 'I'll be on my way. Let me know if there's anything I can do.'

'Make rain,' the old man said.

Eric laughed. 'I'll give it a try.'

Dr Ahmed busied himself making tea. Nick moved out of his way, walking into the family room. The tick of the grandfather clock drew him in.

To his surprise, JoJo was by the clock already, his forehead pressed against the wood, rubbing a section with a cloth. The grain was lighter there than elsewhere, shiny from intense polishing, showing the pale bones beneath. The boy's breath came sharp and unsteady, and Nick saw tears in his eyes.

He knelt down beside him. 'Adeya will be OK, you know. Burns heal.' The enormous inadequacy of the words made him hate himself.

JoJo pushed into the wood with his fingers, a vengeful gesture. Then he said, 'They tease her.' The other hand scraped over his eyes, leaving them red and wet.

'Who?' Nick kept his voice gentle. 'What for?'

'At school. For her bag.'

'Well, she has you to stand up for her.'

JoJo stopped rubbing the wood and turned to Nick. In his face, Nick saw the futility of adolescence, with its impossible explanations.

A sharp breeze rushed between them from the front door. Margaret came back into the room, dragging off her headscarf with fierce exhaustion, her bracelet leaving red imprints against her soot-stained arm.

'They sleep,' she said. Then she covered her face and burst into tears.

Night fell, thick and hot. Nick tossed on the creaking bunk, waking intermittently from dreams of burning. Sometimes it was Madi he hunted in the flames, sometimes a nameless presence, turning wildly until panic spun him back towards consciousness.

Waking for the third time he tasted sweat and smoke. The room's air felt heavy, tangling his arms and legs in a tight, black blanket. He stumbled over to the hose, twisting the tap and splashing his face in water. The bathroom's bare light bulb floated above him, a luminous phantom; somehow it reminded him of JoJo's face.

The water was blood-warm. Closing his eyes, he rested his forehead against the relative coolness of the tiles. *I'm still dreaming.* The cool was a fresh wind on the wild Atlantic shore; he was racing the rollers with Madi, breaking and plunging up the surf line. He felt the spray soaking their backs through to the bone, saw their pale feet kicking up the sand, Madi's cigarette smoke whipping out to sea, carrying away the smell of burning. 'Here, mate, take one. Come on, they're only Silk Cut, for little girls. Don't be a pussy.' Phil had taught Madi to call people 'pussy' by slamming him into the crossbars of the school climbing frame and whispering,'You stink, Sambo. Don't you wash? You smell like a black pussy.' 'We should report him,' Nick had suggested, later on the kissing gate. 'Get him suspended.' But Madi had shaken his head. 'I promised my dad. No more trouble. He's scared they'll send us back.' Instead for a week they'd called each other 'pussy' all the time, to draw the sting – until Madi's weary-eyed, bent-backed father walked into the flat while Madi was scrubbing his arms raw to get rid of the smell of the fishmonger, yelling, 'Come here, my little white pussy,' to Nick over the running of the tap. His father's dry palm had whipped across the side of Madi's face. The boy had already outgrown him, the father whittled away to insignificance, the son just reaching life's cusp. But Madi just stood there, frozen, arms covered in suds, one cheek branded red. And Nick remembered the look that had passed between them – JoJo's hopelessness on a different face.

Rolling back into bed, Nick pulled the pillow over his head. His chest felt raw, his body too drained for sleep. But eventually the rain came, pattering on the glass of his mother's kitchen window. Madi was eating across the table, his bruises black as burns. Nick's father rested one hand on Madi's shoulder, another on JoJo's. 'What were you doing?' he asked Nick, his eyes a challenge. 'Why weren't you there for him?' Nick opened his mouth to reply – but suddenly he was back on that empty shore again, alone. Icy water tumbled around him, swallowing his voice as he shouted their names towards the cold and distant cliffs.

Next morning Nick opened his door to see the butcher, Jalloh, smiling at the gate. A kid lay over his shoulders, thin legs splayed around his head.

'Good morning, Mr Nicholas! Is Dr Ahmed within?'

The house's front door opened – Dr Ahmed came out of the

living room, holding a screwdriver and an oily cloth. 'He is indeed.'

'This goat is for you, sir. From the widow Hanan.'

'Hanan is too kind. I don't want to deprive her of any more of her flock.'

'Don't worry, sir. This one's mother has another still nursing.'

'Well,' Dr Ahmed's glasses had misted into a tired greyness, 'perhaps it's best. We can invite them to a good meal at least.'

When Jalloh opened the gate, Nick started back in surprise. 'He's going to kill it here?'

Jalloh swayed up the path. The small creature on his shoulders had long fine ears dangling around massive black eyes. It examined Nick with innocent interest.

'Excuse me,' said Dr Ahmed. 'I will rouse my wife.' Last night he had put Margaret to bed with a sedative, her face swollen with weeping. The fire had not touched her, yet a part of her soul seemed to be burning with some private grief.

Nick also felt drained – rising before dawn to hack up soot and smoke from his lungs, turning on the hose to douse his face. Then he'd cut off the flow in an adrenalin surge of guilt. *When are they going to start calling this a drought?* He'd watched the yellow drops patter to the floor, a slow, inadequate beat.

He'd called J.P. over the radio afterwards, to update him on the weather and his decision to close the site.

'Assuming we can open again later this week, I'll run out of cash soon,' he'd warned his boss. 'We seem to need permit after permit. Permit to connect to the drains. Permit to link to the electricity supply. Cost of inspections for the permits.'

'Think of it as a public good,' J.P. had said. 'You're used to a private-sector culture. This is different. Every extra stamp on your paper means another family with an income. It's better than Western bullshit, frankly. There, it's just self-importance. Here it's necessity.'

Nick rubbed his forehead, trying to ease a deep needle of pain.

'Look, Nick. What can I say?' J.P. continued. 'In this game we make lots of big investments for small returns. Sometimes you don't see the returns in one year or in three. Honestly, this is why I don't like this midlife tourism. You think nothing is good unless it happens in front of you.'

'That's . . .' His irritated throat cut off Nick's retort, turning it into a cough.

'What's up?' J.P. sounded concerned. 'You're sick?'

'No. We had a fire here yesterday.' Now was as good a time as any. 'Listen, J.P., it's unbelievably dry here. Drought-dry. Are they talking about that in the capital yet?'

'About a drought? No, not really. I mean it's dry – but they know how to manage. They have wells, trucking arrangements.'

'There's no well here. And water prices are going sky-high. Yesterday – the fire – they didn't have water to put it out.'

'OK.' J.P.'s voice crackled down the line. 'Like half of the country. What's your point?'

'My point . . .' Nick paused. 'There's an aquifer here, Eric said. Apparently there used to be a well, too.'

'A well – yes, maybe. Tell me about it when you come through for Christmas. Sounds like you need a break.'

After J.P.'s curt 'Out', Nick leaned his forehead against the radio, listening to the lonely hiss of the line. Suddenly he missed the cool and order of home; he hadn't written to Kate in two weeks. Pulling her stationery towards him, he began to scribble a description of the fire and Dr Ahmed's heroics with Adeya. The nib scratched like the crickets as the generator droned on.

But halfway through he crumpled the paper and pushed it aside. It felt blasphemous to reduce grief and loss to postcard banalities. And it would only worry Kate, give her more ammunition to shoot holes in his decision. 'Mr Indecisive' she'd called him ever since their first night together, fondly, as a mother to a child. She encouraged him to have views and take stands – on politics, home-buying and job-changing – but in her secret heart he knew she liked the scales of choice tilted her way. Their private wedding vows – written at her suggestion just before he left – had been themed *things I promise to accept about you*. 'Anyone can promise to love and honour the good parts,' she'd explained. 'But what about the rest?' Her list had been characteristically full. *I won't pressure you. I won't ask you to be more emotionally open than you can handle. I'll encourage you to stand up for yourself when people push you down.* He'd written a page of compliments, the words flowing with superficial ease. 'It's very sweet, Nick,' she'd said, reading with a rueful smile. 'But hardly the point of the exercise.'

'I don't need to accept anything about you,' he'd assured her. 'You're perfect just as you are.' Now, as then, he experienced the desolation of being most able to express himself when it mattered least.

Margaret was calling him outside to help with Jalloh's goat. She was carrying a bucket for the blood, her eyes puffy. Her head-scarf was dark blue, the colour of grief.

'Eh, Mr Nicholas!' Tuesday came walking up the path behind Jalloh. 'See – we burned the wind away.'

Nick looked up. Jalloh was right. The morning sky was luminous, ghosts of sunlight flickering over an ethereal canopy.

Tuesday stroked the kid, his gold tooth glinting. In his Western jeans and open-necked shirt he was not dressed for slaughter. 'I will eat your leg tonight,' he said, pinching the kid's soft ear.

Jalloh jerked the animal away. 'Join us, Mr Nicholas,' he said. 'You were also a hero of the fire.'

The butcher walked to the back garden. Margaret followed them, drawing her scarf over her mouth, the red beads on her bracelet turned liquid by the light. Nick followed instinctively, fearful but pulled along by her presence.

Jalloh had driven a stake into the ground. With Tuesday's help he drew the kid to him, lifting up its chin, talking to it softly. The big brown eyes fixed on him, a mute and yet intelligent response. Nick remembered the first night here and Jalloh's claim. *The animal knows who is master*. He felt it, too – the calm trance of approaching death. When the knife sliced through the small throat his hands went up to his own in shock, half-expecting to feel life pouring out.

The ground was red in an instant; the kid's tied legs convulsed and buckled as Jalloh lifted it into the air and hung it upside down from the post.

Then Nick was on the ground, coffee and bread surging from his stomach into his mouth. Vomit collected between his hands as he knelt. His heart raced, disorganised and stumbling.

Margaret's hands were soft on his back, soothing, urging him up. He tried to stay hunched over, to hide the vomit with dirt. The ground was rock hard, baked to breaking by the sun. His fingers scraped feebly along it.

I'm weaker than Adeya. Shame forced Nick up. Behind him blood soaked into the thirsty earth.

'I'm so sorry.' He made himself look Margaret in the eye. Her headscarf had come loose, her eyes wide with concern. He sensed Jalloh and Tuesday looking at them.

'I . . . I can't see blood,' he explained, panting. 'It's a phobia. I'm sorry.'

She bit her lip. Dipping her head, she spoke in a whisper. 'You must clean yourself. Go. I will send them away.'

In his room, he leaned against the mirror, forehead pressed to the cool glass. He heard the echoing shriek of children's voices, saw the grey tarmac and its spreading dark stain.

Something was fizzing upwards in his belly, nauseatingly sweet; he pushed it down with slow lungfuls of air.

Breathe, he told himself. *Breathe*. But he couldn't stop the flicker of memory; he pushed one down but others surfaced: the fascination of a bloody knee from a bike fall in the days before fear, the red welling around the point of Nick's Swiss army knife when he and Madi became blood brothers on his thirteenth birthday. The knife had been his father's birthday gift to him, instead of the pocket transistor radio Nick wanted. His chest had filled with disappointment when he opened the wrapping paper and saw it nestled there, red and sleek, as his father said: 'When I was your age I would have killed for one of these.' It was unexpectedly heavy for something so small, mysteriously compact, silver lines folding over and into each other. And then disappointment had turned to shock as his father sat down on the end of the rumpled bed, his faded brown corduroy suit just inches from Nick's knees. 'I got a prayer book for my thirteenth,' he'd said. 'And a room full of old men to hear me sing about God. They all looked the same – the same faces, the same clothes, the same delusions. I knew then I'd have to make my own way. And so can you.' He'd rested his hand on Nick's palm, cool as the metal lying at its centre. 'It's all right here, Nicholas. In your own hands.'

But the knife was gone, like everything else. He'd given it to Madi the very same day – an impulsive apology for their hand-holding argument the week before when they'd both gone home upset and hurt. Madi had met him next morning at the top of his road as usual; but they'd walked in embarrassed silence, school-bags heavy on their backs, the scuff of their feet echoing off the tarmac. And when he stopped at the top of the hill to press the knife into Madi's hand, his own heart lifted at his friend's star-tled look, the reverent way his fingers closed slowly around the flawless red casing, the sudden cast of doubt in his eyes.

'Why you giving me this?'

'Because I want to,' he'd answered. And later, on the kissing gate, they'd laughed in the relief of forgetting, Nick watching Madi draw a red line across his thumb with the long silver blade, feeling the daring excitement of pain, bright red against the grey fields. 'Blood brothers. You do that here in England?' Back then he'd felt nothing but peace as their blood mingled with the clasp of their palms, blurring pale skin into dark.

But those days were done. Nick made his way back to Dr Ahmed's kitchen, filthy clothes bundled in his hand. Margaret stood by the sink, looking out of the window. Her nose wrinkled at the smell as she turned.

'Better wash them at the lake,' she told him. 'In the open air.'

'OK.' Maybe then his shame would evaporate in the desert's blind spaces.

They made their way past Adeya's shuttered house, past the millet fields, scorched and silent. Hanan was at work clearing blackened plants, swinging her machete back and forth in a dull rhythm.

Slowly the land softened, their feet leaving muddy imprints. Out here the world expanded, its horizon swallowed by obscuring brilliance. The lake's dark waters had turned pale gold. Nick felt his heartbeat slow. Squatting down, he began to rinse his shirt.

In the distance he could see the red curtains of the shack where Margaret left food. Binza, he remembered. He'd seen Margaret leaving the house many times since, carrying away bread the family could barely spare.

Now she sat on a lonely boulder, her fingers tracing her bracelet like a rosary. She met his eyes and something like a smile came to her lips. *Look at us both*, she seemed to be saying. She pulled off her headscarf, hair almost red in the light. Escaped strands curled around the nape of her neck and ears; he thought of the long, curled sideburns of his father's few boyhood photographs, his shaved head and downcast eyes drooping like the woollen tassels from his shirt.

'I'm so sorry,' he said. 'I embarrassed you.'

She shook her head. 'They are just foolish men. They see nothing.'

The water was warm on his hands and face. He wrung out the wet shirt and spread it on a rock beside Margaret's feet. Then he put his back to the heated stone, feeling the sun beat through his closed eyelids. The nausea was receding, leaving the hollowness of grief. 'I'm going to stay here for a while,' he said. 'I can't go back yet.'

He waited for her to move. But there was only silence, the faint cry of birds and wind.

Then she said, 'Are you sick, Nicholas?'

He opened his eyes to see her regal silhouette, calm as a priest.

'No,' he said. 'Or maybe – yes. But it's an old sickness.' He looked up at her. 'A penance, you would probably say.'

Her gaze was steady, but he noticed her hand's unconscious impulse towards the red bracelet on her arm. 'A penance for what?'

'For something I did when I was young. Something terrible.' His hands lay in his lap, limp and accusing.

She reached down, the lightest touch on his shoulder. 'The young cannot do anything so terrible.'

'I did.' He swallowed. 'To my brother.'

'You never spoke of a brother,' Margaret said.

Nick shook his head – struggling to explain, even to her.

'I loved him like a brother,' he said, at last. 'And he loved me, I think more than my real family did. My father wanted a saint, not a son. And my mother . . .' He closed his eyes again and saw her – pale hair falling over her shoulders like water. 'She would just paint by the window every day. Like she was expecting someone to arrive.' The colours had seemed so alive when she brushed them onto the canvas, their scent warm and bitter across the table where he'd sit helping Madi with equations. But by evening they would fade away, vanishing into the canvas until only their ghost was left.

'And how did you wrong this brother of yours?'

Grief began to creep up his throat. 'He was a foreigner in our village.' He looked up at her. 'Like you. And the other boys at our school – they bullied him. Beat him at break-times, took his money. Usually the teachers would stop them.'

'Boys fight.' Margaret looked back at him, her face quizzical. 'JoJo and Akim fight every day.'

'Not like this.' They'd circle the playground like wolves, Phil and his friends, made bolder and hungrier by the wounds they caused. *Sambo, stupid black cunt. Go back to Togobogo. Oi!*

Paki. What you doing in a class with kids? You like little boys? That your boyfriend over there?

'It was about a week after my thirteenth birthday.' A good week, he remembered, the scars of forgiveness still red on their thumbs, Madi scoring higher in Tinner's maths test than Phil, thanks to Nick's coaching – Phil's face a violent red as Madi leaned forward to whisper *Sambo strikes back, man* while Tinner read out their marks. 'It was Friday afternoon, so we had plans for after school. You know – head to my mother's garden gate, drink soda, read *National Geographic*. Wild boys, right?' Margaret smiled.

'But at lunch break they came at him.' Nick's stomach clenched. 'Worse than before.'

It replayed as he spoke – the high shrieks of 'you're it' travelling across the playground, the clandestine waft of cigarettes from beside the shed, the twang of elastic skipping ropes. Prefects, deliberately blind, confiscating teen magazines from the girls on the chapel steps. Phil's gang flocking around Madi, Phil heading the pack. And Nick – watching as Madi backed towards the climbing frame, his dark head colliding with the silver arches.

A bottle of Dr Pepper was open in Nick's hand; he could taste its gentle fizz. Madi's bottle was in his hoodie pocket, waiting for the peace and solace of the kissing gate at the end of Nick's garden. A grey wind rose around them. Nick saw Madi look into Phil's face, one unguarded moment of contempt. And Phil's hands slammed into Madi's shoulder, knocking him back against the bars.

Now Madi's gaze swung past Phil; Nick followed his eyes towards Miss Tinner's closed classroom door. Everyone knew she sometimes snuck quick cigarettes there when she should have been on playground duty. *All I have to do is run and get her.* Madi's eyes met Nick's for an instant, his expression blank, before another blow jerked them away. *Get her.* Nick didn't know if Madi had mouthed the appeal, or if it came straight from his own heart. *Get help.*

But then Phil turned around to Nick, his fists clenched. The wind blew cold, Nick's knees bare and shivering in his school shorts. 'Don't you bloody move. Queer. Or you're next.' And Nick's body emptied of everything but the absolute authority of fear.

Phil struck Madi again. This time, his eyes held Nick's – fear finally breaking to the surface.

Don't worry. I'm coming. The wind was behind him, blowing him towards a threshold. Any moment now he would move, he would run to summon Miss Tinner, he would step up. But with each passing second, he found himself still there, motionless.

Madi had given up then; he'd turned away from Nick towards the only escape left, hauling himself up through the climbing frame's steel bars. Laughter chased him. *Look at the monkey!* Two of the boys were already climbing after him. Another ran to the far side for a quick ambush.

At the top of the frame, Madi paused. His eyes searched the horizon. Escaping, Nick imagined – taking wing past the playground, past Nick, past the cold village streets and dark little council flats, past Nick's mother's gentle landscapes – heading outwards to the shores of the sea and its once-beautiful promise.

Phil had nearly reached the top. *Go!* Nick screamed, inside the prison of his mind. *Get away!* Madi twisted round. He shoved a hand in his hoodie pocket, for an instant letting go of the bars.

'He fell.' Madi had slipped like a bird's shadow, plummeting. 'It wasn't a long way down. I thought he would be OK. When I saw all the red underneath him I thought his Dr Pepper bottle must have broken.' The stain had spread slowly from the pocket where his hand still rested. Later, in hospital, they'd unclenched his fingers from Nick's Swiss army knife, the silver blade stuck deep into his abdomen.

Nick's face felt tight, dirty. He wiped it with his shirt, breathing in the smells of mud and heat. A touch on his shoulder – Margaret's hand – restored him to the present.

'You think he would not forgive you?' she said.

'I failed him.' He breathed in, tasting the deep odour of water and warm earth. 'I came here to make amends for that. But everything here reminds me of him.'

She turned her head towards Binza's filthy shack. 'The dead do not want to be forgotten. Maybe your friend is still here, with you.' She reached out her hand; Nick could not tell if she was pointing to him, the land or the sky.

He shook his head. 'I don't believe in ghosts.'

'You are wrong,' she said, her tone insistent. 'There are ghosts everywhere.'

The formless curve of the land stretched away, a white gulf. If ever a place could be haunted . . .

'Maybe I wanted another chance,' he said. 'The desert seemed a good place for a test of character.' He laughed. 'Didn't God like sending people to the desert? The prophets, the tribes of Israel. Poor old Jesus.'

'You shouldn't mock.' She turned back to look at him, stern-faced. 'You don't know what may come.'

Nick laughed, weary. 'It's my father coming out in me.'

'You said he hated God.'

Nick pictured his father writing his daily medical diaries, back ramrod-straight, unbending as Moses re-carving the stone tablets. 'He hated blind faith. A "self-hating Jew", he called himself.' Nick laughed, the sound hurting his throat. 'My father believed in tests, though. His tests were always much harder than God's.'

She nodded. 'I also made my father into a God. JoJo, too, with Ahmed, when he was young. It makes it harder for us, when they fail.'

Her words made him pause. As a small boy he'd woken from terrifying dreams, creeping halfway downstairs to hear the all-powerful reassurance of his father's pen scratching against paper, see the desk-light's yellow beams refracting off his glasses. But Madi's death had widened the gulf between them, filling it with guilt and silence. A year after his funeral,

Nick's religious education teacher read them the story of Jesus and the Temple. 'Jesus was younger than you sorry lot,' she'd said. 'And he already knew more than the scholars.' Nick had felt something stir within him at the drama of Jesus' worried parents – their frantic search for their son, that loving family reunion. In his bedroom, with Madi's *Dark Side of the Moon* poster still pinned to the wall, he'd ached for the same homecoming with his own father – some acknowledgement, some way back into his esteem. On impulse, he decided to learn Hebrew and prepare for a bar mitzvah. He organised everything himself: found a rabbi in the yellow pages and ordered a Hebrew-English Pentateuch translation from the village bookshop. The shop assistant had squinted with suspicion at Nick's careful handwriting. 'That's a first for me, mate,' he'd said. 'Lads your age normally order Jackie Collins under the counter.'

He'd anticipated every possible reaction from his father – surprise, pleasure, even fury – everything except disinterest. He didn't even look up from his desk when Nick told him. 'If this were a true act of conscience,' he'd replied, 'then you wouldn't need my approval.' The Torah finally arrived, a Pandora's box of second thoughts. Today it was somewhere in the house he shared with Kate, still waiting to be opened.

Margaret had closed her eyes, her chin dropping as if in sleep. Silence washed the air between them, a light wind blowing ripples across the lake. Eyelashes shadowed her cheeks; pale fingers stroked the beads on her wrist. Against the sun she could have been one of her own drawings – the same fierce grace of line, the hypnotic contrast of bright and dark.

'So, why do you believe in ghosts?' he asked.

She looked up, her face sharp in the sun's relief. The expression there was so close to hatred it made Nick recoil in shock.

'Because I also killed someone.'

Nick's mouth went dry. 'Who?'

'My child.'

She stood up, pulling her headscarf back around her face. 'Margaret,' he said, struggling to his feet. But she ignored him, turning for an instant towards Binza's shack. He reached out for her hand but her fists were clenched; she wrenched them away. Then she was gone, running back towards the village.

He watched her go, heart pounding. His senses were newly awake to the land's secret menace, the hiss of the wind, the dark threat of the lake.

I also killed someone. He remembered the cross in her garden, the thread of sorrow linking everyone in that house. His mind shied away from possibilities too terrifying to contemplate. But then JoJo's shape emerged in the distance, skipping past Adeya's fields. He raised his arm, a cheerful wave summoning Nick home.

The village council has called a meeting about the rains. Jalloh and Tuesday and Imam Abdi and Mr Kamil – they will all be there. Baba says they want to make trouble, but will not stand and face it. I heard him tell Mama: 'The only thing faster than Kamil's mouth is his car.'

Baba will bring me to the council with him. 'You are nearly a man, Yahya,' he told me. 'One day you must speak there yourself. Nicholas will come also.' He had asked Baba's permission. Baba looked at him for a long while. Then he said: 'Of course, you are most welcome.'

The council meets at the mosque, after prayers. Usually we pray at home, not at the mosque. Mecca is towards Baba's clock. Once I told Bako that Allah lives inside the clock. 'You can hear Allah,' I told him. 'He says, tick-tock, tick-tock.'

Mr Kamil has brought Juma. He looks at me when I walk into the room. He used to look at me like I was a goat and he the dog. But I am different now.

Nicholas sits down with us, at the big table. Juma sits opposite, with Mr Kamil. Imam Abdi has the highest place, at the head. Jalloh is beside Baba. Tuesday is there, too. Today he has buttoned his shirt, because there are no ladies.

A stranger sits beside Imam Abdi. He is fat, like the governor. A rich man. He sees me looking and smiles at me. His teeth are white as a jackal's.

Imam Abdi begins with a blessing. He thanks Allah that He did not burn all the village. He asks Allah to help us with the dry season. He prays for Allah's law to return to us. He talks too long. By the end he is squawking like a parrot. At last, he tells us, 'Allah knows best.'

Mr Kamil, he stands up. He says: 'My friends, Allah knows best. So why does He send the fires to take our fields? It is judgement. We bow to laws that are not His and to corrupt men. We have caused our own suffering.'

Baba raises his voice. He says: 'The ones who suffer most are not in this room. First we must discuss our responsibility to them. Charity pleases Allah more than all other praise.'

Mr Kamil does not like it when Baba speaks. He points his fingers straight out, like knives. He says: 'Dr Ahmed is correct. We must tend first to the suffering. But tell me, where is the root of the disease? The price of water is breaking us. And even then, the trucks do not come. Greed is drinking our water and greed is eating our food. There is a knife at our throats. I can name the knife. Can you?'

'The governor is no friend to us,' Tuesday says.

Baba is translating for Nicholas. But I am thinking of when the governor gave me his cap. He smiled at me then. His teeth were white, too, like the stranger's.

Now the stranger speaks. He says: 'It is true, sir. The governor has not forgiven the rebellion. You will pay and pay, for as long as he lives.'

Mr Kamil bows his head. 'Welcome, Danjuma,' he says.

Now I know who the stranger is. I saw him on the posters in Tuesday's shop. Danjuma is the man who stands against the governor in the election. Tuesday saw us looking at the posters.

He said: 'Is he handsome, this Danjuma? Not so handsome as me, eh?'

Danjuma is handsome. He has a friendly face and his shirt is purple. He clasps his hands and smiles at everyone. He leaves no one out from the smiling.

'Danjuma knows our problems,' Mr Kamil tells us. 'When he is governor, he will give us back justice.'

But Baba, he speaks again. He says: 'The last time our guest's party fought the governor's party, this village paid a heavy price.'

'I know, sir,' Danjuma says. 'Your father was with us, and mine. But that was many years gone. Do we wait for our children to fight the battles that should be ours? I see your boy is here with you.'

He points my way. Baba, he looks down at me. His eyes are hidden behind his glasses. I want to tell him, I am ready, Baba. Ready to fight. But he says to Danjuma: 'I want my son to have peace, food and learning. And I want to leave our dead to rest. I tell you, we must talk to the governor. Ask him to lower the price of water. Give him the chance to hear our concerns.'

Jalloh, across the table, he says: 'Yes, sir.' Tuesday, beside us, he looks here and there like a cat. Imam Abdi, he is angry. He looks like he has swallowed one of Jalloh's goats, and its legs have stuck in his mouth.

Mr Kamil puffs out his big chest, like a rooster. He speaks to Baba in a rooster voice. He says: 'You cannot stop what is coming. There are just six months until the election. We must prepare.'

Nicholas, he raises his hand. 'I will help, if you want,' he says. 'I can speak to the governor.'

They look at him. A white knight, Mama called him. She watches him, like I do. She watches when we are together.

Danjuma, he is watching, too. He asks: 'What can you say to the governor?'

I want to tell Nicholas: be careful of this Danjuma. But

Nicholas is not afraid. He says: 'The village should have its own water supply. There's water underground, a source – or so I hear. We may be able to tap it.'

The men look at each other. Baba, he puts a hand on Nicholas' arm. He says: 'First let us ask for the prices to come down. Elections are difficult times to make big changes.'

'Sure,' Nicholas says. 'We can ask for that, too.'

So Mr Kamil says to him: 'You will go to the governor?'

But Baba, he says: 'I will take Nicholas with me. Together we will see what can be done.'

Later, when we leave, Baba says to Nicholas: 'I am sorry if I am overbearing. But I am afraid of what will happen if Kamil and his friends have their way. They talk of helping people but their real interest is in power. Human nature can be ugly.'

'And it can be noble,' Nicholas says, putting his hand on Baba's shoulder. Baba laughs and looks at me. He says: 'And what do you think of this council, Yahya? Would you like to see Danjuma here, with his loudspeaker?'

I think of the man, of his poster in Tuesday's shop, of his big hands clasped together over his head. Baba's hands held Adeya's to comfort her and wrapped them in bandages. Nicholas' hands can make real things out of numbers, like our castle. But then I think of the governor's hand in mine, and I feel fear.

I take Baba's hands, his good hands. And I say: 'Baba, please. Don't go to the Town.'

Baba takes my face. His touch is warm. He smiles at me, like he did when I was small and Bako was alive. 'Yahya,' he says. 'What has worried you? There's nothing to fear.'

'They are not good men there,' I say. And Baba he squeezes my cheek. 'Wise boy,' he says.

Then he turns to Nicholas. He says: 'This is the most important thing – the moral future of our children. You cannot grow a strong tree with poisoned water. If these boys grow up with anger, what will they learn? What will they become?'

Nicholas nods his head. Then he puts his arm on my shoulder. 'But first,' he says, 'we must make sure they grow up.'

That night in my bed, I ask Mama: 'When Nicholas goes back to England, can I go with him? Like Baba did, to study?'

She touches my cheek and says: 'You are too young, JoJo. There will be time later.'

'When I go,' I tell her, 'I will learn mathematics and build things. And I would send you money, you and Baba and Nagode. And Nagode will come to stay with me, when she is older. You will see.'

Mama turns her head from me. I can see only the shape of her, her back and her cheek. She says: 'I know, JoJo. I know.' Her voice is quiet and I think she is crying. I am afraid to ask her why. Maybe it is for Bako. Or maybe Adeya has become more sick.

Instead I ask her: 'Do you like Nicholas?'

Her head comes up and her voice changes. She says: 'I like him well enough.'

I tell her: 'He's a good man.'

She touches my cheek, her skin as soft as Adeya's goats: 'And I pray you will be one, too.'

After she goes, I pull my blanket over my head. I think of how it will be to live with Nicholas. It is cold in England, and everything is green. I will study at the university. And I will stay with Nicholas and his wife. If they have children, I will be like their big brother.

Next day I tell Akim, at our desks before the teacher comes. I tell him: 'I won't go to the high school next year. I will go to England instead, with Nicholas. The schools here are no good.'

I can see Adeya, listening. Her desk is in front by the teacher, where the girls sit. She turns to me, and I see her face. Mostly she smiles when she sees me. But today she does not smile.

Akim laughs to see her. He says: 'Look – your girlfriend will miss you, eh, JoJo?' He brings his face close to mine and makes his voice high, like a girl's. He says: 'Kiss me, JoJo! I love you. Don't mind my smell. Kiss me!'

My face feels red. I used to think Adeya and me, we would marry. And I kissed her once, on the mouth. She asked me to. So I did. Her mouth was dry, but I liked it. She said: 'Do it again.'

Now all the boys are looking at me. I feel their eyes on me, like ants. My face, it burns.

Adeya is also red. She speaks to Akim in a low voice. She says: 'Leave him be, stupid.'

'You leave him, stinky,' Akim says to her. 'I can smell your shit from here.'

'Lift her dress,' I hear someone call. 'Maybe she only has one hole. You have to put your dick in the same hole she makes her business.'

Adeya looks at me. I open my mouth – but nothing comes.

Akim, he says: 'Better go to England, JoJo, to find a nice woman. Who wants a wife who smells like shit?'

I see her eyes, the look she gives me. Then she turns her back to me. She makes herself small, like a dog when you hit it.

I think: in my bag I still have those stickers – the ones I stole from Tuesday's shop. Flowers and animals. So many times I meant to give them to you.

But now I am looking at her back. I want to tell her: don't cry, Adeya. I want to tell her that I do not care how she smells. That I have cried for her, too, many times. Like when Baba took her to the hospital that time. I cried all night and did not sleep.

But they are laughing around me and I cannot. All that day, I only see her back.

And at night when I sleep, the dreams come. The fires are burning and Adeya stands inside them, on the other side of the lake. I want to reach her. But between us is too much water, and all the water is made from our tears.

DECEMBER

Soon, Nick began to suspect Dr Ahmed was deliberately delaying his mission to the Town. Miss Amina's diabetic foot abscess needed cleaning, Adeya's dressings needed changing, his monthly drop-in clinic at the market was overdue. He dismantled the grandfather clock – forcing the household to step gingerly over weights and tools whose brown patina defied even Dr Ahmed's fevered polishing.

Meanwhile, Nick used the time to learn more about the village aquifer. Eric managed to retrieve an old survey, dating back nearly twenty years. It showed a large water source directly under the village, one hundred metres below in fractured bedrock.

The water of life. With it the land could be transformed – irrigation systems and running taps, reservoirs to slake thirst and extinguish fires.

Nick thought of sharing his discovery with Margaret – but she'd retreated from him since that day at the lake. His overtures were rejected with one-word answers and averted eyes, an invisible curtain drawn irrevocably around her.

With so much else on his mind he should have respected her withdrawal – but instead it left him frustrated, and even bereft. He'd crossed an ocean – left his family without an instant of loneliness. But now he sensed its first cold touches – as she turned her head away passing him in the hall, as her eyes slid from his at the dinner table. He'd confessed his deepest shame to her, a twenty-year scab ripped away. He felt its ache, painfully vivid, like the bloodied knee of a climber or the broken nose of a bare-knuckle boxer. His senses were newly raw and awake; he found himself noticing familiar things as if for the first time – the yellow flag on JoJo's castle, bright shavings of peel on the compost heap, the whisper of Nagode's sleeping tree, Binza's red doorway, sharp tendrils of sight and sound piercing his being.

I killed my child, she'd said. The memory chilled him. Sometimes he was relieved by her absence but other times – at the dinner table or when they passed in the sitting room – he felt the secret touch of her gaze, a pause that stretched between them like an in-held breath.

On Friday, two weeks after the village meeting, Nick returned home early from the Town, bringing Eric's monthly supply list for Dr Ahmed's approval. Friday's sermon was blazing from the mosque loudspeaker; Nick noticed a larger crowd than usual gathering outside as his Jeep sped past.

He pulled up to the house in the choking heat. Pacing up the steps, he rapped on Dr Ahmed's surgery door. Silence answered. The dim sitting room was quiet, the air stale. 'Hello?' Dust motes stirred; Nick's voice came back at him in a flat echo. Moisture pooled on his forehead in the oppressive heat. Perhaps Margaret was sleeping inside with Nagode. An image came, unbidden, long arms outstretched on the sheets, sweat tracing soft lines on their skin.

He opened the back door and stepped out into the garden – nearly tripping over Margaret where she sat on the porch steps. She cried out in alarm, snatching something to her chest, the pencil in her hand clattering to the tiles.

'I'm sorry!' he said, stretching out to reassure her. Colour scalded her cheeks. 'I didn't see you – I was looking for Dr Ahmed.' He brandished the supply checklist. 'Eric's sending someone to get supplies – he wants to know what we need.'

'Ahmed took JoJo to Friday prayers.' Margaret's breath came fast, whatever she'd been holding still clutched to her – a notebook, pressed tight against her skin. 'You came back early.' It was an accusation.

'I'm sorry,' he repeated. Suddenly he felt ridiculous. He fought the urge to grab her, shake her out of this strange pretence of hostility. The castle loomed behind her, dust rising over the ground where they'd danced. *Forget it. She obviously has and so should you.* 'What were you doing?' He indicated the notebook. 'Drawing another story?'

'Nothing,' she said, getting to her feet and pushing past him into the kitchen.

'So I'll look for Dr Ahmed at the mosque then,' he called after her. There was no reply. He gave up, heading down into the garden and out of the front gate.

He could hear noise swelling from the mosque as he rounded the corner. Prayers had just ended and the village men would be gathering their shoes and rolling up their mats, filling the streets with a loose and gentle chatter.

But this sound was different; he could hear dozens of raised voices, punching through the air. Something was wrong. Stopping short, Nick saw files of men marching from the mosque's entrance, heading purposefully into the street.

He barely had time to back away into the safety of the mosque forecourt before they flooded past him, arms jabbing towards the village's scorched fields. Some he knew from Dr Ahmed's surgery: Imam Abdi and Mr Kamil's son Juma, clenched fists pumping over his head. The crowd's leader was shouting into a megaphone.

Nick realised he was trapped, an angry line of men stretching between him and Dr Ahmed's house. He could see no sign of the doctor or JoJo; surely the old man would never take his son to a protest? *Not even if the governor burned his house down in front of him.*

And now another group approached the march from the opposite direction, smaller and more ragged. Jalloh led them; Nick saw the nervous swing of his big arms. They blocked the protesters' path right where Nick stood, hurling insults across the invisible line between the two sides. He could feel the unspilled violence simmering, a pressure-cooker coming to the boil.

One of Jalloh's younger friends pushed across the boundary, fury overlaying his adolescent terror. He launched himself towards the protester holding the megaphone, trying to wrest it from him. But the protester's hand came crashing down, sending metal smashing into dark curls.

'No!' Nick tried to stifle his own cry as the young man fell to the ground. Jalloh stepped forward, then back, undecided as the mob closed in around the fallen boy.

Stop. The word formed silently in Nick's head. But this was no time for heroics. *It's not your fight,* he told himself.

And yet the protester with the megaphone had turned towards him. It was Imam Abdi's Man Friday, Nick realised, who prepared the mosque and cooked the imam's meals, whose cataract-clouded eye regularly required Dr Ahmed's antibiotic ointments.

He advanced, brandishing a burn on his forearm, pale and slick as a knife. 'From the fire,' he yelled. 'You help the governor. You give him money!'

'That's not true!' Nick started to back away; he felt the loom of the mosque wall behind him. Adrenalin surged as he looked towards his only escape route to Dr Ahmed's house, blocked by a wall of menace. 'I'm trying to help!'

The mosque-keeper was in front of him now; his clouded eye filling Nick's view like God's judgment, his breath stale from old food and tobacco. He raised his arms to the parched and empty sky. 'What help?' he screamed upwards – and then to Nick's face. 'What help?'

'Leave him be.'

Nick turned in shock; Margaret stood behind him, head covered with a dark scarf. *How did she get here?* She pushed in front of him, arms unexpectedly strong. The wounded man coughed at her feet in the dust, blood trickling from a cut over his eye.

'For shame.' Margaret pointed at the mosque-keeper, her

voice loud enough to carry with it only a hint of a tremor beneath. 'Another one for my husband's care.'

The mosque-keeper rocked back and forth, one dark eye flicking manically between the bloodied dust and Margaret's outstretched hand. The very sight of it seemed to be another affront to him. He slapped his chest with his palm, despair ringing out with the sound. Stepping forward, he pushed at the air between them, arms waving with frantic energy.

Nick instinctively retreated, but Margaret remained immovable. She pointed at the mosque, reciting a verse in a language he recognised as Arabic, its syllables heavy with warning. He saw confusion on the mosque-keeper's face, the signs of anger derailed. But rage was still thick in the air; Nick had a sudden fear she might over-reach herself. A Christian quoting Muhammad could set the place alight. The thought released him from his paralysis.

'Margaret.' The mosque-keeper had turned away, distracted by the faint sound of a police siren. 'We have to go.' She turned and nodded. 'Follow me,' she whispered.

Then she was moving, her scarf arcing behind her like a bird's wing, away from Dr Ahmed's house towards the low line of walled homes on the road's opposite side. Hurrying to keep up, Nick saw a small gap in the white stone wall between two of the largest houses – one of them Mr Kamil and Aisha's. Behind him the loudspeaker was blasting again, over the screech of car tyres.

'No one uses this way,' Margaret whispered as they squeezed through the small opening, dust coating their clothes. 'But you must keep low or they will see you.'

'I don't understand.' Nick reached out and grabbed her wrist. She stopped, facing him reluctantly. 'Why did you come here?'

'JoJo returned early from prayers.' Her breath was still laboured, sweat further darkening her already sombre headscarf. 'His father found out what was planned here and sent him home. Ahmed has gone to the authorities.'

'You were mad to come out. They could have hurt you.'

'They could have hurt *you.*' The rejoinder was like a slap, quick and harsh; her eyes met his, suddenly furious. Then the moment passed. She took a deep breath, her face softening. 'Anyway. Now we are both well.' She turned towards the alley's end. 'This way.'

The path ended in a heap of rocks; a nimble person could climb these to reach a large hole in Kamil's garden wall. Margaret cautiously peered through it. 'All clear.' She looked back at Nick, a sly sideways glance. 'Is that how James Bond says it?'

Hoisting her abaya up to her knees, she clambered through into the garden. Amazed, he followed, landing behind a dying tree. Margaret had moved over quickly to the wall opposite, which was low enough to climb over. Her lean arms reached up, took her weight and she scrambled over to the other side.

Then he froze, hearing Aisha's voice close by – a scolding tone that grew louder. 'Quickly!' Margaret whispered. He could hear her but not see her. Between the lattice of branches he spied the brilliant green trail of Aisha's abaya, her back to them as she gesticulated at Hanan, dour in brown.

Nick reached for the wall in panic. He knocked a loose stone as he pulled himself clumsily over it, tumbling down into another alley two metres below.

The voices stopped; Margaret pushed him into the shelter of a small overhang, placing her body in front of his. He felt the warm pulse of her breathing, heard Hanan's complaining grumble as she approached, a scuffing sound as she peered over the garden wall into the alley. Margaret looked up to meet Hanan's eyes, raising her finger to her lips. Nick held his breath, transfixed by the swell of her lips around her knuckle, his nerves electric as he waited for the older woman to call out.

A long pause stretched out, broken only by faint tinny cries from the loudspeaker. Thoughts raced. Would Hanan set the crowd on them? Did they stone people here? *But we've done nothing wrong.*

118

Then another scuffle of feet and a heavy thud as Hanan retreated to the foot of the wall, calling out a negative to Aisha. Nick breathed out as the women's voices receded. Margaret giggled with relief, her shoulders shaking. He realised his shirt was filthy, a ripped patch at his elbow. The sweat in his mouth tasted sharp and heady as whisky; he'd rarely felt so completely alive.

'It's been years since I did anything so crazy,' he said, when he got his breath back.

'Me and Sarah, we climbed walls when we were girls,' Margaret said, wiping her eyes. 'We stole guavas from our neighbour's garden. JoJo does it now – he thinks I do not know.'

He smiled at her, relieved. 'Thank you. For coming to my rescue. A real Sir Galahad.'

She snorted. 'There are no knights in this village.'

'Except for Dr Ahmed.' He meant it, but the words stoppered the thrill of the moment, tamping down his joy.

'He's a healer, not a warrior.' Margaret pushed back her headscarf, retying it behind the long curve of her neck. 'He's devoted only to his work.'

'And to you.' The words felt falsely dutiful.

'He cares for me,' she said, the smile gone from her face. 'It's not the same as love.'

He caught her glance before she looked away. The sudden silence was awkward; it stretched out until Nick felt something disturbing insinuate itself into the pause. Then she was gone, moving swiftly through the warren-like paths between the houses.

Finally they stepped into the freedom of open space. Dr Ahmed's house lay ahead under a heavy glaze of light.

He knew that once she crossed that threshold, a door would close in her. 'Margaret – did I do something to offend you?'

'Nothing.'

'That day by the lake – what you said . . .'

'Let's not speak of it.' They'd reached the garden gate. Her eyes stayed resolutely away from him, directed towards the house.

Joy plummeted. Their conversations were like stepping-stones across a flooding river, full of unexpected missteps into cold water. He put his hand on the gate to stop her opening it. 'Tell me we're still friends at least.'

She looked at him. Sunlight scoured her face, irises opaque as an eclipse. 'Yes, Nicholas,' she answered. 'We are friends.'

He released the gate; she went inside. Nick's hands were filthy from the wall. A bucket of soapy water stood near the kitchen sink. As he was rinsing them, he noticed a piece of paper crumpled in the waste-bucket, the pale yellow of Margaret's notepad.

Lifting it out, he smoothed over its creases. Margaret had drawn herself looking away towards the edge of the paper, her tall body curved in a dance. One arm was lifted skywards, the other stretched towards an unseen figure – an anonymous hand, pale and open-palmed, reaching towards hers from a world outside the page.

The protest forced Dr Ahmed's hand; at last he bowed to the inevitable. Nick helped him into the car on the morning of their appointment with the governor, subdued in the stained brown suit he wore to see his patients. Nick read this as a quiet act of defiance.

Speeding up the northern highway, the doctor's eyes looked vacant in the rear-view mirror – lined with moisture, their dark irises tinged with a mottled blue circle.

'When was the last time you came to the Town?' Nick asked.

'Oh, not for a while now.' The doctor seemed to be speaking a beat slower than usual, fixated by the sight of the cars slipping southwards. 'My sister is there. You remember?' Goggo had come for Friday meals twice since Nick's arrival, a gummy old woman sheathed in black.

'Eric said there was some trouble once, between your family and the governor.'

'My father thought he could bring many changes here.' Dr Ahmed turned away from the window. 'He and Danjuma's father were political allies. They spent money and made enemies. There were elections. My father refused to withdraw. In the end there was a riot. People died.' He sighed, studying his open palms.

'I'm sorry.' Impatience spurred Nick onwards, thinking of the aquifer and its boundless possibilities. 'But don't they have a point? The protesters – even Mr Kamil and Danjuma? Why should Adeya lose her crops or children get sick because water is too expensive? Bad leadership kills more people than riots – you must see that in your work, surely.'

'I see many things,' Dr Ahmed told him. 'Mostly what I see is that people do not learn from their mistakes. I told Miss Amina thirty years ago she would develop diabetes unless she stopped drinking sweet colas. But she cannot. I tell men that unless they restrain their sexual habits, they will become diseased and infertile. But they continue. This is human nature.'

Nick swallowed. His father had yelled the same thing during his last visit – barely able to stand but radiating contempt as Nick described some cut-throat business deals among his firm's partners. 'The law of the jungle means everyone gets eaten in the end,' he'd said, fixing Nick with his failing eyes. 'You people never learn.' When Nick protested that he'd nothing to do with his bosses, his father had snorted. 'There's no such thing as an innocent bystander, Nicholas.' The old man's scorn had been a scourge for so long, outliving even the bitter relief of his funeral. That day was still fresh in Nick's memory – his mother shunted aside by a host of barely known relatives, the sad drone of Tahara prayers as Nick washed the withered body in slow strokes – from balding crown to cracked toenails, all that gigantic authority shrivelled into ruin. Later, when they laid his father in the casket and Nick placed the long-rejected yarmulke on the lank hair, he'd felt a vindictive pleasure that the old man could no longer argue about it.

Now Dr Ahmed had his father's eyes, the light turning them grey as stone. 'Human nature is part of God's law,' he said, a touch of sadness in his tone. 'Where there are errors, there will also be consequences. If we have a bad leader, isn't it because we ourselves have not learned to be good?'

The governor was hosting their meeting over lunch. Food was already on the table at his mansion – an international spread of pasta and leafy salads. A vast fish, its flesh brown with smoke, stared up at them from a bed of yellow rice. 'Shipped from the coast,' Eric said in a low voice. 'Too fancy for the likes of us, eh, Dr Ahmed?'

The old man's lips moved to reply, but his mind seemed to be elsewhere. Nick noticed that Eric's language improved around Dr Ahmed. He was not a man to be easily sworn at.

Eventually the governor entered on a wave of activity – thrusting papers back to his scurrying assistant.

'Well.' He encompassed them all with his vast smile. 'I am so pleased you could accept my invitation. And thank you for bringing this most welcome guest. It has been far too long, Dr Ahmed.'

He extended his hand; the doctor shook it limply. 'It has.' His voice had climbed in register. The governor's presence seemed to diminish him, shrinking him into old age.

'Sit, please.' The governor pulled up a seat and started spooning food onto his plate. The fish flaked easily under Nick's fork, but its smoky warmth summoned Adeya's millet fields to mind. He wondered how much of her monthly income he'd swallowed in that single bite.

'So.' The governor turned to him. 'I like your structural changes to our new wing. A much more efficient approach.'

'I hope so.' Nick cast an eye towards Dr Ahmed, eating in silence. 'We're on schedule to finish before the rains.'

'And how do you like the team? I know the company owner well. Not brilliant, but reliable. Personally, I prefer reliable.'

'They're doing fine.' Nick willed Dr Ahmed's eyes upwards – but the older man kept his glance fixed on his plate.

After a pause, Nick continued. 'Actually, I wanted to put a suggestion to you.' Now Dr Ahmed's eyes turned up in a warning glance. 'About health issues here in general. How we could put the money we're saving on the construction project to better use.'

The governor had stopped eating, large hands clasped before him in polite interest. The man's presence radiated outwards like a force field; Nick could almost feel it pushing him back in his seat.

He looked around for support. 'Dr Ahmed, you know more than anyone what's happening in your village.'

The governor's eyes turned to him. 'This man's family and mine go back many years. Some of those were difficult but mutual respect has always been there. If you have something to ask of me, Dr Ahmed, please do not hesitate.'

He held the governor's gaze. 'I have nothing to ask for myself,' he said. 'What I ask is for our village. I come on behalf of the council.'

'Yes. My friend Danjuma was present at your meeting, I hear.' The governor helped himself to another large forkful of fish. 'I was sorry to learn of the fire. Most unfortunate.'

'It will not be the only one.' Dr Ahmed's back was straight as a prisoner's in the dock. 'The rains have failed. The poorest cannot afford to pay the trucks. Now there is no water for their fields. Soon there will be none to wash and then none to drink. And where hunger goes, anger follows. Already there have been protests. Therefore I ask you, in Allah's name: give us a lower price, for this season.'

The governor sat back in his chair, considering Dr Ahmed. The silence between them swelled, filling the room.

Nick's impatience mounted. *We shouldn't have to beg.* It was humiliating to watch Dr Ahmed belittle himself – not an envoy but a sinner dragged to the stocks.

Nick pulled the aquifer survey out of his jacket pocket, and laid it on the table between them.

'There's another option,' he said.

The governor's gaze rested on the survey, like a fly on an abandoned meal. Nick noticed a slight twitch of the arm that bore the gleaming watch.

'Look.' He pointed to the flow of survey lines. 'There's an

underground water reservoir here. Enough for a permanent supply to the whole village. We just need to drill a well.'

'A well?' the governor repeated, the word resonating in his chest.

'We can afford to dig for water,' Nick told him, 'with what was saved on the hospital project.'

'You are an expert in digging wells?'

'No,' Nick admitted. 'But I'm an engineer – I can get it done.'

'How?' The governor leaned forward, turning the survey for a better view. His tone was interested. 'How do such things get done?'

Nick had not come prepared with specifics. 'Well . . . there are different kinds – pump-action, storage, irrigation. I'd have to consult on the best model for this area. But it's quick – a matter of weeks. Months at most. And it's not expensive, not compared to something like this.' He gestured towards the hospital site. 'And the point is – it lasts. We're not talking about a solution to just this drought. It could change things.' He looked at the doctor. 'It could change everything.'

A pause enveloped the table. Even Eric was silent. Only Dr Ahmed stirred. He laid his hand on the survey, fingers spread as if to hide it, the lines on his skin blending with the faded cartography.

Now the governor sat back in his chair, pushing his plate away. Slick flakes tumbled onto the tablecloth, staining it with oily residue.

'So whose proposal am I considering?' The governor turned to Dr Ahmed. 'The doctor says I must reduce the price of water for his village and let others bear his costs. You,' he turned back to Nick, 'have an even bolder plan. A vision. We divert our resources, we make rivers flow in the desert. Like the prophets. Is that the way of it?'

Nick sensed something building in the room – a gathering storm.

'It's a good means to a good end,' he said, doggedly. 'You said you wanted a modern society. In a modern society, people's lives don't depend on nature's whims.'

The governor raised his massive arm towards Nick and tapped the gold watchstrap. 'Did I ever tell you the story of this watch?' he asked. 'It came from my uncle. A graduation present. Originally he wanted to give me a manual watch that some Swiss craftsman worked ten years to make. My uncle was a romantic. In his day we did not have systematic arrangements, like water trucking. We had more of a manual system, you might say. My father was governor then, and my uncle urged him to keep tuning his system to fit everyone's desires. But Dr Ahmed knows what happened next. The adjustments were never sufficient for men like Mr Danjuma. They only created the appetite for more adjustments. In the end the whole mechanism became broken. They tried to take the life of my father. Isn't that correct, sir?'

Dr Ahmed said nothing.

'So when my uncle offered me his expensive manual watch, I said, no – I'm not interested in romantic systems. Give me something that works, that will not break, that can be consistent.'

Now he turned to Dr Ahmed. 'Out of respect for you, I agreed to this meeting. Now you come here asking me to break my word to the people of this region, to fracture our reliable system. Do you know where this path leads?'

Dr Ahmed's head was swaying slightly, as if under the onslaught of a fierce wind.

'Why is it so unreasonable?' Nick felt sweat pooling in his palms as he clenched his cutlery. 'It's just a temporary price drop. You haven't seen the state of these people. They're suffering.'

The governor did not even spare him a glance. 'Doctor, do you speak for yourself? I can forgive your age. But I cannot forgive a man who hides the face of another. So, tell me. Who do you speak for?'

Dr Ahmed swallowed, eyes wide like JoJo's. He was diminishing into a boy before their eyes, his dignity draining away.

'I speak for myself.' His voice was barely more than a hoarse whisper.

The governor stood up. 'Please, finish your lunch.' He left the table, his men following in his wake. The door slammed shut, extinguishing their arguments like a candle.

'Well, that went pretty fucking well.' Eric lit a cigarette as they walked out into the white afternoon. Dr Ahmed's head remained bowed. His frame looked disjointed under his faded brown suit – a discarded wooden puppet propped on a shelf.

Nick reached over and touched the old man's hand.

'I'm sorry,' he said. 'He's a monster.'

Dr Ahmed looked up, his mottled eyes focusing with difficulty. 'No, he is correct. I am foolish. I tried to prevent one bad thing, and I have made another.'

'How can you think that? All that stuff about watches and reliable systems – he just wanted to intimidate you. He knows you're right.'

Dr Ahmed shook his head, weariness creasing his face. 'Please, Nicholas. Let us go home. I am tired now.'

'We'll take you, sir.' Eric slipped a hand under the old man's arm, hoisting him up. 'Don't you worry. One door closes and all that.'

'I'll speak to J.P. before I go home for Christmas,' Nick promised. Noise and dust roared around the rising building, copper wires protruding from the grey slabs like raw innards. Dr Ahmed stopped to look at it. For a moment Nick saw it through his eyes – a grotesque embodiment of struggle and consumption.

Eric left to fetch the Jeep. Dr Ahmed leaned against Nick. His pupils dilated as he stared outwards.

'My mother had a saying.' His voice was hoarse in the high wind. '"From sorrow we come, to sorrow we return. There is weeping at our birth and at our laying out. Sorrow is our midwife and sorrow is our priest."'

Nick was wordless. The wind stung his eyes.

'Islam teaches the same. Sorrow walks in God's footsteps. We do not hide from sorrow. We open our doors and welcome it inside. We say: we have long been expecting you.'

Nick turned away to hide his emotion. The ground beneath him was white, like a shroud.

We welcome in sorrow. The months after Madi died had been filled with it, a river so deep he could have set sail and drifted away. He'd seen his self-disgust reflected in his father's eyes, felt shame gushing out of him like a spring. And even here those bitter waters were still flowing. His father had joined Madi, under the unforgiving ground. Nick had abandoned his mother to silence. Dr Ahmed was shrinking into helpless old age. Adeya's hands were cracking and hardening, like the land where Margaret walked with her ghosts.

Eric pulled up the Jeep. As Dr Ahmed opened the door, he clutched at Nick's hand.

'Do not tell Yahya about today,' he said. 'Please.'

Nick nodded. He knew shame, too. For a moment their hands clasped. And then the Jeep was slipping away, beyond the governor's gate and its soldiers, leaving Nick alone.

It was late evening by the time Nick returned home, climbing wearily from the car. The click of the door sent black birds scudding into the air over Dr Ahmed's garden gate.

He was too tired for any encounters; he was sick and tired of them all: the governor, Eric, Dr Ahmed. Even Margaret. Margaret most of all. He'd had enough of helplessness – he could do nothing more to stop a drought or release her from her self-made prison. In a month he could escape back home to an English Christmas and to Kate, retrieving some perspective, forgetting sorrows that were not his to bear. His own were heavy enough.

The evening breeze was unexpectedly sweet as he leaned on the cooling car roof, wrapping him in quietness. The desert had shed the day's heat, stretching away in long, peaceful curves, gentle as a woman asleep. Colour pulsed over the wide expanse, pale waves deepening to hypnotic blue. The dust storms had cleared from a sky clear as water, small clouds dissolving into silver currents. Eastwards, gathering darkness swept across a horizon studded with faint pinpricks of light.

He balled his fists against his eyes, sparks of colour shooting through the blackness behind the lids. They illuminated a ghost-image of Margaret's face, the too-familiar arc of her smile, rare and breathtaking, her skin patterned with tiny stars. *Stop haunting me.* He tried to rub her away, opening his eyes to flashes of light. The stars were coming out, dazzling in their clarity. *When you wish upon a star.* His mother had loved that song when he was little: another of those sweet childhood lies, like notes for Santa and pennies for the wishing well. But he could sense a different well at his feet now, black and bottomless, pulling him towards its edge. And the wishes he longed to cast into its depths were not a child's. He could not even name them – but he felt their presence in the dark privacy of his dreams.

Enough. He walked up the porch and through the sitting room, following the warm scent of baking drifting from the kitchen. As he opened the door, warily, Nick nearly tripped over Dr Ahmed crouching on the floor. Nagode stood opposite, swaying as she clung to a table leg. Her round face was set in a determined frown.

'Come, daughter.' Dr Ahmed was beckoning with his hands. 'Come on, be brave.'

Nagode's mouth dropped open as she looked up at Nick. Dr Ahmed followed her gaze, delight crinkling the corners of his eyes, the day's setback apparently forgotten.

'She walked just now!' he said. 'Watch – she will do it again. Once they start, there's no stopping them.'

JoJo came running in from the sitting room, bumping into Nick's back. 'Did you see? Nagode made her first step!' He pinched his sister's cheek and she slapped his hand away with a fierce, fleshy palm.

'That's amazing!' Bitterness vanished. Nagode's gaze fixed on

Nick, caught between wonder and terror; baby fat wobbled as her toes kept their precarious grip on the ground.

Margaret was at the sink, long arms beating a bowl of creamy mixture. Nick swallowed the familiar tightness in his throat, walking over to dab up a fleck that had fallen from the bowl's edge. She fell still as he tasted, sweet and rich, with a hint of nutmeg. 'Batter,' she told him, 'for pound cake.'

'A birthday cake!' JoJo was eager to tell him. 'Nagode walked on her first birthday!'

'My god – I totally forgot.' JoJo had mentioned his sister's birthday the week before, during their mathematics session. But no one had mentioned it since.

Nick crouched down by Nagode. He stroked her cheek, where beads of moisture collected like tears. She squinted at him, suspicious. 'Happy birthday, Nagode. I wish I'd bought you a present.'

'Oh, no matter.' Here Dr Ahmed was like a different man; a giant inside his own walls. 'The only birthday we celebrate in Islam is the Prophet's, peace be upon him. But one year is a milestone. Many parents only name their children on their first birthday, if they have survived. And Margaret has her traditions from her girlhood, which we must also honour.'

'Any excuse for birthday cake,' Nick laughed. 'I used to complain I only had it once a year. Every birthday my mother would ask: "Now, what shall it be *this* year – chocolate cake and candles or bread and water?"' He saw Margaret smile.

'My wife will give you her recipe,' Dr Ahmed said. 'And you can pass it to your mother when you return for Christmas. And your wife.' Dr Ahmed insisted on referring to Kate as Nick's wife.

Margaret's busy hands paused to wipe her forehead.

'I'll only be gone for three weeks,' Nick said, carefully. 'We're going hiking in the Lake District.' He forced himself to look away from her. *Remember how much you need a break.* And Dr Ahmed, he suspected, would be politely relieved to be rid of him for a while.

'No!' JoJo's anger rang through the kitchen, generating a sympathetic wail from Nagode. 'You don't need to go to England! It's too long!'

'JoJo, I have to.' The boy's outrage was almost comical. 'I have to go to the capital anyway, to collect more money to pay the hospital bills. And I can even pick you up some new Top Trumps from London. The very latest they have. That's a promise.' He couldn't help casting a glance toward Margaret. But her head was resolutely down once more while she worked the batter into a rich yellow. Disappointment cut through him. *Maybe she really feels nothing, or cares nothing. Maybe she wants to pretend we never spoke.*

'England is beautiful in the winter,' he said to Dr Ahmed, feeling a vindictive pleasure in projecting indifference. 'There might even be snow in the Lakes. Kate and I go every year — we're thinking of having our honeymoon there. And it'll be fantastic to feel cool again. I'm not made for this heat.'

'No doubt.' Dr Ahmed clapped him on the shoulder. 'I hope it refreshes you. To return home is life's deepest instinct.'

The warmth of his hand melted Nick's pique. He could see Margaret's arms moving over the bowl, remembering them outstretched between him and the mob, and Dr Ahmed looming in the foreground, so upright after his crushing day. His heart tightened with affection and remorse.

'But I will miss you.' He dared not look at Margaret again, not with Dr Ahmed standing so close. With all his heart he willed her to hear him. 'And I'll come back.'

He crouched down near Nagode to hide his emotion, reaching out to tickle her bare tummy. She squealed, sending tremors through her firmly planted thighs. 'Na!' she shouted. 'Na!' She glared at him, each eye a lance of suspicion. Her legs twisted on the ground, muscles straining to respond to her will. Nick thought of falcons on display at the county fairs of his childhood, baiting desperately against their jesses.

'Yes,' Nick urged her. 'Come on, Nagode. Come to Uncle Nicholas.'

'Na!' she shouted again, like a battle cry. The round fists released their grasp on the table to clutch at the space between them.

And then she was moving, legs stumbling forward into a suddenly empty world, her face opening with astonishment. Nick caught her just as her delicate balance failed.

Nick looked up to Margaret in instinctive delight. She had turned from the sink to watch them, her eyes wet, while JoJo clapped and hooted.

'You see!' Dr Ahmed slapped his thigh, taking off his glasses to wipe his eyes. 'I told you, it was only the beginning.' He spoke to his daughter from the depth of his feeling. '*Insha'Allah*, the first steps of many,' he said. 'And may they take you only to good places.'

The next morning Nick decided to roll one last die for his well. Dr Ahmed's surgery was empty and Nick was working from home. His head ached and the feeble trickle of water from the hose did little to make him feel clean.

The night before he'd thrown the aquifer survey into the wastebasket. Now he pulled it out, smoothing it over.

Forget about it, he told himself, re-experiencing the bitterness of yesterday's meeting with the governor and Margaret's persistent coldness. In a month you'll be eating turkey with Kate in England. All of this will seem like a dream.

On a whim, he picked up the telephone to make a reverse-charge call to the UK, carefully dialling the code J.P. had given him and he'd promised Kate not to abuse. It was expensive and unreliable – but after a few tries he heard a ringtone, tinny and distant. It was still early; he could picture Kate lying tangled in their ivory bedsheets, energising herself for the morning gym session.

She answered after a few rings. 'Nick!' Her voice was distorted and sleepy. 'I got your letter. Sounds awful. So glad you'll be home soon.'

He tried to remember what he'd written; his mind was blank. 'I definitely need a break,' he said, 'I'm tired. It's too much sometimes, this place.'

'What?' The line was crackling.

'I said, it's too much. I need a break.'

He wasn't sure if she'd heard him as she went on. 'I'm going to book the hotel in Windermere next week. Sam and Julia went there last year. Said we'll love it.'

'That's good.' Suddenly all he could think of was how much Margaret had wanted to see Windermere. *I wandered lonely as a cloud.*

'And I'll schedule a visit to your mum – let me know when so I can put it in the diary. Lots to do.'

'OK.'

'Sorry, Nick, you're breaking up so badly, I just can't hear a word. Maybe wait until you're here?'

An immense weariness came over him. He imagined a different conversation – the kind they'd rarely had and couldn't recreate, finding words that sank beneath the skin to touch heart and nerve beneath. She'd accused him of being walled-off and he'd always known she was right; but now he wondered if he wasn't more like Dr Ahmed's aquifer, waiting silently underground for someone to break through.

A few minutes after they said their goodbyes the porch started shaking – hasty feet pounding towards Nick's office. JoJo came bursting in, shouting, 'Nicholas! Come!'

Nick's heart froze. 'What's happened now?'

'Our castle!' JoJo gulped in exaggerated panic as he leaned on the doorframe. 'Nagode broke it!'

Nick laughed in relief. 'Is that all? You frightened the life out of me!'

A shadow dimmed the boy's eagerness. Nick reminded himself that their castle was more than a game to JoJo. It was proof of something unspoken, of new hopes growing inside him.

'OK, I'm coming,' he said. 'Don't worry, we'll fix it.'

In the back garden, the turret with Margaret's flag on it was missing a chunk from its southern face. Nagode sat by the fractured edge, clutching the broken piece with an expression of grave satisfaction.

'Oh-oh.' Nick rescued it from her, despite her wail of complaint. 'Look who wants to be an architect, too.'

JoJo showed Nick a tub of white, sticky paste placed on a rock. 'From Mama's kitchen,' he said. 'Flour and water, to stick it back. Will it work?'

'I think it will,' Nick laughed. 'Nice improvisation.'

He knelt to help the boy steady the tower as JoJo manoeuvred the piece back into place. He wedged it with soggy mortar, and pasted dried grass over the join. Watching the deft hands at work, Nick noticed new changes in JoJo. Early manhood was filling out the awkwardness of his limbs and stretching his quick mind in new directions.

It was slow work, made slower still by Nagode's relentless assistance. She stumbled around the garden, shrieking in glee, going where she was least wanted. Small fists pushed broken edges out of their careful alignment, and when she stepped in JoJo's bowl of flour and water, he and Nick both yelled in dismay. The sudden noise sent Nagode tumbling; she lay on the ground, howling her distress. Hanan's face peered over the garden wall, on her way to collect the baby for her morning trip to market; JoJo thankfully handed the furious Nagode into her arms.

After another half an hour, JoJo finally stood up, pleased. The old piece was wedged back, the flag restored to its summit. The dried grass made the tower look less English and more African, pale as a cloud on one side, the other infused with the soil's blood-deep red.

'Perfect!' JoJo crowed. He raised his hand to high-five Nick. Instead of returning the gesture, Nick found himself gripping JoJo's shoulder. And to his astonishment, the boy responded, arms reaching around his waist, burying his face in Nick's chest.

'It is good you came,' JoJo whispered.

Nick returned the hug, deeply moved. 'I'm the lucky one.' He rested his chin on the boy's head, feeling a dart of joy in giving what he'd never himself received. *Does Dr Ahmed ever hug you? Or does he expect you to stand alone?*

He kissed JoJo's tight black cap of hair, smelling warm earth.

'You're one of the smartest people I've ever met,' he told the boy. 'You have a brilliant mind, you could do anything. You must always remember that, no matter what.'

JoJo looked up at him, eyes fire-bright. 'I want to be an engineer, like you,' he said, his voice deep with longing. 'I want to work for you.'

Nick smiled down at him. 'You can set up your own company. Then I'll come work for you.'

A strange expression crept over JoJo's face, so sweet and young it made Nick's heart constrict. He could see the boy's forehead crease with anxious expectation. He'd seen that expression countless times, watching JoJo slope off to school each morning, his footsteps heavy as if he carried an invisible weight. Sorrow and doubt were there, and something else, too – a nearly unbearable hope.

'Promise?' JoJo said. 'You'll stay my friend? You won't leave us?'

Nick felt the pressure of JoJo's arms around him, the tide of need blurring past and present, right and wrong. In a few weeks Nick would be home for Christmas; a few months after that, he'd be gone for good. He knew what he should say. But the words would not come. *I'll always be your friend,* he'd pledged Madi on the kissing gate, as they examined the bruises against the dark skin of his arm. *No matter what.*

'I won't leave you,' he promised JoJo. 'But . . .'

'JoJo.'

They both looked around. Margaret stood in the kitchen doorway, her hands twisting together. JoJo disentangled himself from Nick, sensing her strange mood. He pointed to the castle.

'Nagode broke the tower by accident,' he said. 'But Nicholas and I, we fixed it. Now it is even stronger. Look, Mama.'

Her eyes flicked briefly to the castle and then to Nick. He saw hurt and anger – the impulse of a wounded animal.

'You made your clothes dirty,' she said. JoJo looked down at himself, his jeans covered in the mortar's sticky grey. He tried to wipe it off, laughing.

'So what?' he said to his mother. 'They're just clothes.'

'Just clothes.' Her voice was harsh. 'So I can give them to another child, if you don't care about your things?'

JoJo's face tightened. 'I do care!' he said, outraged.

'Then why should you make me clean for you, as if you are Nagode's age? I'm not your slave.'

JoJo was breathing hard. He unbuckled his jeans and pulled them off, legs thin as a foal's. He bunched them up and threw them at his mother.

'Here!' he yelled. 'It is *you* who doesn't care. You want Bako to be alive and not me!'

Margaret caught the jeans by her stomach as JoJo raced out of the garden, pushing past her. She turned her head, her mouth opening – but he was gone before she could speak.

'What the hell was that about?' Nick was furious. 'He's just a kid, he wasn't doing anything wrong.'

Her eyes came up, distraught. In that moment he saw the extraordinary resemblance between mother and son – the boy's face under her skin like soft clay carved into adult planes.

'I'm sorry,' she whispered.

'I'm not the one you should apologise to.'

She bit her lip, wandering over to Nagode's sleeping tree, sweet with the fragrance of dead flowers.

'You are going away,' she said, her back to Nick.

'Just for a few weeks.'

She nodded. 'Your wife will be happy to see you.'

'I told you, she's not my wife.' Kate seemed unreal, a figure inside a snow globe, surrounded by Christmas tree lights and champagne glasses under a falling blizzard.

Margaret picked up the clothes basket at her feet and pushed JoJo's jeans inside it. 'We are used to you being here.' She walked over towards the water bucket, its contents dark with old dirt. 'But you are tired of us, perhaps.'

'I could never be tired of you.' He spoke without caution, infected with her impulsive honesty. The truth was making his heart flood with adrenalin; it pulled dust into his lungs and bloodstream, making him part of the desert's wild expanse.

I don't want to leave. It was a moment of rare clarity; the known and unknown switched inside him and England was now the alien land. It was impossible to imagine re-shaping himself to London life – to carefully ironed bedsheets and bare winter branches, to small-talk amid a growing sense of desolation.

Margaret knelt down by the bucket, setting the clothes basket beside her. One hand rested over JoJo's jeans, fragments of light trapped between her fingers and the denim. The beads on her wrist shifted colour as she ran her hands over the fabric. The gesture moved him, a form of spiritual communication with absent flesh. His anger at her dissolved, as if by a spell.

JoJo's angry passage had kicked a small posy of dried grass and seedpods away from the makeshift cross over what Nick had come to think of as the garden grave. He watched Margaret lean forward to restore it, smoothing the ground in front of the cross, laying the dry bouquet carefully back down.

'Bako,' he said, and he saw her hand go still. 'Dr Ahmed told me what happened to him.'

Her shoulders were rigid, as if she stood at the edge of a deep drop. 'At home we called him Pip,' she replied, her voice almost too low to hear. 'It was my choice. From *Great Expectations*.'

'Is he buried here?'

'It was not permitted,' she said. 'But I took a lock of his hair. Only a small piece.'

'Dr Ahmed said he died of a fever.'

Her head came up. 'The rains failed then, too. The water price went so high, we had to take it from the lake.'

She touched the cross with her fingertips. Small flies circled her, beating shadows into the morning light.

'Akim was the first to sicken. Mr Kamil's youngest. His wife Aisha – she never accepted me. She would turn from me when we passed in the street. Aisha, with her silks and jewels, but not even a high-school certificate.' The words were harsh with mockery. 'I could not bear this nothing village woman to shame me. So I took the waste from our pit. I carried it through the hidden way I showed you. And I spread it in their garden under the clothes line so her dresses would stink.'

In his mind's eye, Nick saw her – a Fury striding through the village with her steaming pot of poison. 'That's quite the revenge.'

She nodded. 'But when Akim took a fever, I knew one of my children would follow. I thought it would be JoJo – he played with Akim. But God's hand passed over him and touched Pip instead.' Her voice had grown quiet.

'He was just a baby. Ahmed tried everything. Every medicine. So . . .' She looked out, her gaze ranging past the garden's crumbling walls to the wilderness beyond. 'I went to Binza. To the witch by the lake. I hoped that her magic would be stronger than God's vengeance.'

Margaret fingered the bright red beads on her wrist. 'She gave me this bracelet to tie on Bako's arm.' She laughed. 'A bracelet – what can that do? But I had to try. I gave her all of our money. For three days Bako wore it, and on the fourth he died. Akim lived, and my son died.'

Nick realised he'd been holding his breath; his grateful lungs sucked in oxygen, drawing deep the fading smells of grass and dust. *There are ghosts here.* He sensed them whispering in the dead branches, bright at the edges of vision. They'd whispered at his father's gravesite, inside the hushed song of the *el maleh rachamim* prayer for the dead – its Hebrew words sounding so bleak and condemning until his father's sister had handed Nick a bound translation as a parting gift. *Illuminate the souls of those we love, like the brilliance of the skies, the blameless ones who have gone to their rest.*

'It wasn't your fault, Margaret,' he said to her. 'It was a virus.'

She tilted her head in amused pity. 'Yes. I did not kill my son.

You did not kill your friend. Even God is innocent. No one is to blame.'

She got to her feet, the clothes basket in her arms. Light fell on her shoulders as a cloud passed overhead. She raised her head at its touch.

'But why do you still bring Binza food?' Nick asked. 'She was a fraud.'

Margaret was silent for a moment, considering.

'When we prepared Bako for burial, this bracelet was still on his arm,' she answered finally. 'I put it there myself. During his sickness I would turn the beads on his skin and pray for them to draw his pain away.' She raised her arm in front of her, twisting the beads to the light.

'When I saw them covering his body with the sheet, I felt they were burying me with him. So I took the bracelet for myself. Because I do not want to forget.' She looked at Nick, unflinching. 'I remember every good thing and also every sin. They are all tied together here, with all of us.' She held her wrist out to him, the beads bright as blood. 'Bako and JoJo. My husband. Aisha. Me. And Binza, too. Binza gave us the bracelet to save his life. So I feed her still. That's all.'

The noon prayer boomed from the mosque, rolling past them on the thermal currents. In song, Imam Abdi's voice lost its bird-like thinness. A penetrating lament channelled a path through Nick into the earth, transforming him into part of the invisible chain linking the deep waters beneath to the sky's high arc.

Then he knew: he had a purpose here, and England would have to wait. The choice felt so easy, so utterly right. *No more skating on thin ice, always afraid of falling through.*

'Margaret,' he said, as she turned towards the kitchen. She swung back to face him, her body drawn in lines of tension. He had a sudden, heart-wrenching impression of youth.

'I'm cancelling my visit to England,' he told her. 'I have a plan, something that could stop these droughts. I'd still have

to go to the capital to see J.P. – but I would be back straight
away.'

Margaret stood motionless, a flush spreading from her throat's
pale hollow. 'A plan?' she echoed.

'A plan to bring a safe water supply from under the ground.'

That made her smile. '"Then Moses lifted up his hand and
struck the rock with his rod, and water came forth
abundantly."'

'Something like that.' He grinned back, excitement pulsing
through him. 'But I'll use a drill instead of a rod. I just need J.P.
to agree. That's why I need to go south.'

'To the capital?'

'Yes, to the capital.'

A strange expression shadowed her face. 'You might have
rain there, even in the dry season,' she said. 'Sarah and I, we
used to catch frogs. There's a pool by our house . . .' Then she
recollected herself. 'But that was long ago.'

'Couldn't I do something for you there?' New ideas were
racing through his mind, thrilling him with their possibilities.
'Take something for someone? For Sarah? I could deliver a letter
or . . . bring back anything you need.'

She bit her lip, doubtful. 'I don't know.' She spoke softly, her
words muffled by the wind. 'Now, after so long?' He followed her
gaze to the little cross, outlined against the shifting brilliance of
sun and shadow. He thought of the ending of her book: two
children, silhouetted against the light, their forms merging into
one.

'Don't you want to lay to rest at least some of your ghosts?'
Her eyes snapped towards him as he spoke. 'You deserve to be
happy too, Margaret.'

The front door slammed – JoJo, walking down to the garden
gate, a fresh pair of jeans on his legs. His mother turned at the
sound, watching him slope slowly away.

'JoJo has never seen the capital.' Now her tone was dark with
thought. 'He knows nothing of any other life.'

She looked back to Nick, her expression indecipherable – and he sensed something forming beneath, a fierce purpose.

'How long?' she asked. 'How long would you stay there?'

'In the capital?' Nick considered. 'Two days. Three at the most.'

'Could you take JoJo?' Her tone was even, questioning – but he felt the hidden urgency. 'He's becoming a man. He needs to know there's more to life than this small place.'

'By himself?' The idea took him aback. 'I could . . . it might be hard sometimes. I have meetings. We'd have to make a plan.'

She hugged the jeans to her chest, head turned; he imagined desperate calculations.

'Then I could come with him. You could take us both.'

He hesitated – unsure; his heart began to beat with the feeling of a world sliding past, a train nearing a dangerous bend in the track. 'But – Dr Ahmed . . . would he agree?'

'Leave Ahmed to me.' Her chest rose and fell rapidly. 'He has asked me to heal this breach with David many times.'

'And you never said yes before?

'I never wanted to go before,' she replied. 'I have slept for thirteen years. But it's like you say, Nicholas.' She looked up at him, excitement mounting in her eyes. 'It's past time to wake.'

She set down her basket as JoJo reached the gate, her body tense with emotion, her face entrancing, flushed – lit from within. 'I must go and tell him. The capital – he will not believe it!'

And Nick watched her run towards her son, calling out his name. He pulled away as she reached him – but she put her hands on either side of his cheeks, pressing their foreheads together, breathing words of apology and assurance.

JoJo's arms hung down for a moment, but then hugged his mother to him.

Alone in the garden, Nick felt their embrace filling up empty rooms inside him. The air was charged with energy – a force he'd imagined but never felt: a living bond between two souls, endlessly broken and remade through love's struggle against fear.

Baba said yes to Mama about the capital. When she came to tell me, she put her hands on my face, and I could smell her tears. 'We will go at New Year,' she said to me. 'A new year, a new start, JoJo.' I could not sleep all that night. Akim was so jealous when I told him! They have so many things in the capital. Swimming pools and football shirts and cinemas. Nicholas will take me to the cinema, to see a film from America. One with girls. Akim, he said: 'Those are only for real men. You're still a baby.' And I laughed because his eyes said he lied.

Before we go, we will eat an English Christmas dinner together with Baba. Jalloh had a big fight with Mama when she told him. He shouted: 'Every week you take my goat! I have saved the best pieces for you!'

Mama, she stands there, her arms folded. She says: 'We are making an English Christmas for our guest. In England they have goose for their lunch at Christmas.'

Now Jalloh is yelling: 'There is no goose here! We are not goose people.'

'Mama says: 'So I will take three chickens. Next week you can sell us goat again.'

Jalloh is not happy. He leans closer to Mama. His hands, they are red from the meat. He says: 'There are no Christians here, woman.'

Mama, she draws up her head. She is not afraid of him. Mama, she fears no one these days.

'Do not test me, Jalloh,' she says. And she makes a quote from the Qur'an. It says: 'Allah loves those who are just.' Baba says it when I say bad things about Akim, or when Mama complains about Aisha Kamil. He says: 'Allah's justice comes from love. And love forbids us to speak ill of each other or seek vengeance.'

Jalloh does not know the Qur'an. So he says he will bring the chickens from his brother in the Town. He does not want to lose our business to Tuesday.

We work all day to make the dinner. Okra and beans and yams. Then we must stuff the chickens. Mama takes tiger nuts from the garden and I cut the stalks and roots. We pound them small. Nagode puts some of them into her mouth. 'Bad Nagode!' I shout. When I say that she laughs. I say it again. 'Bad Nagode!' She says, 'Ba! Ba! Ba!'

We mix the tiger nut with bread and dry plums, and Mama cuts onion. The smell makes me cry. I look and see Mama is crying too. She wipes it with her hand, and I say: 'Bad Mama!' We laugh at each other.

Then we mix up everything together and fill the inside of the chickens. Mama has a needle and thread, to sew the skin closed. The chicken's head falls down onto the table. It looks like it sleeps. If I was that chicken, I would not want to wake.

Baba, he brings candles from Tuesday's store for the table. I was there when he bought them. Tuesday said: 'Dr Ahmed, I hear you are having a festival at your place.' Baba replied: 'Jesus is one of Allah's prophets. I am happy to help my guest celebrate his coming.' Afterwards, Baba said to me: 'Now I have reminded Tuesday of one of our prophets, he is trying to remember the names of the others.'

I say nothing. But I think. Baba knows everything about Allah and the prophets but he does not know the things that Tuesday knows. Baba is like the sleeping chicken. He does not want to see what is happening around him.

Mama brings a red cloth for the table. It has been sewn together, in three big pieces. Baba, he says: 'Oh, my dear. I remember this one!' Then Nicholas, he comes in. He says: 'Wow, look at all this.'

Baba tells him: 'You are receiving an honour today, Nicholas. We are eating our dinner off the blanket that Margaret and I slept under when we married.'

Nicholas, he touches the red cloth, and looks at Mama. 'It is very beautiful,' he tells her.

Now Nicholas, he and Mama have the same smile. Sometimes they have their own language, Mama and Nicholas. They use the same words as Baba and me. But they mean other things.

Mama brings out the food, and we sit together. Baba is talking about chestnuts in England. He tells Nicholas that he did not understand the difference between the horse chestnut and the sweet chestnut. He says: 'I picked some horse chestnuts and cooked them for my friend. How she laughed at me! She said – stick to fixing your patients and leave the cooking to me.'

Our tiger nuts are the same colour as tigers. So the horse nuts must be the same colour as horses. When I go to England, I will ride horses. Nicholas, he knows how to do that.

Baba says to him: 'I am glad that you stayed here for your Christmas feast. But your family must be missing you today.'

I look at Mama, but she is busy pulling yellow meat from the bones, to lay on top of the yams. Mama is happy that Nicholas is staying. And me also. I do not mind about the Top Trumps. Nicholas is better than Top Trumps. And when we go to the capital together, we can find better things there.

Nicholas says to Baba: 'I think England can manage without me for a few months longer. And the nurses look after my mother very well. I don't think she even knows I'm away.'

'Ah,' Baba says. 'The mind is the hardest organ of the body to treat. Even with the best modern medicines.'

Nicholas looks sad. He says: 'This feels like my home. You feel like my family.' He puts down his fork. I think he might cry. I never saw a man cry.

Baba reaches over to him and takes his arm. He says: 'You are always welcome in our house.'

Nicholas, he shakes his head. But then his face changes. Now he is smiling, like Tuesday. He says: 'But you will be rid of me for a few days over New Year. Do you want me to bring back more supplies, if you give me a list?'

'Very many thanks,' Baba says. Last week he was fighting with Miss Amina, I know. He does not have all of her medicines. We do not have enough money to pay for new ones. Baba wanted to buy many medicines – but Mama, she was mad. She said: 'We must pay JoJo's school. We must pay for fuel. And already we fill only

*half a tank of water. Bad times are coming, Ahmed. Let these
people pay for their own medicine.'*

But Baba, he said: 'You know they cannot pay.'

*Now Baba looks at Mama. He asks: 'Are you ready for your
visit? Did your brother David write back to you?'*

'Not yet,' she says. Her eyes are cast down.

He asks her: 'Are you sure it's the right time to go?'

*Now I am frightened. Mama, she also fears Baba will change
his mind. She says: 'I wish to make amends.'*

Baba tells her: 'You have not sinned, Margaret.'

*She is quiet. Nicholas too. Then she says: 'But who knows when
the next chance will come?'*

*Baba is thinking. 'So, Yahya,' he tells me. 'You will see where
your mother was born. You will be my ambassador there. They
must see that we northerners are gentlemen, too.'*

*'Yes, Baba,' I say. But I notice Mama. She is looking at me.
She looks like she is thinking. Then she puts more chicken on
Baba's plate, and he tells her she spoils him.*

*Later Nicholas teaches me how to sing 'The Twelve Days of
Christmas'. He explains what is a partridge, and what is a French
hen. I tell him, if Baba bought any of these for Mama, she would
send him back to the shop. He laughs. In these stories all the
presents are magical, he tells me. If you love someone, then you
don't want to give them something from a shop. You want to give
them something that cannot be bought.*

*At sunset, Mama sends me out with a bucket to bring water for
washing. Now we use our tank water only for cooking and drinking. There is no more water for clothes and dishes. I must go to the
lake. So I run. The bucket is light. I am practising: 'Three French
hens, two turtle doves and a partridge in a pear tree.' The best part
is the five gold rings. If I had five rings I would buy Adeya some
new clothes and ask her to forgive me.*

*The lake is nearly dark. Binza sends ghosts, Juma says, to
drink from the water. And if the lake is dry, she sends them to the
village to drink blood.*

I make the sign of the evil eye towards her place. Stay away, witch. Stay away from us.

I take my bucket to the edge of the water. It feels warm and dark under my toes.

Then I hear a sound. Behind me. Maybe it was a bird. There are no such things as ghosts. Juma is a stupid liar.

The lake is dark. The sun makes the grass here tall and black. They are like knives, each one.

I hear the noise again. Maybe Binza has come out of her place. Maybe she sees me, Binza and her ghosts. I turn around. 'Come out, Binza!' I call, to show I am not afraid. 'Come out!' I say again. My voice sounds small.

'The witch is not here, JoJo.'

I turn around, quick. My heart is beating too hard. I say: 'Who is that?'

Then I see him.

He comes through the reeds, white as stone. He has the knife in his hand and in the other some of the tall grass. He sees me looking at the knife. He laughs. He says: 'Do you still fear me, JoJo?'

Mister shows me the grass he has cut. 'What is this?' he asks.

I try to shrug, like I don't care. 'It's grass.'

'No,' he says. 'This is money in my hand. I will sell it to the ones who make baskets and masks. They will paint them. Then maybe your friend the English, he will buy them for a high price.'

I tell him: 'Nicholas does not want these things.'

Mister shrugs. 'Then some man will. Maybe in the capital, or at the hotels.'

'Why?' I ask him. 'You have money from the garage.' Juma says he makes lots of money. He buys beer from Tuesday and hides it from his father.

Mister sits on the ground. The mud makes his jeans brown. He starts to weave the grass together. His hands are so quick. Even Adeya cannot do it so well.

On the ground he looks smaller than me. I see the back of his neck where his head bends forward. It has pink scars on it, deep, like a lion tore him.

He says: 'This was how I ate when I was younger than you, JoJo. Before I came to the village. I made things to sell. If my things were no good, they beat me and I did not eat.'

I cannot imagine Mister when he was small. He must have been pink all over, like a newborn dog. His tears would have been pink on his skin.

I ask: 'Was it your father who beat you?'

He smiles. 'My mother's husband was not my father. My mother took another man to her bed. A rich man from the Town. Maybe you heard of him, JoJo.'

I shake my head, and Mister smiles. 'No? Well, my mother's husband punished her. He nearly killed us, and from then we had no home. And my true father, he left us to our punishment. One day I will find him again.'

I think of a small dog that I saw Jalloh beat for stealing one of his chickens. The dog cried. Its tail went under its legs, to hide from the stick. I begged Mama: 'Make him stop!' She held me tight. She said: 'Some things cannot be stopped.'

I say: 'It was wrong to beat you.'

Mister, he stands up. He holds out what he has made. It is a cross, like the one Mama made for Bako.

'For you,' he says. It feels smooth when I take it from him.

'Thank you,' I tell him. And he smiles.

'They were right to beat me, JoJo,' he says. 'It was their gift to me. They feared my skin. They called me a bad spirit. But spirits feel no pain. They have no tears and no blood. By the time I was your age, I had no more fear. Now no one beats me any more.'

He looks at me. He says: 'You are a big man now, JoJo. You go to the Town, with the English. You meet with the governor.'

I touch my head. The governor's cap is still there. I wear it nearly every day, after school.

'Nicholas is my friend,' I tell Mister. 'He is teaching me things. He is taking me to the capital. One day I will go with him, to England.'

Mister, he nods. 'Good,' he says. 'You will make a fine white man.'

I feel my face turn red. I say: 'He is my friend.'

Mister tells me: 'The governor laughed at your father. Did you know? He came back like a dog that was kicked by its master. He is afraid to fight. Like you.'

'He's no dog,' I shout. 'And I am not afraid of you!'

Mister comes closer. I feel his breath on me. My heart is still beating. His skin is pink where the sun has burned him. His lips are pink, like Mama's.

'No, you are not afraid,' he says. 'I am glad, JoJo. You grew up. It is time for you to join The Boys, I think.'

I do not answer. The old JoJo wanted to join The Boys. I am with Nicholas, now. And Nicholas is stronger than Mister.

'I cannot join,' I say.

Mister lifts his hand holding the knife. He flips it so that he grasps the blade. 'Take it,' he says.

In my hand it feels heavy. It is warm from his touch.

'Do you like it?' Mister asks. The voice is his, but I feel the knife is speaking. I see how light shines off the metal part. Its shadow stretches long.

Mister says: 'The Englishman is a witch, too. He makes his spells on you. But they will break, JoJo. Believe me. He does not want you. So, afterwards you can come and find me.'

He reaches over to take the knife. His hand is soft, like his voice. Then he goes, turning his back on me. I wonder where he sleeps. Maybe in the garage. Maybe here, by the lake.

The sun swallows him before it falls. And suddenly I am cold.

When I reach my home, Baba is inside, cleaning the grandfather clock. The big box with all his tools is open. He looks up at me from the floor.

'Ah,' he says. 'Yahya. I must speak with you.'

I do not want to talk to Baba. I want to speak to Nicholas in his room. I want to tell him about Mister and The Boys. I want to talk to him about England.

I try to walk away. But Baba, he holds me.

'Yahya, your mother and I have talked with Nicholas. And I'm afraid you cannot go with them to the capital this time.'

My heart, it stops again. Just like when Mister spoke my name.

'Why?' I ask him. 'Why?'

Baba, he takes my hands.

'Yahya, there are too many uncertain things. Your mother must mend her ties with her family. Until this is done, she thinks it will be too difficult to show her son to them. It is a matter best handled by her alone. And then, afterwards, we can all go together.'

'No! I do not understand. This morning I was going to the capital! It was all decided!'

I am shouting at Baba: 'Nicholas told me I could go! He promised! It is not fair. You lied!'

'I am sorry for the disappointment, Yahya.' Baba tries to take my hand again. He says: 'I will take you another time.'

'I want to go with Nicholas!' I pull away from Baba's hand. 'With Nicholas, not with you!'

I see his face. And I think: I am a bad son. But inside my head, I can hear Mister, whispering: 'You see – he does not want you.'

I cannot listen any more. Not to Baba, not to Mister.

I run out of the room, back outside under the dark sky.

I sit down on the steps. I hate to cry. But the tears come.

I see lights in the kitchen where Mama is cleaning. There are more lights in the room where Nicholas works. But no one comes to find me.

I wait there until I am finished crying. I wait while the stars come out. All over the sky they come, one by one. Each one has a name, Nicholas told me, like Adeya's plants. But I cannot remember any of those names. All I remember is that they are all so bright and all so far away.

NEW YEAR'S EVE

Nick and Margaret left for the capital the morning before New Year's Eve.

In the pre-dawn quiet, Dr Ahmed lifted their suitcases into the trunk of the taxi – Margaret standing beside the car door, already searching the southern sky.

'Good luck, my dear,' Dr Ahmed said to her. Nick sensed tension between them, the shadow of anxiety.

'I'll return soon,' she told him.

'Say goodbye to JoJo for us.' Nick offered his hand to Dr Ahmed. 'Tell him again – I'm really sorry.' He'd knocked on the boy's door earlier, to no response.

'He will recover,' Dr Ahmed replied. 'Children have the instinct to forgive.'

As the car pulled away, Nick turned back to watch Dr Ahmed's scarecrow wave. Then they rounded the corner – and he was gone.

The car raced south, hours slipping by on waves of heat. The highway was a thin needle pointing through a vast space, bare as a beaten anvil. White rock broke the ground, like shoulder blades and clutching fingers. Nick thought of buried titans, struggling to break out of their prison.

The air grew heavier as the hours passed: Margaret pressed her face to the window, her breath moistening the glass. Nick watched her as the car bumped and shook, wrestling with his own turbulence. It was only four months ago he'd travelled this same road; but that felt like a different man, or another lifetime. Something in him had changed, or deepened; he was acutely conscious of Margaret's warmth beside him, of his disturbed happiness broken only by the driver's gaze flicking towards them in the rear-view mirror.

The sky curdled and thickened into thunderclouds. As evening fell, the capital appeared in a humid haze of smoke and steel. Dark rainwater ran off the streets as they crossed the blinking red and green of traffic lights where women waited in pencil skirts, shielding their hair with their handbags. A pale, long-haired girl with a backpack stood by a market stall stacked with wooden statues and woven mats. She turned as they passed, catching Nick's eyes through the steamed window. He thought fleetingly of Kate.

J.P. had booked them into the same hotel Nick remembered, its walls slick with falling rain. Margaret looked up at them as she opened her car door.

'I don't remember this place.' Her voice was low, threaded with unease. Dr Ahmed had assured them he recalled the name from university days.

'The decor must have changed.' But still she hesitated. Nick touched her forearm, already dappled with water. It brought back a sudden memory – in the garden on their first morning, bright drops falling from the clothesline.

'It's going to be OK,' he promised. She looked up, biting her lip, tasting raindrops as they rolled over the swell of her mouth. 'Change is why you came here.'

Eric's driver was asking for payment. Nick brought out the last of his cash, peeling off forty dollars. Tomorrow he would replenish with J.P.'s next tranche and money wired by Kate through Western Union.

The lobby was unexpectedly chilling. Margaret had goose bumps; she pulled her scarf over her head, vanishing into a shroud of browns. The drab headscarf and concealing travel clothes had been chosen to reassure Dr Ahmed, he guessed. But suddenly he found them claustrophobic.

'You don't have to wear those here, you know.'

'I am cold,' was all she would say in reply.

After the formalities of check-in, Nick led Margaret to the pool where J.P. waited, smoking a cigarette. Moon-yellow lanterns surrounded the water, dangling from poles in a gaudy web. J.P. beckoned Nick and Margaret as they approached.

'You made it! Amazing! This storm . . . I was sure the roads would be blocked. This weather is a mess, honestly. So, every-thing worked out. Eric's guy was OK? You're tired?'

He ushered Margaret to the table, Nick following behind. A crisp-shirted waiter came for their drink orders. Nick took a beer, as did J.P.. Margaret hesitated.

'They make wonderful cocktails at the bar,' J.P. urged. 'Strawberry, pineapple, kiwi.'

Margaret thanked him, picking up the menu to hide her confusion. Nick knew how she must feel, caught in the friction between two different worlds.

'Try something,' he said to her. 'You're on holiday.'

She laughed at that notion, her face softening.

'Very well, monsieur,' she said to J.P.. 'Choose for me. I will trust your judgement – in fruit juice, at least.'

J.P. laughed with her; one hand smoothed his thinning hair, stirred into unconscious vanity. While the waiter retreated to fill their order, he bent closer to Margaret. 'I didn't know you spoke French, mademoiselle.'

'The nuns at my school said French was the language of seduction.' Her drink was placed on the table, foamy layers topped by pineapple and a striped straw. 'So we came to class ready to be seduced. But we were disappointed.'

'Such a shame,' J.P. said. 'Maybe you were not studying the right subjects.'

'I do not think the nuns approved of most subjects.' Margaret bent her head to sip from the straw. 'It's good,' she told J.P. with a smile. 'A good start.'

As they talked, Nick realised that J.P. was flirting. He leaned towards Margaret, needlessly close, adjusting the collar of his crumpled shirt. Nick felt a brief tug of jealousy. The air was a moist cocoon of scents, flowers unfolding somewhere unseen.

Tomorrow stretched out, clear as the southern highway. First he would win J.P.'s support for the village well. Then he would reunite Margaret with Sarah. Their old sorrows would die with the year.

His eyes travelled to the pool, sparkling under the party lights. The claws of memory had loosened; he had a new purpose, and his heart no longer ached for Madi. He could even forgive his father, imagine them really talking for the first time since they'd sat silently at Madi's tiny, pefunctory funeral. *I understand now. You only despised me so I would redeem myself.*

Margaret was saying she was tired. The rain had given way to a wild jumble of night sounds: croaking frogs, music spilling from the hotel bar, the chatter of arriving guests. She rose, stretching her arms over her head. The slight curve of her stomach was silhouetted against the pool lights. *Three children have come out of that body.* The thought filled Nick with awe, reminding him of life's hidden powers.

'I'll come with you,' he replied. 'I mean – I'm tired as well.'

'OK, so, see you tomorrow morning.' J.P. bent over Margaret's hand. 'And you, mademoiselle.' His glasses grazed her skin. 'Will I have the pleasure of your company again? There's a New Year's Eve party here tomorrow. The usual disaster, no doubt – warm champagne, bad music.'

'No doubt,' Margaret said, slipping her hand from his. Nick felt J.P.'s eyes watching them go.

They walked upstairs and along the hotel's dim corridors. Opposite Margaret's room, a large window reflected the pool below. She looked out, bathed in the flicker of fairy lights, yawning as she rested one hand on the windowsill.

'I could sleep for a hundred years.' she said. 'Such a long journey.' Her mouth curled in a wry smile. 'And all just to come back to where I started.'

Nick smiled too, joining her at the window. 'You should rest,' he said. 'Tomorrow is a big day for both of us. I have to get money for our well. And you'll see Sarah again.'

She shivered, wrapping her arms around herself. Nick remembered the ending of her book: *the start of many wonderful adventures* – words straight from childhood's optimistic heart.

'It's the beginning of a new story,' he promised. '*The Thorn Princess, Part Two.*'

Her palms pressed against the windowpane. 'Thank you.' Her murmured words misted the glass. Then she turned to him and spoke directly. 'Thank you for this chance. If you had not come . . .'

A shriek drifted up from the pool. A woman had fallen in, drunk and stumbling. Two waiters were trying to fish her out with a pool cleaner. Her braids snaked out from her head, a watery Medusa, arms flailing in splashy circles.

Margaret leaned her forehead against the pane to watch them. 'Like a mermaid,' she said, half in wonder.

The waiters were jabbing at her ineffectually with the long pool cleaner. 'I don't think much of her handsome princes.'

'They cannot all be princes,' she said. Colours wove across her forehead, wreathing it in a red and green crown.

Lady Margaret. She was close enough for her warmth to brush his thin shirt; when she reached up to pull off her headscarf he saw the long line of her neck bending forward, wet curls nestled at its nape. Lingering cotton strands clung to the line of bare skin hovering above her abaya, damp in the night's heat. Unconsious, he reached to brush them off. She drew back, hastily; he recovered himself. Apologies formed in his mind – weak against the confused tides of feeling.

'Goodnight, Nicholas,' she said. He thought – hoped – she might say more. Then she was gone, one light touch of her finger on his wrist before she disappeared behind the soft close of her door.

He stayed at the window, hypnotised by tiredness and the pulsing lights. Margaret's touch prickled on his skin. Below, the unknown swimmer was being rescued at last, water clinging heavily to her; even as they dragged her to safety, it threatened to pull her back under its glittering surface.

Margaret's door was still shut when Nick rose next morning. He hesitated outside it for a moment. His eyes felt hard as stones, legacy of a poor night's sleep and muddled, guilty dreams.

A telephone call had broken the news to Kate of his Christmas cancellation, made a week earlier from the hospital site. The connection, usually so precarious, had been brutally clear, magnifying every surprised catch of her breath. He'd described the fire and the riots, the village-council meeting and the governor's intransigence – a story tailored to Kate's mind, which liked its reasons served up black or white. Even as he was telling it, it felt like a lie, or maybe a child's version of the truth. Sins of omission loomed large over his shoulder as he spoke – Margaret and JoJo, Madi and his father, motives too tangled even for him to fathom.

'A well's the perfect solution,' he'd told her. 'But I'd need to build it now, while there's still room to make savings on the site. As soon as J.P. gives me the green light and things start moving, I promise I'll come back.'

Silence filled the line; then he heard her exhale, a weary sound. 'OK, Nick.'

'You're sure?'

'Of course I'm not sure.' Her voice cracked, breaking over the speaker. 'But you'll do what you want. You always do. You can ask me to understand, but you can't ask me to be happy about it.'

'This is important, Kate. You haven't seen how these people are living.'

'I know. I get it. And I'm sorry for that burned girl and for everything that's happening. I'm proud of what you're doing, you know that. But our life is important, too. Isn't it?'

'It's not a competition.' He tried to be gentle. 'We'll still be here, after the well.'

She sighed. 'Your mother's been asking about you, you know. I've gone to see her twice. She's fixated on that drawing she made of you, keeps trying to get me to send it to you.'

'That's not fair.' She knew his mother was his weakness, a guilty wound that never healed.

'How can it be unfair if it's true? She really misses you.' *I miss you.* She wouldn't humiliate herself by saying it, not when he'd just cancelled their time together. But he felt something twisting underneath the anger, the unwanted violence of hurt feelings.

'You've never been completely settled in London.' He could almost see the tears cupped in the corners of her eyes, pale lashes barring their escape. 'I thought you missed the country-side – but it's more than that.'

He opened his mouth to deny it, but suddenly wondered why. He could see her on the clean, cool fabric of their sofa, his diamond on her finger. 'This is not about me – or us,' he said, at last. 'It's a small sacrifice for something bigger. Don't you ever want to feel part of something good – to take a stand for someone else, balance the scales a little?'

'Oh, Nick,' she'd said. 'Who doesn't, sometimes? But not at any price.'

They'd hung up shortly afterwards. 'Good luck with it,' were her final words, artificially bright. But in last night's dreams she'd come at him, weeping, raking his face with curling fingers and filling it with blood. He cried out to stop her, grabbing her wrists as they turned dark, luminescent. They clung onto him, and he was drawn in, his terror turning to need.

He left without knocking on Margaret's door, heading down-stairs to the pool restaurant. The air was damp from new rain. Dark birds roosted on the roof, under a wispy sky.

J.P. was waiting for him with a coffee and *The Economist.* 'Morning,' he said. He wore his reading glasses, sunglasses pushed up over his forehead. 'Sleep well? You look terrible.'

'Not bad,' Nick lied.

J.P. snorted his disbelief. 'Is there something I should know?' He jerked his head up towards the bedrooms.

Nick flushed, furious. 'You have a filthy mind, J.P..'

'Look, I would never blame you.' J.P. sipped his coffee, made a rapturous expression. 'She is magnificent. Not just the looks, which are enough, mind you. She has something else, really. *Un oiseau volant.* What a waste, to be stuck out there in the desert, cooking and cleaning for an old guy! Nothing against Dr Ahmed, but – well, there's no justice in this world.'

There's no justice in this world. Margaret would disagree, Nick knew. *All that comes to us is earned.*

'If you're really interested in justice for Margaret,' he said, 'then listen to some ideas I have about our work there.'

A waiter brought more coffee and some bread rolls. 'God help us,' J.P. said. 'You are Mr Ideas.'

'I thought that was a good thing?'

J.P. put his hands to the sides of his head, palms flapping. 'OK. I am *all ears*, as you British say. Oh, but first . . .' He reached into a backpack by his feet, pulling out an envelope marked with nameless stains.

'This is tranche number two. Thirty thousand dollars. For wages on-site and construction materials.'

'Right.' The notes lay heavy in Nick's hand, slick with an oily sheen.

'So, lots going on, eh?' J.P. continued. 'All on schedule?'

'The first floor should be done by next month.'

'That would be great.' J.P. sipped his coffee. 'So I'll tell the governor end of January for the inspection.'

'What inspection?'

'No big deal. He wants to bring some of his guys, you know, the powers-that-be. A photo opportunity, he said, for the papers.'

Nick had a mental image of silk-clad men lined up on his site, faces pampered and plump, while scarecrow workers choked on dust behind them.

'We don't have time for inspections,' he said. 'And we can't guarantee to be ready by end of January. Put him off.'

J.P. snorted. 'Put him off – you're kidding, right? These things are important for him and important for us, too. It's just thirty minutes out of your day. Why make a fuss?'

Nick spread his hands, unsure of how much to say. 'I just don't trust him. He's using us, this clinic – for some agenda of his own. For *his* people, *his* soldiers and whoever supports him.'

J.P. tapped the desk, nodding slowly. 'That's too simplistic, even for you. You don't like the governor – fine. I told you he was a piece of work. Did he show you his degree from Brown?'

'He showed me his degree, he showed me his empty hospital beds, he showed me everything he wanted me to see.' Nick grew angry, remembering Dr Ahmed crumpling under the onslaught of words.

'I never said he was a good man. They only exist in fairy tales. But he knows how to make things work. Which is a kind of goodness, frankly. The kind that money cannot buy and religions don't teach.'

Nick put the envelope down beside him. He could feel the weight of the notes, lumped together into blocks.

He pushed the cash towards J.P.. 'In the village just down the road from where we're spending thousands on a PR stunt, crops are burning and water is running out. They wait for his trucks to arrive and pay money they can't afford. Margaret – who you were enjoying fruit cocktails with last night – has to get by on a quarter of a tank a week. Her son collects water from the lake for their washing. The same lake that spread an epidemic in the village a few years back. Her baby boy died. So, tell me again about how there's no justice in the world.'

Nick's heart was pounding; the resident crows shrieked and leaped suddenly skywards, woken by the warming sun. J.P. took off his reading glasses and rubbed his eyes. Without them he looked vulnerable: a child's blue orbs nestled in a man's lined face.

'Nick, look. I've known these people longer than you. I remember the epidemic, don't think I will ever forget.'

'So.' Nick tapped the envelope. 'A few thousand dollars could balance the scales. They're walking around on top of water they can't reach. It's not even the water . . .' He was desperate now, looking for a way to explain. 'It's *him*. It's the way he keeps them dangling in a noose.'

J.P. cleaned his glasses and put them away in his shirt pocket. He pulled his sunglasses down from his forehead, turning his eyes opaque.

'I agree, something more could be done,' he said. 'But let me be very clear with you. You are not in the Wild West – the Lone Ranger. You are part of something that involves many people who also have rights and expectations. Just because you do not eat dinner with them every night does not make them less important. We have committed to a project.'

'But . . .'

'No *but*.' J.P. raised his hand. 'We have committed ourselves to something that requires finishing. If you want to be a man of honour, then keeping your word is the first place to start.'

I did give my word – to Margaret and JoJo. I promised I wouldn't abandon them. It was a bond as real as the cement and mortar of their castle, as real as Margaret's touch on his hand last night, as real as JoJo's new-found faith in his future. Guilt pricked Nick, remembering how easily their conversations had slipped from *when I go back to England* into *when we go back.*

'We could do both,' he insisted. 'We could finish the hospital and build a well with the money we're saving.'

'Any money saved must be returned so we can agree with the governor how to spend it in his region. I promise, I will even come myself and bring an army of experts.'

'It's not good enough, J.P..' Nick stood up, furious. 'We need to act now, not later. During the dry season.'

J.P. sighed. 'Listen to a wise head. Be upset if it makes you feel like a good guy. But accept: you are just one small corner in a big world of trouble.'

Nick felt the cold prickle of sweat on his skin, an ugly premonition of failure.

'They're our friends,' he said, in a last appeal against the dawning realisation that J.P. might not be persuaded. 'If we don't stand up for them, then who will?'

J.P. got to his feet too, signalling for the bill. 'If they are all like your lady,' he said, 'then I think they could well stand up for themselves.'

Margaret met Nick at noon in the lobby of the hotel. She broke into the storm of his thoughts like a bird of paradise, brilliantly wrapped in a sky blue skirt patterned with crimson flowers. The white cotton of her blouse scooped low around her neck, baring dark shoulders, tiny filaments of light gleaming on them in the lobby's chill. She'd taken off Bako's bracelet, her wrist strangely bare without it.

'You look beautiful,' he said.

Her smile was nervous. She smoothed back newly braided hair and plucked at the skirt as it rustled. 'I wore this for Sarah's school graduation,' she said. 'It was my mother's. I preferred Western clothes. But Sarah is more traditional.'

'I'm sure she'll be thrilled,' he assured her, holding out his hand. Margaret laid hers in his and squeezed it tight.

The taxi drove them through the city's chaos, following Margaret's halting directions. On her lap she clutched a bag of gifts, an anxious frown on her face whenever she looked at them. Most were handmade or looted from old family treasures. JoJo had written a note to his uncle, including a careful drawing of a house under Nick's guidance. On the bottom it read: *Our family home where we will be pleased if you visit us.* Dr Ahmed had sent his own, more eloquent letter and an expensive memento from his youth – a porcelain statuette of Mary and Child, bought years before at Portobello Market.

Margaret had struggled the longest to find a gift she deemed worthy. But then she'd remembered a gold cross Dr Ahmed had given her on their wedding day, hidden in a cupboard for thirteen years away from Imam Abdi's sceptical eyes. She'd told Nick how, on the morning of her conversion to Islam, before reciting the Shahada, the testament of faith, her husband-to-be had placed it quietly in her hand. 'For solace,' she'd said, running a thumb thoughtfully over its spiny arms. Dr Ahmed gave her permission to sell the cross at the capital's central gold market, converting it into something new for Sarah's neck.

The gold merchant smelled of sweat; his stones glimmered with suspicious brilliance. Margaret was instantly entranced by a bird-shaped charm, its eyes bright with tiny rubies. She held it against the dark glow of her skin, admiring how the wings shone in the unforgiving neon light.

'This is Sarah's style,' she whispered to Nick. 'She loved birds, I think. I'm sure she did.' Nick murmured his agreement, watching the gold wings dip and soar over the hollows of her throat. *Un oiseau volant,* he thought.

The bird was wrapped in cream paper, the cross relinquished. Margaret's delight was transfixing as she took hold of Sarah's gift. 'She will love it,' she told Nick again, her body electric with emotion. She was laughing as they climbed into the taxi, slipping the gift into the bag. Nick caught a glimpse of bound yellow paper nestled among the offerings – her storybook, a red flower crayoned on the corner.

They headed away from the city centre. Tall office blocks gave way to low villas with pink- and peach-painted stonework. Flowering vines tumbled over the walls, voluptuous as open mouths.

Finally, Margaret leaned forward. 'Please, stop here.'

The car rolled to a halt outside a white bungalow. Its paved courtyard was bare, grass pushing through the cracks. A small fountain lay silent at its centre, a winged angel pointing skywards.

The front gate was wedged shut. But Margaret slipped her hand under the trellised ironwork and Nick heard a sharp click as the lock gave way. 'There's a trick to it,' she said. Her shoulders rose in a deep inhalation – and she stepped through.

Nick stood behind the open gate, letting her walk ahead. The front door was brown and solid-looking, thick as the walls. She glanced back towards him for reassurance. 'Go on,' he urged.

Margaret knocked on the door with the flat of her hand. After a few seconds a woman's voice answered, muffled behind the wood.

'Who is that?'

'It's me,' she called back, pressing her mouth to the door. 'Me. Margaret.'

The voice said something indistinguishable. Then the door swung open, stopping halfway.

A young woman peered from the gap: tall as Margaret, with the same haughty curve of cheek and forehead. Her face was larger, fuller, its skin smooth as new-baked bread. The tops of her breasts swelled over her blouse, hair fanning out behind her in a soft, dark cloud.

'Oh my God.' The woman put her hand to her mouth. 'My God. Margaret!'

'Sarah.' Margaret was laughing, hands held to her chest as if her heart might burst out. 'Sarah.'

Sarah looked from Nick back to Margaret, the turn of her head echoing Margaret's wild grace.

'You returned,' she whispered. And then she burst into tears, pushing through the door and falling onto her sister's shoulder.

Margaret stroked Sarah's hair. Her eyes were closed, but Nick saw tears staining her cheeks. 'Forgive me.' Her voice was hoarse in her throat. 'I never meant to be so long.'

Sarah disentangled herself, her face red and swollen. Pale marks shone on Margaret's arms where her sister's fingers had gripped them. Sarah wiped her running nose on her wrist. Margaret lifted a corner of her skirt to dry her sister's eyes.

'Still not a real lady,' she said, in a shaky voice. 'Always without a handkerchief.'

The same laugh burst from both of them. But it flickered out quickly in Sarah; she reached over to Margaret with the haste of fear. 'Margaret,' she whispered again, running her hands over her sister's forearms, fingers clenching flesh, 'you are not a ghost.'

'No.' Margaret grabbed Sarah's hands, holding them to her throat. 'I'm here.'

'Why did you not write to me?' Sarah's chest was heaving with agitation, her voice catching on the words. 'I thought you had died.' As she spoke, she craned her head over Nick's shoulder, checking the road outside.

'I wrote,' Margaret said, and Nick thought of her desperate, unsent message. 'But I could not post the letters. I swear I missed you every day. I call my daughter by your name in my heart.'

'Your daughter?' Sarah put her hand on Margaret's stomach. 'Meg, you have a girl.'

Margaret put her hands on top of Sarah's. 'I have a girl,' she laughed. 'She looks like Mama.'

Wiping her eyes, she smiled at her sister. 'And now we can be healed,' she said. 'I will make amends to David. We can visit our mother together.'

At David's name, Sarah stepped away from Margaret's hands. She clung to the doorframe, her eyes downcast.

'He was so angry with you, Meg,' she said, her voice low and suddenly accusing. 'He forbade me to study. He said all you learned at school was how to be a whore.'

Margaret tried to touch Sarah's face again. But this time the girl jerked away. 'You don't know, Margaret. I stayed here with nothing, without even a man to marry me. You didn't even tell me goodbye.'

Margaret drew herself up, her head high. 'I did not want you to stop me,' she said. 'I was too angry with David. He lied, Sarah, about so many things. And I thought . . .' She bit her lip, dropping her eyes. 'I thought that you could still be happy without me.'

Sarah looked at her, incredulous. 'How could you think so? You were like my mother.'

The door remained half-open, Sarah's tall frame blocking the entrance. Margaret reached out to touch her sister's round cheeks, tears gathering around her fingers.

'I'm thirsty, Sarah,' she said. 'Let's go inside and drink while we wait for David.'

Sarah raised her own hand to her face, laying it over Margaret's. For a moment they were both still, a tableau of peace.

But then her palm started moving, down to Margaret's wrist. Gently, she pulled her sister's hand away.

Margaret's face turned pale. 'What is wrong?' Her voice was calm, but Nick heard panic underneath. 'Why won't you open the door?'

Sarah had started crying again, water leaking from her nose. Margaret seemed to stumble, and only Nick's hand on her shoulder prevented her from falling.

'Open the door, Sarah,' she said, louder this time. 'Please. Open it.' Nick could feel the tremors underneath his hand.

'You must go.' Sarah's arms were crossed over her chest, her whole body trembling. 'David is coming soon. He will kill you if he sees you.'

'I'm not afraid of David.' Contempt made Margaret's voice harsh. 'Don't fear him, Sarah. He cannot hurt you if I am here.'

But Sarah shook her head, nervous eyes darting to the road. 'You must go,' she begged. 'You must.'

'I don't understand.' Margaret took Sarah's chin in her hands, forcing her attention back. 'Why are you afraid?'

Sarah's wide eyes were fixed on her sister's now, like an animal in a trap. Under the film of tears, Nick saw guilt flicker.

'You should have come sooner,' she said. 'I would have gone with you. Now it's too late.'

Margaret dropped her hand. 'Who is coming, Sarah?' she asked, her voice soft.

'My fiancé.' Defiance crept into her tone. 'David told him you are dead. So his parents would forgive our shame.' Then her face crumpled and she started to weep again.

'You ran away with a Muslim, Margaret!' The words escaped between sobs. 'You are not even properly wed. For so long I couldn't marry. *Because of you.*' She spat the words. 'It was you who took everything – who got what you wanted.'

Margaret's eyes had been glazed, unfocused – but this brought her back to herself. She brushed away tears, her body straightening into its familiar, lonely lines – as tall and spare as a winter birch. 'So many years, Sarah,' she said, quietly. 'And still you have not forgiven me.'

Her sister stared back at her, chest rising and falling, cheeks blotched red as if she'd been slapped. Her nostrils flared. 'You chose, Margaret.' She turned her head away. 'Now let me have my choice.'

Margaret nodded. Her hand left the doorframe and hovered over Sarah's, like a benediction.

Sarah grabbed it, brought it to her lips and kissed the palm. 'Go now,' she said. 'Go, before they get here.'

Margaret turned back towards Nick, as if in a dream. He saw her pick up her little bag of offerings and walk down the steps, a violent slash of colour against the patio's pale tiles.

'Margaret!' Sarah's call was high, urgent.

She stopped again; Nick saw that slight turn of her neck he'd come to know so well.

'Is he a good man, Margaret?' The girl's voice was thick with tears. 'Are you happy?'

He saw Margaret smile. She looked skywards, eyes bone dry. At last they dropped to the bag swaying from her hand.

'Yes, Sarah,' she called back. 'I am very happy.'

Then she walked out of the gate, ignoring the hand Nick offered her and climbing into the waiting taxi. Her fingers loosened as she stepped inside, the bag of gifts slipping down into the dust.

The street blurred past the car window, house after silent house. Nick asked Margaret if she was OK. She nodded: 'Fine.' But she did not speak again.

Steel-and-glass pinnacles were visible in the distance. Clouds gathered, forecasting another storm to come.

They pulled up outside a small church, its white stucco adorned with peach turrets. A bronze cross on the highest one blazed into radiance against backlit clouds.

'You can wait here,' Margaret told Nick.

'But I want to come with you.'

'As you like,' she said.

The cemetery was tucked away from the road. He traced Margaret's steps, through tooth-like rows of stone interspersed with sad sculptures. The ominous afternoon glow summoned colours from the white marble: tangerine, rose, marigold; they could have been children walking through a garden of death.

Margaret stopped at a low gravestone of grey marble, carved into a heart shape at the top. The inscription read: *Miriam, Most Beloved Wife of Jonathan, mother to David, Margaret and Sarah.*

Underneath, the stonemason had etched a Madonna, her head bowed in sorrow. It looked so much like Margaret that Nick's mind reeled with sudden terror. He reached out to take her hand, to feel the reassuring pulse of warmth within her.

She let it lie there, wrapped up in her memories. He waited, feeling silence stretch with the shadows.

'I did not think so much time had passed.' Margaret spoke at last, her fingers heavy in his: 'I was only leaving her for one angry moment. When you are young, you cannot imagine forever. Even when they told me God lasts forever, and heaven lasts forever – I would think they just meant a long time. That forever would change into . . . something else.'

She reached to touch the marble heart over her mother's bones.

'I cannot recall her face,' she said, her voice low with anguish. 'It's as if she died again.'

Nick searched for words of comfort.

'She probably looked just like you,' he said. 'That means JoJo and Nagode look like her. Their children will, too. A part of her is being born again and again.'

Margaret drew in a slow breath. 'Mama believed only the spirit is immortal. She thought she would rise and leave nothing behind.'

Nick thought of Madi's grave, lying in strange ground so far from his home. *Where did your spirit go, Madi? Did you leave the earth? Or are you still here, waiting for me?*

'I don't know if souls are real,' he said. 'Or where we go when we die. But the part that loves stays with the living – I believe that. Your mother's love for you – it's in everything you do – how you sing to Nagode, how you care for JoJo. You keep her alive, and so do they.'

Her laughter was incredulous as she lifted her eyes to meet his. 'Is that what they believe, your people? The Hebrews – they believe that spirits walk with us?'

'No.' The gravestone was darkening as evening descended, casting a shadow over the bare plot. 'They believe we sleep, to wake on the Day of Judgement.'

She laughed again. 'But every day is a Day of Judgement.'

Her hand slipped out of his, leaving a hollow absence. *There's no justice in this world.* J.P.'s words this morning now seemed prophetic. Their wild plans were all buried in the earth. They would return the way they came, empty-handed.

Margaret bent to kiss the gravestone. As she pulled up, she said, in a conversational tone, 'Do you know why I was so angry in the garden? When you and JoJo mended the castle?'

Nick shook his head, and she continued. 'I was jealous. Because he is still young. He is still free to choose his own path, to show everything within him.'

'You are free,' he told her, through the ferocious beating of his heart. 'My father used to say: cowards make their own prisons. And you are the bravest soul I've ever met.'

She dropped her head, and he thought she would cry again.

But then she turned to walk back towards the last gleam of daylight, past the little church and its emblems, a lonely figure among greying stones.

Nick dropped Margaret at the hotel and went on to Western Union. Kate had sent him a thousand dollars and a conciliatory note that read: *Happy New Year next one we'll celebrate together hope it's giving you what you need.*

He considered calling her – but she would be at a party already. He could not face shouting down a bad phone line, every word misheard, tangled agonies of hesitation and repetition. He could imagine her only in fragments – a flash of long hair, the imprint of her lips on a wineglass, laughter from someone slipping out of sight.

It was nightfall when he arrived back at the hotel. A dark sunset had spread across the sky; its dying glow was mirrored by lamps, springing to life around the pool, intersecting worlds of half-light and luminous shadow.

They'd arranged to meet J.P. at the bar for dinner. Nick could not bring himself to go upstairs and change. The air was oppressive. He hadn't eaten since breakfast and his stomach churned. He asked the barman for a beer and drank it fast – cool and light. He ordered another. The lightness in his stomach spread to his head. The sky was velvet and heavy, a curtain drawn against prying eyes.

He did not want to see J.P., to make polite conversation when all was confusion. He could see the course being planned for him: he would spend J.P.'s money on the governor's hospital and go back to England. He would marry Kate in a marquee in his mother's garden and hold dinner parties while Margaret fought and dreamed her life apart from him. The idea was strangely desolating.

People were pouring into the courtyard – light refracting from their wrists, their hair, the jewels around their necks. Waiters moved through the crowd in smooth circles, carrying champagne. A woman stood with her back to him, her dress flame red. Her skin was a flickering black in the uneven light, her head tilted in laughter. She was night and heat embodied; arousal stirred as he watched the curve of her body. *What's wrong with me?*

Making his way to the pool, he dipped his hands in the water – dark and blood temperature. He splashed it into his eyes, rubbing until they stung.

J.P. arrived as the music began, dressed in white trousers and a pale blue linen shirt.

'Hey, you didn't change?' was the first thing he said when he saw Nick. 'And where's your beautiful lady?'

'She'll be down soon,' Nick replied.

J.P. laughed at the expression on his face. 'Did you start your celebrations early?'

'I'm not drunk.' Nick tried to smile. 'It's just been a long day.'

J.P. took him by the shoulder. 'Relax, Nicholas. Really. Let the world go for one night.'

'I'm OK.' He could not shake his sense of disconnection; he felt himself in free fall, above a world held down by the weight of rights and wrongs.

J.P. looked concerned. 'You are doing a great job, Nick. You are more than OK.'

A waiter passed, carrying a silver tray laden with glass flutes. Their bubbles streamed upwards in tiny gaseous explosions. 'Here, have a drink. *Santé!*' J.P. tipped his glass towards Nick's, joining the silver chime of toasts rising all around them.

The champagne was warmed by humidity; it was like sipping air and light. J.P. greeted the hotel manager. Nick looked up at the windows of the first floor, willing Margaret's presence.

He saw her emerge a little later from under the archways. She was wrapped in a long, dark robe and her head loosely covered, framing her face in shadow. Her eyes searched the room; she found him and raised a hand in greeting. He recognised the familiar red beads back in place around her wrist.

J.P. returned from the bar with two more glasses of champagne. Margaret seemed to draw him like a magnet, upsetting his balance. He shouted to her above the music's din, raising his arms in welcome and spilling frothy liquid all over his suit. 'Oh, no, so sorry,' he said, as Margaret reached them. She laughed at his distress.

'Is this how they celebrate in France?' she teased. 'They have so much champagne that they throw it away'

'Take mine,' J.P. said, pushing a half-filled flute towards her. 'Really, please. I'm an idiot.'

Margaret took the glass and touched it to his nearly emptied one. 'Cheers,' she said. He laughed. 'Cheers indeed.' He turned the glass upside down to drain the last few drops into his mouth. Margaret just lifted hers to her lips without drinking.

'Excuse me while I fill this up.' J.P. was swaying slightly, looking around for the waiters with their trays. 'Don't go anywhere,' he said to Margaret, wagging his finger at her.

'I am right here,' she replied.

Nick watched J.P. disappear unsteadily into the crowd, his balding crown glistening with sweat, 'He means well.'

'Everybody means well.' She lifted the champagne flute and turned it around, watching the liquid fade from gold to grey and brighten again. Then she put her lips to the rim and swallowed a few drops. Her forehead wrinkled, and Nick laughed outright at the surprise on her face. 'I thought it would be sweet,' she said. 'I remember it being sweet.'

'When was the last time you drank champagne?' But he regretted the question immediately – why ask for memories that could only wound? *Let the world go for one night.*

She looked at him, solemn and remote. Champagne lights were dancing in front of his eyes, like spirits conjured from unseen worlds.

'Let us pretend,' she said. 'I will pretend that this is the first time I have drunk champagne. You will pretend this is the first time you have seen me. Tonight is for forgetting.'

'I'll drink to that,' he answered, raising his own glass.

This time she drank deep, draining half and wiping spilled drops from her chin. She laughed – half pleasure, half a gasp for air.

J.P. came back too soon, wanting them to eat at the barbecue. Smoke was rising by the pool's edge in spirals of charcoal sweetness. Nick was suddenly ravenous. The meat was served on the bone; it burned his fingers. Margaret ate beside him, smoke billowing around her. J.P. managed to ensure her glass was always full.

The band had moved on to slower tunes, striking up incongruously into 'New York, New York'. J.P. went to find a toilet. Nick turned to Margaret. Her eyes were half closed, as if dreaming – her lips parted, head swaying in time to the song.

'Excuse me,' he said to her. 'Do I know you?'

Her eyes widened as she turned to him, looking puzzled. Then she smiled and said, 'No, we've not met.'

'You're a stranger here, like me?'

'Perhaps it's so.'

He grinned at her, and she shook her head in mock disapproval. Reflections from the pool played over her throat as she turned back to watch the band.

'But will you dance with me anyway?' he asked her. 'If your card isn't filled?'

She turned back to study him. 'I don't know how to dance.'

He shrugged. 'Neither do I.' He held out his hand. 'My name is Nicholas.'

She hesitated, then took it. Her pupils were dilated in the low light; she stared through him without seeing, focused on something beyond them both.

They walked into the maze of swaying backs. Hidden in the middle of the crowd, he put one arm around her waist and lifted the hand that held hers.

He could not hear the music, only his heartbeat in his ears – disorientating. *Dance,* he told himself. *Move.* But something unbridgeable was between them, even in the midst of pretence.

They were only inches apart, but those inches were endless – a gulf separating worlds of thought and deed.

Behind her the orange lamps sent light in rivers over the upper floors. Black birds huddled in their nests – some crouched and formless, some stirring in restless anxiety. Nick saw one teetering on the edge of the gutter, opening and closing its wings.

'Nicholas,' Margaret said to him. She'd returned from wherever her mind had been; her hand was withdrawing from his.

Desperation filled the widening space. He could not tell if it was tugging him forward or pushing him back. 'Margaret.' He put his hand to his eyes. 'Margaret, I . . .'

'Where the hell were you?' J.P. stumbled into them, wrapping his arms around their shoulders. Nick realised the music had stopped. Voices were raised in excitement; around the courtyard people's eyes were turned to the sky.

'It's the countdown,' J.P. said. 'Prepare for a new year, eh?' He pulled Nick into a bear hug without waiting for an answer. '*Allez, allez!*' he yelled towards the lead singer, who checked his watch. Nick saw his boss sweep Margaret against him, tucking her under the patch of sweat around his armpit.

The singer began to count down from ten. The crowd joined him – bellowing out the numbers.

Nick saw Margaret's lips move, her eyes raised as if in prayer. He followed her gaze. The sky was deep and formless – a closed door without even a star in it. *There's nothing up there.* To his astonishment, the thought called tears into his eyes. For the first time in his life he wished it were different – that someone was listening, that he could know the right thing to ask for.

Zero – and glee erupted all around them. J.P. kissed them on both cheeks and they kissed each other automatically, barely registering the touch. A high shriek was followed by a burst of red light. The fireworks began, showering colours down like rain. The dark sky became a garden flowering with blue and yellow and green, cascades of light leaving bright trails on Nick's retina. Margaret watched, enraptured.

'Look,' she said – not to him or J.P. – perhaps to herself. 'The sky is talking.'

Nick made a decision. *I have to go. Now, while I can.*

He turned to J.P. and said goodnight. 'But why? It's early. Now we start the real fun. Dancing and everything.'

Nick shook his head. The world was spinning. 'Too much to drink,' he said. 'I have to lie down.'

He turned to Margaret. 'Goodnight.' She looked at him, puzzled. The scream of fireworks filled the air; light framed her in a pulsing corona. He made himself walk away before she could speak – headed out of the crowds towards the darkness of the lobby, reaching the long cocoon of the stairwell.

Sounds faded behind him, a muffled peace. Gentle laughter and faint crackles followed him up the staircase.

'Nicholas.'

He stopped. Margaret was standing at the bottom of the stairs. Her scarf had fallen around her shoulders.

'I do not know the way,' she said, placing one hand on the banister, looking up at him. 'I am dizzy.'

He paused, the sense of déjà vu overwhelming. For an instant he was the one trapped at the top of the climbing frame, searching for any safe way out.

'I'll help you,' he said. She climbed the steps towards him and they walked together to her room.

The sounds of celebration followed them from the courtyard, dwindling as Margaret gave him her key and he unlocked the door. He stepped inside, into the dark room with its drawn curtains and ceiling fan humming faintly. He was drifting away from his body; he almost didn't feel her fingers reach his face, the touch of Bako's beads cool on his cheek, the electric pressure of her lips, the sudden warmth of skin beneath his hands. And then the door closed behind them – crashing over them both, like the break of a returning wave.

JANUARY

Nicholas is late to pick me up from school. The other students already went home. He promised to take me with him to the Town today. Mama said it's OK for me to go. Since she and Nicholas came back from the capital, she says yes to everything.

Today is an important day, Nicholas says. The governor is bringing some village heads and even the emir to see the hospital. Nicholas says they will take pictures for the newspaper. I brought the governor's cap to school with me so I can wear it in the photographs.

Some days I am still angry with Nicholas for leaving me behind. I thought I could not forgive him. The day he left, I pretended to sleep when he came to my door. I stayed until I heard Baba come back into the house. Soon I heard him open the toolbox for the clock.

Later Hanan came to collect Nagode. I heard her speaking with Baba in the kitchen.

She said: 'There is talk, Baba. Bad talk. About your guest.' She calls him Baba sometimes, to show her respect. Adeya has no real baba. He was a stranger from the south, like Mama. He left one day and did not come back.

Baba's voice sounded tired. He told Hanan: 'The Prophet, peace be upon him, says that Hell is reached fastest through the harvest of our tongues.'

'Do not be angry with me, Baba,' I heard Hanan say. 'I do not want you to suffer as I did.'

'Only the innocent suffer,' Baba says to her. 'For the rest of us, adversity is necessary.'

Hanan does not understand when Baba speaks this way. I do not either.

But I am thinking of Adeya and her baba. Did she cry, when he went? Does she still wait for him?

Adeya does not come to school any more. Baba says they have no money after the fire. And she cannot write with her burned hands. Each day I see her desk, where she used to sit. I cannot forget her face when I let them laugh at her.

After Hanan went home, I came from my room. There was Baba, on his knees. He had opened the side of the clock and was pulling something from the inside. He was pulling and pulling, but it would not come.

'Ah, Yahya,' he said. 'Hand me the pliers if you would.'

I brought them to him. Together we worked quietly. Baba, he does not talk. I missed Nicholas. He talks to me all the time. And just then, I felt fear. Suppose he did not want to come back? Suppose he did not teach me any more about trigonometry and pi. I would not be an engineer. Then I would stay here forever, with Baba and this clock.

Then I wanted to run after Nicholas, to call him back. To say: I am sorry I was angry. I promise I will not fight any more if you come back soon.

My throat hurt from swallowing. I could not help asking Baba: 'Why did Adeya's baba not come back to them?'

I saw Baba stop for one moment. He said: 'So, you are worrying, too?'

I did not understand. So I asked again: 'Do you know why?'

Baba took off his glasses and leaned his weight on the clock.

He said: 'Each of us is a mystery, Yahya. We expect understanding from others when we do not even know ourselves.'

I wished Baba would answer me. So I said: 'Maybe he was tired of this place. Maybe he wanted his home.'

Baba started pulling on the clock's insides again. He said: 'There are people like that, always running. We humans want to be birds, flying where we like. But this is not what Allah intends.

He made us more like the tortoise. A tortoise cannot run from what it carries on its back.'

Then he said: 'There!' I heard a clicking sound. And the clock, it started to tick again: tock, tock, tock. For two days this was the only sound in the house.

But on the day Mama and Nicholas came back, we came alive again. Mama was laughing like she had the fever. She hugged me and asked so many questions. She took Nagode and squeezed and kissed her so much that my sister started to cry. Mama closed her eyes, as if she could not hear. I said, 'Careful, Mama!' And she opened her eyes, like someone waking.

When Baba came, Mama started to talk fast to him. She was telling him about my uncles and aunts in the capital. She said they thanked him for the gifts. He asked her, 'Did you see David?' She answered: 'He was travelling. I saw Sarah. But I am glad to be home.'

Baba, he smiled at that. But under his smile he looked sad. He said: 'We missed you, my dear. Isn't that so, Yahya?'

I said: 'I missed you, Mama.'

She knelt down and kissed me. I could not tell if she was smiling or crying. She took my chin in her hand. She said: 'You are growing tall as a tree.'

I asked her: 'Did my aunt Sarah like my letter?'

Mama, she smiled at that. It was a funny smile. She said: 'She liked it very much, JoJo. You write so well.'

'Do I have cousins?' I asked her, but she had already moved away.

So I went to see Nicholas in his room. I knocked on the door. There was no sound. I went inside.

There he was, sitting on the bed. His face was in his hands as if he was very tired.

I said: 'Nicholas.' He looked up, quick and surprised. He said: 'JoJo. Mate.' Then he hugged me. Like Mama – so tight, I thought my bones would break.

I asked Nicholas about the capital. How big is it? What do they have there? How are the buildings? Nicholas told me about the fireworks and the skyscrapers and the university and stadium. I showed him my workbook for the trigonometry. He said he was proud of me.

I said: 'Baba has been missing you too. Even Miss Amina was missing you! She told Baba you promised to buy milk from her goat and you did not. She says you Christians cannot be trusted. You are all thieves.'

Nicholas, he laughed. He said: 'Well, I must go and see your father.' He took a deep breath when he said it. Then, at dinner-time, he was very loud and happy. We were all together, like one family.

The next day Nicholas started to teach me again. I showed my workbook to Akim. He said, 'What kind of writing is this?' I told him: 'This is the quadratic equation.' Akim, he is no good at sums. So he pretended to laugh. 'This is girl's writing,' he said to me. 'You are becoming a girl, JoJo.'

I told him about the well, too, the one Nicholas and I will build together. It has been so long since the rains. Everything died and the dust hurts our eyes. The teacher closes the window in my class, but still the dust comes in. Every morning I write my name on my desk in dust. Some days I write Nicholas' name, or Adeya's. Once I wrote Bako's name, but then I rubbed it out. The dead are spirits, Juma used to tell us. They watch us. The witch, Binza – she brings them. Sometimes her place looks far away. But now the lake is small. And Binza's place, it is getting nearer every day.

From here, beside the school gate, I cannot see the lake. Just the road, the empty road, and the mosque ahead of us. My shoes hurt from standing here, waiting. Nicholas promised it would be our first trip together since he came back, just him and me. I do not think he would forget. Nicholas does not forget things, like Baba. He is not old.

I can see men leaving the mosque – Mr Kamil and Imam Abdi, Akim and Juma behind him. They will be going to speak about the drought. Akim tells me sometimes Danjuma sends a man, too.

The price of water is too high. Soon there will be sickness, Imam Abdi says. The sickness will be like a fire from Allah.

Akim comes running. 'Hey, JoJo,' he says. 'Did the white man forget you?'

I tell him: 'No – we are meeting at my place.'

Juma laughs behind him. 'Mr Nicholas is making his business with a different boy today.' He rubs his fingers together so I know what he means. Last week he showed me some magazines he stole from Tuesday – the ones in the back, with the milk powder and cola. Men and girls, and everything. They had a smell on them. The pages, they stuck together.

'Your dick must be tired from those magazines,' I say to Juma. He makes a snorting sound.

Akim does not smile. I know he joined The Boys. He cut two lines into his face, one on each cheek, like the old people do. He put ash on it, but it got an infection. Mr Kamil had to bring him to Baba. Mr Kamil beat him, he told me, for costing money. Mr Kamil is village head, Baba says, so he can afford to pay.

I start to walk with him, back to my house. Juma goes ahead, to Tuesday's shop.

Then I see Mister. He comes out from Tuesday's door. A big bag is over his shoulder. His shirt is closed today. The knife, it is hidden, and the scars from his beatings. But Mister, he is the knife himself. White and cold.

Akim stops still beside me. Juma is shaking Mister's hand. He calls: 'Akim! Get here, boy.' But Akim, he does not move.

I ask him: 'Why don't you go with them, Akim?'

Akim says nothing. He looks at the ground. His face is red from the knife, where it cut him.

Then I understand. I say, very quiet: 'Tell them we are going to my house. I will ask Nicholas to take you to the Town with me.'

Akim looks up. Now his face, it twists like a snake. He says: 'I do not want to go anywhere with you, JoJo. I am a man now. I am saving the village. While your baba plays with his clock and your mama fucks that white man.'

I hit him. We fall onto the ground and my mouth is full of dust. My hands are hard. I hit and hit and I do not need to stop. Akim's skin tastes of salt. His body is thin. I can hear nothing except his crying.

Then I feel someone lifting me up. It is Mister, laughing. He holds me by the collar of my shirt. I try to pull free from him.

'Hey!' he says. 'Wild boys! Look at these two. Two dogs, eh? Come on, dogs, let us see you bark.'

Akim is lying on the ground. He is white from the dust. I try to spit on him. The water, it burns my mouth.

'Hey!' Mister is speaking again. 'It is finished now.'

'You are crazy,' Akim says to me. He is crying, his face red.

Juma is looking at me and at Mister. Akim coughs and tries to stand – but Juma does not go to help him.

I can feel water coming from my nose. I lift my hand to clean it. There is red mixed with the dust.

Mister takes me by my school shirt. He holds me close. He is warm. His eyes, they are blue. I look at them and I feel quiet.

He says: 'Is it finished?'

I nod my head.

'OK,' he says.

He lets me go. My body hurts. My hand hurts. Something inside hurts, but I cannot feel where.

'Cut him,' Akim says. 'He's a traitor.'

Mister walks over to Akim. Akim, he grows small. Mister says: 'Do you tell me what to do, boss?'

Akim's eyes, they are white. Once I saw a dog that caught its leg in a trap. It had eyes just like that.

Mister says: 'JoJo is no traitor. He is a fighter, like us. We are waiting for him. He will come when it is time.'

I say nothing. I want to be home. I want to feel Mama's hands and have her wash my face. I want to know why Nicholas left me again.

'See you later, boss,' Mister says.

I run. My eyes are full of dust. The mosque is quiet in the square. They have all gone home. Tuesday's shop is closed and the sun is too bright. I see Jalloh's car parked behind there, and another car I do not know.

I can still feel the blood coming from my nose. Mama will ask questions. I run past Miss Amina's house. Beyond there is Adeya, and Binza. Beyond them are the spirits that drink at the lake.

I run to my garden and open the gate. The car the fat man gave Nicholas is there, but Baba's car is not.

I go around the back to wash my face before they find me. It is quiet in the house. There are sounds in the kitchen, but they are small. I wonder if Nagode is there, crying alone.

I am afraid now. Where is Mama? But then I hear her voice. It sounds like she is singing. It is a sad song, with no words, like crying.

Then I hear another voice. Nicholas. He says one word: 'Beautiful.' Then he says it again.

I walk very slowly to the kitchen door. I cannot even fit my fingers into the crack. But I can still see them.

Mama, her eyes are closed. Nicholas is pressed against her, like the people in Tuesday's magazines. And Nicholas is saying the same word again and again. He says: 'Beautiful, beautiful, beautiful.'

Something slammed; Nick heard it through the rush of his blood. Was it a door, or an engine? He pushed himself back from Margaret. Her eyes opened, caution giving sudden definition to her face – that reserve he loved so much in its dissolution.

Now her arms untangled from his. 'Is he home?' she said, voice hoarse, her neck flushed from the pressure of his lips.

'He has his market surgery after prayers.' Nick could see nothing through the dim cotton curtain, just shadows moving on the road. 'He can't be back yet, Margaret.'

She breathed out slowly. Her fingers covered her face, clenching into the halo of hair, head bowing to rest on his chest. 'We are doing wrong,' she whispered.

We are doing wrong. The moisture on her breath warmed his skin. He'd carried guilt every day since boyhood, a parasitic worm winding around every other sensation. But the slam of Margaret's hotel room door had killed it dead. When he returned to JoJo's eager arms, to Dr Ahmed's welcoming handshake and Kate's stationery on his desk – his shame had been nothing compared to the ecstasy of a life sentence unexpectedly commuted. He'd touched her tears as loneliness melted from her in the merging of breath and bodies, feeling the dizzy faith of the high-wire walker. They'd sworn not to touch each other after their return – a promise broken the very next day, in the hot, dark air of Nagode's room. He'd become hardened to greeting Dr Ahmed every morning with the taste of her lips still in his mouth. 'He cares about me,' Margaret had said. 'It's not the same as love.' Love was reason enough to believe this was still goodness, as if they'd crossed into some secret, more hallowed universe blind to sin – like children playing in a sunlit meadow while tall, unconquerable cliffs loomed over them from all sides.

'This isn't wrong,' he whispered, insistent, his chin resting on the back of her head, hands stroking the angles of her back. As she'd unwound beside him into sleep that first dawn, he'd stroked the year's fresh light as it illuminated pathways on her skin, feeling the spirit flowing under the flesh.

Margaret broke away, turning back to the kitchen sink and the half-peeled vegetables smelling of wet earth. She started flensing a yam – chocolate flakes peeling back from pink flesh. Their vegetables lay in a bowl of scummy water, brought from the lake. They were lucky still to have water for washing; Nick had long since swapped his shower hose for a stale bucket that collected flies every night.

He moved to stand close behind, watching the hands that had explored every inch of his body under the hot, quiet darkness, a hunger with no hint of shame. Outside, the bones of Miss Amina's porch were flaking under the lash of the wind. Two days ago he'd seen her beating dust from her favourite orange abaya as rheum streamed from her eyes. She'd brandished the fabric at Nick and Dr Ahmed as they passed, making futile jabs at the burning sky. 'She is right,' Dr Ahmed had said later. 'I cannot remember a worse season.'

Margaret glanced over her shoulder towards Nick, her smile almost shy. 'Is your mother a good English cook?' she asked. 'The kind who makes puddings for her little children and then beats them and sends them to bed?'

Nick stroked her back. 'Is that what English cooks do? Like African cooks roast their enemies for dinner?'

'Some people need roasting.' Margaret wiped her hands on her dress, leaving tear-like spots. 'I can teach your mother how.' She looked up at him, shafts of sunlight highlighting the smile-lines around her eyes and mouth. 'If I meet her one day.'

Nick's throat tightened. He imagined them together walking in his childhood garden, Margaret's fire infusing his mother's drowning spirit, a joyful coming to life.

'You'll meet her,' was all he could say in reply. She reached up to his face, her thumb wiping away imaginary tears. Nick caught it, smelling the musty sweetness on her skin, under dark tones of stagnant water. Madi had said the same thing once. 'I like talking to your mum,' he'd admonished Nick, in a moment of unguarded seriousness. 'She knows what you mean without asking anything.' All the things that made Nick pull away from his mother – the bewildered disorder of her clothes and hair, the sudden collapse of her sentences into yawning pauses, the times he'd walked into a silent room to find her motionless there, a sliver of emptiness – none of that had mattered to Madi. His own mother was a dark absence, a void they skirted around by unspoken agreement. No pictures hung on the brown walls of the council flat, no keepsakes were visible on the scratched cream of the coffee table donated by the Salvation Army – just the scuffed, frayed spines of Madi's father's books. 'She ran off when I was a baby,' Madi had said, in the early days. 'She had a boyfriend. But if she hadn't gone, maybe my father would never have taken the boat here. We'd have stayed. And then I'd never've met you.'

'Don't you have your big appointment in the Town today?' Margaret asked. She would sometimes step away from him, as if to remind herself she still could. 'It's already late.'

'Oh my God.' Remorse twisted in him. 'I was supposed to pick JoJo up from school. This ridiculous bloody inspection – I can't believe I forgot!'

'Then go,' she said. As he passed her, she grabbed his hand, bringing it to her lips.

He ran out into the yellowing garden. Even Nagode's tree had shrunk into skeletal faintness; its delicate fronds rattled with every lift and sway of the wind.

As he passed, something else called his attention – a presence or absence in the garden's shade. It broke into his haste, like a cold voice calling his name.

Under the half-shadow of Nagode's tree a pile of dirt lay in irregular pieces – part stone, part gravel, part sandy earth. A small stick had been snapped at its centre, fragments of bright cloth peeping out from the rubble.

JoJo's castle. One outer wall still stood and a couple of inner chambers. But the careful turrets, the stones that formed the support walls, the central tower that had taken a day to set in place – all lay scattered.

A terrible fear started to swell in Nick. *That slamming door.* But no, surely JoJo was still waiting for him at school? And why would he come in through the back door and not the front?

Nick pulled his keys from his office desk and hurried out to the Jeep, sweltering in the dead heat. He felt the grind of the gearbox as he turned the ignition, yellow dust trails blasting behind him as he sped past the mosque and down towards the village school.

But the gates were shut and the playground silent. A deep brown haze loomed over it – his father, leaning down from his desk with a thunderous face. JoJo was nowhere to be seen.

We are doing wrong. Nick leaned his head on the wheel, the heated rubber branding his skin. And these were the bitter consequences: distraction, lies, oblivious cruelty. *Bad deeds breed.* It had been one of the old man's favourite sayings. Nick had heard him utter it countless times – over the morning paper's latest iniquities, or to crush one of his son's feeble acts of rebellion.

It was too late to search for JoJo: the governor's inspection was imminent and Nick was running late. He headed out onto the northern highway, the tarmac a shimmering ribbon ahead. Dust flew in through the ancient air-conditioner, parching his throat. *Water, water everywhere, Nor any drop to drink.* His Jeep was a tiny white boat sailing over silent oceans just meters beneath.

He reached the site half an hour before the governor and his circus. Nick's men had worked through Christmas and New Year against a punishing schedule, trying to get the ground floor photo-shoot ready.

Eric stood under the scaffold of the gaping entrance, signing a docket for four huge crates. Generators, the governor had insisted on them, power thirsty, high-end imaging appliances. Nick had argued, 'The power drain will unbalance your whole system. Maintenance will cost a fortune. You'll have a show-piece, but no show.'

The governor smiled at this. 'Worry less and build faster,' he'd advised.

Eric waved to him from the container. 'You're fucking late,' he yelled over the fury of the drill. 'The boss will be here soon. And Tricky Dicky wanted to talk to you, but he fucked off home. Too much waity waity.' Tricky Dicky was Richard, the construction firm's boss and shiftless provider of cheap labour.

'I was writing reports,' Nick lied.

He gestured to a banner being unrolled over the bones of the clinic entrance, an oversized governor smiling down at a little girl in a white gown, her wheelchair sleekly state-of-the-art. In her lap she clutched a teddy bear; they both stared up at their benefactor, plump and admiring. Below, the crew was wreathed in yellow dust, scarves wrapped around their mouths, bloodshot eyes straining against the gritty air.

'It's inhuman to make them work today,' Nick muttered. 'I can barely breathe.'

'Yeah, well.' Eric spat on the ground. 'It's our big afternoon, isn't it? Not to mention completion on fucking schedule. With the weather like this we could be getting sandstorms right up to the rains. If there ever are any rains.'

'Sandstorms?' Nick imagined the heat rising in a cloudy fist, choking the last of the lake and the dying millet crops.

'You've not seen one of the really big buggers. We're not usually in line for them here, but this year who fucking knows?'

Nick shook his head. 'Can you come inside? I want to talk something through.'

The silent corridors were air-conditioning cool as Nick entered his office. He laid J.P.'s cash envelope on the table, counting out five thousand dollars: two for rental of the digging machines, one for the foreman and the rest to be spread among the crew, tens of dollars each. The little bundle of money looked pathetic, crumpled against the smooth grey of the desk.

'So,' Eric said, after they'd made their monthly tally. 'I hear J.P. gave your well the old heave-ho.'

So Eric and J.P. were talking on the side. 'And what else did J.P. say?'

'That maybe it's something to look at next dry season.'

'I'll be gone by then.' The fact hit him like a punch to the stomach, delivering its brutal reality-check.

'Good for you. I'm stuck here till I fucking die.'

'But how long would it take,' Nick persisted. 'From start to finish?'

'To put in a well?'

'Yes.'

'Near Dr Ahmed's place?' Eric pursed his lips. 'A couple of weeks for the permit, a few more to drill. You're not exactly talking top-of-the-range kit out here. Ramadan is coming at the end of March, finding workers then is like getting blood from a fucking stone.'

Ramadan lasted a month, Nick remembered. 'So it could be done in May? After Ramadan?'

'Better not to drill in the wet season. If the rains come, you're fucked. And if they don't come, then the whole place is fucked.'

The rains. 'So April would be the latest to finish the build.'

'Finishing in March would be better.'

'We're already mid-January. That's just a few weeks away.'

Eric frowned. 'This is theoretical, no?'

'Yes . . . I don't know.' Nick stood up, crossing to the window. 'They really need that water.' The air swirled thickly outside. He touched the hollow centre of his chest, where Margaret's breath had blended with the salt of his sweat.

Eric watched him, eyes narrowed. 'You ever hear that saying: "man cannot live by bread alone"? The same goes for water.'

Nick ignored him. The moving dust clouds were hypnotic, shadows ebbing and flowing across the sun. 'And how much would it cost?'

'For a medium-depth well, motorised with a good flow-rate? Around twenty thousand all-in. Good enough for drinking and cooking for maybe five hundred families.'

Nick turned to him. 'So if I gave you twenty thousand, could you do it? Organise it and supervise?'

Eric raised his eyebrows. 'Do you personally have twenty thou' spare to build a fucking well?'

'I might.' The legacy from his father had been little short of that. He'd put it into a fund, with some of Kate's money from her grandmother. They'd planned to build a house one day, designed by him, decorated by her.

A shout of alarm drifted through the haze. The throb of

189

engines slowed and stopped and voices began calling across the site. People were running towards an area blocked from Nick's view. One man unwrapped a scarf from his head; Nick saw it snatched frantically from his hand.

'There's been an accident,' he told Eric, in sudden certainty. They both ran for the door and out into the choking heat.

The worker who'd fallen from the first floor had landed by chance on a sand pile. He looked more ghost than human – thin and grey, his legs pale branches sticking from his cut-off jeans. His eyes blinked slowly, dazed and red under the cropped fuzz of his hair, his mouth making small, animated twitches like someone conversing with unseen forces.

Nick pushed through the crowds, the stench of ash and dry sweat filling his nostrils. 'Dry,' said a workman as he knelt down, patting himself on the head for emphasis. 'Too dry.'

'Where's water?' Nick demanded. Someone held a bottle to the man's lips. He did not swallow. 'Wait,' Nick said in frustration. 'You'll choke him.' He looked up at the hospital, incredulous. Had anyone gone to get a doctor?

More shouts – this time from the soldiers at the checkpoint. Nick looked behind to see the governor's car pulling up – a silent black Land Rover, followed by several others. The rear door swung open and the man himself emerged, his long robe trailing in the dirt. Other doors were opening; men darted forward holding cameras. Nick knew instantly who the governor's guests were. They moved with the slow assurance of wealth, pressing forward with dignified curiosity.

'What has happened here?' the governor asked Nick, without a word of greeting.

'He fell,' Nick said. Eric added, 'Dehydration. This weather's no good for afternoon working.'

The governor nodded. 'Where are my doctors?' No one replied. The governor roared out over the courtyard: 'Where are my doctors?'

The suited young men by his car jumped in alarm. One was sent running into the hospital. The governor knelt in the dust by the injured man, putting his hand on his forehead. Cameras snapped around them. He spoke quietly, and the man's eyes refocused, his lips pulling back in a rictus smile.

'This should not happen.' The governor spoke to Nick. 'You must take better precautions.'

Nick swallowed his fury. 'You told us to maintain our pace. You vetoed a morning-only schedule.'

'And now I am telling you to take better precautions,' the governor replied, getting to his feet as two white-coated orderlies and a doctor squeezed past.

He raised his voice. 'Go home,' he called to the filthy, sweating workmen. 'Now! Stop your work and go home. I will take care of him.' The command was shouted again in the local dialect, and a murmur rose from the crowd – cheering broken by coughing.

The governor turned to the men behind him. 'This is my right hand,' he told them, gesturing at Nick. 'He runs a tight ship.' Laughter and murmurs of approval broke out. 'But we must also take care of our sailors, eh?'

Nick was forced to shake hand after hand, feeling the moist fullness of the flesh, thanking them for coming, hearing the steady click of camera shutters.

'We will reschedule our event,' the governor said into Nick's ear, gripping his arm. Then, louder: 'When you are finished, join us inside for some refreshments.'

Nick watched as the governor herded his guests back towards the mansion, his clothes stained with dark patches of the workman's sweat. Fountain spray drifted towards the facade in white plumes, its coolness a slap to the face. His thoughts swarmed, binding to each other in a chain of dark connections: the charred fish staring eyelessly up at them from the governor's table; pus leaking from Adeya's burned hands as JoJo wept; JoJo sloping off with a bucket to the lake that killed his brother; Bako's cross in Margaret's garden, the blood-red beads on her wrist.

191

The dehydrated workman was on his feet now, arms slung over the orderlies' shoulders. Eric started laughing as they stumbled together towards the hospital entrance, the man's feet dragging in the dirt. 'Ah, the irony,' he said. 'The only way that unlucky bugger could ever dream of seeing the inside of the governor's hospital is nearly to break his fucking neck building it. Life is full of surprises.'

Nick smiled faintly in reply. And in a deep corner of his mind, a braver version of him wrapped his hands around the governor's thick throat and squeezed and squeezed until nothing was left of him but empty skin.

The sky to the west was reddening as Nick drove home. Eric's words bounced inside his mind like arcade pinballs, maddening him with repetition. *Twenty thousand spare to build a well.*

At last he could bear it no longer; he swung off-road before reaching the village, heading towards the sun's open mouth.

The lake emerged, barely an oily slick on the ground. He felt the mud become soft, sucking at his wheels. The open window in the cooling air, with its brilliant song of insects.

Water stretched out around him – the land's empty mirror to the sky. Old plastic bags clung to dried bushes, ripped on their thorns, fluttering in the wind like tattered flags.

Twenty thousand spare to build a well. His savings were a world away – intended for a future with Kate, to make rooms for their children to sleep in and gardens where they would dream of retirement.

But he'd set that future ablaze in Margaret's arms. And for the first time, he understood the fire might burn more than him.

I'm sorry. He saw Kate, standing at the airport, watching him leave. Her eyes locked on his, accusing. Blue numbers ran down her face from the announcement board overhead, counting down endless departures.

To get the money would mean more lies and betrayals. He'd given Kate power of attorney before leaving; now he'd have to talk her into liquidating their bonds and wiring the money to him. One part of his mind ran through schemes and scenarios while another cried out in protest. He felt dizzy, a compass needle spinning back and forth between two opposite poles of right, like the *tick tock* of Dr Ahmed's grandfather clock. But time was running out.

Nick's hands gripped the steering wheel, damp and slick against the worn rubber. The violence of his feelings frightened him – welling up from some deep pit within, a darkness he'd never known was there. *That ridiculous clock.* He could almost see it, right there in front of him in the growing dusk, its pendulum swinging sadly. What Dr Ahmed knew, or suspected, Nick did not dare to imagine. The old man was no fool. 'My husband may choose not to see,' Margaret had said. 'But his heart knows more than his eyes.'

What would Dr Ahmed do if he discovered the truth? Hunt them down and drive them out? *He doesn't really love her*, the dark inner voice urged. *He'd rather be a saint than make her happy.* But Dr Ahmed wasn't the only one he'd wronged. JoJo's broken castle loomed in Nick's memory, an icy question. Sunlight glinted off its scattered stones, bright as the diamond on Kate's ring finger. *If you do something wrong out of love, can it still be all wrong? Or does love make it a little bit right?*

Against the glare of sunset an old woman was wading through the plants, hair and face ash-white. Her robe was hitched up to her thighs over twisted, tree-stump legs. Behind her, the red curtain of the witch's hut flapped open.

Binza. Even at this distance she radiated a malevolent energy. It repulsed him; but he felt an eerie sense of confederacy, too – they were the last living things between the village and the void.

Binza picked her way into the watery mud, her waddling gait uneven. A bag dangled from her waist. Her lips opened as she bent to pluck things from the water, drooping like a voracious flower. Nick thought of Baba Yaga, the Russian witch in his mother's books, whose house chased children so that she could devour them in the forest's depths.

Something powerful stirred within him then, a righteous anger. *Margaret came to you for help, and you failed her too.* Binza was just another false prophet, her magic as hollow as the red beads that could not tie one little boy to life.

Then the witch stood and turned towards him.

Her eyes were grey as the lakewater, her gaze physically unpleasant like a cold hand reaching inside. *She's just an old woman. A lonely old woman.* Sun shone through the tangled strands of her thinning hair – her face like a spider's in a glowing web.

Hatred seized him – for her, for the malevolent land, for the callous forces that punished without reason, that conspired with greedy men to crush people's lives and plunder their hopes.

Sickened, he turned the ignition and put the Jeep into gear. The wheels bit deep into the ground. Binza faded from view, her eyes flashing once in the rear-view mirror before they were swallowed by the sun's glare.

He passed the empty millet fields and Adeya's house, its curtains drawn. Dr Ahmed's Ford was parked in front of the gate, the light on in his office window.

As Nick walked along the porch he heard the creak of the garden door as it opened. Margaret's back was to him as she walked down the steps with a bucket of black kitchen water, her form silhouetted against the dusk. Nagode was tied to her back in a dark scarf that flattened the swell of her breasts.

Need flooded him; he crept up behind her and felt the stiffening of her body as his arms slid under hers. Nagode breathed, warm and soft between them.

'Hush,' he whispered, as Margaret twisted around, eyes wide as they darted to the kitchen window. 'No one's there.'

Nagode reached out from behind her mother. 'Ni,' she crowed. Her face had thinned recently, high cheekbones emerging from its soft, round depths.

Margaret smiled in the darkness. 'No one except Nagode.'

Nick touched the small hands; they grasped his finger with youth's casual ferocity. 'Nagode won't tell,' he said. 'Will you?'

Margaret's mouth moved onto his; he smelled the bucket's odour – rot, mud, the richness of moisture.

'I was expecting you home before now,' she whispered. 'I waited for you.'

'I know.' He longed to promise a time when they would not have to wait, or hide – but the future seemed impenetrable, a sandstorm blocking the sun.

'Let me help you with that,' he said instead, taking the bucket from her. The liquid inside was too thick and filthy to be considered water even in these desperate times. She watched him pour it out onto the soil.

'Tomorrow JoJo will have to get more.' Her hand reached behind to touch Nagode's foot – a compulsive reassurance. 'This drought is even worse than the last.'

'I'll get more if you need it,' he said. 'We could go to the lake together.' They'd found a dip behind one of the rocks out by the water's edge, where only the sky could see them.

He saw her blush with understanding. 'So noble,' she teased. 'Is there no more challenging quest for this knight to prove his faith?'

'Try me,' he said, in deadly earnest.

After Margaret had returned to the house, Nick unlocked his office door.

A kerosene stench lay heavy in the air. He flipped the generator's ignition and sat back, the whine of the turning engine lacing the room with petrol-fumed light. The radio was a hulking black presence, one red button blinking on and off like a warning.

Nick knelt to open the safe. The code was Madi's birthday.

Inside, the remainder of J.P.'s cash lay in neat bundles.

Twenty thousand spare to build a well. He pulled out the bundles one by one, stacking them on the desk.

That last glance of Binza's face in his rear-view mirror

returned as he counted them, her expression twisting to some-thing like laughter.

Let her laugh. *Twenty thousand spare to build a well.* The money lay under the flickering light. To Nick, it looked like the only green thing left in a dying world.

I hide in the reeds, where Nicholas cannot see me. I watch him where he waits, in his car. We are so close I could hit him from here. I reach down to take a stone in my hand, hot from the sun. I could throw it. I threw my shoe to break the school window. I was just a boy then. Now I am a man. Now Nicholas is the glass, and I am the stone.

If he sees me, he will tell me more lies. Lies about going to England. Lies about how I am clever. He will tell me we are friends. Lies and more lies, so that so I cannot hear the truth.

But I hear. I hear him start the engine and drive away from the lake. And the stone is still here, in my hand. I feel a pain, a sharp pain. But men do not cry.

The pain is everywhere, like the sky. The voice in my head says: 'Stupid, stupid JoJo.' Maybe this is the reason. Maybe this is why he did not want me.

I still have my schoolbag. Nicholas' workbook is in it. I can smell vomit on it. I was sick before, from crying. I came to the lake, to wash the vomit away. But the smell is still with me. I think it will never leave.

The pages are open. So much time I spent with Nicholas, making these lines and these angles. I did not play football with Akim, I did not go to Tuesday's shop and read those magazines. I stayed with you, Nicholas.

I close the book in my hand. Nicholas, you are a liar. You will never take me to England. You will steal Mama from me and take her instead. Baba will let you, because he is weak. So I must be a man. You will see.

I throw the book as far as I can. It lands in the water. There is not enough water to make a splash. I can still see the corner of the book. It stands up in the mud.

'Eh, boy.'

She makes me jump. I did not know she was so close. She has no teeth in her mouth. Her legs are white and brown, like a disease.

'Get away from me,' I say to Binza. I hold up the stone. 'Get back.'

She starts to laugh. It is not a real laugh. Nicholas has a real laugh. He puts back his head and he laughs from deep down. Binza makes a dry sound – like ah, ah, ah.

She says: 'Eh, boy. Be careful with your step here. Do not disturb the spirits.'

'There are no spirits,' I tell her.

She looks out to the water. 'There are so many spirits,' she says. 'So many.'

Her voice is sad. Her eyes are white like her hair. There is white spit on her lips.

'They come to drink,' she says. 'The dead are always thirsty. Listen! You can hear them.'

She puts her hand to her ear. But I hear nothing. Just the mosquitoes. They whine like Nagode. And the wind, too, it hisses. Together they make a song. There are no words to it. But it makes me sad, and I feel I will cry again.

Binza says: 'See, boy. You hear them too.'

I tell her: 'The dead go to Paradise. This is what the Qu'ran says.'

Binza makes another laughing noise. 'There is no Paradise,' she says. 'They are waiting for us here. They wait for us to join them.'

'Imam Abdi would put you in prison,' I warn her. 'You are speaking against God.'

Binza opens her arms. She has a bag tied to her clothes. It moves. I do not want to see what is inside it. She says: 'The fools will come to me. Their spirits will drink here, too.'

I can still hear them whispering. Like Mama singing to me and Bako, when we slept in the same bed. 'Hush,' she would tell us, if we would not quiet. 'Hush.' The spirits say it too. 'Hush.' They hiss in my ears.

Now I am crying. I cannot stop. I wipe my eyes, but more tears come. I ask her: 'Does Bako come? Does he wait for me?'

She does not answer. She is looking behind me. She makes a hissing noise, like the spirits.

I turn.

He is there. White, the same as her. I can feel the stone in my hand. It is cold now, cold and hard.

'JoJo,' he says. 'You came to find me.'

When I saw Mister the first time, I feared him. Now it is different. I can taste the fear but I cannot feel it. The fear is far away, on the other side of the lake.

'You come here at night,' I say to him.

Mister, he nods. He says: 'What do you want with me, JoJo? What does the doctor's son want?'

I cannot answer him. I do not know. I want to tell him what I saw in the kitchen, with Nicholas and Mama. I want to tell him about the lies and about England. I want to tell him about Baba, how the love went out of him when Bako died. I want to tell him about Bako, about how he comes to drink at the lake and wait for me because I wished he would die when Mama loved him best.

But I say nothing. I look down to the ground, to the mud and the water.

Mister, he walks to me. He takes my hand with the stone inside it. And with the other hand he takes the stone.

He says: 'A stone is for children, JoJo. A stone is for games. You are becoming a man now.'

Binza, she shouts. 'Leave him!' Her voice is like a frog. It croaks. 'Let him be!'

Mister looks at her. 'Go,' he says. His voice is gentle, but Binza, she crouches down like a dog. 'Go,' he says. 'I will come soon.'

Her mouth, it moves. But she does not speak. She turns her back to us and starts to move away, like a shadow.

'Who is she to you?' I ask Mister. He looks after her as she goes.

He smells of oil and metal. But I think he looks smaller than before. He looks sad, like me.

'She is my mother,' he says.

I cannot believe him. I remember what he told me – that his mother had sinned with another man and this is why no one would save her. I thought his mother must be beautiful, more beautiful even than Mama.

I say: 'She is too old. How can she be your mother?'

Mister's voice is different when he answers. It is quiet like Adeya's.

'She did not look so old when she birthed me,' he says. 'Or when they drove her to this place from the Town. They beat her and called her whore and witch and made her naked on the ground. I was small, but I remember. It is the curse that turns her skin white and makes her grow old too fast. I have the same curse.'

He holds out his white arms, with the pink patches where the sun has burned him.

'Touch them,' he says to me. 'Do not be afraid.'

I reach out my hand. The burned places, they feel smooth. Soft and hard at the same time. I look up at his face. I ask: 'Does it hurt?'

Mister, he smiles at me. 'I do not feel them,' he says. 'The pain has gone. I turned it into my strength. It was the only way for me.'

He drops my stone on the ground. I watch as the mud takes it in.

He says: 'You still feel the pain, JoJo. I understand you. I was also betrayed. My true father left us to the dogs. But the dogs will take him too one day. He thinks he is strong and safe in his big house. But I grew stronger than him, stronger than this curse, stronger than every dog in this place.'

Mister clenches his fists as he speaks. He breathes fast, like Bako when the fever came. The pink scars stand up on his arm, like snakes.

'You said I was too weak for The Boys,' I tell him. 'My father is weak. My brother died.'

'It was a test,' he says. 'Look at me, eh? You think I am the lucky one? You had a brother. You have a father. I have no one. Just The Boys. Just you.'

I want to take his hand, to touch where the pink scars finish. I want to call him my brother, because I also have no one. But maybe Bako is here, still thirsty. Maybe he hears us.

Mister opens his hands. On his palms, the pink marks have turned red.

'I was not born strong, JoJo,' he says. 'I learned. I can teach you, too. If you are ready.'

The sun has set and the spirits are quiet. There is nothing around us, just the whiteness of his face.

'Teach me,' I tell him.

FEBRUARY

They brought a new rig to the well's deepening hole on the last day of February, after hitting water-bearing rock at fifty metres.

The drill site was marked with a ring of orange flags – cut from Miss Amina's old abaya. Nick had supervised while Adeya tied them onto sticks and planted them carefully in the earth. Water cycled in and out of the depths from two pools of black slurry, lidded by mud walls.

Eric's crew was racing to finish before the end of March brought the holy fast of Ramadan. Over three weeks, sand had given way to dark clays, broken stones and now this fractured, forbidding granite. Eric's inexperienced operator had battered his ancient rig against it – until it gave up in a strangled grind of metal.

It was another expense to add to a lengthening list. The new surveys had provided the first hiccup. Instead of confirming a good water yield at thirty metres, they projected having to drill down to the aquifer at almost three times that depth – a six-week process. Nick was horrified when the surveyor broke the news. Eric shrugged. 'The best-laid plans,' he answered. 'That's what you get for doing things on the fucking sly.'

In the end, J.P.'s twenty thousand dollars had been all too easy to take. By the time Nick handed it to Eric, it didn't even feel like theft. It was only a loan, he reasoned; he would repay it from his father's inheritance as soon as Kate could liquidate their bonds. His father would have wanted such a memorial. For the first time in his life Nick found himself yearning for some way to bridge the gulf between the living and the dead, so he could find the old man and tell him.

He'd steeled himself to write to Kate, faxing a message to her office via Eric. The first attempt to speak to her over Dr Ahmed's hissing landline had failed, understanding possible only in fragments. She seemed to hear that he needed more money for something very important; he learned that a new business pitch at her office meant delaying his visit home until after March. Even her voice sounded unreal – made of static and echoes rather than human warmth.

His letter repeated much of what she already knew about the village and the drought, layering grief already felt here with fear of worse to come. He softened J.P.'s position on the well with half-truths, blaming bureaucratic delays for the funding shortfall, implying that their money might be repaid in the future. He fought back against his conscience as he wrote; the stakes were too high. He finished by telling her to cash in his bonds and wire the money to him as soon as possible. He couldn't bring himself to read the final version.

Afterwards, he'd gone to find Margaret. JoJo was at school and Dr Ahmed due back from his monthly clinic at the market. She'd been in the bedroom, rubbing a laughing Nagode with a damp cloth. 'Take her to Hanan and meet me by the lake,' he'd said. And he'd waited there, watching Margaret pick her careful way through the reeds, her scarf streaming skywards. She'd grasped his hands as she reached him, recklessness in her fingers as she pulled him into the concealed hollow on the desert-facing side of a rocky hillock. Her abaya rode up above her legs as he pressed her into the dirt, cradling them as they moved on top of her outspread scarf, only dust and the sky as witness.

Afterwards he'd put her palm to the earth as he explained his grand design to her. She'd pressed it flat, as if feeling a heartbeat. 'So much water,' she'd whispered. 'So close.'

'It's what my father would have wanted me to do,' he'd said. 'Something that matters.'

The earth in her fingertips had been dry and light as she sat up and sprinkled it on his chest, a light wind playing with the knots of her hair, drops of moisture beading a channel between her breasts. 'So this is for him?'

'No, it's a present for you,' he'd answered, only half-teasing as he stroked the contours of her cheeks and lips. 'You asked me to prove myself.'

That had startled her. 'I'm not your judge, Nicholas.' Her hand had pressed into his heart, gritty with dirt, the skin of her neck and shoulders darkly flushed, her shadow warm as it fell over him. 'We left judgements behind us.'

'You're the only judge who matters to me,' he replied. And as he pulled her to the ground a song from childhood played in the back of his mind – a psalm of David they'd taught him in the chapel choir. *My soul thirsts for you, my flesh yearns for you, in a dry and weary land.*

Eric had also been a willing accomplice – raising no more than an eyebrow when Nick proposed his scheme. 'Are you going to tell J.P.?' Nick had asked then.

The friendly blue eyes had turned impenetrable. 'Is there a reason I shouldn't?'

'Everything else goes on as normal,' Nick reassured him. The pace of construction on the hospital had slowed under the new 'mornings only' work policy, giving him a month or two's grace to replenish J.P.'s funds.

Eric looked away, rubbing the bristles on his face. Turning back to Nick, he jabbed a large, accusing finger. 'You're a fucking idiot, you know?'

'I know,' Nick said, relieved. 'Thank you.'

The permit to drill had been the biggest hurdle. How could they get a permit for what the governor himself had forbidden?

In the end, help had come from an unexpected quarter – Mr Kamil's friend Danjuma.

It began with an unexpected invitation to dinner. Nick had arrived at Mr Kamil's bungalow to the fading sounds of Imam

Abdi's muezzin call. Aisha Kamil's house had carpets and cheap chandeliers where Margaret had only tiles and bare bulbs. She'd sat in purple silks, Juma and Akim in sullen attendance beside her, clicking her fingers to hurry Hanan who'd cooked the meal and was now dutifully spooning it into guests' plates. The maid looked harassed as she passed Nick, her round face squeezed into the severe black ring of her abaya. Dr Ahmed was at the table's other end; he murmured thanks as she reached him, before scooping up his rice in a slow, methodical forkful. The prayer hummed through walls lit gold by the evening, a song now so familiar – the Magrib, sung at the sun's death.

Nick had tried to persuade JoJo to come, too; but the boy had refused. His interest in coming to the Town with Nick had nosedived since their return from the capital. He claimed to have joined a school club that made him late most evenings, studying the Qu'ran with Akim. Dr Ahmed accepted this with his usual air of genial distraction, busier than ever with his drought-afflicted patients. Nick had been more perplexed. 'If that's what you want,' he'd told JoJo with a smile, a clumsy attempt to recapture the old warmth. 'Although in my opinion there's more to learn from algebra than from hadiths.' To his horror he sounded just like his own father.

JoJo had responded with a blank, teenage shrug. It hurt Nick and troubled him; he sensed deception there – but while deceiving so many people himself, he had no courage to enquire.

Dinner at Mr Kamil's was soured yogurt and dried yellow dates, followed by one of Jalloh's last goats flavoured with groundnuts. Tuesday brought his few remaining cans of Fanta. 'Maybe next month I will have more,' he said without conviction, pouring a trickle of blood-temperature liquid into each glass. Its sweetness revived Nick. The choking heat of the hospital site had threaded weakness through him, making the world feel shaky and unsure.

Mr Kamil raised his Fanta glass to Nick. 'I hear,' he said, 'that you plan to give us a Ramadan gift.'

Confusion must have shown on Nick's face, for Mr Kamil

laughed. 'Forgive me,' he said. 'A bad joke. I mean – this well you are donating to us. If it can be finished before Ramadan, then many of our problems will be solved.'

Nick was only mildly surprised by Mr Kamil's knowledge of what should still have been a secret. The only visible sign of the well so far was a pole marking the drill-site on the village outskirts, within sight of Binza's shack. He had been waiting for Eric to produce the drilling permit before announcing the project formally to the village council.

'Who told you?' Nick kept his voice low. He was aware of Dr Ahmed's attention, a forkful of stringy meat pausing on its way to his lips.

'We heard you need a drilling permit.' Mr Kamil eased himself back into his chair, his belly rising in his seat. 'Most of these officials are the governor's men, bought and paid for. Mr Eric, he is very right to be careful.'

'Most,' said Nick. 'But not all?'

Mr Kamil grinned. 'Yes, not all. Some are already our friends. They are supporting Danjuma – and Danjuma wants to help you.'

'That's kind of him.' He vaguely remembered the man at the council meeting – plump skin and smooth words.

'I am serious, Nicholas,' Mr Kamil said, his voice falling. 'This is a good initiative and Danjuma supports it. I trust Danjuma, truly. So I hope you will soon have news.'

Mr Kamil was as good as his word. Eric returned from the Town two days later with a permit and a rig. Speed was important, he said, and a certain amount of discretion. Nick laughed at that, despite his anxieties. 'How can you be discreet with a massive drill?'

Slowly, the great machine pounded its way through the earth. Children came after school to watch, wide-eyed and eager-fingered. Wonder drew them in as the ground split under the assault. They scrambled around the slurry pools' treacherous walls to peer into their unreflective depths. The rig operator was often forced to leap from the cabin, shooing them away from danger.

Adeya was often among them, her wounded hands hidden under the lumpy folds of her dress. During a quiet moment, Nick lifted her into the drill cabin, feeling the lightness of a body that took up so little of this land's endless space. Her hands emerged from under her abaya, stiff with ugly ridges of scar tissue. She reached out towards the dials, her face transforming with an almost religious awe.

'It is like an animal,' she said to Nick. 'It is alive like us.'

Her dignified amazement touched his heart. 'Would you like to learn how one of these works?' he asked. 'You could be an engineer when you grow up.'

At this, her face clouded over. 'Yes,' she said, dropping her gaze. Stupid, he berated himself. Blind, cruel. How could Adeya with her damaged bowels and burned hands ever learn how to be an engineer? *There's no justice in this world.* As the drill kicked back to life, he imagined the heavy cable smashing through the chains that weighed her down, breaking through into unseen possibilities.

The collapse of the rig could have been a disaster but Eric was on hand again. A new team arrived, 'borrowing' another from one of Eric's friends working near the capital. A surprise guest came with them – Danjuma himself.

He arrived in a black car, stirring great blasts of dust into the already over-charged air. Nick saw Mr Kamil and Imam Abdi hurrying towards it, a small crowd coiling behind them.

Danjuma was easy to pick out – a head taller than Nick, barrel-chested under his Western suit, skin shining through the dirt-clogged air. Mr Kamil and Imam Abdi clasped hands with him, leading him over to Nick.

'Well, sir.' Danjuma removed his sunglasses and waved to encompass the new rig, the cement mixer and the crowd. 'You are doing great things, I see.'

Nick mustered a smile in return. There was something about Danjuma, a glossy hunger, that raised his hackles.

'Nice to see you again, too,' he replied.

Danjuma laughed and turned to Mr Kamil. 'Only the English use this word. Nice. I like it. Neither this nor that.'

The other men from Danjuma's car were moving among the crowd, distributing leaflets. Nick saw a flash of the broad smiling face on the front page.

Mr Kamil said, 'Danjuma wanted to see your progress.'

Eric had insisted no one learn of Danjuma's hand in the drill permit. 'Worse than a slap in the face *and* a kick in the balls,' he'd warned.

Nick had no trouble agreeing; he would much rather forget about the politician altogether. He remembered Dr Ahmed's fork stopping mid-air at dinner; it brought back that old feeling of foreboding – of consequences sweeping towards him.

'Welcome to the site, Mr Danjuma,' he said. 'We're about to start pounding again, as you can see.'

'Ah, yes,' said Danjuma. 'You had some delays, I hear.'

'This is the most difficult part,' Nick explained. 'These hard rocks are weathered – they have cracks, through which the aquifer can flow. But they're tough, and the rigs here are pretty old. They can't cope if the rock is really stubborn.'

'I see.' Danjuma's expression was alight with interest. 'I am sorry for our stubborn rocks. And the people are more stubborn than the rocks!' Laughter spread from Mr Kamil and Imam Abdi in a human wave.

A group of boys hovered beside the drill rig. Nick recognised Juma and Akim. The tallest among them was an albino, his skin shockingly white against the red of the cabin. A young man stood next to him; alarmed, Nick realised it was JoJo. But this was not the JoJo he thought he knew – not the eager boy with his home-made mortar and book of sketches. This was someone else: a young adult, deep in watchful silence.

What changed, JoJo? Nick wanted to ask him. *Where did you go?* But the questions felt dishonest. He knew what had changed: he could still feel the boy's arms, tight around him in the garden, where the castle now lay broken. Now, between Margaret and the well, he barely had time to do more than wave him hello when they passed in Dr Ahmed's corridors. When he'd asked JoJo about the broken castle, the boy had refused to meet Nick's eyes. 'Akim did it,' he'd claimed. 'It was an accident.' Nick's planned reassurances had withered inside him, noticing how narrow JoJo's face had grown, how sharp – as if all his possibilities were converging in a single direction. He'd offered to help fix it, but the boy had shaken his head. 'I am busy today,' he'd replied, already halfway out of the door.

One day, Nick thought, *I'll be able to explain everything, and you'll understand.* The well was for JoJo, too – a more substantial gift than empty promises about his future, which no earthly power could fulfill.

Nick waved him over. The boy made no move at first. But then his albino friend nudged him. So he came, in a slow saunter. The others followed. Only the older boy was smiling, pale eyes alight like a wild animal's.

'Hey.' Nick put his hand on JoJo's shoulder as they reached him. The boy tilted his head to look at it. 'Do you know what that man's doing there?'

He pointed over to where the engineers had finished fitting the sleek new drill hammer to the cable. The mouth of the hole was open; JoJo's eyes followed the drill as it vanished inside.

'It will break the rocks,' the albino said. 'You need to force them away.'

'That's right.' Nick turned to look at the strange boy – or man? He seemed almost ageless – those disturbing eyes, the smooth skin. But that wounded pink flesh was so vulnerable – like a baby's just emerged from the womb.

'Who's your friend?' he asked JoJo.

JoJo looked up at Nick. His every gesture seemed unnaturally slow, his eyes empty of expression. Nick stifled the urge to feel his forehead, as Dr Ahmed had done on that very first evening.

Eventually JoJo spoke. 'He's called Mister. He works with Juma.'

Nick extended his hand. 'I'm pleased to meet you, Mister. We haven't met before, have we?'

Mister's grasp was warm. He met Nick's eyes with composure.

'No, you did not see me, boss,' he said. His English was fluid, although heavily accented. He pointed towards the rig operator. 'I know this work. Once I worked with the same.'

'With drilling?'

'Yes, boss.'

Nick looked back at JoJo's group of friends. They were lined up, like a scout group. Mister put his hand on JoJo's other shoulder, a gesture that matched Nick's. 'Will you let us start the drilling, boss? I can do it, easy.'

Nick shook his head. 'No, I'm sorry.'

Mister was not discouraged. 'Ask him.' He jerked his head towards the rig operator, who was looking their way. 'He knows me. He will let us.'

Nick hesitated, then met JoJo's eyes. *Fine.*

He walked over to the operator. 'Can these boys help you?' he asked. The man shrugged.

'OK,' he said.

Nick called back to JoJo, 'You can come.'

Out of the corner of his eye he saw one of Danjuma's men pulling a loudspeaker out of the car. Another was setting a small podium down in the dirt.

JoJo came with Mister, climbing up the rig's side. Eric kept the crowd well back. Danjuma himself had stepped up onto his makeshift podium, flanked by Mr Kamil and Imam Abdi.

Mister turned to Nick. 'Thank you for this, boss.' The boy's hair was gilded by the brutal sun; he resembled some ancient magician or god. 'The next time, *I* will help *you*. If you find more rocks in your way.'

The operator called out to Eric, who gave the thumbs up. Silence rolled outwards from him; the air stilled like an in-drawn breath.

And then JoJo's hands moved, guided but assured. He gripped the ignition lever, pushing with all the force in his young body.

The noise was as powerful as a blast, a roar of tortured rock racing through them in a pressure wave. Above it, Nick heard the clamour of the loudspeaker – Danjuma's voice booming above chaos.

He knew he should be listening, but a part of him was still mesmerised by the hammer's fury, the sense of powerful forces set in motion. Small details commanded his attention: the black smoke drifting from the generator towards Binza's shack, JoJo's hand resting on the rig level and Mister leaning in behind him. They looked back towards him, and the light in their eyes reflected the engine's shimmering heat.

After the drilling, we meet behind Tuesday's shop. Mister told me: 'I know all of Tuesday's secrets. I know the women he goes with. I know the things he brings here. So Tuesday will never speak of what we do. He knows if I tell, they will kill him.'

Tuesday gives things to Mister, to keep him happy. One of the things is the bang powder. It is white, like flour for bread. Akim calls it bang powder because it makes you run like a bullet. Mister puts it into cigarettes for us to smoke. The first time I said to him: 'I don't smoke. It's bad for your health.' Because this is what Baba always told me. He said: 'For God's sake don't take up this habit, Yahya, or it will kill you as sure as the sun rises.'

Mister, he put the bang cigarette down on the barrel. He had made one cigarette for each one of us. I was drinking cola. I remember it tasted sweet.

Mister said to me: 'Your baba is right, JoJo. This one will kill you. It will put a fire in your chest and in your heart. It will burn the weakness from you. And you may die, too, it's true.'

Then he told us about a country where they take the bravest boys, the best ones, and make them into fighters. These boys dressed only in white, he said, like the bodies of the dead, to show they were not afraid to die. He said: 'This way they were more powerful than other men. They had power like the spirits have.'

He makes me think of Bako – of the thirsty spirits at the lake, drinking with Binza. Or of the sounds Nicholas and Mama made in the kitchen together. And I thought: I want to feel this power. So I took the bang cigarette. We smoked them, and I felt the fire inside me. But later I was sick and so tired. My skin felt like ants bit me and I could not scratch them off.

Every day we smoke like this. Most days I do not go to school. Mister, he trains us. We have to climb walls into houses and not be seen. We have to take things from the market, like cassettes or shoes. We have to fight each other, to test our strength. Because I am the newest one, I watch. But when the smoke is in me, I want to fight. Mister made Akim fight Juma. He gave Akim the smoke and he gave Juma none. Akim beat him, and Juma was shamed to be beaten by his small brother. But Mister, he laughed. He said, 'We are all brothers here.'

Today behind Tuesday's shop, I ask Mister to let me smoke. 'Later,' he says. 'We have to wait for our guest.'

My head, it aches. It aches all the time. Sometimes I think I see Baba looking at me. If I told him my secret, would he kill Nicholas? If I was a man, I would take the knife myself. When I smoke, I feel like I could do it. In my head sometimes I fight him. But sometimes I ask him to take me with him when they go. And we run and we run and we do not come back.

Then Mister stands up. He says: 'Quiet, all of you.'

And a man comes in.

Danjuma carries a big bag on his shoulder. He is not so big as the governor. But he is young. He looks around us and says: 'A salaam ou aleikum. It is my honour to meet our soldiers.'

'We are not soldiers,' Akim says. 'We don't take orders from the Town.'

Danjuma laughs and Mister, too. Mister says to Danjuma: 'My men are still learning many things, boss.'

Danjuma nods his head, with a big smile. He says: 'You are soldiers, eh? Your uniform is inside you, hidden.'

Mister, he says: 'My men are ready for you, Danjuma.' And Danjuma, he looks at us. He asks us: 'Do you know what is coming?'

Juma and Akim and the other boys, they say nothing. But I have been listening. I know what Danjuma wants. So I say: 'The elections are coming.'

He looks at me. His eyes, they are thirsty, like the spirits. He says: 'What do you wear on your head?'

I put my hand to my head. There is the governor's cap. I take it off and look at it. I can see the letters, big and red. And the bear's mouth is red, too.

Danjuma asks me: 'Who gave that to you?'

I do not fear Danjuma. I say: 'The governor.'

He asks: 'And what do you think of the governor?'

I try to remember him, his voice, his watch. He smiled like a man who is never afraid.

I say to Danjuma: 'He has power and we are weak.'

Danjuma says: 'You are a wise fellow. But soon we will not be weak. With help from you, if it's God's will.'

He lifts up the bag and puts it on the barrel. He says to Mister: 'Open it.'

Mister reaches his hand inside. What comes out is black against his white skin, long and black. It is a gun. There are others inside. Some are long and thin. Some are small and fat.

Mister, he takes one of the small ones. He puts it in his belt, beside the knife. The other Boys, they come round the bag. They all want one. But Mister says: 'Wait.' He looks to Danjuma.

'You will not wait long,' Danjuma says. 'But we need more money for his private guard. His two captains are the key. They can bring their loyal men. But they ask a high price to join us. If you can find some means for them, then tell me. Maybe this

well-builder. He pays his workers in dollars, American dollars. Where does he keep those dollars?'

Mister says: 'I will find out, boss.' Danjuma is not afraid of Mister. I do not know which one should fear the other.

Then Danjuma looks at me. I have not come to the bag. I am thinking about the drill today. I felt so strong, like the power came from my hands. But we only broke stone. I look at the gun in Mister's belt. I think: how does it feel to break a man? To send a bullet into him and break him?

Danjuma, he asks me: 'What about you, soldier?'

I do not know how to answer him. I look at the cap in my hands. Danjuma leans over and takes it. He puts it back on my head. He says: 'Maybe you will give this back to the governor. Maybe very soon.'

Margaret served a family meal that night to celebrate the well's renewed progress. Nick sat on the porch while she prepared, watching the sun's slow fall. The sky was pregnant with dust, dark seeds scattered across a garden blooming with violet, orange and pink.

This was Nick's favourite time of the day. The soft bray of goats floated over the flap of Miss Amina's fan and the early flutter of moths. He heard Margaret singing, the melody familiar as a hymn. A trick of the moving air lifted her voice from the window, an envoy heading into the night.

Quiet bliss filled his body as he listened, a peace so deep it was almost sleep. Margaret's voice, the distant desert birds, the mosque incantation as the first generators lit with their deep hum – they wove through him and each other, merging and falling apart, until it seemed the desert itself was singing.

Dr Ahmed appeared, a long shadow in the doorway. 'Dinner is served.' The electric light drew tired lines on his face. 'Margaret has made us a good supper.'

Their little table was set with red yams, heavy green spinach and pieces of flat bread, surrounded by a bowl of buttermilk and some sweet dates. Each bowl looked half-full – scant rations for four hungry mouths.

Dr Ahmed would have given Nick the biggest portion, but he held back – blaming a sore stomach. An old can of Fanta was waiting for him in the office. There was no meat at the table these days. Nick suspected that all of Dr Ahmed's spare money was going elsewhere – paying for Miss Amina's medicine and extra water for Hanan.

JoJo sat silently at one end of the table, Dr Ahmed at the other. Nick and Margaret faced each other across its centre. Nagode sat on her mother's knee, seizing pieces of buttermilk-dipped bread with eager fingers and mashing them into her mouth. She held one piece up to her mother; Margaret bent to take it in her mouth, gently biting Nagode's fingers and causing the little girl to crow with glee.

Dr Ahmed laughed with her. 'She will make you fat, Margaret,' he said. Nagode's black eyes turned to fix on her father's plate. To Nick, her skin seemed the same the rich walnut as the grand-father clock.

'Eh, daughter!' Dr Ahmed made a big show of guarding his food with his hands. 'Eat your own. Don't be stealing mine. This is not a good start.'

'She's learning one of the basic lessons of life,' Nick said. 'Always try for as much as you can get.'

Dr Ahmed nodded, looking rueful. 'These lessons are not set in stone, though. They are not God's holy Commandments.' He glanced at his wife, with the half-smile that usually accompanied any acknowledgement of her birth faith. Warmth softened Margaret's face at the small kindness. She reached across the table, touching his hand with hers.

'No, indeed they are not,' she said to him.

Nick felt a twist of jealousy. She's his wife, he reminded himself. And she'll be his wife as long as I stay here, unless I can set her free somehow. He knew absolutely that Margaret loved him. She had told him – if not with her words then with her eyes and hands and body. Their relationship was a private church in which he could unbutton her dress under the dim light of his locked office, feel her heart beating through her palms and breasts, and still feel pure.

Looking for a change of subject, he turned to JoJo. 'Did you enjoy the drilling today? It's more powerful than you think it's going to be.'

JoJo's eyes were on his parents' joined hands. Nick saw him look at his mother, his expression blank – almost cold. Then he nodded. 'It was good. I liked it.'

'Who is your friend? A new one, or just someone I never met before?'

JoJo bent over his plate, eyes fixed on the wall. 'He is a new friend.'

'How did you meet him?'

JoJo looked at Nick, a slow, considering gaze. To Nick's surprise, he didn't answer. Dr Ahmed cleared his throat and said, 'Yahya, rudeness is not allowed at this table.'

'It's OK.' Despite his resolution at the drill site, Nick found he didn't want a confrontation with JoJo. 'It's not my business.' JoJo gave a thin smile.

'Who are these new friends, JoJo?' Now Dr Ahmed was using his most unhelpful, authoritarian tone. Nick willed him to let it drop, but the old man continued, oblivious. 'This club with Akim is taking too much of your time. Who joins you there?'

'Don't worry about it, Baba,' JoJo replied, voice calm.

Dr Ahmed shook his head. 'That is the answer of a boy, not a man. You are thirteen this month.' He turned to address Nick. 'In cultures like this one, children must become adults very young. Resources are scarce and life depends on our wise use of them. Children must learn judgement and reason quickly. The great religions came from the desert – this is no coincidence. The Jews were first. They mark the thirteenth year with a special ceremony.'

'The bar mitzvah,' Nick said, automatically.

'Yes, this one,' the doctor said, shaking a fork in JoJo's direction. 'It means "son of the law" in the Hebrew tongue. It means a boy of thirteen can no longer hide behind the excuse that he is young. He must account to God for all his actions.'

JoJo's eyes were locked on his plate. Nick thought of the impulsive boy he'd first met – who would still run to his mother for comfort, who'd dreamed of driving a Jaguar and designing his own buildings. *Growing up kills something inside us.* He tried to remember his own adolescence, which began in a haze of grief and guilt. The knife that pierced Madi had killed him, too – or the person he was becoming.

'Happy birthday, JoJo,' he said. 'For whenever it is.' JoJo's head came up; Nick saw lines hardening across his face, sensed some inner strain, as if powerful forces were wrestling within him. He had a sudden rush of pity – for JoJo, for his own thirteen-year-old self, for all children caught as life's tide unexpectedly turns, sent surging out on journeys they'd never imagined.

'One of JoJo's friends has albinism,' he said, trying to change the subject. 'Does he get a hard time here or do people accept him?'

To his relief, the question distracted Dr Ahmed. 'Sadly, it's true,' he said. 'We are a superstitious people underneath our pieties. A lady hereabouts also has this condition. They call her "witch". They have called her this for so long that she believes it herself.'

'Binza.' Nick felt something in the room grow taut as he spoke her name. Margaret's eyes flickered up to meet his.

'It means witch in our local tongue,' Dr Ahmed explained. 'But I knew her before, when she was just a girl in this village, who never played with the rest of us or went to school. Children can be too cruel. Superstition drove her away to the Town, but she did not prosper there either. She married one of the governor's bodyguards. But later I heard he accused her of witchcraft. He said she had seduced his patron and that their young son was not his blood.'

'Binza had an affair with the governor?' Nick was astonished.

'These were only rumours.' Dr Ahmed sounded sad. 'Albinos are so easily accused and not easily defended. All I know is that she returned here beaten and bloody. The child she'd birthed – he was not with her. I don't know what happened to him. But from then on she embraced this name: witch. She would not accept any help from me.' He shook his head. 'Progress is very slow, painfully slow.'

'This Danjuma seems all for progress,' Nick said.

'They are all the same as each other,' Margaret said, as Nagode tried to climb on to the table. 'None have a drop of goodness in them.'

She so rarely expressed her opinion on politics that Nick was surprised. She was looking at JoJo, he saw; JoJo just stared at the floor.

Dr Ahmed spoke slowly. 'My wife is right. There is no goodness in that man, no more than in the governor he hates so much. Hate is the first sign. Nothing good was ever built from hate.'

They cleared the table. JoJo went to his room while Margaret washed up, Nagode at her feet. By now Dr Ahmed would usually be in the living room, reading or fiddling with the clock's mechanism. But today he procrastinated, lingering in the kitchen. When Nick finally headed out to his office, Dr Ahmed followed him onto the porch.

Generators were churning the hot darkness, a faint glow on the western horizon all that remained of the sunset. Dr Ahmed leaned on the porch's wooden strut, looking out over empty miles.

'When I was a boy,' he said, 'the millet fields were on the other side of the lake. It was much bigger then. We had an irrigation system. White birds would come every season to eat fish from the lake and small shrimp. You would not believe it, but it was quite a nice place.'

'I do believe it,' Nick said, his voice soft.

'I had good memories.' The old man sighed. 'Maybe too good. I returned here because of those memories. I forgot to see what was before my eyes.'

Nick felt the weight of Dr Ahmed's weariness, filling the night around them. 'You dedicated your life to this place,' he said. 'That's a great thing. A good deed to be proud of.'

'Perhaps.' Dr Ahmed looked up, the pale lights of the village reflected in eyes that were suddenly watery. 'But even good deeds are not immune from consequences. Sometimes they are good for some but not for others. I love my wife, you know.'

Nick was shocked to stillness. Guilt twisted inside him, sudden and brutal, driving home the scale of his betrayal.

'I love her,' said Dr Ahmed. 'And I know that she is unhappy here. Love wishes happiness on the beloved. So how can I say I love her when I know she grieves and I do nothing to comfort her?'

Nick wrapped his arms around his chest. The urge to unburden his heart had never been stronger. He could do it – confess everything, offer his life and a new start to Margaret and JoJo and Nagode, relieve the pain for all of them. The moment stretched out to fill the formlessness around them.

Then Dr Ahmed sighed, his hand heavy on Nick's shoulder.

'You are a good man,' he said. 'You have a good heart. But do not make my mistake, I beg you. See what is really here, not what you wish could be here.'

'What do you mean?' Dr Ahmed's arm weighed him down, pressing him into the earth.

'The reasons you are digging this well.' The aged voice was faltering, schoolteacher English growing uneven and jagged. 'Maybe they seem good to you. But you are digging into ground that has not been touched for many years.' His eyes gaped wetly into the failing light. 'You do not always know what lies beneath.'

Nick breathed against the racing of his heart, burning with

words that he dared not say. *See me as I am*, he wanted to scream. *A liar, a thief.* But what did those names matter? Why should he care what he became, if it meant Margaret could be happy? An ache spread from his ribs, like the sharp cut of a blade. He willed it to grow, imagining a knife piercing through bone and muscle into some hidden rot, the poison of guilt draining out.

'I'm not a good man,' he said. 'I never have been. But I can still do this one thing.' A hot wetness was stinging his eyes; he rubbed it away with a fierce swipe of his hand. 'You won't have to pay the governor's blood money for his tankers. Your children will be free from him. They'll have clean water to drink.' He rubbed his head with his hands. 'Your white birds might come back.'

Nick felt the old man's fingers pressing through his thin shirt. He experienced a moment of dissonance, present clashing with past. It was his father's hand on his shoulder, trying to steady himself during the breathlessness in his final stage of heart failure – an accidental connection that seemed to mock them both.

'I do not want to discourage you,' Dr Ahmed was saying. 'Even I myself do not know sometimes.'

Margaret put her head out of the front door, holding Nagode. She paused when she saw them both standing there. 'There is tea,' she said, subdued. 'If you would like it.'

Her husband looked up at her. Nick did not dare.

'I would,' Dr Ahmed said, releasing Nick's shoulder. He bent his head – a half bow, his shoulders laced with tiny night-flies 'Goodnight,' he said. 'Goodnight,' Nick replied.

Dr Ahmed eased past his wife and vanished inside. Margaret hesitated. She looked up at Nick; her eyes seemed full of unspoken fears.

'Nagode wishes to say goodnight, too,' she whispered.

He walked over and clasped the chubby fist waving over Margaret's shoulder. Nagode grinned, and for the first time Nick saw JoJo in that frank, astonished smile. 'Ni,' she said. Nick leaned in to kiss her forehead, smelling the rich sourness of buttermilk. She gripped his hair and pulled it with cunning tyranny.

'She is perfect,' he said to Margaret. She smiled, and he saw tension release its silent hold on her. She bent to rest her cheek on her daughter's head. 'She is,' she murmured. 'She came straight from God. Maybe He was making His amends to me. Or maybe I have not yet paid for her in full. I do not know.'

Margaret bit her lip and he brushed the mark with his fingers, forgetting for a moment where they were. Her eyes closed at his touch. After she went inside he stayed for a while, watching the desert sleep, listening as she sang Nagode into a fathomless ocean of dreams.

Today I am thirteen. A man. Mister will take me and Akim into the desert for our test. Ramadan begins soon, Mister says, and after this the elections. The time for soldiers is almost come.

Akim and Juma get money on their birthdays, always money. They buy sweets with it and magazines.

But Baba, he never gave me money. Only books. One was a book called Peter Pan. *Some boys lived with their leader in a land of magic. They never grew up. I thought this was the story of Robin Hood, which Mama told Bako and me, but Baba said it was not so. Peter Pan and Robin Hood are very different, Baba said. Peter and his boys love nothing except fighting. They are no better than those they fight. But Robin Hood loves the people of his land. He is not fighting against just one man. He fights for all men.*

When I woke this morning, I saw another book on the floor by my door. I picked it up. It had a thick cover, from leather the same colour as old blood. It smelled like Baba. An old-man smell.

Inside the cover was Baba's writing. I read the first line. To Yahya, my beloved first son.

Then I could not read any more. I closed the book and put it down. I went to look in the mirror. There was my face, the same as the day before. How can you tell that you are a man? Where are the signs? If the outside is the same, can the inside be different?

Mister says he can tell, always. The test is the proof, he says. After the test, I will know.

Our test today is in the desert. We go out past the lake. The water is nearly gone. The sun has eaten it all. At home we drink only a little water each day. We all wash from the same bucket. Mama uses the same water two times to cook the yams and the rice. The yams taste of rice and the rice tastes of yams. All the food tastes the same, and all the faces look the same. When Nagode cries, I think how her tears would taste if I drank them from her face.

Binza's place looks empty from here. The red curtains move – but it is the wind. My eyes hurt from the light and the bang cigarettes that we smoked. The light is yellow and brown. It fills the whole sky.

We come to a place where there used to be a lake. Baba told me that this old lake was once part of our lake, but then it died. Now it is just nothing, not even the ghost of a lake.

'Look,' Mister says. He points ahead of us.

I can hear barking. There are brown dogs in the dead lake. They are eating something. A bird. One of them has the wing in its mouth. The feathers are black and grey.

'They are hungry,' Mister says. 'They have started their dinner early.'

Akim, he laughs. He says: 'A stinking bird for dinner! Good food for a dog, eh?'

Mister, he comes over to Akim. The sun is falling on him, and his face is white. I know the sun brings him pain. It is the pain that makes him strong.

'You are a dog,' Mister says. 'We are all dogs. We all eat this meal every day. We eat worse than this.'

Akim twists his head away from Mister. He fears him still. Mister knows. He laughs at Akim. He turns to me this time. He says: 'What about you, boss? Would you like to taste dead bird?'

I tell him: 'I won't eat it.'

Mister leaves Akim and comes to me. He reaches behind him to show me what he carries in his belt.

Danjuma's gun. It is smaller than I remember. The metal is black and thirsty. It drinks the light.

Mister says, 'What about it, JoJo? If I tell you to eat, will you eat?'

I am looking at the gun. I wonder where the bullets are. I wonder how it feels when they go inside you. Does it feel cold? I would like to feel cold, even for one second.

'No,' I answer him.

Mister, he raises the gun and points it at me. 'Eat, JoJo,' he says.

Akim starts to laugh again, but Juma hits him.

I am looking only at the gun. The mouth of the gun is black and deep. It gets bigger and bigger. It goes deep into the earth.

I am not afraid. I feel my heart beating so fast. But this is from the bang cigarettes. It pushes my fear somewhere else, with the dust and the light.

'Well?' Mister says. He is not smiling at me now. His hand is white on the gun, but his mouth is black. He is the mouth of the gun and I am the bullet.

I look at him and I say again: 'I will not.'

Mister, he smiles and nods his head. He turns to the other Boys and says: 'See, this one? He is nearly a soldier.'

I think of the word that Nicholas used. The Hebrew word. I tell Mister: 'A son of the law.'

Juma, he laughs. He says: 'JoJo the prophet.'

I don't look at Juma. I say: 'It is what the Hebrews say when a boy becomes a man.'

Mister, he nods. Then he says to me: 'If you are a man, then prove it.'

He takes Akim by his shoulder. Akim, he is restless from the bang cigarettes. I see him twitch and move his feet. He wants to be doing something.

Mister, he says to Akim: 'Your father thinks he is a big man. But he is just like that bird. The dogs are eating him every day. They will keep eating, until we take their teeth.'

Akim screws up his face. He wants Mister to say he is brave like me. He shouts: 'I will kill them! I am a soldier too!'

Mister, he looks at me. 'And what about you, boss? Can you catch me a dog? Or are you a boy still?'

The light is too bright. It fills my mouth, and I cannot speak.

Mister, he comes and puts his arm on my shoulder. Very quiet, he says to me: 'There is only one law, JoJo.'

He shows me Danjuma's gun, black in his belt. And then he steps back.

Akim is already running, into the place where the dogs eat. I wait and look around. The wind beats inside my ears, like a drum. The bushes here are sharp. They have needles in them. I bend and take two. They cut my arms as I pull them. I ask Mister for his knife to cut the second one. It feels cold in my hand.

Now the dogs are running from Akim. Some are small, and fast. But one is bigger than the rest. Her teats sway near the dust, like a monster. Her mouth is open and she snarls at Akim. The bird has dropped from her mouth. I can smell it from here. Sweet, like cola. She smells like death. The smell brings vomit into my mouth. She is like Binza and Mister. She is one of the spirits.

I give Akim one of the branches and say: 'Go that way!' He does not understand me, so I show him. He goes behind the dog. She runs to the side, but I run after her. She runs to the other side, but Akim is there. He shakes his stick at her. It makes a hissing noise, like Binza when she saw Mister.

The dog tries to run back, but I follow her now. I am running fast around her. I reach out with the stick to hit her, so she will turn her head and snap at me. We are like brothers, fighting. I am Bako and she is me. I push her with the stick and she turns her head to snap at it. I run around her and make her turn until she is dizzy. The sun comes through the dust and we are choking, both of us. I can hear The Boys cheering us. The other dogs are close by. I can hear them calling their sister. They are calling her home, but I have her, and I will not let her leave.

We go around and around. I swap the sticks from one hand to another. She will get tired soon. I am tired. Even with the bang cigarettes, I am tired. I do not know how to stop her from running. She is still growling and barking, but sometimes she whines.

Then Akim, he comes, with his stick. He creeps up behind her, while we are chasing each other. He hits her hard, with his stick. He hits at her back legs. She is yellow like the dust, but I see red come where he hits her. She turns to him. She is ready to fight. I can see then that she is brave, even braver than me, braver than Akim or even Mister. She will not give up.

But she stumbles when she turns. And Akim he comes in with his stick. He hits her again and again. And she falls onto the ground. Even now, she fights. She tries to get up. The legs at the back, they do not work. She pulls herself with two legs. She is trying to run away. Go, I want to say to her. Go. But it is too late for going.

Mister, he comes up to us. Akim is so happy. He is dancing. He holds the stick out to Mister. There is blood on the end.

'Here,' Akim says. 'I did it. Did you see?'

He turns to Juma and the other Boys. He holds the stick in the air and jumps up and down. He shouts: 'Did you see it?'

Mister says: 'I saw it. But it was JoJo's plan first.'

I am so tired, I cannot hold my stick. I want to sit down in the dirt, like the dog. I try to breathe, but the air is too thick. I feel water on my face. It is sharp, and it cuts me.

Mister, he reaches over and takes the stick from me. He looks in my eyes. He says: 'Now, we must finish it.'

I know what he will give me. I do not want it. But it comes anyway.

'Take it,' he says.

I cannot. I do not want to. Now The Boys are silent. Even Akim, he is silent. They all look at Danjuma's gun.

'Take it,' Mister says again. 'This is how we finish it, JoJo. This is the only way to finish it.'

I look at her, on the ground. She is still moving. Her eyes are white. Her teats are so long. They are on the ground, in the dirt.

Maybe this morning there were babies on them. Now there is only dust.

I take Danjuma's gun. It is so heavy, like a rock. Mister, he folds my fingers around it. My first finger is on the trigger. This is the only part I know. I know what happens if I move that finger.

Then he pulls something back on the gun. And there is a sound, a metal sound. Nothing I ever heard before makes such a sound.

He lifts my arm until it points at her. Then he moves away from me.

There is nothing around me now. We are alone, she and me. But I do not think of her or of Mister or of the gun. I think of the book that Baba gave me for my birthday. I wonder what story was inside it.

But I must not think of that. I tell myself: she is the illness that took Bako. She is the dry land and the men who steal from us, those men in their suits who said Baba must not work at the hospital. She is the storms that come and the fires. She is the one who called Adeya names and made her cry. She is Nicholas putting his hands on Mama in the kitchen. She is Mama begging my forgiveness. And I cannot forgive. I will not.

Her eyes, they see me. They are white all around. I cannot look at them. There is water on my face, and it runs into my mouth. It tastes bitter and warm. But the gun is so cold. Like the snow Nicholas said comes in England. It is the only cold thing in all of this place.

I fire.

In the evening Mister sends us home. The sun is red, and soon Imam Abdi will sing from the mosque. In all these houses, the people will start their meal. But not me. I am not hungry. The bang cigarettes burned my stomach. Their smoke tastes like fire.

There is a light in Adeya's house. It dances and moves in her window. I try to rub my eyes but I see only more shadows. Maybe the spirits are coming here. They are tired of waiting for us. There is no more water at the lake. So they are coming here to find us.

I see one – there, standing by Adeya's door. Dark and small, like an animal. I wave my arms at it. Go, I try to shout. Go. My tongue is heavy. It does not work. But the spirit is not afraid. A real animal would fear me. A real animal would run.

The door opens and Adeya looks out. Her mouth moves; she is speaking to me. But that is not her voice. It is only the singing from the mosque. I laugh at Imam Abdi's voice coming from her mouth. She looks at me. I think she is saying: 'JoJo, wait.' But the spirit is walking away from her, back towards the lake. And I have to follow.

There is the well, in front of the sun. The sun has grown big, like a balloon. It has split into two suns. One is like a shadow of the other. It swallows the drill that breaks the rocks. Somewhere there are men talking. Maybe it is Nicholas. But he cannot see me. He never sees me any more.

She is there. The dog is right there, on the bank above the water pits. She waits for me.

I shout to her: 'I am one of The Boys now! I am not afraid of you spirits! I passed the test.'

But now the sun is down, and everything is cold. The cold is calling me from under the ground. The well is like a mouth and these pools of water are its eyes. But these are not eyes for seeing. They are for hiding. They hide the spirits.

I will call them out. 'Come and find me, if you want me!' I will not run.

So I lie on the wall beside the pool. Down I look, into the black water. It is far below, and it smells strange. Not mud and grass, like the lakewater. A cold smell, from deep in the ground.

This is where the spirits hide. I can see them moving. I lean further forward. I call: 'Come out! I am waiting for you. Come!'

I hear my words come back to me. They are laughing, those spirits. They mock me.

I lean over further, down into the darkness. I want the laughing to stop. I want to pull the spirits from the black water. My head is so heavy. It is pulling my body in.

And now I cannot stop it. I reach out with my hands. I must find the edge of the wall. The stone is wet and my hands slide on it. It tears my skin, like the fire tore Adeya's. Inside something is shouting: 'Get back!' I do not want to fall. I do not want to join the spirits.

But I am already falling, sliding down the bank. The mud is hard and wet. My fingers cannot hold on. I feel my body moving, sliding and sliding. My heart is beating, beating – and I scream. But there is nothing to hear me.

I put my arms over my face as the black water fills my mouth. Something has taken me, something has my legs and shoulders. The spirits have me. I fight them, but their fingers bite down, on my legs and my shoulders. I do not know if I am falling or rising. There is cold all around me, and light. Please do not make me open my eyes. I do not want to see the spirits. I do not want to join them.

But now I can feel hard ground. My skin is cold, and I can taste the black water. But my mouth is empty. Something is hold-ing my arm. Someone. I can feel their skin. It warms me. Through my fingers I can see a torch. And the face behind it is Nicholas'.

His face is white, white as the spirits. He is speaking. But the beating inside me is too loud. I can only feel him, holding onto me. I can feel his fingers. Tight, so tight, like they will never let me go.

MARCH

The well reached its target depth of ninety metres at the height of the dry season, a few days before Ramadan. The crew worked feverishly to finish before Imam Abdi announced the start of the daily fast.

High excitement spread through the village. Aisha Kamil sashayed to see them through the dust, bearing a bowl of Ramadan sweets. Akim tossed them to an eager mob of children, bright fistfuls of cellophane filling the air with festival colours. Adeya crept around behind Akim, her burned fingers like shiny pink snakes as they slipped into the bowl — stealing a handful for the too-timid smallest children waiting at the melée's outskirts.

As Ramadan's dusk neared, men began scanning the sky for the sliver of a crescent moon. Work pounded on around them: the great red beast had been hauled away and disassembled, replaced by new machines driving compressed air down the hole. A mixer churned cement for grouting. Mud, flushed from the depths, was darkening the desert. An open tube twelve inches wide protruded above the surface like a new blood vessel, carrying life from the silent aquifer. A ten-thousand-litre water tank squatted on the earth beside it — grey and hulking, like a sad beast of burden. Adeya's mouth had turned into a perfect round O on seeing it for the first time.

The pump had been lowered into the well's depths — an electric lung, driving water up to the parched surface. A diesel generator would power it day and night; the council would take levies, Mr Kamil had assured Nick, to buy the fuel. The pump's seal was a gasket sandwiched between two expensive steel plates. Eric had imported them from the capital, paying smuggler rates. 'The most valuable pieces of metal I own,' he'd grumbled. 'If I find a nice girl they could be a fucking wedding ring.'

On the day of the first pumping test, the village turned out to witness the moment of truth. A long hose had been attached to the pump, snaking three hundred feet to the bare remains of the lake. If all went well, a flip of the generator's switch would send the first water flowing from the earth's depths down to the lake, pure and unstoppable. If not . . . Nick did not dare to imagine what might come next. *The last hurdle*, he reassured himself, as the crowd began to gather on the baking ground, an agitated blur of heat and hope. Eric's technicians were fiddling with the pump's pressure gauge. Its thin metal bones looked so fragile, almost apologetic, against the enormity of the task.

Mr Kamil was waving at Nick, Aisha by his side. He saw Jalloh with his red hands and heavy brows standing behind the throng of heads – and Tuesday, smiling as his eyes swivelled from face to face.

A pale flash caught his eye at the edge of the site. JoJo's friend, Mister. He'd come more than once to watch the progress of the well, his presence tangible like a weight. Today he was silent, taking a cigarette from Juma. They were the same height and build – but Mister loomed larger, a low-sun shadow. He caught Nick staring at him as he raised the cigarette to his lips.

'You want one, boss?' he called across the scrum, lifting the pack to Nick.

'You should stop,' he called back. 'They'll kill you, those things.'

'Yes,' Mister said. 'I know.' Beside him, Juma laughed.

Something drew Nick's attention from them – Margaret approaching from the path that led to Dr Ahmed's house, heads turning as she moved through the crowd. She'd changed out of the dark houseclothes he'd left her in that morning. Now her hair was wrapped in a brilliant headband, a vivid jacaranda red that seemed to shout its presence. A blue scarf trailed behind her like a covering sky.

Celebration colours. They moved him deeply – he hadn't been sure she would come today. There'd been a strange tension between them earlier that morning – the unspoken knowledge that the well's birth was the prelude to other great changes in their lives, foreshadowing difficult choices. She'd appeared unexpectedly at his office door before he headed to the site, casually, as if just passing.

'So, Sir Galahad,' she'd said, their old joke. 'You achieved your quest.' Her chin was lifted in a tremulous smile, her body taut as a violin string.

He had not dared to take her hand, aware of Miss Amina's fan flapping curiously from her watching porch. He barely knew what to say; they'd never talked about what came next. Any future they imagined in those stolen moments by the lake under the sky's vast canvas was far distant, the misty impression of a crystal ball – two old people tending roses in his mother's garden, Margaret's sketches on the wall next to her framed doctorate, and Wordsworth on the bookshelves. The immediate future was taboo; Dr Ahmed and her children cast long shadows over it, and there could be no painless path through.

But he'd answered, in the hope that the words would make themselves truth. 'Margaret, this is only the beginning. For you, for the children. For all of us.'

Now she looked up and smiled across the construction site, as if he'd just spoken her name – as if his mouth were still pressed to the hollow of her ear or the pulse between her breasts. And again he experienced the thrill of a connection that overturned every childhood certainty – that mocked the years he'd spent burying himself in formulae and chasing scientific proofs when this deeper, vaster world had been just at hand, its nameless forces waiting to remake him.

A shout from Eric reminded him that the pump was about to start. The air swelled with the generator's roar, Eric's technicians hovering over the surface gauges, a keening sound like the agony of birth.

Suddenly, the hose began to vibrate. Nick watched as it stiffened and filled. *Water.* His knees shook with relief, head spinning as the adrenalin dropped away. *It's working. It worked.*

Eric threw up his arms. 'Done,' he shouted. 'Done, you bastard!'

A cheer started, pounding Nick with a visceral joy. *Listen*, he told his father and Madi's watching spirit. *Listen.* It was a beautiful sound, flooding through the old channels, washing out the debris of loneliness.

He turned to see Mr Kamil beaming at him, hand outstretched. '*Masha'Allah*, you are a clever man, Nicholas,' he said, grasping Nick's elbow. 'I knew it . . . I knew you would do good things for us.'

'Well fucking done!' Eric said, slapping Nick on the back. 'A good job.'

'There's still more to do,' he replied, fighting to stay afloat on a rising tide of triumph. 'We have to finish the pumping test and connect the tank. But in a day or so we'll be drinking free water. Then we can think of the next phase – irrigation and crops.'

He sensed Margaret near him, listening outside the circle of men. Her arms were around Adeya, their light hairs trembling in the hot wind around the red of Bako's bracelet.

Nick walked over to them, trailed by Mr Kamil. Adeya's face was flushed red. She dropped her gaze in embarrassment; Nick touched her lightly under her chin.

'You can plant your millet again, Adeya,' he said, tilting her face to his. 'And give them new names.'

The girl blinked, moisture pooling in her eyes. 'Yes, Mr Nicholas,' she said. He saw Margaret's hand touch Adeya's cheeks, catching the tears as they fell.

Mr Kamil put his hand on Nick's arm, his palm moist with sweat.

'We must have prayers and then a meal at the mosque,' he said, brimming with satisfaction. 'I have special food coming from the Town. And a special guest!' He raised his voice and waved to the crowd around him.

'Eh!' Tuesday nodded alongside Mr Kamil, like a deputy cheerleader. 'Danjuma! Danjuma!' Others took up the chant. 'Dan! Ju! Ma!' A pocket of stillness caught Nick's eye – Jalloh, frowning, thick arms dangling by his sides.

A voice rang out – sharp, sounding a note of alarm. 'Hey!' Eric was standing next to the sealed well, shading his eyes as he looked northwards. His other hand was raised, pointing into the afternoon glare. 'Hold up, boys and girls,' he called. 'Something's coming.'

Something's coming. Hairs prickled on the back of Nick's neck. He followed Eric's finger towards the distant ribbon of road connecting the village to the horizon.

At first he could see nothing – just blank, blinding desert.

But then shapes coalesced in his vision; a cloud of dust drawing near – a convoy – cars or trucks, leaving the highway to cross the sand towards them. Their sides shone through the haze of sand, sleek as a raven's wing. Only one man could have sent them.

As the governor's Land Cruisers closed in, Nick's mind flicked to the safe in his office. *How much money do I have left?* No more than two thousand at the last count. He'd been expecting Kate's reply to his letter every day, anxiety growing with every successive, silent sunset. By now she should have liquidated their bonds and wired the money to Western Union. She'd do it – he was still confident. But in the past week, he'd decided to ration his funds. The hospital construction had gone onto half-day rates. Tricky Dicky had been furious, stalking him with accusations from his car to the office. In response, Nick had shown him the wages bill. 'There are twice as many men listed here as we have on site,' he'd yelled back. 'I can pay full rates for half of them or half rates for all of them.' Nick suspected the slowdown in cash was making it harder for the foreman to skim his take.

'I knew this was coming,' he told Eric, swallowing the plunge of his nerves. 'It's Tricky Dicky, making a fuss about nothing. He's probably complained.'

Eric nodded. 'OK. Well, lucky the governor's an understanding fucking fellow.'

Nick breathed in, dust sharp in his lungs. *I'm not afraid.* He turned to Mr Kamil. The chanting had stopped. Mr Kamil wore a dogged look: arms folded, robe clinging to his stomach. 'The jackal comes,' he said. 'But the lions do not run.'

'Please, Mr Kamil. Let me handle him.' Nick wished them all away; Dr Ahmed had achieved nothing, and Mr Kamil was no substitute. The doctor had wished Nick a cordial 'good luck' this morning, excusing himself from the well-capping ceremony to clean his surgical tools with the last of his iodine solution. Miss Amina had another abscess in her foot, and a boy from JoJo's class needed a deep splinter drawing. Nick had not protested.

The Land Cruisers were drawing nearer and a pickup carrying armed bodyguards. They rocked across the scrubland, the scars of their passage twisting back to the highway.

Aisha hurried off, pulling Juma and Akim with her. Margaret looked at Nick, her hand on Adeya's shoulder. Go, he mouthed. Go.

She bit her lip, scarf slipping as she rubbed sweat from her forehead. One hand reached quietly to his wrist, transferring a jolt of courage.

'Come,' she said to Adeya. He watched them leave, like a garden moving through the dry landscape. Tuesday had vanished. Jalloh stayed, his head raised; he watched the governor's car approach like a dog hearing footsteps at the door.

Mister stayed, too. As Nick's eyes flickered over him, he dropped his cigarette, squashing it with his bare heel.

The convoy stopped on the other side of the well. Nick waited, his chest tight. Adeya's flags snapped frantically in the wind's blast – orange leaves in a silent field.

The window of the middle Land Cruiser rolled down. Cool air spilled from the dark interior. A man's figure sat in the back seat.

Cheap showmanship. It made Nick feel bolder.

He walked over and laid his hand on the hot metal. Inside, the governor was reading papers. He wore a suit: heavy brown pants stretched over his large legs, a brown jacket, double-breasted. His white shirt was closed at the neck with a pin.

His eyes flickered upwards briefly. 'Ah,' he said. 'Nicholas.'

'Sir.' Nicholas kept his voice low and respectful.

The governor shifted one paper aside. Nick felt the silence stretch between them. *It's a tactic,* he told himself. *Be calm.*

Finally the governor looked up, taking off his glasses. His gaze passed over Nick, to the parched desert and the last vestiges of the lake, drying and cracking on the earth.

'We have never had such a dry season,' he said, as if speaking to himself. 'I remember when all this was green.'

'Dr Ahmed told me,' Nick said. 'He said you could fish in the lake.'

The governor's head shifted on its powerful neck. 'And how is the good doctor?'

'He's well.' The false concern poured onto Nick like gasoline, waking his anger. *I will not give you one inch, you bastard.*

'And I also have not seen you at the hospital for a while,' the governor continued. 'My foreman tells me that we are behind schedule. And his men have not been paid.'

'I paid the team a few days ago. But the foreman wants me to pay ghost workers. And I'm afraid I can't do that.'

'I see.' The governor looked down at Nick. Rising heat from the engine blurred his features. But Nick could smell the man – a cocktail of gasoline, dust, sweat and cologne.

'You have been very busy with your well, Nicholas,' he said, pointing his finger out of the window like a pistol. 'And I see one of your workmen is a ghost, too.'

Nick's gaze followed the governor's. Mister was standing by the unfinished generator. To Nick's shock, JoJo now stood beside him. He was jolted by the similarities between the two boys – the same jagged lines of early manhood, the same aura of contained force. The governor's cap was perched on JoJo's head.

Now Nick felt the first trickle of fear, like rain in a thunderstorm. 'The well is finished. I'm paying for it personally.'

'I understand you.' The governor did not look at him. 'And yet still we are behind schedule.'

'We'll get back on in a couple of weeks.'

The governor craned his head around, back towards the village. The mosque had come to life, the last prayer before Ramadan running ahead of the sunset. The wind rose in competition – rattling the scrubland's skeletal bushes and setting the dogs howling.

Nick saw the governor laugh and nod his head, as if understanding some hidden message.

'Do you understand what our imam here is singing, Nicholas?'

'No.'

'It's about submission to God. The first pillar of Islam. My father was a very religious man. And as a boy, I thought he could never be wrong. But at Brown, they killed my delusions from the very first semester. A painful lesson, but important. Do you know what it was?'

Nick said nothing. The well's freshly sealed cap was reflected in the car's wing mirror; he saw the elephant tank squatting beside it, the bare wiring of the generator. *So close. We are so close to success.*

'They taught that the universe is built on order,' the governor was saying. 'Gods have whims, they are capricious. Their followers inspire chaos – the evidence is all around us. But order is written into nature. We all depend on it. Me. The Town, this village. Even you. We spoke about this before. But I'm not sure you listened. Which is a pity.'

The sand hissed through the lake's dead stalks. Nick's mouth was dry.

'This land could be green again if the well works,' he said. 'That's got to be worth a few thousand dollars and a couple of weeks' delay?'

The governor gestured to his driver. Nick heard the Cruiser shift into gear. The engine began to keen, high and urgent. The window wound upwards, nearly trapping Nick's fingers. He snatched them back in shock.

The window halted as the governor turned his head. From below Nick could see the powerful planes of his face, cheekbones broad as a bull's under a marble-smooth forehead.

'People tell me what you are doing here, Nicholas.' His gaze tipped towards Jalloh, standing a few metres behind them. The big man blushed.

'And I know you mean well,' the governor went on. 'But I wish you had listened to me. When I cannot communicate with a man in words, I have to find other ways.'

He tapped the driver. The vehicle reversed, forcing Nick to step back. One by one, the other Land Cruisers followed, speeding off into the distance. The last to leave was the small contingent of armed men, dust swallowing them as they headed north.

Eric walked Nick back to Dr Ahmed's house, the heavy tread of his boots eating into the ground. The world was so dry that the ground seemed barely to cling to it, once-dark millet fields rising in layers of gold and light. It hid their feet as they walked, wading slowly into a strange sea.

Eric swung his broad arms, waving at Miss Amina on her porch as they passed. She stopped the tired drifting of her fan. Nick saw languid flies settling on her headscarf, crawling down loose strands of grey.

At the garden gate to Dr Ahmed's house, Eric stopped – putting his hand on Nick's shoulder. His broad face was red, sweat pooling in his beard. The blue eyes narrowed as they looked down at him.

'This business with the governor . . .' he said.

'It will be OK.' Nick didn't want to hear anything more. 'I'm sorting it out.'

'I never said a word to J.P.. You can count on that.' Eric shifted uneasily on his feet, fingers digging into Nick's collarbone. 'But you're a fucking idiot if you think that dickless foreman hasn't. Their headquarters are in the capital, remember?'

'I've not done anything wrong.' Nick wiped the sweat from his own forehead, trying to recall the arsenal of explanations he'd gathered when this all began. He'd been ready for any challenge, almost disappointed that none had come.

'I'd get on the blower to J.P. today, if I were you,' Eric was saying. 'Because the truth is we are really fucking behind. And I'm not going to be the last person he hears it from. I have more than your fucking problems to worry about, understand me?'

'I promise I'll call him. Just give me another couple of days.' If the money arrived in the capital this week, J.P. would never need to hear from him.

Eric dropped his arm and looked back towards the well, hidden in the shimmer of afternoon heat.

'You've got balls, I'll give you that. They would have been waiting for their own water supply here till the Day of fucking Judgement.'

Nick closed his eyes, remembering what Margaret had said by her mother's grave. *Every day is a Day of Judgement.* 'Imam Abdi said the fires were Allah's judgement,' he reminded Eric. 'For bowing to a godless man.'

Eric snorted. 'Their Allah has a lot to fucking answer for. The governor's right about that, at least.'

Dr Ahmed was not in his office. Nick opened the door to his own room, the air stale with old breath and gasoline but a relief nonetheless from the crucible outside.

He sat down at his desk, head in his hands. *Kate will answer soon. She will.* The pressure of her silence was building like a bubble, distorting today's victory with fear. But, he reasoned, that was only the old poison of his self-doubt – of the boy standingly helplessly by the climbing frame, too terrified to disobey. His hands dropped to the table, palms facing upwards. He almost laughed at the sight of them; how puny they seemed, to be attempting so much.

Sliding his arms down the table, he rested his forehead on the

242

warm, chipped wood. The whir of the fan seeped into his brain, soothing him, blowing his thoughts over and over, like autumn leaves chasing each other down a winding country lane. As he drifted, he felt them rising on warm currents into a lightening sky. *We won. The well is built. Relief is on its way.*

He woke to a hand on his shoulder. Dr Ahmed's face loomed above him, his reading glasses dark. His throat was sore and his thoughts scattered.

'Nicholas, I am so sorry to wake you.'

'No.' Nick tried to sit up, stretching his aching back. 'I didn't mean to fall asleep. I haven't been sleeping well.'

Dr Ahmed, too, looked exhausted. His hair had grown, a wiry bush above his head. He smelled strongly of sweat. His head seemed to tick constantly with tiny, staccato jerks, some faulty inner mechanism finally seizing up. *The Tin Man*, Nick thought. *Binza's the Wicked Witch and the governor's Oz the Great and Powerful.*

'I have a letter for you from England,' the doctor said. 'They sent it from your office this morning. Perhaps you want to read it?'

'Thank you.' Nick's heart leaped to life. *Kate's reply, at last.*

'I may have to travel to the capital tomorrow, to collect an instalment of cash,' he told the old man. 'By the time I get back, the well will be up and running. We can all celebrate with a glass of cold, clean water.'

Dr Ahmed nodded. 'Congratulations.' His voice was gracious. 'They had to postpone today's celebration, I hear. An unexpected visitor upset all plans.'

'The governor tried to intimidate us,' Nick said. 'But it's too late for that.'

Dr Ahmed smiled as he straightened. 'I am glad to hear it.' He placed a letter on the desk. 'Happy reading. I will see you at dinner.'

Nick waited for him to leave. Then he tore open the letter, thrilled to see Kate's neat cursive under the N&K embossed initials.

Dear Nick, it began, *I'm sorry this is late, but honestly I had a lot of thinking to do since we last spoke.*

It went on, and he could almost see her – bent over the paper, brow furrowed, hair a smooth cascade down her back, cool sunlight gracing her with its pale halo.

At first she didn't refer to his request. She was worried about his mother: a change of medication had made her unusually agitated; she was constantly asking for Nick, for his father, hating the clinic, begging for her garden at home.

It's too much to expect of me, she wrote. *You can't be a saint doing wonderful things for other people while you're being unkind to those closest to you. Maybe it's hard to hear. But that's what marriage is supposed to be, isn't it? No rose-tinted glasses, seeing things as they really are? Telling each other the truth, no matter what?*

He felt a cold premonition as he read on. Kate was worried about him. She'd agreed to support this dream of his and she hoped he was proving whatever he had to prove. But she could not in all conscience just send him all his savings on a whim.

I'm your fiancée. It's awful what's happening there, and I'm very sorry for them all. But we have our own future to think of, and our own family. We have to make these decisions together, not thousands of miles apart. Come home. Come home and let's talk. What could be more important than that?

He didn't bother to read to the end, letting the paper fall to the desk.

Come home. That was Kate all over, Kate the parent looking after a wayward child, protecting him from all but the most middle-class of errors. *Come home.* He knew she believed she loved him. And at one time he'd marvelled that a woman like her could choose him, when she could have had anyone. But now he understood: it had been a gamble, a blind roll of the dice as uncertain as his own when he'd handed over J.P.'s money. And in the end, both of them had lost.

So ... there would be no money from London to pay back what he'd taken. Maybe two thousand dollars was left in the safe. It would not be enough to finish the hospital.

What now? He could fly back to London, to Kate's door, and beg her. But he knew he would fail. The gulf between them was much wider than thousands of miles. He wished he could spare her the coming pain – prayed for it to be short, like the burn of a hot knife cauterising a wound. One day he would be nothing more than a faint scar, the first on that smooth white skin, for another man to soothe one day as she lay in his arms.

Once J.P. learned of Nick's theft, he would face criminal charges. The only way to protect himself was to run – back to England, out of arm's reach, until he could return the money. For an instant this hard truth lanced through him, so violent that he wondered if this was what his father had felt when his heart finally exploded, dying alone, without his wife or son or one of the hundreds of patients he'd cared for instead of paying attention to his family. *See, you old bastard.* Nick screwed up Kate's letter and threw it on the floor. *I abandoned my family. I stole from the rich and gave to the poor. And now I'm alone. I became you at last.*

The light was off in Dr Ahmed's office. Nick ran into JoJo as he searched through the corridors of the house. The boy was hurrying away, head down, the governor's cap on his head.

'Where are you off to?' Nick asked him.

'Nowhere,' was JoJo's short reply. The cap with its ridiculous bear logo was pulled slightly to one side. Nick half wanted to reach out and straighten it.

'That's what I used to say to my father,' he said. 'Nowhere means: somewhere I don't want to talk about.'

JoJo looked down, his hands in his jean pockets. He shrugged, but stayed where he was.

Nick searched his memory, desperate for some way past the sly nonchalance back to the boy he remembered.

'I miss you,' he said at last. 'I miss making our schematics.'

The boy stayed silent. His foot scuffed over the tiles.

'Now that I've finished the well, I'll have more time,' Nick went on. He touched JoJo's arm, fingers cautious. 'I'll make more time, JoJo. It can be like before.'

The boy's eyes turned upwards – an unguarded moment. Nick stepped back in shock at the anger they held. A memory returned of the night JoJo had nearly fallen into the reservoir pit – of the boy's fingers clenching his arm, nails black from the muddy wall. He'd answered none of Nick's frantic questions – *what were you doing? Didn't you hear me say it was dangerous? What happened to you?* He'd only looked up with these very same eyes, like dark holes filled with fury.

Now JoJo pulled his arm away from Nick with a sharp jerk.

'I'm going out,' he said. He pushed past towards the door, and Nick heard it slam.

The hall was silent, apart from the slow tick of the grandfather clock. Nick walked slowly into the dark and pushed open the door to Margaret's room, where Nagode still slept.

Margaret lay on the bed, the baby curled up beside her. Her arm with Bako's bracelet was flung up, pale on the underside, reflecting the window's faint glow.

Nick had only seen Margaret asleep once, in the hotel in the capital. Then he'd lain watching her, awestruck by the beauty of life's unconscious rhythms. Now her lips were relaxed as her chest moved with the pulse of breath and blood, the embodiment of peace.

He sat down on the bed and her eyes opened, full of sleep. 'Nicholas,' she said, reaching up to him, touching his cheek. 'You should not be here.'

'I know,' he said. 'I've done many things I shouldn't.'

She studied him, face thoughtful. 'Today was your triumph. But you're sad. Why?'

Even good deeds are not immune from consequences. Nick tried to smile. 'I wanted to make you proud.' He touched her fingers, tracing the skin between her breasts, the hardness of the breastbone and the dark swell of nipples still tender from Nagode's mouth. 'To make up for all your regrets. But maybe I've just given you more of them.'

She sat up, bringing her lips to his. He felt the warm curve of her forehead pressing into his. 'No,' she said. 'I have paid with a thousand sorrows for this one joy.'

Nagode stirred between them, breath escaping from her lips in a faint cry. His heart thudded against his ribs, feeling the air catch between Margaret's open lips as he kissed her. Her eyes were open, and he remembered how they'd closed when he was inside her, surrounded by the smell of her, pressing her arms into the ground as Bako's bracelet branded both their skins.

'Margaret,' he said, pulling back. 'We're going to have to make some decisions.' He rubbed his hands along her back, feeling the curve of her spine. 'Things are happening – and I have to know: do you want to make a life with me?'

She turned her head away, biting her lip. 'Please, Nicholas. Please, not now.'

'Now.' He took her face in his hands. The room felt hot and cold at once, heat shivers spreading through his body to confuse his senses. Even the mechanical tick of the clock in the lounge had fallen out of sync with Nagode's even breath. Margaret's features seemed to shift and change before his eyes, sliding from fierce youth to the soft surrender of old age.

'I don't want to go back to England without you,' he said, words halting in the incoherence of his thoughts. 'I don't want to be anywhere without you. But I may not be able to stay here.' She opened her mouth to ask a question; he put his fingers to her lips.

'I can't explain everything now. But you and me and Nagode and JoJo – we're going to have to make a choice very soon.'

Tears came to Margaret's eyes. 'Ahmed is a good man,' she said, her voice hushed. 'He does not deserve more grief.'

He brushed her tears away with his thumbs. Remorse lodged in his throat, a leaden lump. *I'm so sorry.* He wondered if the old man would ever be able to forgive them. *If anyone could, he would.*

'He told me that love meant wishing happiness on the beloved,' he whispered, finding his voice. 'He said he knew you were unhappy. He tried to rescue you once, but it didn't work. Now he has a second chance. We all do.'

His pulse pounded in his ears, strong as the grandfather clock's tick, a tide of seconds flooding past. He took Margaret's hand. His face felt hot and dry and her palm moist as rain. He knelt beside the bed and looked up at her.

'I swear, Margaret, I will love you all my life. And Nagode and JoJo – we'll open the whole world to them. You can go back to university and get that doctorate. You can grow old with me, teaching English literature students something real about life. We can visit your daffodils every year.' Her hand was on her chest; he took it, holding it tight. 'It can all happen.'

'It's a dream,' she said. 'This is what we did in another life.'

He shook his head. 'This is our life.'

She was crying, one hand on Nagode's arm, the other hot inside his.

'This place was my exile.' Her breath was hoarse. 'My punishment. Like the Hebrews in the desert – they reached the Promised Land but were afraid to step across.'

'Maybe they were right to say no.' *Jews invented doubt*, his father would say. Nick almost laughed at the memory. 'Maybe they'd had enough of God's promises.'

She smiled through her tears. 'But their children found it at last.'

He took her chin in his hand. 'So can we. I'm asking – will you be ready? When it's time, will you come with me?'

She looked down at him, doubt tracing her face. For a moment his heart faltered.

But then she looked up. Dropping his hand, she wiped her cheeks and then laid her palms flat on her lap. Her eyes met his; he saw fear there – but also purpose.

'I am ready,' she said. 'I've been ready for too long.'

I ask Mister: 'How can you know Jalloh is a traitor?'

Mister, he says: 'Watch his eyes. His mouth lies, but his eyes cannot.'

'And his table,' Juma says. 'His table tells us, too.'

Mister, he smiles. He says: 'You are right, captain. Jalloh's table tells us everything.'

Now I understand. There is no more meat in the village. Jalloh's animals, they all died. Hanan has only three goats now – the oldest ones. The young ones died first.

But Jalloh still has meat at his table. Tuesday said that one of his ladies ate meat at Jalloh's house. Mister says it is our meat Jalloh eats. The flesh from our bones and the blood from our skin. The governor, he pays Jalloh to eat us.

'Tonight,' Mister tells us, 'it's time for Jalloh to pay back what he owes us.'

I ask: 'Pay back the meat?'

The others, they laugh. But when I took the test, they did not laugh. My finger still feels cold, from the trigger. I point it at Akim, and he stops laughing. He sees. He remembers what I want to forget.

Mister, he says to them: 'You are fools. JoJo knows. Yes, Jalloh must pay in meat.'

'We will do it after Mr Kamil's iftar feast,' Mister says, 'the one to honour Nicholas and his well. The food is from Danjuma's men. Danjuma himself, he cannot come. They watch him,' Mister says. 'The governor watches Danjuma. He knows his time is coming. But even the governor cannot watch every man.' That is what Mister tells us, as we smoke. We are the secret that Danjuma keeps.

I must go to the feast with Nicholas and Baba. These days he sleeps all the time. Even when he wakes, he is still sleeping.

But today he woke up. He woke because the clock, it stopped.

I notice it first. I am standing by the door, ready to leave for the iftar. But then I hear the silence. And I say: 'Baba, the clock.'

He goes to the clock and puts his hand against the wood. He is feeling for the heart, the way he does with people. He is listening with his hands.

Mama comes into the room with her best clothes on. A long dress, blue with many colours. She is like a sky with birds flying all over her. Today I think she is beautiful. She smiles at me and takes my hand. She is a fool, like Juma. She sees nothing. But I take her hand anyway.

Then Baba puts his back to the clock. And he says: 'I do not want you there, Margaret.'

Mama, she is surprised. She takes her hand from me. She says: 'What is wrong?'

Baba says: 'I do not trust these men. It is my duty to go. But you must stay safe here, with Nagode. That is my wish.'

Mama feels anger, I can tell. She says: 'Aisha will go. I gave Nagode to Hanan already. I am here all day. I speak to no one.'

Baba, he hits the clock. Bang! Not with a fist. His hand is open. He is standing in front of the clock and he hits it behind him, like he is hitting the wall. He shouts: 'Obey my wish, Margaret. For God's sake!'

I never hear him shout. Not since Bako died. Mama, she takes a step back. She looks at Nicholas. He is silent.

I want to scream at Baba: Look at them! Look at them! Can you not see? But I will keep my silence. He does not deserve to know. They are all the same as each other.

Now Mama is very angry. But she will obey Baba. She turns around and goes into her room. Nicholas and me, we follow Baba out of the door. The clock, it says nothing.

There is meat at the feast. Lamb, not goat. Danjuma's gift. There is yellow rice and yams and buttermilk and flat bread to soak it. Men bring it to the mosque on trays from a van. They eat like dogs, Mr Kamil and Imam Abdi and all of them. They bend their heads over the food and it falls from their mouths.

I want to eat, but I am not hungry. I smell the lamb. It smells alive still. It is the same size as that dog. The meat from our bones and the blood from our skin. This is all I can see. I want to leave this table. Leave this place. But I have nowhere to go.

'Eat, Yahya.' Baba is talking to me. 'Eat. We may not see another meal like this one.'

Nicholas, he says: 'There is enough water in our well to irrigate all these fields for years to come. This meal is the first of many more, I promise.'

Baba, he does not reply. But Mr Kamil, he hears, and he stands up. Everyone goes quiet. Tuesday, and Jalloh. Miss Amina. Everyone.

Mr Kamil is still wearing his peacock clothes. He is smiling. He smiles like Akim. He says: 'Nicholas. You came to us a stranger. But today you are part of our council and our family.'

He says: 'Allah knows best. The Qur'an teaches us that water belongs to Allah. Allah alone chooses where it flows, and Allah alone owns its supply. The drought has caused much suffering here. But adversity is Allah's gift to the sinner, to make him humble. But when we return to Allah's path, He rewards us. He sent Nicholas by His goodness, to restore His gift to us. So we thank you, Nicholas. Please.'

Mr Kamil wants Nicholas to stand up and speak. Nicholas' face is white. His snowman face. Today he looks like he is melting. He stands up and holds the table. His legs look weak.

He speaks in a quiet voice: 'I'm honoured to be here with you. I was a stranger once, but I don't feel like one any more. I feel . . .' Nicholas stops. He looks down. His voice sounds strange. I think of Adeya when the smoke took her voice, how she tried to cry but could not.

Nicholas is speaking again: 'I feel like I had to come a very long way from my birth home to find my real home. My own father – he was a local doctor, like . . . like Dr Ahmed. If something was wrong – with a person or with a system – he would *always try to fix that. He was a good man who tried to teach me how to be like him. I was a bad student.'*

He stops again. He looks at Baba. Baba, he is staring at his plate. He stares like gold is there, not rice.

Nicholas says: 'I hope that no matter what else comes we have fixed something wrong here and made it right. I hope that some of our sorrows can now be forgotten and never repeated.'

Nicholas looks as if he would say more. But now Mr Kamil is clapping, and Tuesday is following him. They clap their hands like birds beating the air when a cat comes near.

Nicholas, he sits down. He looks at Baba, and his face is sad. I do not think Baba wants to see him. But Baba turns his head to Nicholas. He raises his can of Fanta. He says: 'To your well, Nicholas.'

Nicholas takes a can and touches it to Baba's. He says, his voice very quiet: 'To you.'

The men who brought the food go home after dark, in their vans. I go home with Baba and Nicholas. They are talking now. They talk about nonsense. Nicholas is asking about Miss Amina and her foot. Baba is explaining to him why diabetes is bad for walking. They are not talking to each other. These are just words that mean nothing.

At the house, all is silent. Mama must be sleeping.

I say to Baba: 'Will you fix the clock now?'

He looks into the room, the silent room. I cross my fingers. If he goes to bed now, I can leave to join Mister. Then Baba drops his head. He says: 'In the morning, Yahya.'

When the house is quiet, I go.

The darkness is full of shadows. Out by the well, there is one light alone. The shadows follow the light. I do not want to go there. The dog is there, with Bako and the thirsty spirits.

We meet behind Tuesday's shop, to smoke some bang cigarettes. The smoke makes me live again. I feel my heart. Before it was dead, like Baba's clock. Now it beats so fast I cannot breathe.

Then Mister gives Akim and Juma a big metal bar from the garage. The ones they use to tighten the wheels. I saw Juma using them many times. He puts four bottles on the bucket. The bottles are empty. They say Sun Beer on the label. But they smell of the spirits he uses for cleaning.

Mister takes a can of oil from the floor. Juma holds a lighter above us, so we can see more clearly. Mister slaps his hand down. He says: 'Take that away.'

He pours oil into the bottles. It looks black, and smells like the bang cigarettes. I breathe it in until I feel dizzy.

When he is done, he puts a small piece of cloth inside each bottle. He will have two and Juma another. Then he gives one to me. Akim, he looks at me. I know what he thinks. He does not want the metal bar any more. He wants the fire in his hands, like me.

But Mister does not see Akim. He only looks at me. 'Aim well, boss,' he says.

The night is different as we run. I am different. I do not fear the spirits. I feel the fire in my hand. Now I am one of them. I am the most dangerous one.

There is Jalloh's place. He has no goats left to warn him. There is only one dog. But when he sees us, he whines. 'Run,' I whisper, with the spirits. 'Do not come back.'

Jalloh sleeps above the shop. Baba has bought nothing from him for one month now. His shop is closed. But Jalloh is still fat. He still eats meat. So it is true what Mister says. He gives our secrets to the governor.

There is no one to see us. Only one light, from the mosque. It makes us white, like Mister. Like we have all become spirits.

'Go,' says Mister. And so we go.

Juma breaks the window of the shop with his stick. The glass falls on the ground. Juma hits and hits until the hole is big. I see the hole swallow him. Then he is inside.

'Come,' Juma says.

I am dizzy from the bang cigarettes. My heart is jumping inside me. It makes me laugh. The bottle in my hand shakes. Mister, he grabs my wrist. In the light, his skin looks like mine.

253

'Be steady,' he says to me.

I try to stop my laughter. I look at him, at his white face. Like Nicholas.

He puts his hand on my shoulder. He says: 'Are you ready, boss?' I nod.

And so we go in. First Mister. Then Akim. Then it is my turn. Juma, he pulls me through the hole. Then we are inside.

The room smells of old blood. There are two chairs and a table. The tiles are white. On the wall there are pictures of Jalloh and some old man and woman. He laughs in the picture. In the corner there is a television. It is new. The box lies beside it. Behind the television is a door.

This is where the blood smell comes from. This is where Jalloh kills the goats and cuts them into pieces.

The smell of blood makes me sick. But Juma and Mister have already started work. They take their sticks and break the pictures on the walls. They break the television. Juma opens the door to the blood room. Whatever is there, he will break it too.

My heart is beating fast, too fast. Akim is beside me. His eyes are big. He holds the metal bar in his hand. But his face is tight, like it burns him.

Then I hear it. Something is roaring, roaring – something hungry coming for us. Jalloh – he comes down the stairs, with his hands out. Like a bull, he comes for me.

I throw my bottle. It misses him. He screams and kicks me. Akim, he is screaming too. The floor is slippery. I am falling.

Then Mister is on Jalloh and Juma too. He is so strong – but the metal bars are stronger. His hands go over his head, and he screams. I cover my ears. Something comes up inside me. It comes into my mouth and I vomit on the floor.

Jalloh is standing. I can see his feet. His arms reach towards Juma. Like he wants to eat him. I see white, white in his eyes. Juma is in the corner, with blood on his lip.

Jalloh says: 'I will kill you!' His voice is like the horn from those trucks on the highway.

But Juma, he shouts back. 'We will burn you, traitor. Allah's fire is coming!'

Then he lights the cloth on his bottle. He throws it at Jalloh. Jalloh moves, and it misses. The floor, it starts to burn.

'Get out, JoJo!' I try to move. My leg hurts. There is smoke, and I cannot breathe. I get up and try to run. I do not know which way is out. I do not know.

But Mister he pulls me, and there is the door. Someone has kicked it open. I run out – but still I am lost in the smoke. I cannot see Mister or Juma or Akim. I am alone. And maybe Jalloh is inside becoming a spirit. He saw my face. He knows me.

My fingers pull me along the wall. I am coughing from the smoke. My heart beats so fast that I think it must stop. My leg is hurting. I want to rest.

And then I see them – the boxes Jalloh used to keep his chickens. They have straw inside. It is dry and dark.

I climb in and pull my legs up. Close your eyes, JoJo. I close them, tight. I will stay here until the spirits go. Until the light comes and they return home to wait again.

When I wake the light hurts my eyes. I can taste smoke on my tongue. It tastes of ashes. Inside I feel cold, where the bang cigarettes have left me.

I am so tired. I want my own bed. I can smell Jalloh's chickens, the dead chickens that used to live here. It makes the sickness come again. In England, Nicholas says, the chickens are fat and their eggs are brown. The children cut bread and call it soldiers. Their soldiers are made from bread and their knives are just for the eggs.

Then an arm comes in. It grabs me by my shoulder. There is a face then, black with smoke and with one eye closing. There is something on it. White and red – a bandage, fresh.

Jalloh sounds like a dog snarling. He pulls me from the coop and I fall onto the ground. His arms are thick, like the trees. I cry to him: 'Stop! My leg hurts.'

He kicks me again. 'Walk, you piece of shit!' He curses me and pushes me with those hands, the killing hands. I have to get up and walk. Jalloh is pushing and pushing. If I stop once, I feel his hands.

Tuesday and other men from the village are standing by Jalloh's house. Their eyes, they follow me, past the square, past Miss Amina's house. The sun is up, and it stings my eyes. There is my gate. I want to lie on my bed and close my door. I want Baba and Mama. But I do not want to go inside there.

'Ahmed!' Jalloh is yelling now. 'Ahmed! Come get this piece of shit son of yours.'

The door, it opens. Mama is there. She looks still asleep. Her scarf is not even on her head. She is wearing her blue sleeping gown. Dark blue. Like the water under the ground.

She says: 'Hush, Jalloh. Ahmed is sleeping. He just slept now.'

Then she sees me. Her hand goes to her mouth, and she comes running. She runs to me and opens the gate. But Jalloh pulls me to him. I feel his heart, his angry heart. His arm is around my throat.

He said: 'He was with those robbers.'

Mama shakes her head. 'No,' she says. 'No.'

'Yes.' He shakes me. He says: 'Tell her.'

I say nothing. I feel water in my eyes. I cannot move.

'What are you doing, JoJo?' She is crying now. 'You are just a boy. He is just a boy.'

She is speaking to Jalloh, pleading with him, her hands on his arm. She weeps so well, I can almost believe her myself.

Jalloh says to her: 'I should call the police. Call the governor's men. He will go to jail. Better now than later.'

'No,' says Mama. 'I beg you, Jalloh. We will pay for everything. I promise.'

He lets me go and pushes me towards her.

'Your father is the only good man in this place,' he says to me. He points to his eye, to the bandage there. 'You shame him.'

And then his finger is pointing at me. Fat and black, like a hole in the air. He points it in my face. And he says: 'Next time.'

He goes.

Mama and I, we are still. She is holding me. But I cannot feel her hands. I cannot feel anything.

She takes my face and kneels down.

'JoJo,' she says. 'Why?'

I want to go inside. I want to lie down. I want her and Baba. But I can have none of those things.

'I saw you,' I say.

She goes still.

'I saw you with Nicholas. I saw you.'

She drops her hands, kneels on the ground. I could kick her and she would fall.

She says: 'My God.' Now her face is in her hands. 'Forgive me. Forgive me.'

Now I am angry. 'You lied!' I am shouting. 'You betrayed us!'

She looks up at me. Her face is like Binza's. It is old.

'I did,' she says. 'I betrayed you.'

I do not want to hear her voice. I put my hands on her shoulders. I squeeze them until I hurt her. I want to break them. But they are strong, too strong.

'It was him,' I tell her. 'He made you.'

She shakes her head. No. But I shake her too and shout: 'It was him!'

'No, JoJo.'

Her hands come up again to try and touch my face. I move my head, but she will not stop trying.

'It was me,' she says. 'I loved him. I did not want you and Nagode to grow up here. I thought he could rescue us.'

'You loved him more than me,' I say. I do not want to cry. There is water on my face, black from the smoke.

'Never,' she says.

'Stop lying!' I scream at her. She deserves the spirits. She loved Bako best. And then she let him die.

'You would leave us,' I say. 'You would go with him!'

Her hand finds my cheek. The touch hurts my skin. But I cannot break away.

'A lifetime of my happiness is not worth one second of yours,' she says.

Her face is turned up. The sun is on it. There are no tears in her eyes. She is calm, calm like water.

'You stole him from me,' I say. Now I am crying. I cry for the books, our drawings and the castle. 'He was my friend and you stole him.'

The door opens. Nicholas steps out in a shirt and his jeans. He rubs his eyes to try and see us. The light is in his hair. He says: 'What's going on? JoJo? Margaret?'

I turn and run.

'JoJo!' I hear Mama scream. I feel the pain in my leg. Like broken glass. But I run.

I run towards the well. I run past Adeya's house and her goats. Behind me, I hear Nicholas calling: 'JoJo! Wait!'

The air over the well is white. It blinds me. I am coughing black water. My heart is bursting. But he will not catch me.

And then I hear them. Screams. But not from me. Voices are calling. I stop.

Behind the well, trucks are coming. They are driving out of the desert – one, two, three, four. I cannot see how many. Inside are the soldiers.

Now Nicholas comes running beside me. But he is not looking for me any more. He is looking ahead, to where the soldiers are coming. The governor's men.

Hanan comes and Adeya and Mr Kamil – they all come. I hear shouts from everywhere, and curses.

But the governor's soldiers do not look at us. We are ants, the insects of the field. And they are the bulls here to stamp us out.

The soldiers make a ring around the well, with their trucks. Dust rises from under the wheels – it comes to cover us all. And then they jump down, one and then another and another and another. And in every hand there is a gun.

APRIL

The first death knocked on their door in the middle of a suffocating night. Frantic banging penetrated Nick's dreams, waking him into darkness.

The inside of his mouth was dry and itching. Nameless wings rattled against the windows. Sweat-stung bites scratched to bloody holes. They itched, little legs crawling over him.

Somewhere, a woman was wailing. The sound raked his spine with ice-cold fingers – high-pitched, but with a strange, deep resonance. For the first time since childhood, he remembered being afraid of the dark.

I must get up. His head felt dangerously light – a balloon connected to his body by fraying strings of will.

Stumbling into the office past the radio's silent hulk, he turned the handle. On the opposite side of the porch he saw Dr Ahmed's front door standing open, candlelight throwing two strangers into harsh relief. The man looked strangely bulky, wrapped in a stained satin bathrobe. Light glinted off the grease on his hair. *Tuesday?*

Behind him, a woman in a pink dressing gown clutched at his back, her body bent almost double. Her hair was coiled into ferocious braids that shook as breath escaped from her in rapid bursts. *Aieeee.* The noise was halfway between a word and a scream. *Aieeee.* She clutched her stomach and squatted on the ground.

I've seen her before. One of Tuesday's ladies, Nick remembered. JoJo had pointed her out in the salon a lifetime ago, braiding Aisha Kamil's hair with bold, thick fingers.

'Please, sir,' Tuesday was saying to Dr Ahmed. His voice was hoarse. 'Please, sir.' His arms seemed to be wrapped around his waist, dangling at odd, floppy angles.

Nick willed himself to look closer. *Those are not Tuesday's hands.* They were too small, too pale, tiny palms held upwards to catch the fading light.

Horror bloomed inside him, cold and sickening; the darkness yawned. He gripped the porch rail, wood flaking under his hands.

Dr Ahmed was speaking with quiet compassion. Nick didn't need a translation. Somewhere in the emptiness those little hands had opened up and let life go. *Meat, not flesh.* Jalloh had explained the difference, one day. 'Doesn't it upset you to kill them?' Nick had asked, as the living kids nuzzled into Jalloh's hand. He had laughed. 'While they live, they are my friends,' he said. 'But once I take up my knife, they become meat.'

Now Nick saw Margaret behind the candle flame, Nagode's sleepy head on her shoulder. The wavering light painted shadows in the hollows of her eyes. He saw her reach over to the small body, tweaking aside a corner of the damp covering sheet. Whatever she saw made her step back. Her hand rose to cover Nagode's face – an instinctive warding off. Bako's bracelet was red against her skin. Her eyes found Nick's, wide with sudden fear.

Dr Ahmed was trying to take the bundle from Tuesday. But Tuesday clung on. A fold fell back, revealing round baby cheeks and a thick knot of hair. The eyes were open, staring calmly upwards. 'Please,' Tuesday repeated. 'Please.'

The braided woman was sitting on the ground now, her expression bemused. She studied her empty arms, manicured fingers curling like dried leaves.

As Dr Ahmed pulled desperately on the bed sheet, a faecal stench rose into the air. The doctor turned to his wife. 'Remove Nagode into the bedroom. Do not come out.' Margaret obeyed without hesitation, vanishing into the dark doorway.

Dr Ahmed stepped back from Tuesday, who seemed to

crumple as the strong arms released him. He opened the door to his office and said, 'Take him inside, Tuesday. Go ahead.'

So Dr Ahmed knew that Tuesday had a son. He'd probably handled the delivery and told no one.

The shopkeeper staggered in. Nick looked up at Dr Ahmed, helpless. The old man's face was lined and grey. 'Stay out here, Nicholas,' he instructed. Then he took his candle into the deeper dark of the clinic, closing the door.

Margaret was waiting in the kitchen, Nagode on her hip. She pulled Nick close as he came in, forehead resting on his shoulder. Her breath burned his skin and he felt the wetness of tears; they anchored him to a world that was reeling away.

'JoJo knows,' she said.

Something cold trickled between them, freezing Nick's heart. 'What did he say?'

'He saw us. I don't know when. A long time ago.'

Nick felt dizzy. 'And he didn't tell anyone?'

Margaret drew back, raising her eyes to his.

'He told us every day,' she said. 'But not in words.'

He held onto Margaret, unable to speak, mesmerised by the redness inside her lips spilling over onto her skin like falling blossoms. It reminded him of the jacaranda tree outside the village, on the brink of its glorious flowering.

Sounds came from the hallway. They stepped apart as Dr Ahmed walked in, drying his hands on a towel.

'We have run out of iodine,' he said. 'I don't know how we will get more, unless they open the roads.'

Nick cleared his throat, searching for words.

'I didn't know Tuesday had any children,' he said.

Dr Ahmed sat at the table, a weary folding of his limbs.

'You cannot sow so many fields without reaping a harvest in one,' he said. 'She pretended the boy was her sister's. And Tuesday would visit and give him sweets. I told him not to. The child's teeth were very bad. But love never listens.'

'I'm so sorry.' The words were useless. Dr Ahmed laughed – a humourless sound.

'We will all be sorry soon,' he said. 'The boy had cholera.'

Nick heard Margaret gasp behind him. Another face appeared in the doorway. JoJo, his legs emerging from his shorts like stalks.

Cholera. On that terrible first day, the governor's men had moved systematically through the village. They'd broken the well's generator, tearing the hose and letting water drain uselessly into the sand. They'd looted the market and Tuesday's shop and smashed Imam Abdi's room beside the mosque. Hanan screamed as they shot the last of her flock. Wild dogs barked after them, driven to frenzy by the crack of bullets and stench of blood.

Aisha Kamil met them with insults and brandished a cooking pot. The butt of a gun slammed her in the stomach. They'd kicked the legs from under Mr Kamil as he raced to defend her, smashing boots into his teeth as he lay in the dirt. Then they'd riddled the water tank with bullets, sending precious liquid gushing over the roof tiles.

When they reached Miss Amina's house, Dr Ahmed stood with his hand on her arm as they ripped the cloths from her porch and broke her chair. They moved on to Margaret's garden then – boots stomping over Bako's fragile cross and the remains of JoJo's castle.

Nick had been forced to stand and watch them carry away his kerosene and diesel, rage expanding inside him. His senses were heightened; small details seemed vividly unreal – the crimson lines in a young soldier's eyes, the dizzy contrast of his black and white scarf, the sharp, shadowed angles of his khaki shirt. Nick's whole body screamed for vengeance – he wanted to fight back, like Aisha Kamil. Only Dr Ahmed's strong hand and JoJo's terrified face saved him from a gun in the stomach.

The soldiers set up camp by the well, using stolen fuel to power generators that roared into the night.

The village council gathered in the mosque, in a room that stank of fuel and sweat. Tuesday suggested going for help. 'Who are you counting on?' Dr Ahmed asked. 'In the south, they will tell us it's not their concern. And the ones to the north are already here.' He pointed through the wall, out towards the well.

Tuesday tried. He wasted the last of his petrol, heading south in his brown Toyota with its leopard-print seats. Nick watched it sputter off in a cloud of dirt. But he returned before afternoon prayers. 'They closed the roads,' he panted. 'They are keeping us here.'

As the sun sank over the village it stretched bloody fingers out in a wide circle. All directions now looked ominous and forbidding.

Before dawn on the second day, Margaret, Nick and JoJo went together to the lake, taking every bucket and container. The last of the fuel would be used for boiling and storing. They walked together without speaking, bubbles of thought colliding in silent friction.

The air by the lake was fetid and heavy, the water thick as it pooled in Nick's bucket. The world seemed dead. Only the distant red curtain on Binza's shack was alive, twitching with the breeze like a heartbeat.

Nick felt the presence of the well, a mosquito pricking his back. Imaginary thirst crawled up his throat. *Pure water, just a hundred metres beneath us.* He'd punched through the earth to find it; he'd cast his old life into the depths. And yet still it lay there, unreachable. *Stolen.*

They boiled the lakewater and added the last of Nick's water purification tablets, just to be sure. Dr Ahmed wanted to share them with others, but Margaret became hysterical at the suggestion. 'Remember your son,' she said to him, fists clenched. She wasn't talking about JoJo, Nick knew. JoJo knew it too. The boy turned away as she spoke, striding out to wherever he went these days. Nick wanted to call him back – but his courage failed. *He knows*, Margaret had said.

Instead he spent the evening helping her to re-create Bako's broken cross. The original was wounded beyond repair; only scattered shards left. The ground was hard and unyielding but eventually a makeshift replacement leaned out of the earth at odd angles, a twisted facsimile of mourning.

Later, in the silence of his office, Nick tried to call Eric on the landline. The generator was almost empty and the radio lay dead and silent. The phone clicked and whirred, until Nick hurled the mouthpiece onto the desk. He knew he should fire up the generator, turn on the radio and call J.P. But he was afraid. *Remember that well you told me not to build, with the money I stole from you?* The damage was done, the price would have to be paid – but J.P.'s part could be paid later.

As clouds massed in a thunderous evening sky, Nick imagined a huge form seated above them, leaning down to block the light. *The governor just wants to teach us a lesson. In the end he'll release us. And I'll face whatever I need to face.* Nothing would stop him taking Margaret to his mother's garden where the roses would be newly in bloom. They would sit on the kissing gate together and look over grassy fields instead of dust. No price was too high for that.

The lake was now their only lifeline – a pilgrimage site for rich and poor alike, gathering in the cool of evening, fasting and sleeping through the days in a cruel parody of Ramadan's voluntary abstinence. Adeya collected water for her mother and Miss Amina. Schoolteachers bent and filled alongside their pupils. Tuesday's ladies came, painted toenails squelching into the mud. Aisha came with Hanan, their sandals dark with filth, and as they hauled grey liquid back to her house Nick saw fear scored into Aisha's face around the dark red of her lipstick. He knew what she was thinking. *How long before this too runs out?*

Tuesday's child was barely a few hours dead when the banging on the doctor's front door sounded again. Dr Ahmed looked up from the face of his grandfather clock, polishing cloth in hand.

'Ahmed!' a voice yelled. 'Open up! Open, eh!'

Mr Kamil appeared in the doorway, nose still red and purple from his beating. When he opened his mouth, Nick saw dark holes where teeth had been.

'That rogue Tuesday has closed his shop and taken the food!' Kamil's voice squeaked through his wounded sinuses. 'First we have thieves breaking into houses. Now Tuesday gives every last thing to that whore of his. I could take some men and retrieve his goods, what do you think? This is an emergency.'

'His boy died last night, Kamil.'

The man's eyes widened, one hand clutching at his chest. But then he drew himself up. 'This is Allah's judgement. He was an adulterer and a criminal.'

'Cholera killed the child, not adultery.' Dr Ahmed stood up to him. 'We must stop people going to the lake. They have infected the water. We could have a big outbreak. Today even, or tomorrow.'

'Where will they go, if not the lake?' Kamil's question startled Dr Ahmed into silence. Kamil rubbed his bent nose, his unwashed body reeking of desperation.

'Danjuma will fix this,' he said. 'They are writing his name on the walls in red paint. He will come, any day now.'

'Danjuma is powerless,' Dr Ahmed replied. 'By now he is in prison or worse. You know this as well as I. His goods will have been seized, his money taken. We might as well wait for Yahya to rescue us.'

Nick's head had started to ring – a faint, rhythmic sound. He closed his eyes for a moment, feeling the shiver of the fever that seemed to come and go.

The ringing grew more insistent. He opened his eyes. 'My telephone,' he said, amazed at the overwhelming rush of relief he felt. *Eric, at last.* 'Excuse me.' He almost knocked over a chair in his hurry to get out.

The phone trilled on the desk. Nick grabbed the handset, his whole body aching. 'Hello?'

'Nick. Fucking hell, is that you?'

'Yes.' *Thank god.* He heard the crack of relief in his voice. 'Eric, we're in real trouble here.'

'No fucking joke.'

'A child died last night. Of cholera. That makes the governor a murderer.'

'So, what did you expect?' Eric's voice was faint, drowning in static. 'I haven't been able to reach you for fucking days.'

'They took our fuel and cut off the roads. It's a siege. Does J.P. know?'

Eric snorted. 'You need to find some juice for that radio and call your boss. It's time to confess your sins, boy.'

'My sins are the least of my problems.' Nick felt the burn of frustration; lifelines surrounded him but each was sliding out of his grasp. 'Children are dying here. I have to speak to him.'

'To who? J.P.?'

The receiver had become heavy in Nick's hand. 'Not J.P.. I need to speak to the governor.'

Silence crackled down the line. Nick waited, his breath's moisture oddly comforting on dry lips.

'I'm not sure that's a good idea.'

Cramps swirled through Nick's bowels, clenching his stomach. He could still see the child's hand flopping towards him in the shadows, spreading its curse to all of them.

'You said I should confess,' he said, swallowing down his nausea. 'I will – but to *him*, not J.P.. He wants a pound of flesh – I'll give him mine. He'll see me, Eric. I know he will.'

'OK.' Eric's voice was hollow across the miles. 'Come to the north road checkpoint tomorrow at afternoon prayers. You'd better be on time.'

'I'll be there.' Nick didn't want to put the phone down; it was a precious link to an ordinary world turning blithely far away.

'Eric . . .' he said – but the static drowned him out. He heard a voice say, 'OK, then. Tomorrow. 'Bye.' The line went dead.

He stood for a moment, the receiver humming in his ear. The

sound seemed beautiful to him, an almost sacred song. *If only I could pray.*

'Who are you meeting tomorrow?'

Nick looked up in surprise. JoJo stood by the door. His T-shirt was loose on his body, the governor's cap on his head.

He saw us, Margaret had said. *He knows.*

Nick set the phone down on the desk. 'The governor,' he replied. 'I'm going to see him.' Nausea and adrenalin chased each other around his veins; the boy's outline filled the doorway, monstrously huge. *I'm delirious.* He wanted ice-cold water, to drink it down and feel its cool splash on his face.

JoJo nodded. 'You are the governor's friend.'

Nick leaned against the desk, pressing the heel of his palm into his aching forehead. 'Why would you say that? You know it's not true.'

JoJo laughed – an ugly snigger. 'Yes. I don't know anything. I am just stupid JoJo.'

How did things come to this? Nick forced himself to look at JoJo. The unstable light played tricks with the boy's outline, dissolving and re-forming it. He tried to focus on the hands splayed on the doorframe, remembering with what assurance they had grasped a pencil to draw angles, or how he would rub his forehead with his knuckles while trying to solve a tricky equation.

'You know that I love your mother.'

The words came from nowhere. They flooded out as if a dam had burst, finally overwhelming him.

JoJo straightened. A shadow crossed his face. He folded his arms in front of him – a young, sombre judge.

'Love,' he echoed. 'Like the people in Tuesday's magazines.'

'Not like that.' Images confronted him, twisted and horrifying, sending shame through every channel of Nick's being. *I'm crying.* The water burned his eyes. 'You can't imagine yet, JoJo. One day you will.'

Through the roar of the fever chills, he heard the boy say, 'I don't love anything.'

Nick tried to breathe in calm. 'I know it feels like that now.' His voice was cracking. He opened his palms, offering them upwards. 'And I'm sorry, JoJo. I'm so, so sorry.'

Silence fell between them. Nick knew his words must ring empty to the boy – this young man – gazing at him with such contempt. What was the point of these justifications? Loving Margaret had been as inevitable as the tide coming in – and if time could circle back to New Year's Day, he could not make a different choice: he couldn't feel there'd been a choice to make.

There was no easy way to explain this to JoJo, but Nick felt he had to try. 'When I was your age I thought I wouldn't be able to love anything – not even myself. I thought my last chance had gone. But Margaret – your mother – she saved me from that.'

JoJo jerked his head on hearing his mother's name, mouth twisting. His disgust pierced Nick's heart, a brutal mirror to his own sins – the corrupting lies, the casual betrayals.

'Please don't blame her, JoJo. She's suffered so much.' The boy looked on, impassive as an angel. 'This wasn't her fault.'

JoJo laughed, an ugly sound. 'But she says it was not your fault. So who is to blame?'

Nick shrugged, exhaustion stealing over him. 'I don't know. Fate, I suppose.'

'What's Fate?'

A wry smile crept onto Nick's dry lips. 'It means: how things turn out. Another word for God. Or luck. Or universal forces. It depends if you believe things happen for a reason, or if they just happen.'

JoJo's eyes met his. 'So Fate sent you to take Mama.'

'No,' Nick whispered. He felt dazed; the few feet between them could have been a hundred miles. 'Maybe there's a reason all this happened – but I can't understand it yet.'

'But you will take Mama when you go.'

Nick looked up to meet the boy's eyes. 'I want to take all of you, JoJo.'

For the first time Nick saw the cold adult mask shift, a glimpse of painful confusion beneath. The boy looked down, uneasy. 'What if I want to stay here?'

'*I* can't stay here.' The words felt unreal even as Nick voiced them. 'I committed a crime. The money I was supposed to spend building the hospital – I used it to build the well instead.'

JoJo kept his arms folded in front of him. Nick noticed the way his fingers locked onto his own flesh. His eyes were in shadow.

'Where did you get this money?'

'I stole it.' Nick pointed to the safe. 'From there. Not all – there's a little left. Two thousand maybe.' He rubbed his forehead against the terrible itch burrowing inside.

'You stole like Robin Hood?' JoJo's voice was still tremulous with childhood – but Nick heard something deeper building beneath.

Nick laughed. His throat burned, sinews straining in his neck. 'Just like Robin Hood.'

'So it was good stealing, then?'

'I thought so.' The question overwhelmed him with sadness. 'I thought I was putting something right. For all of us.' He dipped his head under the weight of memories – sins of action and inaction linked together, heavy as a chain around his neck.

'Only thieves steal.' JoJo's voice was a challenge. 'Maybe they will put you in prison.'

'Oh, JoJo.' Nick rubbed his temples, exhausted by explanations. 'Maybe some things in life are more important than laws.'

'So you are in trouble?'

'Yes. A lot, unless I can pay it back.'

'Are you afraid?'

Nick struggled for an answer. *Am I afraid?* He lived inside a spinning cyclone of hopes and fears, all whirling past him too fast to count.

'I'm afraid you won't forgive me,' he said, at last. 'Maybe I deserve that. But only you can decide.'

'Mama says she will not go with you.' The boy's eyes did not waver.

Nick swallowed. 'We can't decide anything now, JoJo. Not yet. When this is over, I'll talk to you and your father. I'll answer any questions you want. But please – wait.'

JoJo looked on in silence. Then he released his arms, and began to turn around.

'Nagodeallah does not eat tonight,' he said over his shoulder. 'She cries all the time. Baba, he says we must stay away from each other. In case she is sick.'

Then he was gone from the doorway, leaving only the empty sky.

Nagode cried through the night. Her sobs reached Nick's window, sharp slivers shredding his sleep. Before dawn her cries lost their rhythm, becoming ragged and faint.

Nick opened his door into the milky air. His chills were back, frightening and powerful. The world was hot, but felt icy cold. His stomach cramped as he entered Dr Ahmed's house. The slick cool of the door handle burned and abraded his skin. Nothing was as it should be. *I'm dehydrated,* he told himself, clutching at drifting straws of reason. *But it's not cholera. Cholera has no fever.*

A candle still burned in the living room. Nick steadied himself on the grandfather clock as he passed. The wood felt soft under his hand, ripples of grain blurring like moth's wings. They seemed to dissolve under his touch, his fingers slipping through to the cogs and wheels beneath. He imagined the faraway London workshop where the clock was made – a delicate system of right angles and circles and symmetry conjured out of a simple tree trunk. The thought made him laugh aloud. *And, now, here you are, thousands of miles from home. And you don't even tick.*

Dr Ahmed stood in his dim bedroom doorway. He turned at Nick's approach, face bleak.

'She does not do well.' The reek of diarrhoea drifted up the hallway, in slow pulses of fetid air. 'She's making a lot of water.'

Nick felt a selfish dread. He looked into the little room. Margaret lay next to her daughter, one hand resting on Nagode's stomach, another on the pulse at her wrist. Candlelight crept over the bed sheets. Nagode's eyes were half open, following little flickers on the wall. Her face was beaded with sweat, an orb of dark gold melting slowly into the sheets.

Cholera sucks the body dry, he remembered. The baby's living reservoirs – her skin, her lips, her small hands – were being drained to emptiness.

Then Margaret moved her hand from Nagode's – and Nick saw them: the red beads tied onto the child's tiny wrist. The sight flooded him with unreasoning terror.

'I'm sorry.' He could not stay there one minute longer – the air was full of horror. 'Let me know what I can do.' Dr Ahmed's lips turned up in a ghost of a smile as Nick bolted towards the front door.

Outside the sun had risen. Pale but burning, it turned the world ash white.

Nick walked down the dead front garden and through the gate. The wind was rising with the heat, blasting dust from all directions. Miss Amina's broken chair still lay tilted on her porch. One leg rolled backwards and forwards, creaking with the random gusts. No goats brayed; even the dogs were silent.

Adeya and Hanan's house was shuttered. Their fields looked savage, stumps of millet poking up like amputated fingers. *She gave them all names.* But that was another world, as remote as anything he'd left behind in England.

The well was hidden behind a wall of trucks. Around it, the governor's soldiers were eating breakfast. Nick saw hands passing bread around, and flasks. One man shared a cigarette with his comrade. Tendrils of smoke leached out between the folds of his checkered scarf, as if the skin inside was steaming.

The itch in Nick's brain was close to unbearable. *Aren't these people human?* He wondered what would happen if he offered to take them to the little room in the back of Dr Ahmed's house and showed them the child vanishing into the bed sheets. Would they think of their own children, their little brothers and sisters? What would they feel?

'Don't go.'

Nick looked around, shocked. The white boy was standing next to him, his shirt open. To Nick's feverish eyes he seemed constructed of parched earth and heat – the elements in all their fury.

The boy nodded his head towards the soldiers.

'They will not help you.'

Nick opened his mouth to argue. But weariness pressed into him. The pink scars on the boy's skin were electric ribbons, the hilt of his knife a dark snake writhing from his belt.

'The girl is dying,' the boy said. *Mister. His name is Mister.* 'JoJo's sister. He told me. The mother, she weeps.'

Nick could not answer. His chest was tight, his neck muscles like iron bands. His eyes were drawn to the horizon, already erased by the heat haze.

'And more are sick in the village.' Mister laughed. The sound rose through the wind's hiss, stirring Nick to rage. That laugh was the world laughing back at him, ridiculing all his hopes and efforts.

'What the fuck are you laughing at?' he shouted, his voice hoarse. 'What do you want?' There were sores in his mouth, the iron taste of blood. He wanted to hit this ghost boy, to exorcise him from his thoughts. His fists clenched and unclenched; a small presence in the back of his mind, perhaps his father's, shook its head in disgust.

Mister was unfazed. 'I want nothing. But what about you?' He pointed to the men around the well. 'Do you want them to leave? To have the water and fuel and medicines again?'

Now it was Nick's turn to laugh. 'Right. You're the magician. You tell me how to make that happen.'

Mister put his head on one side. Then he reached behind his back and brought out a small bottle of Johnnie Walker Red Label. 'Abracadabra! Isn't that what the magicians say?'

Nick took the bottle almost by instinct. It glowed rich amber in the light. 'Where does this come from?'

'From Tuesday's place. I know his hidden things.'

'You stole it.' Nick tried to hand the bottle back, but Mister put his arms up, backing away.

'Yes, boss.' He smiled, a slow, red smile. 'We are both thieves, you and I.'

The chills redoubled, pushing up spikes of fear. 'JoJo told you.'

Mister bowed, pink scalp showing under the white curls. 'Sir Robin Hood,' he said.

'Don't you dare mock me.'

'I do not mock you,' Mister replied. 'I respect you. You are brave, sure. But are you brave enough?'

'Brave enough for what?'

Mister turned his head a few degrees. The men around the well had finished their morning meal and were stretching their legs in the sun. 'To make them leave.'

Nick squinted into the killing light, trying to catch sight of the well. 'How can I make them leave?'

'They are loyal to one man, while he pays them. If that man is no more, they will turn to another who can pay. Someone who loves us. You know him, I think.'

A slow pulse of dread pushed through Nick's chest. He looked down at Mister, not daring to understand him. 'You mean, without the governor, these become Danjuma's men?'

'Between one day and the next.'

'So why doesn't Danjuma just pay them himself?'

'They took him, boss.' Mister smiled. 'The governor's soldiers keep him. But these soldiers – they wait for word from us.'

Small shadows whirred between them – blowflies, searching for carrion. Nick felt one settle on his cheek; he tried to brush it away, with an arm heavy as lead. 'What has this to do with me?'

Mister shrugged. 'Only a little money, for some of these men,' he said. 'And I can make the governor go.'

'Go?' The light was blinding, tangled up with the flies and the buzzing of the wind. 'Go where?'

Mister's voice was soft. 'Go.' His hand swept across his throat and carried on upwards, towards the white sky.

Nick felt his gaze dragged along with it until the light scorched his retina. *Go*. He'd walked here with Margaret and JoJo once, gathering pebbles to decorate their castle. JoJo had raced ahead in exhilaration, Margaret's scarf a stream of colour flooding the sky.

Now he turned away from Mister, towards the house, towards the dark little room and its smell of decay. Behind him, Mister stood wreathed in light and smiles, a young Dionysus.

The house seemed to retreat before him as Nick neared it. The air was thick, as in dreams of paralysis. The whisky bottle swayed in his hand like a pendulum. His feet dragged as he walked, each step heavy with the effort not to look back.

The house was all quiet and stillness. Margaret's bedroom door stood open; he stepped through. She lay on her back beside Nagode, hands clasped between them – and his heart nearly stopped. *Too late,* a cruel voice whispered, until he saw the slow rise of their chests.

At rest they were so similar. He could see Margaret's strong jawline under Nagode's cheeks, waiting for life to sculpt it out of softness.

Then Margaret opened her eyes. She turned to her daughter without a word, checking her pulse.

'I was praying,' she said. Her voice was clear, normal – as if she'd said, *I was cooking*.

Nick nodded, rubbing his chest. For the first time in many months, he was lost for words with her. *I held you in my arms and watched your face loosen,* he wanted to say. *We talked about your family, about Wordsworth and Shakespeare. We dreamed of where we would go together, and what we would do. I could smell you on my skin at the office and taste you in my sleep.*

But now there was this terrible sense of drifting apart, of a world coming unmoored. He buried his face in her neck, breathing her bitter, salty smell; a distant part of him was conscious of Nagode's wet sheets. And yet Margaret's arms were around him and he felt their breath synchronising, the reassuring immediacy of touch – and for a moment he was secure.

But then her arms loosed. She pushed him back and turned away, towards her daughter. Nick saw her fingers brush Bako's bracelet, bright on Nagode's wrist.

'I'm not a fool, in this at least,' she said. 'It cannot make her live. But if she goes ...' She swallowed, steadying herself to calmness. 'If she goes, perhaps it will guide them to each other.'

Nick laid his hand over hers. 'This is not your fault, Margaret. God is not punishing you. Or us.'

She turned to him, studying him in the candlelight. Her pupils were huge, but intently focused – as if he were a book in a foreign language. 'We reap what we sow.'

Nick clenched her hand, feeling the grind of bones. 'We didn't sow this. The governor did.'

She shook her head, pulling her hand away.

'None of you can see the truth,' she whispered. 'If JoJo asks why it rains, my husband will tell him about the clouds. You will tell him about the oceans and winds. But who gave us water in the first place and made us need it so much?' She was crying now, tears making luminous traces on her cheeks.

He leaned in towards her, but she pushed him away. 'No, Nicholas,' she said. 'We had a season. But it is over.'

Her words dropped onto him like stones, crushing some deep, sustaining hope. 'Nagode won't die.' The words felt false and desperate; his mind raced, grasping at straws. 'And this is even more reason to come with me. To keep her and JoJo safe.'

'If she dies, there will be two children under my garden,' said Margaret. 'I will eat and drink them every morning, and I will know my penance is done.'

'No.' Nick pushed himself off the bed, fury accelerating from a dark, hidden place within. 'You think some God would be happy to see you suffering here for the rest of your life? You think Nagode would want that? It's bullshit and you know it.'

Footsteps cut into his consciousness – Dr Ahmed coming up the corridor.

'Is there trouble?' The old man put his head around the door. Nick could not answer; fever still beat in his brain, raw and wounded. He knew how it must look: her tears and his in the charged air. But he was past caring. His mind reeled; he almost longed for discovery.

But then Nagode stirred, a soft cry escaping her blistered lips. Sanity returned, the raking touch of remorse. The baby lay unnaturally flat, as if starting to release her hold on her body. He had a sudden image of her stretched pale on a winding sheet in the mosque's back room, Margaret slowly untying the beads from another child's wrist.

He turned to the door. 'I'm going to speak to the governor,' he told them. 'I need to get to the checkpoint by afternoon prayers.'

Dr Ahmed stood in silence for a moment, considering. Then he said, 'Take my car. It has some fuel still. Yours is empty.'

Thank you. Nick opened his mouth but the words shrivelled in his throat. Dr Ahmed's eyes were calm voids.

The car keys were on a shelf behind the grandfather clock. As Nick's hands closed on them, he smelled the fresh polish. A buffing cloth lay there, brown with old wax.

The clock gleamed in the room's half-light. Its face was bone white, solemn. It filled Nick's vision, the circle with its eternal numeric procession restoring a memory of calm and order to the chaos of his feelings.

Please. The word swelled from him, an impulsive prayer. *Let Nagode live. Bring back Adeya's crops and Dr Ahmed's white birds. Let JoJo grow up safe and happy. Let him learn to love someone, so he can understand and forgive me. Set Margaret free. Please.*

Silence flowed from the clock in reply. It spread over him and through the room, drowning out the howl of the wind battering against the walls.

The white wind blew through the village, a relentless hiss against Dr Ahmed's car. The market stalls were empty, bags of trash tumbling across the street.

The closest checkpoint was a mile away. Nick felt strength return to him as the car bumped and groaned towards it. The chills had faded, his senses calmed.

He slowed as two soldiers walked into the road to wave him down. Across the checkpoint he saw the white shape of Eric's Jeep, its engine humming.

A teenager in fatigues pulled open Nick's door, indicating he should get out. The muzzle of a rifle slapped against his thigh as he stood. 'Thank you.' Nick's voice rang clear through the flat space. The soldier pointed to the barrier where Eric waited and jerked his head.

Eric didn't look at him as Nick swung into the passenger seat. He put the car into gear, swinging back north. They travelled in the cloudy wake of a pickup truck carrying armed men. Another followed close behind. 'Escorts,' said Eric. 'Lucky us.'

The highway was empty, closed at both ends. 'He took no chances,' Eric explained. 'If you want to go south from the Town, you have to drive way out east first. Another whole fucking day on the road.'

'I didn't expect it to come to this,' Nick told him.

He looked through the windscreen at the soldiers just feet away. One returned his glance, hunched over, head jerking to the highway's rhythm. Silence filled the car.

At last the convoy crossed the Town's borders. The highway slowed and swelled into shops, into roadside flowerbeds and people. *Life goes on.* Nick leaned his forehead against the window, eyes trailing people as they went about their business – laughing, reading newspapers, buying shoes. He wondered if they would care if he showed them a picture of Tuesday's son lying lifeless on Dr Ahmed's table, or Nagode dying quietly in her stinking bedroom just a short drive away.

Something vicious began to bubble inside Nick, stirring memories long-sealed. He was back in his mother's kitchen, roses climbing outside the window, his father home early from work to eat tea with them, asking Madi whether things were improving at school, probing beyond the boy's hesitancy, asking whether he was glad he'd come to England despite everything.

'We're not always the kindest people,' Nick's father had said. 'Not always welcoming to strangers. My own lot got their share, when I was a boy. Jews are foreigners everywhere. Not that we were perfect. There were brutes inside our community and brutes outside. It was hard to choose between them sometimes.'

Madi had been dubious, his face troubled. 'My father says we're lucky,' he'd said. 'He says we're safe here. But – well – he still gets mad sometimes. When people round here think we're stupid, I tell him: they can't help it. They don't know you were a teacher. They think all taxi drivers are stupid.'

Nick could still see Madi's eyes, lowered and fixed on the table while he scratched a piece of blue paint off the edge, another of life's inconsequential details. 'I know we have to get used to it,' he'd said. 'But I see what it does to him – he's angry all the time. Like he wants to smack something.'

Now Nick remembered the satisfying force of that word – *smack* – picturing his own fist in Phil's face, wiping off the bully's sneer. He'd been eating a Jammy Dodger while his father spoke to Madi; he could still taste the factory pink of the jam, fiercely sweet, see his father's hand as he laid it briefly on Madi's head. 'Unfairness is universal,' he'd told them both. 'But, fortunately, so is justice.'

The iron barrier before the governor's residence swung up as their convoy approached. To Nick's right, the hospital complex loomed against a hazy sky. The unfinished clinic jutted from its side, ragged plastic sheeting fluttering in empty holes.

Nick pushed his hands into his pockets, digging for confidence. *This has to work.*

The guard jerked his gun for Nick and Eric to follow him. They walked past the heavy doors and along the hallway with its silent marbled walls. Another set of doors swung open at the end onto a long room where sound echoed from the vaulted ceilings.

The governor sat facing them, dressed in military greens. Nick had time to count every bronzed button as his footfalls reverberated against the walls.

He stopped in front of the chair. The governor was engaged in quiet conversation with a staff member, his head turned away. It struck Nick as a petty kind of arrogance. *I can wait you out, you son of a bitch.*

But as the minutes ticked by, his temper began to fray. Dr Ahmed's clock was running its countdown inside his head; back in the village, the seconds of Nagode's life were draining away. *Whatever arguments we have to make, whatever punishments are coming, let them come now.*

'You've made your point,' Nick said aloud. The governor's eyes flickered upwards, settling on his face. Water churned inside his stomach – an echo of the morning's chills. He clenched his legs, and found they were trembling.

'Please.' He tried again, his tone lower, more conciliatory. 'You've made your point.'

The governor tilted his head, heavy brows furrowed.

'What point was I making, Nicholas?'

He looked up to the airy ceiling. *Give me the right words.*

'Dr Ahmed's daughter, his baby daughter,' he said. 'She has cholera. She's dying. The lake is infected.' He swallowed down the caustic burning in his stomach. 'If you're so angry – and I understand why you would be – then take it out on me. Not them.'

The governor leaned forward, a dark mass in the centre of the room.

'You think this is revenge, Nicholas? You think: here is another petty ruler who subjugates with collective punishment.'

'This is absolutely collective punishment.'

The governor pointed his finger at him in a stabbing gesture. 'You insult me. You think you are some hero in one of your fairy tales. But this is my land, my people. My blood. I care for every drop. You – you care only for your own skin.'

Nick clenched his fists. The room smelled of disinfectant and the oily waft of some unknown fragrance. Vomit curled into his throat.

'You're the one killing them.' He longed for the courage to punch this man, wishing that he'd come like Madi with a knife instead of on his knees. 'You're the murderer, not me.'

'Wrong again.' The governor leaned back. 'Tell me, where is the money for the children's clinic? The one you promised to build us?'

The chills were back full force, splintering Nick's bones from the inside. 'I can get that money back. I just need time.'

The governor nodded. 'So, take your time. And when you next come, bring back what you stole from us because you think you know better.'

He waved his arm in dismissal. Nick felt a hand on his shoulder – one of the young guards, bristling with authority.

'Wait!' The hand was tugging him but he held his ground. The governor turned away; panic seized Nick – there was too much left unsaid. 'Don't you understand?' He was screaming now, the words choking him. 'They're dying already!'

He threw the guard's hand off his shoulder. But another wrapped around his neck, squeezing his windpipe. Hard metal pressed into his back.

Now the governor stood up. Nick had forgotten how tall he was, larger than Danjuma or Dr Ahmed. His outline blurred before Nick's eyes as he approached, deeper than the well, immovable as a rock.

'Our new hospital will treat children with cancer,' he said, as

Nick fought for breath. 'Sometimes the treatment will be very drastic and there will be pain. But the cancer must die for the child to live.'

He made a gesture, and Nick was freed. He gasped for air as he clutched his throat; his skin felt slippery, loose.

The governor turned away, walking back to his seat. Then he stopped, the strong muscles of his neck twisting as he looked back. 'Dr Ahmed would tell you I am right,' he said. 'So please give him a message from me. Tell him his old friend sends greetings. Tell him – I wish his daughter well.'

Eric dropped Nick off at the checkpoint in silence. A cloudy evening was setting in, covering the land in colours of ash and smoke.

Nick glanced up as he stepped from the Jeep. 'It looks like rain.' The air was growing heavy, static building between sky and ground. He could almost feel the water falling onto his face, warm and rich.

But Eric shook his head. 'Electric storm,' he said. 'A good night to stay inside.'

Dark forms were hurrying through the streets, a handful of people caught out after dusk. *A good night to stay inside.* The words played inside his head over and over. *Hurry*, he thought as he passed them. *Hurry.*

Above Dr Ahmed's house the sky was purple as a bruise. Inside the candlelight was gentle. Dr Ahmed sat hunched on the sofa, his can of polish in one hand and a buffing cloth in the other. The old man looked hollow, a stretched shape over brittle bones. *Polishing his clock while his child's life ebbs away.*

Dreading the answer, Nick asked: 'How is Nagode?'

'Still living.' Dr Ahmed looked up, his glasses smudged with grease. 'No better and no worse. Praise Allah for that.' Nick could not bring himself to reply.

'The young are stronger than we imagine.' Dr Ahmed's eyes

fell to the cloth lying on his palm, as if he were weighing it. 'They can endure what we cannot.'

'Is Margaret with her?'

Dr Ahmed's body grew even stiller. 'She will not leave her side.'

His voice was so heavy that Nick felt a strange compulsion to take his hand and kiss it. If only there were a way across this strange gulf of silence and complicity. *I love my wife, you know.* Somewhere the right words existed to explain that they were not rivals, but partners in the same quest – that each needed the other to succeed.

'How was your meeting with the governor?' Dr Ahmed's tone switched to strained breeziness.

Nick shook his head. The cold was still within him, gripping his muscles and contorting his thoughts. 'A waste of time.'

'A pity.' The two words cut Nick; his father might have said the same. Not in all the years of his son's missteps had he ever descended to the banality of 'I told you so'.

Nick looked down the little hallway, towards the closed door of Margaret's room. He wanted more than anything to go to her, to lie down with her and share her sorrow. Dr Ahmed's presence barred the way. But another shape sat huddled by her door. 'JoJo?'

The boy looked up, silent, his arms around his knees.

Behind them, Dr Ahmed said, 'I cannot let him inside. But Yahya wishes to wait there.'

The chill was in Nick's heart, freezing pain into numbness. 'He loves his sister.'

'He loves us all.' Dr Ahmed stood up and walked to the clock, resting the cloth against its body.

The bottle of Johnnie Walker stood on Nick's desk in the office where he'd left it. The liquid was cool and gold in the light, but it scorched his throat as it went down.

At a quarter empty, his head was already pounding along with the thunder outside. Resolution was heating up inside him: he flicked on the HF radio, fired up the generator and called J.P.. The handset felt hard against his mouth as he waited for a response. *Come in. Over. Come in. Over.*

Suddenly, the static broke. 'Nicholas? Is that you?'

Nick leaned his head against the receiver. 'J.P.. It's me. I should have called, I know. I'm nearly out of fuel for the generator. There's . . . there's real trouble here.'

J.P.'s voice came through, harsh over the breaking frequency. 'Nicholas, please tell me you didn't take that money?'

Everything hurt. Nick pressed the receiver to his chest, trying to breathe. Then he raised it to his mouth again, the Johnnie Walker slurring the words on his tongue. 'I have the money in England. I was going to pay it back. I still can. J.P. – I don't know what to say. I couldn't just stand by.'

The static hissed at Nick. *'No way, mate.'* Madi was standing in the corner, smiling. *'Never thought you could.'*

The line crackled into life. 'I cannot speak to you now, Nicholas. There are laws here, too, and penalties. I could put you in prison.'

Nick felt the threat bounce off the armour of his desperation. 'So be it. Can you help us here? The governor has cut off all supplies. People will die. They're already dying.'

'I have to consult. Then I will come north. With the police, Nicholas. Do you understand me?'

That will be too late. 'I understand you,' he said. His heart was taking wing, lifting him above fear.

'You're a fool, Nicholas. Out.' The line went dead.

He let the receiver fall on the desk. The safe was under his feet. He opened it and pulled out the small bundle of notes. He laid them on the desk beside the telephone. *Just a little money, and they can become Danjuma's men. Between one day and the next.*

No. He picked up the mouthpiece and dialled Kate's number. The wires strained to make their connection, searching over thousands of miles for one pinpoint echo of response.

At last, incredibly, he heard a ringing tone. It would still be afternoon in London. She was out, probably at a friend's house.

Or maybe visiting his mother, holding her unresponsive hand, chatting aimlessly about new clients or fabricating wedding plans.

But she answered after a few rings. 'Hello?' Music played in the background; he heard the hum of voices. 'Hello?'

'Kate.'

'Who is this?' Her words were fracturing over the line into staccato bursts. 'Nick? Is that you?'

'Yes.' His voice sounded broken, even to himself. 'It's me.'

'God, Nick. Oh, god – I was just . . . it's so frustrating! I can't hear you – it's Sam's birthday, he came to do a barbecue.'

He laughed, suddenly drunk. The sun would be shining, the air chilled with a residual nip of winter. Kate would be light and pretty in her flimsy dress, bare arms challenging the spring goose bumps and a glass of wine in her hand.

'Nick, about the money. Don't hate me, please. I just – please come home. Please. We can't do this over the phone.'

'I know that.'

'Sorry, I . . . what? I can't hear!'

'I know.' He was crying now – weak, useless fever tears running into the handset. She was in another universe; they had separated into two bubbles of existence, floating off in different directions. He tried to transport himself to their garden: the neat floral borders, the pale chime of glass against glass, the smooth touch of her hand. Teflon-coated, it slipped out of his and left him standing there, invisible.

'I want . . . talk.' A song was playing behind her, achingly familiar. Someone else laughed, close to the receiver. 'Sam . . . tell me . . . you . . . OK?'

'I'm sorry, Kate.' His voice was barely a whisper. 'Nick!' he heard her say as he put the receiver down. It knocked the whisky bottle, making a hollow ring.

Picking up J.P.'s money, he stepped out onto the porch. The night was full of heat, a directionless, rumbling darkness. Flashes of lightning sent insect wings into panicked spirals around his head. Nick stood in the doorway, feeling the alcohol stalk the fever through his limbs.

Bodies were moving at the edge of his vision – Hanan, with Adeya beside her, walking slowly away from the house. They would have offered to nurse Nagode, he realised. Of course they would have come – and of course Dr Ahmed would have turned them back. Adeya walked more slowly than her mother, her shoulders bowed, the scarred ridges of her hands hidden under long sleeves. He saw her look back for a moment, face wet in the lightning's afterglow.

The hair on his arms stood on end. The darkness had a red tinge. The sky was breaking into rolling shapes, like writing underlined in white flashes. The governor was the thunder. Mister was the lightning. And the rest of them, they were just insects spiralling oblivious, drawn blindly into the storm's mouth.

Fury filled him: at the storm, at his own helplessness. Lightning mocked him as it struck due north, the only signpost in the formless night. *You only care for your own skin.*

You're wrong! he screamed, a voiceless cry that hurt. *I love them!* He flung his arms out, setting his body in front of the porch, in front of Margaret and her children, in front of Adeya and Miss Amina, in front of Madi and the climbing frame.

The thunder laughed back at him. *You're drunk,* Madi said. *Smashed. I know,* Nick replied. *I'm sorry.*

The rest of J.P.'s money lay crumpled in his hand. Less than two thousand dollars. He felt the hands on his windpipe again, choking the air from him. *You're a murderer,* he told the governor. *Wrong.* The governor's voice ricocheted through the air. *The cancer must die for the child to live.*

Nick's feet carried him along the porch to the back of the house. They passed the swaying branches of low, dead trees and JoJo's ruined castle, bringing him to the boy's bedroom window.

You're mad. Stop. Stop now. Someone was crying out to him – a boy's voice, a child frozen by the climbing frame. But Madi whispered in his other ear. *Go on, mate. I dare you. I double dare you.*

He tapped on the window. There was a second of silence. And then he saw JoJo's surprised face.

'I need Mister,' Nick said. He tried to focus through the blur of the whisky – and saw JoJo's face crease in puzzlement. 'I need him right now. Where is he?'

'Wait there,' JoJo mouthed at last.

The boy met him in the back garden. He wore the governor's college cap, a large Coca-Cola T-shirt and low-slung jeans.

'What do you want with him?'

Nick put his face in his hands. *What do I want?* he asked his father. *What do you think?* But for the first time in his life, the old man was silent.

There was no point in waiting; time was running out. Nick forced himself to speak. 'Mister knows what I want,' he said.

JoJo hesitated. Then he said: 'Come.'

The child drinking Coke on JoJo's T-shirt had yellow hair and a white smile. It waved at Nick, toasting his success as he followed JoJo out of Dr Ahmed's garden, into the street and through the village.

Time slowed. Nick had to force one step to follow another; with each he felt the world turn a fraction under his feet, a relentless onward movement. He focused on the blond child on JoJo's T-shirt, following him through Tuesday's unlocked front door, past the dark and pillaged shelves and into the rear courtyard.

Mister stood up as Nick came in. The air here had a sharp, chemical reek. It woke the alcohol in Nick's veins, sending his head reeling.

The Boys gathered around. Nick saw Akim and Juma and others from the village. But Mister stood out among them, a lonely pillar in the sand.

'Hey, boss.' Mister spoke to him, unsmiling. 'What is it you want here?'

The others were not real; Nick could only see Mister, could only feel the strange force pulling them together, stronger than anything he'd ever known.

There was a moment of hesitation, the last echoes of doubt. But he'd gone too far; there was no turning back. He felt JoJo's eyes on him.

What do I want here? Nick reached into the back of his jeans; he brought out the dollars, slick with his sweat. Holding them out to Mister, he fought the protest of gravity as it tugged against his arm.

'I want justice,' he said.

Mister gives Nicholas' money to Juma. He says: 'This is for the governor's men. You know which ones. Half for the captain watching the governor's house. Half for the captain holding Danjuma. Make sure you see Danjuma's face before you give the captain the money.'

Juma says: 'First let me smoke.' He wants a bang cigarette. But Mister takes him by his shoulder. He says: 'Juma, eh! Use your head. Remember what Danjuma said. We are his soldiers. He cannot move tonight, but we can. When I come to the Town later, all must be ready.'

Juma has his head down. He is angry. But Mister puts his hand behind Juma's neck. Black skin on white. He says: 'My captain.' And Juma, he starts to smile. They laugh, the two of them. Mister, he stands up now. He says, 'Go now, captain.'

Akim complains: 'Why does Juma always go? What if they see him on the road?'

'They will never see him,' Mister says.

He takes one of our last cigarettes and gives it to Akim. Juma's friend Buffalo says: 'Eh, Akim, share with me.' Akim says: 'Wait your turn, long-nose, or smoke your dick.'

'Fuck you,' Buffalo says. He likes the American films that Mister gets from the Town. He pretends to talk like those films. Buffalo's real name is Abubakar. But in The Boys he is Buffalo Soldier. He played me a song with the same name, on Mister's stereo. 'He sings for us,' Buffalo told me. 'For all the slaves. He

289

was a lion, like us.' I used to think he was clever to think these things. Now I do not care.

Mister is looking at them. He smiles when they fight. Like Baba used to smile at me and Bako. 'They are just boys,' he would say to Mama. 'They have to fight if they are to grow.'

Mister sees me looking. He says: 'Boss, do you want Akim's smoke? It's yours. Take it if you like.'

I want to smoke. I want to. My head hurts without the smoke. My bones are like stones in the ground. But Akim is staring at me, waiting for my answer. His mouth is open. Inside he is pink and white. I can see all the way down his throat.

I say to Mister: 'Akim can smoke.'

Akim thinks I laugh at him. He makes a face and turns away from me. Buffalo helps him to light the smoke. 'Fuck,' he says, when the light burns his fingers. Fuck. He likes that word.

The smoke is lit now. But I cannot smell it. I sit and put my head onto my knees. I can smell Nagode. Not how she is now. Now she smells like Bako. But before she smelled like milk. She and Adeya, they have the same smell. Adeya milks the goats and she brings the milk to Mama. Mama drinks the milk and gives her milk to Nagode. They all smell like milk. Sometimes if I close my eyes, I cannot tell which one of them is near me.

Mister touches me on my head. 'JoJo,' he says. His voice is quiet.

I do not answer. I am thinking of Nicholas and Mama. 'I love her,' he said. Like this tells me the answer to everything – like we are one of his quadratic equations, and he is x and Mama is y and if you make all the calculations in the right way then everything becomes clear.

'Do not be sad, JoJo.' Mister is talking now. His eyes are white. They see everything.

He says: 'You need to keep the fires hot, JoJo. The fires are your strength. You cannot put water on a fire.' He touches my cheek with one finger. Gentle. Like Mama's hand.

'I want to walk,' I tell him.

He looks at me for a moment. Then he nods. He says: 'Walk, it's OK.'

I turn to leave. Akim and Ibrahim are sharing their smoke. Mister, he says: 'Wait.' He comes to me and puts something in my hand.

It is a watch. It is not heavy like Danjuma's watch or like the governor's. It has a small face and electric numbers that flash: on, off, on, off. The strap has a picture of a laughing mouse in red pants. Mickey Mouse. I know him from the comics we used to read before. Bako and me.

'You can read this?' Mister is asking me.

'Yes, I can.'

'Before it says three here, you must be back. Can you remember?'

He puts his hand on my shoulder. I feel it there, heavy. It pushes me down.

I look at his eyes. I am thinking: when will my eyes look like this? When will I have no fear?

'Yes,' I tell him. 'I can remember.'

'Good,' he says. 'We have work to do, you and me.'

Outside Tuesday's shop there is nothing. There is no noise, nothing from the generators or the lights. The only sound comes from the sky. It speaks and we listen.

The mosque has no light any more. Imam Abdi, he sleeps at Juma's house. I cannot go to my house. Nicholas is there, with Mama and Nagode. If I go back, they will tell me she is dead. Then Mama will go with Nicholas. And Baba will be broken, like his clock.

My feet want to move. They take me south, towards the school. Towards the capital. But now I will never go there. They will go and I will stay. I will stay with Mister, and I will have his eyes one day, and boys will come to me and I will teach them things. Not like Nicholas, with his books and his equations. I will teach them about the spirits and the fires.

I come to the wall of the yard. A long time ago, I climbed here, to throw my shoe. *Right here is where I put my foot. You can see, there is a mark. A hole where the wall has crumbled. When other children come to play here, they will not know my foot made this hole. But I will still be here.*

'JoJo.'

I jump. Did the spirits follow me here? I turn and say: 'Who is that?'

Adeya comes down the path from the village. Her abaya falls all the way down from her head, like water. Her dress is weeping onto the sand.

'Eh, JoJo. What are you doing here?'

I do not want to tell her. 'Go away, Adeya,' *is all I say. I turn back to the wall. I must not see her. She must not see me.*

She says: 'I cannot sleep.'

Then she comes to stand by me, to look with me over the wall. She keeps her hands inside her abaya. She is always hiding her hands now. First her body and now her hands. One day she will hide her face, too. Then Adeya will become a spirit, like the rest.

'I came from your mother's house,' *she said.* 'My mother watches Nagode while she rests. But your baba would not let me inside.'

'Does Nagode live?' *These words come without me thinking. I can feel Adeya close by. She is smaller than I am. I could carry her easily, now that I am growing strong.*

'She lives.' *Adeya speaks quickly.* 'She still lives, JoJo.'

I want to cry. But Mister says we must not put water on the fires inside. Instead I say: 'You must go from here, Adeya. It is a bad night.'

Adeya, she nods her head. Her foot, it makes circles on the ground. All lines from the middle of the circle to the edge will be the same length.

'Will you not come too?' *she says. Her voice is quiet.* 'Come back with me. Hanan, she will stay at your house until dawn. You can sleep in our house, JoJo.'

I cannot, I tell her. I have work to do.

'Work with those boys? They are the bad ones, JoJo.'

'You know nothing,' I tell her. 'Leave me alone.'

Adeya's face is round, like Nagode's. She is made of circles. But when she is cross, she gets lines that are straight and deep. She makes those lines now, and she folds her arms.

She says: 'Don't you speak to me like some big shot. I know you, JoJo. These boys, they are playing with you.'

Adeya, her hand comes out from her dress and touches my arm. Her scars are pink, like the flowers on Mama's scarf.

I am trying to think of Mister and Nicholas and his money, and Juma on his motorbike. But inside my mind I can only see Adeya, with her hands out to me, open.

'Come with me, JoJo.' She is saying it, over and over. Her voice hurts my head. She is bringing the water up from inside, she is trying to stop the fires. 'Come with me, JoJo. It is not good to be outside tonight.'

I grab her by the shoulders. I see it then – the fear. She looks into my eyes and she sees white, only white.

I scream: 'Get away from me! Get away!' I push her. And she falls.

The air goes out of her. Her hands, they go to where the bag is connected to her insides. She pulls herself around the bag. She makes a circle on the ground.

I stand above her. And now the sky and I are shouting. We are shouting together. 'See! See!' I shout. But I feel like this is not me. This is not my voice. I stop, and there is no sound. Just Adeya. She is crying.

I turn and I run. I run away from her – but there is nowhere to run, except back. Back to Tuesday's looted shop and to Mister, who waits there for me.

The wind follows me. It sends things to trip me. There are branches that cut my legs. There are wires that twine around my feet. The place where Jalloh keeps his hens, it is turned over on its side. And it rattles, like a sick person.

Now Mickey Mouse says three. And when I come in, Mister, he stands up.

'Are you ready, JoJo?' he asks. The other boys, they say nothing. They are not the ones chosen.

I am not ready. No, never.

But then I remember how I pushed Adeya on the ground. And I say, 'Yes. Yes, I am ready.'

Mister takes me to his workshop. There is Tuesday's bike, waiting. It shines, silver and black. Reflected in the chrome I look big, like Danjuma.

He climbs on and starts the engine. The bike makes a noise like the goats, when Jalloh turns them upside down.

Mister says: 'Get up behind me, JoJo.' So I climb on. I put my hands on his shoulders. Between us is something stiff and sharp. I take my cap, the governor's cap, off my head. I tuck it into my jeans, so I cannot feel the knife. 'Be careful,' Mister tells me. 'And hold tight.'

We ride west – out into the desert, until we see the lake. I see Binza's place. The red curtain goes in and out, like a tongue.

'Where are we going?' I shout into Mister's ear.

'We cannot take the road,' he calls back. 'So we must find a way without roads.'

The way without roads is long. We go around the lake, over stones until my bones feel like they will break. When it hurts too much to stay silent, I cry out. And Mister, he laughs.

'Eh, JoJo, it hurts, eh? Don't be ashamed. We are making you again. We will make you strong.'

'Why not take Akim?' I ask Mister as we go.

'That one? He is nothing,' Mister says. 'He never felt the fire like you and me.' Mister points east. 'Look,' he says. 'The road to the Town.' And there it is, with no cars and no soldiers. We left them behind. Now there is nothing to stop us.

'We will come into the Town this way,' Mister says. 'They will never see us. Near the Town there are other roads – small and not watched.'

'Why did no one come this way before?' I ask him. I can see him smile.

'They came, boss. Many times, to bring our smokes and fuel.'
Mister lifts his packet of cigarettes, holding them tight against the
wind.

He says: 'And now it is your turn. To become a real soldier. And
it is my turn to pay my blood debt.'

I ask him: 'Which debt?' But I already know.

'To my father,' he says. The back of his head is white in the
dark around us.

The road is silent. Now we go more slowly, and the way is
smooth. My ears, they are singing from the wind. I take my cap
out of my jeans and put it back on my head.

Soon we reach the quiet roads, turning and turning through
houses. The houses are close together and made of fine stone.
They are tall with high windows and bars to guard them from
strangers.

I can smell flowers in these gardens. Something sweet still grows
here. There are dates on the road. And red flowers on the walls, with
yellow mouths. Laughing lilies, I remember. Mama, she loves these
ones. But they only grow for us when the rains come.

At last, we stop. Mister, he tells me to get off. He pulls the bike
against the wall. There are lights here, bright lights. The bike
makes a shadow, big and black.

Mister says: 'We wait.' So I watch the sky. The storm has passed
away south. Above there is quiet, and a moon. Yellow, like a husk
of corn. Like Nagode's milk.

My body is still shaking, and I am so tired. I stand against the
wall. In my head I fly to the moon. The moon is a lake. The water
is white and sweet to drink.

Then Mister, he pinches my arm. I am awake, straight away. A
man is coming to us. A soldier – one of the governor's men. I want
to cry out, but Mister, he hushes me.

The soldier comes to stand in front of us. He looks at me. His
eyes are black inside yellow, like the well inside the land.

He asks Mister: 'Who is he?

'My man,' says Mister. 'Is it done?'

The man says nothing. Then he turns his head to look down the street.

'Go inside,' he says. 'The house is the first one.'

The first house is the one with the laughing lilies. I want to pick one as we open the gate. I would have given it to Mama. But that was before.

I whisper to Mister: 'Someone will see us.' Rich men, they always have someone guarding.

Mister, he smiles. 'Not tonight,' he whispers back. 'Tonight they will all be blind.'

And then I understand the secret. The money Nicholas gave Mister has paid the governor's soldiers tonight. It has paid them all to be blind.

The garden is quiet and green, too green. Aloe and date palms. A path points to the front door. A man stands there, watching. Mister puts his hand behind his back. He looks at the man. I hear my heart, like the engine. Then the man opens the door and stands aside.

The doorway is a black mouth. It swallows us. Inside is a carpet. So soft. I can smell dinner. Rice and meat. There is one candle and a big glass light with many colours. It sends shadows onto Mister's face. It makes him look like a painting.

Behind one door, a woman is making noises. Ah ah ah, she says. Like a song with no words.

Mister puts his hand on the door. I want to pray. Do not open it. Please. Do not. I am not ready.

But Mister, he pushes it open.

I can see over his shoulder. I can see the bed and the woman on her back.

She is fat, like Tuesday's ladies. Her skin shines like someone has polished her. Ah, ah. She is singing. Above her is someone's back. It is shiny too, like Baba's wax. It moves with her singing. Her eyes are closed and she puts her hand up over her head. Her palms are pink. Her fingers are full of rings and the nails are purple like dung beetles.

But the cold air comes with us and her eyes – they open. She sees us and her mouth makes a shape. O. The shape is a circle like her eyes. She is not beautiful now. She is one of Jalloh's goats, meat and bone.

The governor turns around and he sees us. His chest is thick with hair, black hair that goes all the way down to his legs. His body is wet.

He sees Mister. His eyes go wide, like a goat's. Mister, he smiles. He says: 'Yes, Baba. It's me.'

Then the governor sees me. His eyes stay on me. And then I know. He sees his cap. The one he gave me, sitting on my head.

He makes a deep sound, like Buffalo's lion. And he comes towards us, comes from the woman, with his hands out. I do not move. I hope he takes me. I pray that he kills me and puts me in the garden to sleep.

Mister takes out his knife as he passes, steps behind him and cuts his neck.

The governor does not know what Mister has done. He reaches me, and takes my shoulders. He looks into my face and his mouth is moving. There are no sounds coming from him any more. The sounds come from the woman. She screams and screams.

I can hear her, but I cannot look anywhere else. He is still holding me. He still wants to tell me something. He is a spirit now. He speaks the tongue of the dead.

The governor falls. Mister comes to us. He pulls the governor's hands off me. He kicks him in the stomach again and again. He shouts: 'Here's my stick, Baba. How do you like it? Now it is your turn.'

The governor falls on his back. No one is here except the woman. She crawls on the bed. She cries like Nagode, like Adeya. Like Mama, the day I told her what I saw.

Then Mister, he gives me the knife. It is cold in my hand. I kneel beside the governor. Blood is coming from his neck. He bleeds like Baba's clock – tock, tock. But the clock is nearly broken.

Mister says: 'Now, JoJo.'

I am dreaming. Just like when I was swimming on the moon. I still dream now. And soon we will wake. And go to school. The rains will come. The flowers will grow back on Nagode's sleeping tree.

Mister puts my hand with the knife over the black hair on the chest. I feel him pushing it down. It is like cutting cement when it is still wet. We made cement for the castle. It must dry before you can shape it. But not too hard, Nicholas told me. Soft but firm, like Nagode's skin.

I let go of the knife. It stays there, standing straight up. The woman, she makes no more sounds. Mister takes my cap from my head. He hangs it on the knife. I can see the bear. Its mouth is open and nothing comes out.

Our hands are wet and red. Mister's hands open and close, like he is holding something tight. His face is the fire, but there is water on it, too. He kicks the man again with his foot. Nothing. He is meat now. His spirit has gone.

'Come,' Mister says to me.

The garden smells so sweet. And the moon is still bright. I hear men, coming closer, their steps heavy on the road. They are not spirits; they are real. They call us and Mister answers them, his hand on my back. I look up and see a face, smiling at us. His mouth speaks my name; he has white teeth and he holds a hand out to me. Danjuma.

I go on my knees in the road. I vomit until there is nothing left inside me. I vomit until I am empty. As empty as my hands.

THE FIRES

The sun stabbed at Nick through the high window. He flinched, feeling hard floor beneath him. His arm connected with something cool and smooth beside him – the whisky bottle, which toppled over with a hollow clink.

His eyes were made of glue and wire, the bed a hazy shadow, dead insects crumpled underneath. Somewhere a voice was shouting, a distant, dream-like sound.

He forced his eyes open, head pounding. The empty bottle was a sickening yellow, making his stomach heave. He'd drunk his way to its bottom, dreaming of dawn coming gently and someone's arms around him.

The hum outside was growing. He staggered to his feet. Vomit coated the floor, and he stank of spirits. A bucket of brown water sat in the bathroom corner – blood temperature, thick with dirt. He rinsed his T-shirt and his face. Yesterday's chills felt remote, a distant tremor. He could still feel the imprint of J.P.'s money, itching against his skin.

Footsteps came, pounding up the porch steps. His door rattled. 'Mr Nicholas!' The voice was muffled, but familiar. 'Mr Nicholas, come and see!'

Nick opened the door slowly, gritting his teeth against the daylight. There was Tuesday, wild-eyed, one gold tooth showing in a hysterical grin. He reached out and grabbed Nick's forearms. 'Come!' he repeated. 'Come now!'

People were thronging outside Dr Ahmed's house; there was a strange aura of celebration. Hope touched his heart. *Nagode must be better.*

'Nicholas!' Now it was Mr Kamil, waving from the garden gate. 'They are gone. *Gone*. Go and look.'

Gone? Nick's mind tried to grope through the fog of alcohol and confusion. But then Dr Ahmed's front door opened. The doctor stepped out, red-eyed from sleeplessness. 'Nagode is resting,' he told Nick. 'The crisis passed in the night. She will recover.'

'Thank god.' Relief weakened his legs, making them tremble. Dr Ahmed put his hand on Nick's shoulder. 'There is other news,' he said. 'Go to the well and see.'

Nick made his way down the steps, followed by Tuesday. Mr Kamil clapped him on the arm, and Imam Abdi bobbed his head. Aisha was there, with a befuddled Akim, her face broad with joy. Miss Amina waddled along next to them, grinning toothlessly, holding her abaya out of the dirt. A stream of people pushed them ahead down the dirt path, like a wedding party.

Hanan and Adeya were standing on their porch; the girl leaned out towards the lake, her hands resting on an orange robe hung to dry over the porch rail. It streamed in the wind as they flocked by, a brilliant flag of victory.

The well was silent, the elephant tank squatting meek and grey beside it. A dark bird flapped on the pump; it called out, loud and disconsolate. Tyre tracks headed northwards, vanishing towards the highway.

Elation swelled inside Nick – a terrifying, ecstatic bubble. *Gone.* Twelve hours ago the soldiers had been here, as real and immovable as the stones. He dropped to the ground, knees thudding into the dust. *It's over. They're gone.*

And then the next thought came rushing in, ice-cold and dazzling. J.P.'s money had worked its dark alchemy somewhere and freed them. *Mister came through. I saved us.*

Hands snuck under his arms, pulling him up. 'We beat them,' he heard Kamil shouting. '*Al-hamdullilah.*'

Imam Abdi had started to sing, his voice soaring up and down like a kite. Others joined him – some clicking their teeth and blowing air between their lips in exaggerated shivers. Aisha opened her arms, throwing back her head in an ululation that sent the crow screeching into the air.

Nick turned to Mr Kamil. 'We have a lot of work to do,' he said. 'The pump, the electrics. We need fuel, repairs. I have to call Eric now.'

'Go ahead.' Mr Kamil grasped his hand. 'May God reward you.'

The garden path was outlined in brightness. Nick pushed the front door open and saw Margaret there, standing beside the grandfather clock. Her eyes were sleepy, her hair tousled and soft. Her abaya was sky blue, patterned with tiny flowers around her bare feet.

She held out her hands and he came towards her, leaning forehead to forehead. Her breath was buttermilk, sour from sleep. To Nick it was like drinking joy.

'She will live,' she whispered. 'God spared her.'

Nick touched her face as she spoke, sensing the electric thread of thoughts tracing patterns inside her.

'Where is Dr Ahmed?' he whispered.

'Out with the sick.' She drew back, looking through the brightening windowpane. 'Some may still die.'

'The siege is over. We can get the well working. We'll have clean water to drink in a day. Eric will bring fuel and medicines.'

'I know,' she said, a sad smile on her face. Her palm was moist as it touched his cheek. 'My love.'

He felt a sudden rush of panic. The warmth reminded him of loss, of her words during Nagode's sickness. He grabbed her wrist, holding it tight.

'Everything's OK, Margaret,' he said. 'We can start again now.'

Gently, she detached herself. Light filtered in through the window behind her, like a loving hand.

'Please, Nicholas,' she said, her voice low with emotion. 'Do not test me. I made my bargain when Nagode was dying.'

'But now she's not dying.' A deep ache was winding through his joy, entangled so tightly he could not tell one from the other. 'And you're allowed to be happy.'

'There's sorrow on every road.' She twisted her fingers together, like Adeya. 'I promised God that I would not run from my share. That I would stay and face my penance.'

God. The word woke a futile jealousy. 'Margaret, *I* made this happen, not God.'

He pointed out of the window, towards the ongoing sounds of jubilation. 'The governor would have let Nagode die. No one in this whole village could stop him. Some men – they said they could stop him, find a way to help Danjuma take power. They needed money – so I gave it to them.'

Margaret's brow creased, sunlight playing on her face. 'I don't understand. You gave Danjuma money?'

A memory forced itself on him: JoJo and his Coca-Cola T-shirt, standing next to him in that acrid backyard. Nick shut his eyes against it.

'It doesn't matter.' He took Margaret's hands in a last appeal. 'Don't you know – I would have done anything, paid any price, to protect you? How can you keep every promise except the ones we made?'

'Those were dreams.' She returned his grip, a furious pressure. 'This is real life. Are you ready to be a father to my children? To JoJo and Nagode? Can you know what would it be like, to take them from their home and make them grow up as strangers?'

'I'm ready,' he said, with desperate conviction. 'I will be there for them, no matter what it takes. Isn't that why I did all of this?'

The smile she gave him in reply was so sad his heart quailed within him. Dropping his hands, she reached up towards his face.

'No, Nicholas,' she said, cupping his cheek with the lightest consoling touch. 'We wanted to be the only people in the world. But we are not.'

He shook his head, a protest too deep for words. The trill of the telephone broke through; Dr Ahmed's unreliable landline was ringing. Margaret crossed to pick it up. 'Hello?' Her voice sounded raw, trembling – she lifted one hand to wipe the damp hollows under her eyes.

A man's voice answered through the receiver. 'Please wait,' she said.

Nick took the receiver from her hands. 'Eric?' His voice seemed not to belong to him; it rang out, calm and even.

'Nicholas, fucking hell! What's happening there?'

'The siege ended.' He licked dryness from his lips. 'The soldiers left this morning. What's happening in the Town?'

'All types of fucking madness. The governor's dead.'

Nick opened his mouth, his mind blank. *Dead?* He sensed Margaret, listening near him.

'They say one of his whores killed him. Then Danjuma turned up at the residence, with half the governor's men.'

'Danjuma lifted the siege?'

'There's been no time for him to do anything. No one knows where the rest of the governor's men are. This isn't over, Nick.'

A chill began to creep down his spine.

'Listen, keep your radio on today. Use up all the rest of your juice. In case anything happens. And tell Dr Ahmed – you understand?'

'I understand. Thank you.'

Eric snorted. 'Swim together, sink together. I'll be in touch.'

The line went dead. Nick replaced the receiver, his arm heavy. He turned to Margaret, saw her stiffen at the expression on his face.

'The governor is dead,' he told her.

She put her hand to her mouth. 'Dead – how?'

'Killed.' Something had lodged in his throat, hard and foul. 'They don't know who did it.'

'God help us,' she said, wrapping her arms tight around herself. 'What will they do now?'

What will they do now? Dark possibilities churned through Nick like a storm of wings: he felt the stain of J.P.'s cash in his hand, the strange, burning stench in the yard behind Tuesday's shop, Mister, tall and white as an avenging angel. 'The governor was a murderer,' he said at last, tasting the true horror of that word for the first time. 'An evil man. He got what he deserved.'

From the window he could see Dr Ahmed walking back up the garden path, a black form against the daylight. An inner voice screamed against the old man's approach, coming like Death himself to put an end to all arguments and choices. 'May God spare us from the same,' Margaret whispered, as he turned the handle of the front door.

It is not yet daylight when we reach the lake. Mister, he stops the motorbike. He says: 'You can walk from here, JoJo.'

'Here?' I look around. There is no sound. No wind. No voices of the spirits. I can see the red curtain on Binza's place. Maybe the governor's spirit is here already. Maybe he waits, somewhere by the water.

I tell him: 'I do not want to walk.'

Mister has his back to me. He looks towards Binza's place. Maybe he wants her to hold him and sing to him, like my mama does. Maybe he wants to wake up later and tell her, 'Mama, I had a bad dream.'

'Go home, boss.' Mister turns away from Binza's place. His voice is quiet. 'Take rest,' he says. 'Even knights must rest.'

I watch him go – out, towards the lake. The sky has no colour, and the moon is small and white.

I start to walk. My hands are sticky. I cover them with mud, so I cannot see the dark stains.

The sun brings a new wind. It's a devil wind. It speaks in the branches and the reeds. The spirits are talking.

I hold up my hands and show them. 'See,' I shout. 'I am thirsty too! I will come to you soon. We will drink together.'

The spirits are sad. They cry, like wild dogs. That dog is still here somewhere. This makes me sad, too. I remember how we chased her. She did not know. She did no wrong.

I wish I could find her. I want to tell her what Baba told me. We are all travellers on the same road, and every test is a gate we must pass. If we are wise and do good then Allah gives us the key. But if we fail the test, Allah makes us wait on the road, until we learn better.

So, maybe there is a JoJo still here. He is waiting to pass through the gate. If I could find him, I would tell him to stop and turn back. I would tell him to leave Mister and Akim. I would tell him to take the dog and go with her. Back to Baba and Mama and Nagode.

Then I hear a sound across the lake. Adeya has come to wash her clothes in the water.

I call to her. 'Adeya! Adeya!' She looks up. I see her stand. She does not move. She fears me.

'Adeya!' I wave. 'Please Adeya. Please come.'

She comes, very slowly.

'JoJo,' she calls. 'What do you want now?'

I say nothing. I cannot say: help me find where I am waiting.

'Eh, JoJo,' she says, coming closer, looking at my face. 'What happened to you?'

I whisper: 'We went to the Town. Mister and me. We went together – a secret way.'

She looks at my hands and then my face. She covers her mouth. I think she will cry again. But she does not. She looks at me. She is looking for the old JoJo – but he is lost somewhere.

I say: 'I am sorry I pushed you.'

Adeya keeps her hand on her mouth. But then she looks at my eyes. And I know she sees me there. If she sees me, I am not lost. I must be here, with her.

She puts her hand down. 'I forgive you,' she tells me.

I whisper: 'Adeya, I am afraid. I am afraid of the spirits.'

And she says, 'There are no spirits here.'

Adeya, she listens when I tell her about the dog. She tells me what I must do. Together we look for the bones. The birds have picked them clean. The head is so small it fits in my hand. The other bones are curved and thin, like yellow writing. She was so fierce before, when she fought me. But her spirit is gone, and these pieces are just lines and numbers, like the drawings that I made with Nicholas.

I want to dig her a hole in the ground, like Bako had. But the ground is too hard. Adeya, she says: 'We can build her resting place with stones.' I use one stone to make a bed in the ground. Then we bring other stones to put around her. The mud and the blood, they come off my hands as we build. The stones and the ground take it all.

At last, Adeya, she takes off her headscarf. Her hair is short, like mine. She ties her scarf to a stick and puts it between the stones.

'There,' she says. 'Now she is not forgotten.'

I say: 'Hanan will beat you about your scarf.'

Adeya, she laughs. When she laughs her whole body moves. And her nose, it turns up like a cat's.

She says: 'I will tell her the wind took it. Allah sends the wind, so it must be Allah's will.'

I pretend to speak with a girl's voice: 'Allah likes my hair, Mama! I cannot go against Allah!'

She punches my arm and I pretend she hurts me. I say: 'Hey, watch out, boss!'

Then Adeya, she bites her lip. She says: 'I must go now, JoJo. But you – you must promise something.'

I tell her: 'I will promise whatever you want.'

Adeya, she looks to the north. The soldiers are gone. But the devil wind is still there, making circles in the dust.

She says: 'If those men come back, do not fight them. Come to me instead. Come to find me, JoJo. And together we will run.'

Late afternoon, the sun started its earthwards fall. Nick slumped on his desk, head on his arms, light reddening the window.

The telephone rang, chiming through the walls of Dr Ahmed's house. Footsteps hurried down the porch soon after, followed by a knock at the door. Dr Ahmed politely put his head around it. 'Nicholas, your colleague asks if you will please turn on the radio.'

Nick looked at the box beside him, the receiver limp on its top. 'OK. Thank you.'

Dr Ahmed nodded, turning to leave. *He wants me gone*, the ugly voice whispered. *Now that he's won.* But then Nick felt ashamed, remembering the outstretched hand across the garden gate on his first day, the scent of flowers. *There were no roses*, he thought. *But somehow I remember roses.*

'Dr Ahmed!'

The old man stopped, eyes turned to the floor.

'How is Nagode?'

He saw a smile steal across the weary face.

'She strengthens. Not all have been so lucky.' Dr Ahmed looked up at Nick, straightening his back. 'But maybe better times are coming.'

'*Insha'Allah.*' The old man's smile widened at that; he waved his finger in mock triumph. 'Eh, from the atheist, this is a very good sign!'

As soon as Dr Ahmed left, Nick flicked on the radio and called Eric, who picked up immediately.

'What's so urgent?' Nick asked. 'Why couldn't I speak to you from the house?'

Eric coughed. 'It's shitty, but I didn't want them to hear.'

'Hear what?'

'They're coming. Tonight, most likely.'

Nick went cold. 'Who? J.P.?'

'Not J fucking P. The governor's men.'

The governor's men. They had been boys, no more than boys, Nick remembered, young bodies in green camouflage, nervous eyes.

'There were riots here today – Danjuma's men against the old guard. Apparently there's a hideout or something out in the desert. They're going to take the fight to Danjuma, like Custer's Last fucking Stand.

'But why would they come here? What do we have to do with anything?'

'Don't be stupid, Nick. Everyone knows where the killers came from. I bet Dr Ahmed could give you their names and addresses. There are no secrets.'

Terror broke over Nick in a wave of sweat. What had he unleashed?

'We have to tell people,' he said, the receiver slick under his hand. 'We have to get people out, right now.'

'Hey!' Eric's voice crackled over the line. 'We've no time, so listen. I'm going to come to you now. I can pick you up and take you south. I can even put you on a fucking plane in the capital. Fuck J.P. and fuck all of this.'

'But what about Margaret? And – and Dr Ahmed and the children?' Nick stood up, watching the sun's bloody fingers creep under the door. 'I can't leave them here.'

'We can fit them in the car. Get them ready if you can. But you've got half an hour, tops.'

'OK.' Nick's mind raced for options. 'Danjuma – he's a friend of theirs. Of Mr Kamil and all the rest. Can't he do something – send some protection?'

The line crackled at Eric's belly laugh. Nick saw him, bent over the receiver in their air-conditioned office, wiping tears from his red eyelashes. 'Oh, Nick,' he gasped at last. 'You mean well and you're a smart fellow. But you still don't fucking know anything.'

The sun was low in the sky, the evening prayers dissonant with their clash of call and echo. Five o'clock. Maybe a little earlier. Wood smoke curled darkly over homes and gardens, threading the air with ashen sweetness.

Nick ran across the porch to Dr Ahmed's front door, bursting into the sitting room. Margaret sat on the low sofa. In her arms,

Nagode's round head was bobbing – a slow, sleepy rhythm. She'd lost her baby fatness, planes emerging from the roundness of her cheeks – a woman's face on a child's body. JoJo sat on the floor beside her, stroking her feet with a hesitant forefinger.

Margaret looked up, her smile radiant. 'Look at her,' she said. 'Look how strong she is.'

'Like her mother,' Nick said. He stooped to touch the small head, slick with dark curls. She looked up, a soft glance of recognition.

Dr Ahmed entered with a spoonfull of viscous black liquid. He knelt down by Nick, pushing it into Nagode's unresisting mouth. 'There, girl, there. Swallow it down.' Nagode's expression turned to outrage; she began to cry. Margaret hugged her. 'Ahmed, not now, please.'

Dr Ahmed cleared his throat, casting Nick a stilted smile.

'When I was a boy, my mother gave me justicia mixed with honey for every ailment. It was a very good treatment, or else I was a very good patient. Either way, I am alive and well.'

'You don't believe in those things,' Nick said quietly.

Dr Ahmed shrugged. 'When my medicine cabinet is empty, I believe in what I must.' He straightened, and his voice became more jovial. 'But perhaps tomorrow we can get to the Town, and take Nagode to the hospital there.'

Nick stood up, too. 'Dr Ahmed, that was Eric on the telephone. He's on his way here, right now, to get us all.'

Four pairs of eyes locked on him, blank in incomprehension.

'He said the governor's men are coming.' Nick swallowed. 'They think his killers are hiding here.' He could not meet JoJo's eyes.

Margaret laid her cheek on Nagode's head, hands tracing the soft bones of her daughter's back. Dr Ahmed's face was pale against the evening shadows. 'You are leaving?' the doctor asked.

Frustration scorched Nick's stomach. 'We're all leaving. Eric says he'll take us to the capital. It's not safe here.'

'And then what?' Dr Ahmed walked towards Margaret and put his hand on her shoulder. Beside him, the grandfather clock stood tall and silent.

'I don't understand.' Nick's heartbeat was becoming a hammer. 'What do you mean?'

'We will have no place to live there, no money. You will not be able to help us, Nick. This you know well.'

'J.P. will help you.' The dizziness was returning, the world tilting beneath him.

Dr Ahmed shook his head. 'J.P. owes me nothing. I will not make my burdens his.'

'What are you talking about?' Nick was shouting now. 'This is your family. Your children. For God's sake, just come!'

'No!' Dr Ahmed's voice rang like the crack of a gun. The old man's hand came down in a fist, beating into his palm – a fury so raw that Nick felt his own rage quail and grow still.

'Do not lecture me, Nicholas. You are my guest, not my teacher. You have your own home and your own life. But everything of mine is here. Everything I have given to this place and these people. We will not go with you to become beggars at the door of J.P..'

'I don't mean to lecture you.' Nick was pleading now; they were two ships passing so close to each other but somehow driven by different winds. 'I'm trying to keep you safe.'

Dr Ahmed came over to him and bent his head. Their eyes met, dark into blue.

'I also want to keep us safe,' he said. 'And I fear that the real danger hides in here.' He tapped Nick's chest. 'And not out there.'

Nick looked towards Margaret, watching them in silence. Her blue dress shaded to purple in the failing light, Bako's bracelet in its place around her wrist.

The sight of her overwhelmed him, this woman he loved; in that moment the whole of his life, his path to this point, seemed to be written on her body: her dress the flick of colour on his mother's canvas, her eyes the dark liquid flowing from Madi onto the playground floor, her red beads the sway of Binza's curtain, her lips the wings of black birds circling a hotel swimming pool.

'Margaret,' he said. 'Please.'

She pushed herself to her feet, Nagode resting under her chin.

'I must stay with my family, Nicholas.' Her pupils were large in the darkening room; he could not see if they were wet or dry.

JoJo stood in the corner, his back against the grandfather clock. The space between them seemed full of dark flecks, as if the unsaid truths were crystallising, becoming visible.

'JoJo.' The boy's head came up, his gaze blank, looking without seeing.

'I'll go for help,' Nick promised. 'But I'll come back. OK?'

JoJo said nothing. His expression shifted in the half-light, glimmers of disbelief easing across the indifference.

'You had better get ready.' Dr Ahmed spoke into the silence. 'You have a long journey ahead.'

I am asleep, Nick told himself, as his feet carried him out of the room, as he piled T-shirts and his passport into a bag. *This is a dream*. His limbs had the strange fluidity of a dream. They moved without a will of their own, lifeless as atoms pushed and pulled by unfeeling forces.

Eric pulled up outside the house at sunset. Nick heard his horn, setting dogs howling at the desert's edge.

Nick emerged, a bag over his shoulder. Eric wound down one window and thrust his arm out, slapping the door.

'Come on, let's be going now,' he yelled.

Miss Amina sat on her porch, smoking from her pouch of herbs. She scowled at the noise. Nick looked into the gathering darkness, towards Adeya's house. A line of pale light marked the gap between Hanan's curtains and the window. Could he at least get them? Or why not Miss Amina? Or Mr Kamil and Aisha and Akim? Confusion gnawed him, its teeth sharp. *If I have the power – what's the right choice? Save some? All? Or none?*

He walked down the steps and the garden path. Time was a flood, sweeping him along. His hand was on the gate latch, flicking it upwards. The gate swung open and he stepped outside.

Eric had opened the passenger door. Nick climbed slowly into the seat. 'There we go,' Eric said. 'Not so hard.'

Margaret stayed by the door with Nagode, one hand on JoJo's shoulder. He could barely see her in the dusk. Dr Ahmed walked down to meet them. He leaned over the bonnet and offered Nick his hand.

Nick took it, feeling the electric pressure as their palms met. He'd shaken his father's hand during their last, awkward visit – a mechanical movement of tendons and muscle. But now he remembered why as a boy he'd found Madi's handshakes more intimate than hugs. It was the firing of millions of nerve endings together, the violence of bare contact dissolving barriers between thought and skin.

'Travel well.' The bite of Dr Ahmed's fingers travelled up his arm.

Nick swallowed. He knew there must be a key to this moment – but he was grasping in the dark.

'I hope you fix your clock,' he said. 'It's worth cherishing.'

'I will.'

Nick looked over to Margaret and JoJo on the steps. Dr Ahmed's eyes followed his.

'I only wanted good things for them.' Nick felt numb as he looked back at his host. 'If I caused you pain, I . . .'

Dr Ahmed turned away, his back a solid shadow.

'I told you once that time judges us more honestly than men.' His voice was hoarse. 'Maybe life will surprise you, Nicholas. Maybe you are better than you know.'

Then he was walking away, a tall line against the gathering dark, moving up the porch steps. Nick tried to wave to Margaret,

Nagode and JoJo, but their forms were blurring together into a single outline.

Eric put the car into gear. But then a shape detached itself from the doorstep – Margaret, running down through the gate past her husband towards Nick's open window. Her scarf fell back as she ran, her hair a dark halo in the rising wind.

She put her hand on the edge of the window and leaned towards him, a violet line between her lips where they parted, her face alive with its own light.

He lifted his hand to hers, oblivious to Dr Ahmed, to Eric, to everything except the sense of this moment stretching on its way from present to past.

'Remember our garden,' she told him, hushed, her words falling over each other. 'You know – in that other life, when we grew old, you and me? Don't forget.'

'I won't.' There was no more time; she touched one finger to his lips, stepping away from him. Eric put his foot on the accelerator – and she vanished.

I see him go. I think: he will be out of the village soon. And tomorrow he will be leaving. Leaving on a jet plane. Bye bye, Nicholas. Bye, mate. Soon I will forget you and all of your lessons.

Baba says to me: 'Come inside, Yahya.'

Mama, she says: 'Ahmed, if they are really coming, what shall we do?'

Baba, he looks at me. Then he says, 'They will go to the square, like the last time. We must gather the council and the police and reason with them there. You and the children should stay here where it's safe.'

'Not all men can be reasoned with,' Mama answers. And Baba, he nods. He says: 'I know, my love.'

I see her eyes. She is crying. My love. I wonder if I will ever say it. I can try it sometime. I can say, 'Adeya, my love.' She will laugh at me, but she will like it. She will pretend to laugh, and I will pretend to be joking.

Mama, she wipes her eyes. She gives Nagode to Baba. She says: 'Go to your father.' Nagode puts out her hands and says: 'Baba!' He loves this. Once I was small like her. Once I also did those things.

Baba, he takes Nagode and kisses her. He holds her tight. He is crying under his glasses.

He says: 'I would not have stopped you, Margaret. You are free, always.'

Mama, she bites her lip when she smiles. She puts her hand on Nagode's face.

'I am free,' she says to him. 'And I am here.'

She is touching Nagode's face, and Baba is holding Nagode. He looks at me and says: 'Yahya. My son.'

I can hear there is water inside him, not fire. He puts his arm out to me. I come to him, and he pulls my head to his chest. I can smell the polish on his shirt. I can smell Nagode's legs. I can feel his hand tight on my shoulder. And Mama's hand is here too, and we stand in our house, together, like a baobab tree.

Darkness touched down as they drove south along the dirt road, headlights on full beam. Eric's hands were white, gripping the wheel. Nick sat in silence. The world seemed on pause.

I'll get help and come back. But what was one more broken promise among so many? Blackness swished past the window, hot and relentless.

A ridge marked the end of the dirt track; a pothole had opened in the tarmac beyond. The tyres screamed as Eric forced the car over it, sending punishing jolts through the suspension. When the rear wheels finally settled, one side tilted towards the ground.

'Fuck,' Eric said. He pulled up the handbrake and got out to check the wheels. 'Fuck!' he yelled, from the back of the car. 'Fucking driving at night in this godforsaken place.'

He came to Nick's window.

'I have a spare in the back,' he said. 'Give me a hand, eh?'

Nick climbed out of the car. Eric's back was to him, broad in the red flash of the hazards. He took a torch from the boot and handed it to Nick. The light was a narrow beam, boring into Eric as he hauled out his toolbox.

Streams of warm wind blew past them, but Nick was shivering. The torch trembled in his hand.

'Do they really know who killed the governor?' The question burst from him, even while he dreaded the answer. He saw Eric's back tense.

'They say one of Danjuma's people. From the village.'

Nick swallowed. The darkness closed in, tense and silent. Suddenly he could not bear it any more – this agonised wait for judgement, a hidden sword ready to fall.

'I know who killed him,' he said.

Eric stood up slowly, the jack in his hand. He turned towards Nick, the torch flooding white light up onto his face.

'I don't want to know.' Eric's voice was quiet. 'I'm no one's fucking priest. You understand me?'

Nick swallowed. More moments slid past on the wind, too fast to catch.

Eric turned back to the broken wheel. 'What's done is done,' he said, fitting the jack to the metal frame. 'We'll fix this and be on our way to the airport. You can say hi-de-hi to your lady in England for me. There's been enough damage here already.'

I smell them before I hear them. They come with smoke and fires.

Baba, he stands by the window. Mama is singing to Nagode, the same song we sang with Nicholas, the one where the man does not want to leave his woman, but he leaves anyway. He says goodbye and takes his jet plane and flies away from her and all of us. And even though he says he may come back, I know he never will, because he says 'goodbye' – and people who come back do not say this. They say: 'I will see you again.' And Nagode, she sings with Mama. She puts her hands on Mama's face and sings: 'Na na na, 'bye.'

Then we smell it.

Mama, she stops singing. She says: 'Something is burning.'

Baba, he looks out of the window. He says: 'There is a fire in the market.'

We come to the window. Behind Miss Amina's house, away to the north, the sky is red.

Then I hear it. Crack crack crack. It stops. Then it comes again. Crack crack crack crack.

I say: 'Mama!' Mama, she puts her hand on my shoulder.

'Ahmed,' she says. 'Ahmed, what is happening?'

Baba says: 'I will go to Kamil's house. We will call the council and find out. We will meet these people, whoever they are – and see what they want.'

'No!' Mama and I, we shout it together. Mama, her eyes are big, like Nagode's. She says: 'Are you mad? Stay here, for God's sake.'

'I have to go,' he is saying. 'I must. We must stand together.'

In the red light he looks old, so old. I cannot let him go outside. Outside there is Mister and Binza and the thunder and the lightning. Outside are the spirits. Outside is the gun, with its hungry mouth. It will swallow him and he will not come back. 'No, Baba,' I say to him. 'Please.'

Mama, she takes his hand. She says: 'I stayed with you, Ahmed. Now you stay with me.'

Other sounds are coming closer. I hear someone, screaming. It is a woman. 'Adeya!' I run to the door. 'That's Adeya!'

'No,' Mama says, taking hold of me, one arm around my chest, another on my forehead. I can see Bako's bracelet, red, like the fires.

'It's not Adeya,' she says. 'It comes from the mosque. But they will come here, Ahmed. Soon.'

'I don't understand,' Baba says. 'Why are they doing this?'

Mama looks at me. I cannot answer. There is a hole deep inside me, full of water. I will drown if I fall in.

She puts her finger on my heart, and I feel her there. She says: 'Men's reasons are worthless. We must wait for God's.'

The sounds are nearly in our street. I run to the kitchen and open the door. I see them – across the garden wall, over Nagode's

sleeping tree. Cars, their lights bright, and men. They carry fire,
and they are shouting. There is red in the sky.

'Baba!' I shout. 'They are outside the garden! We must go.
Now, now!'

'Come here, Yahya!' he calls to me, and I run.

He is on his knees – he has opened the big box, the one with the
tools for fixing his clock. All of the tools, they are on the floor. The
box is open, like a hole. Like the grave they put Bako into.

And then I know what he wants.

'No, Baba,' I say. 'No way.'

'Yahya, you must,' he says. 'You and Nagode. Get in here.
Right now.'

'No!' I am crying. 'I want to stay with you! I can fight! I can
fight!'

'Yahya,' he says to me, 'JoJo. Listen to me. Listen!'

Then he says: 'This grandfather clock, what makes the tick?'

'What?' I am crying still.

'Answer me!' I can see his eyes. They have a grey circle around
them. I look at the circle and I say: 'The machine inside.'

'And what makes the machine work?'

'The weights,' I say. 'The earth pulls them down. This is what
Nicholas taught me.'

'And the force that makes the weights fall down, where does it
come from?'

'I don't know,' I say. 'I don't know, Baba.'

He puts his hand on my chest. His hand is warm. He says: 'All
things come from the same centre. What drives the clock also
drives the sun and the rains and your heart and mine. We are all
joined in this place. We are never, ever alone.'

I do not know what he means. But from love, I nod my head. I
step into the box. Mama runs to us, with Nagode. She puts Nagode
in the box beside me. Then she takes Bako's bracelet from her arm,
and ties it on mine.

'It will keep you safe,' she says. 'As long as you wear it, I am
with you.'

319

Then Nagode is in my arms, and we are lying down in the smell of oil and metal. And Nagode's face is on my chest, and I can feel the water from her mouth and hear her heart. I see Mama's face, her eyes the same as mine. Then the lid comes down, and we are in darkness.

Eric tightened the last screw on the tyre. 'Done.' He stood up.

Nick looked down the highway. Time to go. He'd imagined a different homecoming. He'd seen it: the green rise of an English spring, going together to lay flowers on Madi's grave, leading Margaret through his mother's garden towards the kissing gate to meet the path to the sea.

'Ready?' Eric slammed the boot shut and began to walk back to the driver's side-door.

Nick took a breath.

Across the road the jacaranda tree marked the village outskirts. Before it had been bare and studded with buds. Now every branch was wreathed in living flowers, brilliant red against the dark.

As he stood there, an inner pendulum suspended its long, upwards arc – poised before surrender to the earth's pull.

The words came without thinking, becoming truth in his mouth. 'I'm going back'.

The pendulum was swinging downwards now, accelerating through the air in the terrible lightness of free-fall. His feet were already moving, the smooth tarmac reverting to rough stones.

He heard Eric yell after him, words telescoping, like a siren shooting past. 'Don't be fucking crazy! They'll kill you.'

'Tell J.P. I'm sorry. I have to go.'

'Nick!'

But he was already running, back into the blind night, towards Margaret and JoJo and the distant line of red.

Tock, tock, tock. This is how we wait. I whisper in Nagode's ear. 'Hush, Nagode.' Tock, tock, tock. Her body, it shakes. She is hot and we sweat. We are water and breath and hearts – nothing else.

I hear voices shouting outside the house. They shout: 'Come out! Come out!' And I think: they know. They have found us.

The voice is nearer now. The door breaks, it breaks open. They are inside. They are in here with us.

The voice shouts: 'Where is your boy? Where is he?'

Baba says: 'Please. We are not your enemies. There are no enemies here.'

'Where is he?' the voice shouts, again. Now there are more sounds, other voices. The soldiers, the governor's knights. I can see them in my head. Their long legs. Their long guns. Then I hear Mama – she cries out. She screams like Nagode when something hurts her.

'Leave her be! No! No!' It's my father. He is crying too. Baba is crying: 'Allah is great! Allah is great!'

There is a crash, and I close my eyes. I pray. Not Baba's clock. Please, he loves his clock. Nagode, she makes her water quietly on my leg. 'Tock, tock,' I whisper to her. 'We must be quiet. Tock, tock.'

I speak to Nagode until I feel her stop shaking. I whisper that song, the one Nicholas used to sing to us. Kiss me! Smile for me! Promise me you will never let me go!

I whisper until I hear it go quiet outside. There are no more noises, no more sounds. All is quiet. Except for our hearts. They go tock, tock, just like the grandfather clock. And I want to tell Baba – you are right. Nagode and me, and you and the clock, we became one and the same, we are joined together. When he opens the lid I will tell him. Until then, we will wait.

A car skidded past Nick on the road, and then another – men leaning out of the windows, back wheels sliding off the dirt track.

He ducked as they flew by, urgency battling with terror. The sky was lit; houses were burning ahead, near the village square. JoJo's school was in flames to his right. Men stood beside it smoking cigarettes, leaning on their guns.

Not that way. But which? Chaos sucked him into its vortex; the village was a labyrinth, its paths filled with murder. The mosque was ahead, and then behind, and the air was dense with smoke and ash.

Suddenly he saw the gap in the wall beside Mr Kamil's burning house. Margaret's secret way. He squeezed inside, climbing into the garden, racing past the crackle of cindered boughs, scrambling over the wall on the other side.

He ran on, winded – and then Miss Amina's house was there, right in front of him. The door was open, swinging off its hinges. A shapeless bundle of cloth poked through the doorway.

Nick's mind went blank. Light swarmed across the body, an orange glare from Hanan's fields up ahead. Laughter drifted down on the smoke, and cheers. His stomach heaved, bile dropping onto the dirt in small, sad drops.

I can't. His body swayed and his hand reached up, meeting cool brick. Dr Ahmed's wall. Margaret's garden.

His hands traced the smoothness of mortar and roughness of stone. No two the same. His mind drifted; he closed his eyes, his body emptied of will. *I showed JoJo how to make bricks out of pretend concrete.* He remembered how the boy's fingers had moved over the wet sand, uncertain at first, then with blossoming assurance.

His breathing slowed, and he opened his eyes. *Time to go.* His hand reached the top of the wall and he pulled himself up, feet scrabbling for purchase. The garden was silent under the flickering lights, the kitchen door closed. He pushed it open and walked inside.

A shape by the wall was Dr Ahmed. He sat upright, eyes fixed straight ahead. The grandfather clock seemed to grow from his back, its white face bearing silent witness.

Margaret lay relaxed on the floor. 'I'm here,' Nick said, rushing to her side, one hand reaching for her cheek, the other for the bare curve of her shoulder, its skin flushed and reddened where her dress had been ripped away.

Unconscious, he thought, as his mind reeled and his legs gave way. He landed beside her. *Dreaming*. Her lips were parted, her eyes half open, staring at the ceiling in quiet wonder.

Her lingering warmth seeped into him, as on their New Year's morning – when the sun had seemed to rise inside the walls of their room. His hand went to her chest, imagining he could still feel the soft movement of breath, look forward to a morning still to come where she would wake and stretch and turn to him smiling. *This is what we did in another life.*

The void was still inside him, the cold rush of the pendulum on its relentless earthwards slide. He felt the warmth of her cheek as he stroked it, her skin still full to his touch. Beneath him, a terrifying wetness had soaked through the rug; he could smell its red, metal stench. *I did this, Margaret*, he'd boasted earlier that morning, in this very room. Despair pressed him down like a crushing stone. He couldn't move, couldn't leave her; as long as he stayed by her side none of this was real – no full-stop, nothing fixed or irreversible. But if he moved, if he opened the door, then Time would find them – would come surging back in an unstoppable flood to carry them finally away from each other. It would be like killing her himself.

Or there was another choice. He could walk out into that screaming night, through the fires and deadly fury. He could feel it, waiting for him out there in the darkness, a hammer ready to fall. *No one could deserve it more*, the ugly voice whispered. There'd be a too-brief moment of pain, a cheap penance for his sins. And maybe she'd been right – maybe somewhere beyond it he'd still be able to find her and beg her forgiveness.

His hand moved over the lips still breath-warm and down the soft swell of her arm – her favourite blue scarf, the one she'd worn to the well-capping ceremony, lying stained and crumpled beneath it like a blanket – to rest his hand in hers as it lay open in welcome.

Nicholas. The word was urgent, commanding. He fought against it, wanting to rest with her longer. *Nicholas, look*.

His eyelids were heavy, but he forced them open. *Look*. Her wrist came into focus; luminous and bare, only faint marks where Bako's bracelet used to be.

And then his eyes moved across the still arc of her breasts to where Dr Ahmed's tools lay, emptied onto the floor. Beside the clock sat the large wooden toolbox, its lid closed tight.

He lifted his dazed body. The door was in front of him – he could still walk out to the fires or stay here with Margaret and sleep until daylight.

But the pendulum sliced downwards, relentless. It shattered the grey pane between him and the present; he crawled over to the box and flung open the lid. And JoJo leaped out, screaming, a tiny screwdriver in one clenched hand framed by Bako's red beads, Nagode's wrist held tight in the other.

The light comes in, and I am ready. I hold Nagode with one hand and with the other I strike. Go for the face, Mister taught us. The eyes first. The eyes have no defence.

I can smell him, this one. I can smell his fear. Nagode is crying. I want to tell her – I will protect you. But then I hear: 'JoJo! JoJo, stop!'

I have his face in my hands. His skin is white. He holds my hands back and says: 'JoJo! It's me. I came back.'

This is a dream. I am dreaming that I see them both, there on the floor. Nicholas, he takes my face and he says: 'No! Don't look. Don't look at them. Look at me.'

I look at his eyes instead, his snowman eyes. He takes Nagode from me. I have no strength left.

He says: 'We have to go. They might come back. You have to come with me.'

And then I remember. I say: 'Adeya! I promised to find her.'

He shakes his head. 'We can't find anyone. We have to go.'

'No!' I shout. I grab his arms and shake him. 'I promised! I must!'

He closes his eyes. He says: 'I will go. You stay.'

I cannot stay here. Not here. 'Please,' I say. 'Take me. Take us.'

I see him look where I cannot. Then he says, 'Come with me. Come fast.'

He picks up Nagode. 'Close your eyes,' he says. 'I'll lead you.'

I close my eyes and he takes my hand. I feel something soft under my foot. 'Step up,' Nicholas says. 'Keep going.'

When we are out of the room I open my eyes. We are at the back gate. There is light everywhere. In the garden, on my castle. On Bako's cross.

Nicholas gives me Nagode and climbs over the wall. I hand her to him. Then it is my turn. His arms are strong when they catch me.

The spirits have come. They are all around us. I hear them, laughing and calling. We go round the back way, past the fields. They set a fire in the fields. The spirits are dancing there. I see them in Nagode's eyes.

'Look!' Nicholas points to Hanan's house. There are men outside. The fire is eating the roof.

'I'm sorry, JoJo,' Nicholas says. His face is black from smoke, like mine. He takes my shoulder.

But I am thinking. Adeya is clever. She would know to run. She would go somewhere and wait for me.

So I say to him: 'One more place. Come!'

And I start to run. I run through the dark and the spirits and the fires. Nicholas, he chases me. I shout: 'Adeya! Adeya!' I am not afraid, because the spirits are with me. They will help me. Bako and Mama and Baba – they are with me. I hold out my arm with the bracelet on it. So they will see me when I come.

Then I hear my name: 'JoJo!' Now I see Adeya. I see her! There, where we buried the dog. She is hiding behind the stones.

She runs to me, and I feel her arms go around me. She cries: 'Mother would not come! I had to leave her.'

Nicholas is with us now. He pulls us apart. I feel his hand on my shoulder, hard. 'They're coming,' he says. He points back to the village. 'They're coming.'

Adeya sees them at the same time. Cars with bright lights approaching fast. They have music playing. We are the dogs and they are the sticks.

'Go,' Nicholas says. He pushes us and we run. By the lake it is still dark. Binza's place is close. The ground is wet and pulls at us. Adeya, she is crying. 'I cannot,' she says, 'I cannot.' She holds her side. Nicholas gives Nagode to me. He picks up Adeya and now we run again.

My foot catches on a stone, and I stumble. Nagode falls under me. She weeps. 'Hush, Nagode,' I beg her. 'Hush.'

Nicholas, he says: 'Wait.' He pulls something out from his jeans. A torch. It makes a small light. He shines it around, looking and looking.

Then Adeya, she screams. The light shines on a spirit. The spirit points to me.

'Bang!' the spirit says. Then it laughs.

I want to run, but nothing will move. The spirit, it says: 'Boss, you came to me. My captain.'

He has a dark hole in his stomach.

He says: 'The Boys fought well. They killed Juma and Ibrahim. Are you happy, JoJo? Now there is only you.'

I look at him. He is fading, he is joining the spirits. But in his other hand, there is the knife.

I say to Mister: 'Come with us.' But he laughs and then coughs.

'They cannot kill me, boss.' He points the knife at my throat.

Adeya, she is crying. But the knife is all I see. It is so close now. The blade is red, like the fires. It is red from the governor. From the dog and from Juma and Ibrahim and from Mama and Baba and all of us.

'This is yours, my captain,' Mister says. 'You are a soldier, JoJo. We are the only two left now.'

'Leave him alone.'

Nicholas stands in front of me, between me and the knife. The knife is in his face. But still he stands.

Mister turns the knife. He says: 'JoJo, come.' His face has water on it. He cries. Mister cries.

'Get back,' Nicholas tells him. 'Get away from us.'

Mister does not listen to him: 'Are you hiding, JoJo? Stay with me. Do not leave me alone. My soldier. My brother.'

I can hear the cars coming behind us. Closer and closer. Adeya's hands are on me. 'They're coming,' she weeps. 'They will find us!'

Nicholas turns to see the lights. There is no way back and no way forward. I think – I will have to be the one. I will take the knife so that Nagode and Adeya can be free.

Then Nicholas, he steps forward. He steps up to the knife. He opens his arms. And Mister, he goes inside them. Nicholas' hand is on the knife as they fall together. His hand hits Mister's face with the torch. The ground takes them both, and the torch, it spins away.

I shout: 'Nicholas!' But I only hear a sound, a sound like the dog, when she lay in the dust. 'Nicholas!'

Then Binza is there. Binza, the witch, with her white hair. She comes from the dark, and the torch shines on her. I think: she has come for us. She comes to take us to the spirits.

But she leans down to her son. She pulls Mister's hair, pulling him back. Mister screams. Nicholas, he comes to his knees. His hand is on his side and his eyes are closed.

Binza, she takes the knife from Mister. He is weeping now, weeping and trying to hold her hand. She slips the red knife inside her dress. Then she points north, towards the well. She says: 'Go that way.'

Nicholas stands. His side is red, like the knife. His eyes are bright, like fever eyes.

Binza picks up the torch. The lights are coming, coming around the lake. They are looking for us.

Binza shines the torch at me. She shines it onto my arm, where Bako's bracelet is. She gives the torch into that hand. Her hand, it touches the beads. Her hand is soft, like Mama's.

'Run now,' she says to me. Her voice sounds like beetles walking on stones. 'Run now. I will send a spirit to guard you.'

She leaves Mister, she leaves him to the ground. I see her running, running straight towards the lights. She holds up her hands. I cry for her to stop – but she has gone.

And Nicholas, he takes me. He pulls me away from her and Mister, from the dog and The Boys – and together we run to where the spirits will keep us safe.

Nick saw Binza vanish into the brilliance of the headlights. Pain pulsed through him, deadly and deep. He was light-headed; he dared not sit in case he never stood again.

Run now. The words blazed in front of him, out to the north where the well lay.

He grabbed Adeya's arm and ran. The ground was uneven; JoJo stumbled under Nagode's cumbersome weight, his knees raw from the stony ground. Nick willed himself on, feeling strength leak out of him.

I must not fall. But tidal forces were pulling his thoughts down to a black hole of grief. They traced the edge of Dr Ahmed's living room, the soft line of Margaret's arm on the floor. All at once the strength left him and he collapsed.

'Up, up!' Adeya screamed.

His mind was dark, flooded with sorrow. *I made love to her here.* His hands touched the hard earth. *We looked at the sky and made impossible plans.*

He felt JoJo's hands on his shoulders. 'Nicholas.' The boy's face was scrunched in desperation, his breath coming in rapid gasps. 'Where do we go?'

Where do we go? *Home*, he thought, in the delirium of heat and blood loss. *To the kissing gate. To a green field.*

He looked up and saw the grey hulk of the elephant tank by the well, only a hundred metres away from them. *There.*

He pulled himself to his feet and saw the lights approaching again, bright cones of terror. 'With me,' he told the two children, hoisting Adeya into his arms. He felt the water running beneath him, pulling him on, as if his last reserves of will had been waiting there in the depths.

The elephant tank was on its side, concrete feet smashed to fragments. Someone had ripped the pump out of the well, exposing the dark hole underneath.

He laid Adeya down in the deep shadow of the tank, her abaya merging into the ground. 'Stay there,' he said to her. She nodded, laying her head on her hands, body heaving with stifled sobs.

'But there is no space for us,' JoJo said, voice cracking with panic.

The lights were closing in, and there was nowhere left to run. Tall reeds had crept back around the well's circumference, the lake slowly claiming back its own.

Nick pulled JoJo towards them. He pushed the boy down onto the ground and laid Nagode beside him.

Vehicles were coming closer; he could hear the hot scream of their engines, the angry roar of wheels accelerating on dirt. The three children lay in the dust, half-hidden by the reeds.

Nick's head swam; his body was growing light. He held his side in agony. *I will send a spirit to guard you.* He wanted to believe that Margaret was still nearby, or Madi, or even his father, some greater force sent to shield them from evil. But the night was silent and deaf to prayers. And as Nick lifted his palm from his side to see the scarlet bloom on the death-pale skin, like a red lion rampant on a white field, it struck him – an understanding so clear, so ironic, that he almost laughed. No hidden powers were rushing to save them; the only shield left now was him.

He pulled off his shirt and threw it as far away as he could, scooping up heaps of dust to camouflage his skin. Then he laid his body down on top of the children, spreading his arms to cover them, feeling the warmth of the wind on his back.

Around them the Land Cruisers hooted and searched. But now he felt immune to them, invisible. His being filled up with the chaotic tumble of four hearts against each other, slowing, breath by breath, into a common rhythm.

And then there was a warm touch on his skin. And another, and another, and another. Heavy wetness dropped from his hands to JoJo's and Nagode's, mixing with blood as it rolled onwards to the earth. The world exhaled, a sweet rush of sound. And at once, water was everywhere, inside and out. Rain at last, all around them, falling in its own unfathomable time.

THE RAINS

Hands lifted him off the ground amid cascades of blue light.

They held him up against metal – a vehicle, still warm. Men in grey uniforms moved through the dawn.

Something was pressed against his lips – water, gushing down his throat, choking him with sweetness.

He glimpsed JoJo, a fragment through moving forms. The boy was staring ahead, mesmerised by covered white stretchers carried past him, dappled by silent rain.

And then he was gone.

Then there was a long road, potholed and rough, jarring his bones. He lay on a bed that rumbled and juddered. Margaret lay beside him and stroked his head, her bare wrist marked with small indentations. 'You lost Bako's bracelet,' he whispered, breathing her in. 'Where did you put it?'

'I gave it to you, my love,' she replied with a smile.

Then another bump rocked the ambulance and her image blurred, slipping away from him.

He laughed as they carried him in through the gentle swoosh of hospital doors, past the gleaming floors and the empty beds. He was still laughing when they put the drip in his arm, sending him to sleep.

When he woke, he asked for JoJo. The nurse's face was blank as her uniform. 'JoJo,' he said, to everyone who came in. 'Dr Ahmed's son. JoJo.' They worked in silence, their eyes sliding over him but never settling. His existence was reduced to numbers; he was a mathematical expression, an equation of pulse rate, blood pressure and oxygen flow.

J.P.'s was the first familiar face. He sat by the bed, head down, twisting his glassses in his hands. Nick watched through half-closed eyes as the lenses revolved, catching the overhead light. 'What happened to you, Nicholas?' His voice was faint, as though carried from another shore. 'What did you do?'

The heavy embrace of drugs was pulling Nick down to a place without voices or questions. He struggled against it with all his strength. 'Where is JoJo?'

'Safe,' J.P. answered, as Nick fell back into the dark. 'Saved, thank God.'

At last the police came. Nick travelled south in the back of an armoured van, bandages white against his hands and stomach. A young officer sat beside him, nodding in sleep. The land was wide and bright, the horizon brushed with gold. The hard world dissolved as they rushed through it, melting back into life.

The deputy consul had a balding crown and an air of practised sympathy. He talked earnestly about arrest warrants and extradition processes as Nick watched a fly dance over the drifting brown hairs. When asked whether he would rather face charges here or at home, Nick saw the fly settle, translucent wings tense with daring.

'Home,' he answered. 'I want to go home.'

Weeks of waiting stretched ahead of him. He spent them in detention, making regular calls to Kate and taking visits from J.P. and Eric. Kate wept down the phone; it was the first time he'd ever heard her cry. *Why didn't you talk to me? Why didn't you say something?* He had no answers; he felt like a child, re-learning a lost language.

J.P. and Eric were easier. They brought newspapers and cans of cola and chocolates to share with the guards. His room was quiet and clean, the routines strangely relaxing. They talked about the weather – the end of the drought – their words flowing over the surface. They asked nothing and Nick demanded nothing in return.

Only once, as Eric was leaving, something lifted from the depths: 'Who else died?'

Eric paused. 'A few. It could have been worse. Tuesday and one of his girlfriends. The elder boy of Kamil's. Miss Amina and that maid whose field burned – Hanan, Adeya's mother. Some of the older boys who tried to fight back. They say around twenty in all. That old witch out by the lake. By the time Danjuma's men arrived, it was all over.'

Nick nodded, wordless. Twenty names, thrown down into the dark.

'Danjuma is even going to fix your bloody well. It's his well now, of course. There'll be rationing or similar. But he has big plans – irrigation systems, agriculture. A swimming pool, so I hear. He's draining the lake. You won't recognise the place soon.'

A swimming pool. Nick would have laughed if there'd been any laughter left in him.

'And what about JoJo?' His fingers clenched the desk, feeling the bite of metal and wood. 'Where is he?'

'He's fine.' Eric's eyes met his. 'Dr Ahmed's sister took him – the one who lives in the Town. She has all three of them. JoJo and the little girl and Adeya, too. They're going to a private school, a fancy one for rich kids. Danjuma is setting up a fund. They'll get the best of everything. Medical care, university – all the trimmings.'

'JoJo always wondered why his father wasn't good enough to work in that hospital.' Mentioning Dr Ahmed was like breaking a spell. Margaret's name he could not yet say.

'Well, if the boy wants to be chief surgeon now, I guess he will. Adeya too. She's getting those hands of hers fixed. They're both smart kids.'

Nick nodded. Exhaustion washed over him – and something else, harder to define: the numb relief of a drowning man who finally surrenders his struggle for air.

'I took everything from them.' The words came before he could stop them, burning his throat.

Eric stood for a moment considering this.

'When you left me that night, I thought you were fucking stupid. Throwing your life away for nothing.' He shrugged. 'But as it turns out, who knows? There could have been more than two bodies in that house.'

That night Nick cried himself to sleep. He dreamed he stood at the lake, rigid and tall. Dr Ahmed sat in quiet contentment at his feet, Margaret laughing over by the bright water, beckoning to him. Something inside was broken; his heart was still and locked in silence. *Wake*! He willed it to beat with every fibre of his being. *Wake up!* And then from somewhere he heard a voice. *I am coming!* JoJo was running to him, breathless, a screwdriver in his hand. *Look, Nicholas! I came back!*

And then the last day came, and there was no time left.

Nick stepped out of the detention centre, carrying a small bag of possessions. The police car drove him to the airport under the boughs of blossoming trees. The traffic sang, horns and voices spreading cheerfully through the smoke. He looked upwards, to the wisps of vanishing cloud. A line of birds followed them; he watched the silhouette break the air like ripples on water.

English police officers met him at the terminal doors, their faces puffy with heat and sleep. One crossed meaty arms over a stomach bulging from black trousers. The other was well muscled, head shaved to gleaming baldness.

They handcuffed him after the customs formalities. 'For the look of it, mate.' One hand on his back, another on his arm. He remembered the baby goat across Jalloh's shoulders, helpless and trusting on its way through the garden.

Finally they stood on the runway under the sun's blaze.

The plane ahead was white and lean as a swan. People queued on the stairway to the open cabin door, a trailing line of colour.

The hands were heavy on his shoulders, and the sun dazzled his mind. *What happened, Nicholas? What did you do?* If he closed his eyes he could still sense Dr Ahmed's room where he'd lain next to Margaret's body, still feel himself there beside her, more vivid than a memory. It was almost enough to make him believe he'd never left her – that this odd and empty world around him was nothing more than the soul's journey of penance, some strange, dying dream. But a cold voice told him it wasn't so: a nameless force had propelled him out of the door that night, driving him away from Margaret through the fires and Mister and Binza and then abandoning him there like a stopped clock. And he could neither thank it nor blame it, for he could not understand its purpose.

Another car was pulling up beside them. Its brown sides were marked with the red stripe of the police force.

A door opened and a uniformed woman hoisted herself out, saluting her colleagues. Nick's eyes followed her as she walked round to the rear doors. There, she stopped, looking into the back seat. Her hand rested lightly on the doorhandle, as if waiting for a sign from within.

Firm hands returned to his shoulders; he looked back along the tarmac towards the waiting plane. 'Come on, mate,' someone said. 'You don't know how lucky you are. You could have been stuck here.'

Somewhere a machine's roar cut off, pitching them into a sudden gulf of silence. The absence of noise pressed on Nick's ears like a vacuum; through it, he heard the faint echo of birdsong. A woman's shape mesmerised him, curved against the light like a question mark. He realised he was holding his breath.

The policewoman stepped back; then the car door swung open, pushed from the inside. Nick squinted at a figure moving in the back seat. As he watched, it separated into two smaller forms, their arms tangled around each other.

'JoJo.' Something moved within him, a thump of emotion like the first turn of an engine.

JoJo would not look at him. His long legs unfolded as he climbed slowly out of the car. Nagode clutched onto his arms. Nick saw her twist around in confused recognition.

The last signatures were being scribbled onto papers transferring custody. Noon was nearly on them, the sun at its zenith. It traced the balanced lines of JoJo's face, the new definition of his jaw. The battle between child and man had been blasted away, revealing equilibrium beneath.

'JoJo,' Nick said again, softly.

JoJo handed Nagode to the policewoman. He dug his hands into his back pockets.

Nick felt his captors pulling him backwards, towards the plane. *I'm not ready.* His chest pounded; he could still feel the echo of two other hearts beating within him, pumping life through his veins.

'JoJo, please.' He resisted the pressure dragging him away. 'Please.' He'd promised never to ask for anything, neither absolution nor understanding. But JoJo's silence undid him. And now he felt it – the staggering weight of loss, a profound emptiness in hands that had once been full. *Love stays with the living.* That's what he'd told her – but now she was gone, and he could not feel her at all except through this crushing, brutal pain. His knees almost gave way with the weight of it, unable to put it down, but knowing it was more than he could bear.

It was too much; he wrenched his body away from them, turning towards the plane.

But then he heard his name. 'Nicholas.'

JoJo was looking straight at him, eyes meeting Nick's through the sun's brilliance. The young man's hands emerged from his pockets, holding something out towards him. It lay at the edge of his fingers, a dark shape in a pool of light.

Bako's bracelet.

JoJo walked towards him, shaking off the policewoman's warning grasp. The birds wheeled and called as Nick reached out with his cuffed hands. And then he felt the beads fall like an abacus into his palm.

They curled there, small dots of red. *All the good deeds, and all the bad*, he remembered. One for JoJo, one for Adeya, one for Nagode. He ran his fingers over each smooth surface, his mind making its own count. One for Dr Ahmed. One for Binza, one for Mister. He touched the first and last, bringing the two ends of the cord together. One for Margaret. And one for me.

He looked at JoJo, who looked back, eyes solemn.

'Are you sure?' Nick asked.

JoJo shrugged. He bit his lip, a gesture so like his mother's that Nick's whole being thrilled with sudden joy.

They stood in silence, the crows reeling above them. Then, JoJo reached over. He touched the beads lightly – tentative fingers hovering just above Nick's hand.

'I fixed Baba's clock already. Adeya helped me.' His voice was deeper now, but quiet. Nick felt the electric pressure of his fingertips, the inexpressible passing through a world of flesh and blood. 'Adeya and me, we went back to school. Maybe one day we will build another castle.'

'You'll build many things,' Nick told him. 'More than I ever will.'

JoJo nodded. His eyes were still bright, but grief rolled over them like passing clouds.

Nick closed his hand over the beads, absorbing their vanishing warmth. JoJo blinked, gathered water spilling from the corners of his eyes. To Nick's amazement, the boy smiled then – as if a quiet trickle of feeling had woken within, flowing from a source long denied.

'Mama gave it to me when we were in the box.' It was quietly spoken, as if in a cathedral of memory where only they sat. 'She said to wear it until she came back.' His mouth was trembling; his fists came up to rub away tears – then, slowly, returned to his sides.

'She did not come back,' he went on, raising his face to Nick's. Now the restraint of manhood was in every feature; Nick saw him breathing sorrow inwards, turning it to strength. 'But you did. You came. So you can take her with you.' He nodded at Nick's closed hand. 'Like you wanted to.'

Nagode was stirring behind them, arms reaching out to her brother. 'JoJo!' she called. He responded instinctively, turning towards the cry as a father would. Then he paused, his body halfway across the space between them. 'Goodbye, Nicholas.' The boy's face was hidden, but Nick heard something strong and new in his voice – the force of decision. 'I'll see you again.'

Then he was running back to his sister, lifting her out of the policewoman's arms, hugging her as she began to laugh.

I'll see you again. As Nick turned towards the waiting aeroplane JoJo's words rolled ahead of him, leading to unknown places. He followed them, Bako's beads rubbing against each other in his hand, the cord stretching and yet refusing to break.

The line of migrating birds raced him as the aeroplane breached the pull of gravity. Their wings dipped as he rose to meet them, perfect in their symmetry. And at the moment their pathways crossed, he saw each separate form blur and merge in their onward flight, transforming into a single wave of life.

'Here? This is the one, Uncle Nicholas?'

The young girl's feet are bare. She's standing in the long grass by a kissing gate, pointing to a red climbing rose. Her legs are already soaking wet with dew.

'Shouldn't she should put some shoes on, darling?' the old woman asks Nick. 'They just came off the plane yesterday – she'll catch her death.' He answers: 'Mum, you worry too much.'

It's an early-summer morning – warm, but full of moisture. The old woman has been telling her guests to wrap up ever since they woke. 'But youth never listens,' she whispers to Nick. 'At thirteen I knew everything, too.'

Now she calls across the garden. 'You'll catch cold, dear. You're not used to English weather yet.'

But the girl only laughs. 'Don't worry, Grandmother. I'm strong.'

'Are you OK, Mum?' Nick holds the old woman's arm.

'I'm fine, silly,' she tells him. 'I look better than you.' It's true. Lines are growing into his hair and across his face like grey wire. 'Like someone started to draw over you,' she'd told him once.

'I wish they could,' he'd replied. 'Draw a better version.'

She's touched that he still worries about her. He checks her pills every morning, in case she forgets to take them. 'They're important,' he reminds her. 'They brought you back to us.'

'You brought me back,' she tells him on his blackest days. 'As soon as the judge let you out, you came and took me away from that dreadful place. Whatever else you did – remember, you did that for me.'

These days she has to lean on him to walk. And she gets cold so quickly. But it's not the terrible, long, white cold of the ward; now her world has colours in it. Sometimes she imagines how they would look on a canvas. Sapphires and silvers. A vast blue filled with light – like a sky, coming nearer to her every day.

Today the same blue is opening above them all in the garden. The girl's brother is dark against it, tall as a hazel tree. He doesn't speak much – but when he does, it's slow and rich. Over last night's tea he showed them sketches from his portfolio, building designs he made during his architectural apprenticeship. 'They're like paintings,' the old woman told him. 'They have souls.' And he'd laughed – but she heard something else under the sound, angry and red, like a wound.

The two of them arrived from the airport after a day of anxious waiting: the girl so happy – bright as a flower, touching everything in the kitchen and telling jokes. But the brother sat slowly down at the table, Nick silent as a shadow opposite, meaningless sentences passing between them. Sometimes the brother tried to smile at her – and the old woman was reminded of that other boy who used to sit on the very same seat in her kitchen all those years ago. His smile had been sad, too – a smudged charcoal line. Nothing in life is ever really over and done, she'd told Nick that ten years ago when he first brought her back home, when loss still burned in him like an unquenchable, devouring flame. She'd said: 'Even if you paint over something it doesn't mean it's gone. It's still there, part of the picture. All our living is really re-living.'

This girl is living for the first time. They can all see it in her – that flowering of life. She stands at the kissing gate in the sunshine, touching the climbing rose Nick planted the day he brought his mother back home. An unlikely rose, planted in the frosts of a brutal winter – that grew into glorious colour.

Petals fall around her as the girl pulls off one of the rose-blooms. 'I love the red,' she says. 'It reminds me of her.'

'You don't even remember her,' the brother tells her. The old woman hears colours in his voice – rain colours, deep purples and blues.

The girl shakes her head. 'I do,' she says. 'In my way.'

Now Nick is at his mother's side, pushing up her sleeve very gently. A bracelet shines on her wrist, its beads red and bright.

'I'm going to miss it,' she tells him, wistful.

He touches her cheek. 'But you're so much better now, Mum,' he says. 'You don't need it any more.'

'And you'll have me.' The girl takes her other hand. She's going to be as tall as her brother – long bones, like the brushes artists use for the finest strokes.

'For now,' the brother says.

At last the bracelet comes undone. Nick turns to his friend, holding it in his hand. 'I would pay any price to change what happened. You know that. Anything at all.'

'I want nothing from you,' the tall man answers, his head lifting, like a challenge. 'We have our own lives now. I'll be a junior partner soon. I'm building a house for Adeya. Once she finishes her training, we'll marry. Nagode can live with us, when she gets tired of the weather here.' Then he laughs. 'The English love to offer to pay for things that can't be bought.'

But he did pay, the old woman wants to tell him. He paid when they locked him up, when he sold his house in London and sent all the money away, when his girlfriend tried for a while but couldn't stick with him. His winter came too early, you see, and she wanted her time in summer. Look at him now, she wants to say. He's still paying, every day.

'I did not approve of this plan at first,' the man is saying. 'There are plenty of good private schools back home. But Nagode insisted.'

'It's my adventure.' She smiles at him, and he softens.

'Your adventure.' He takes her hand. 'Mama would be happy. The world is yours to conquer.'

The girl takes the bracelet from Nick, and brings it to her lips. 'Tie it on for me,' she asks.

His fingers shake as he makes the knot, but she's patient. The petals smell sweet falling from her hands; the bruised ones smell sweetest.

When he's finished, she touches the beads, her eyes closing.

'Good morning, Mama,' she says. A flock of swallows dives as she speaks, something startling them from their roost. Nick watches them go. His hands are on the kissing gate, gripping tight.

The brother turns to the old woman.

'Watch over Nagode for me,' he says to her. 'Until she returns home to us.'

The girl goes to put her arms around him. Then she pulls away, like someone who doesn't want to cry.

Nick turns back from the kissing gate. 'Come on, then,' he says to Nagode. 'Let's make a start.' There's a smile there, trying to come through. Give it time, the old woman wants to tell them. Time is life's best medicine.

But instead she takes the girl's hand, still moist from the morning. Thirteen is just like early summer; everything in you is still waiting to wake.

'We'll go inside and have some tea,' she tells her. She points to the sky; it's hazy with clouds, but the sun's breaking through. 'I'm not sure how it's going to turn out today.'

Nagode squeezes the old woman's palm. 'Wait and see,' she says.

ACKNOWLEDGEMENTS

This story began life on the remote desert border between Nigeria and Niger, delivering polio vaccines during an outbreak under the eye of a fearless local doctor. One night, she invited her naïve charge to a meal. There, she tried to educate me on the terrible dilemmas she saw playing out between the West and the rest of the world – in the fault lines between different values, between good intentions and harsh realities. I hope this book does justice to her message.

Eric Fewster of Bushproof was an invaluable resource on the technicalities of well-drilling in Africa in the early 1990s. He did his best to correct several misguided assumptions on my part. Errors that remain are mine alone.

My family, my agent and my editor in their different manners made this a better book. Throughout the writing process, their collective faith in me helped me keep faith in the story.

Finally, to those many people I met on my United Nations journey, people from both East and West – doctors, volunteers, peace brokers, relief workers, activists, engineers, teachers and entrepreneurs, each in their own way striving to shape a better life, putting themselves and their choices to the test every day – I salute you.

ALSO BY

CLAIRE HAJAJ

ISHMAEL'S ORANGES

Shortlisted for the Jewish
Quarterly-Wingate Prize 2016

A finalist for the Authors' Club
Best First Novel Award 2015

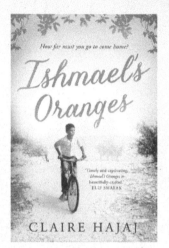

It's April 1948, and war hangs over Jaffa. One minute seven-year-old Salim is dreaming of taking his first harvest from the family's orange tree; the next he is swept away into a life of exile and rage. Seeking a new beginning in swinging-'60s London, Salim falls in love with Jude. The only problem? Jude is Jewish.

A captivating story about love and loss, *Ishmael's Oranges* follows the story of two families spanning the crossroad events of modern times, and of the legacy of hatred their children inherit.

'Timely and captivating, *Ishmael's Oranges* is beautifully crafted.'
Elif Shafak, author of *Three Daughters of Eve*

'Richly, hauntingly written...immeasurably beautiful.'
Independent

ONEWORLD